THE MEISTER OF DECIMEN CITY

THE MEISTER OF DECIMEN CITY

BRENNA RANEY

CamCat
Books

CamCat Publishing, LLC
Brentwood, Tennessee 37027
camcatpublishing.com

Hardcover ISBN 9780744307702
Paperback ISBN 9780744307719
Large-Print Paperback ISBN 9780744307726
eBook ISBN 9780744307733
Audiobook ISBN 9780744307740

Library of Congress Control Number: 2022944563

Book and cover design by Maryann Appel

5 3 1 2 4

TO THE PEOPLE WHO CAN NEVER FIT THE NARRATIVE.

LOVE YOU.

ISSUE 1

DINOSAURS ON MAIN STREET

*R*ex made a list of her obligations from most pressing to least pressing, with *deal with the dinosaurs* at the top. It was a stress-managing exercise her high school counselor had suggested. It hadn't worked then, and it wasn't working now.

The TV over her workbench screeched, and she looked up. The news was still showing live helicopter footage of the dinosaurs tearing down Main Street. As a velociraptor-looking thing—someone in the lab was watching too much *Jurassic Park*—crashed through a line of abandoned cars, the Lightning zapped onto the scene. Rex winced as the superhero punched the raptor in the face, electric flickers bursting from the impact, and reporters broke into happy hysterics.

The *ding* of the lab door made her jump, but it was just Flora striding in with a jet-black hair swish.

A pair of metal eyes hovered after her, a robotic voice calling, "I couldn't keep her out, Doctor." Despite having written the subroutine for Aya to say exactly that, Rex didn't find it funny.

"When you said you were working on the dinosaur project, I thought you were researching how the dinosaurs died, not unleashing a dinosaur-themed apocalypse," Flora said.

"This wasn't intentional," Rex hissed, moving to the end of the workbench to flip through her notes. "They shouldn't have gotten out."

Flora adjusted her glasses and rested her other hand on her hip. "You need to deal with this before the Lightning traces them back to the source and beats your face in with her taser-fist of death."

"I'm trying!" Rex tossed the notes away. "What *did* kill the dinosaurs? The same thing would work now, right?"

"Climate change?"

"Shall I run simulations on potential asteroid impacts?" Aya offered. The two eyes bobbed next to each other over the workbench, a trick with magnets that had been hell to work out but looked really cool. Still, Aya's two staring eyes was getting to Rex in a way that one staring camera never had. She snatched up the to-do list and scribbled *give Aya eyelids* at the bottom.

Screams erupted on the television as a news chopper dipped too low and a variety of dinosaurs with some truly impressive back legs leaped high enough to catch one of the helicopter's ski-looking thingies in its jaws.

"I don't remember making so many," Rex muttered as she rushed to the chemical zone to mix a hasty genetic destabilizer, pausing only to shove goggles over her buzzed, blonde head and cover her freckled hands with a snap of gloves.

"You got clone-happy." Flora followed her past the line of red tape on the floor with quick little steps in her pencil skirt. Rex wondered how she was still so intimidated by professional dress after seeing Flora in it almost every day for five years. "I warned you. The whole city warned you. It's in point three of the latest truce agreement—"

"The clone clause—yes, I know." Rex didn't have genetic material to form the base of the destabilizer at the home lab. It was all in the Peak Street facility, which they shouldn't have been able to escape from if her lab techs had followed her damn instructions.

Rex dropped into a chair and ran her hands over her face, pushing the goggles up. "I'm just going to take the Exo-suit and go punch dinos with 'Ning." The hero couldn't zap her if they were fighting side by side, right?

Shit. She was so screwed.

"I will call up the mecha," Aya said, cueing the hum of moving floor panels.

"You can't Voltron your way out of every problem," Flora said.

"But I can Voltron my way out of this problem." Rex was already stepping around the hollow robot rising out of the floor—mostly used for wrangling hostile test subjects from the bottom of the ocean and breaking safes that she had forgotten the combinations to.

"Hey." Flora put a hand on her arm before she could slide it into the myoelectric sleeve. "If the Lightning tries to fight you, don't stick around. There's no shame in running away."

"There's so much shame in running away."

"There's more shame in getting your ass kicked by a superhero. And frankly, I don't think you need more brain damage."

"A real friend would support me." Rex strapped herself into the suit's harness and straightened her spine for the neural uplink.

"I try. Call me later to let me know you're alive."

←⟳⟳⟳→

Punching dinosaurs wasn't as satisfying as Rex had hoped. In practice, it was basically animal abuse.

No basically about it, she thought as a feathery thing went down with a squawk. She tried to reassure herself that knocking them out to be re-contained was better than letting a SWAT team shoot them. The area had been evacuated, so she didn't see a reason to put them down, anyway.

When she showed up, the Lightning met her eyes, sort of—her yellow costume covered her whole body, including her face, and Rex's suit had robot eyes that didn't line up with the pilot's. Then she nodded once and turned her back, which Rex took as silent acceptance of their team-up. It was probably for the best that they split up—that yellow costume was really tight, and Rex had trouble keeping her eyes up when they were face-to-face for any length of time.

The Lightning was a bright streak in her peripheral vision, zipping from building to building using her Static Cling and tasering the crap out of the dinos too fast for the Exo-suit. That left Rex to deal with the heavy hitters, who had no business being so bloodthirsty considering their build and metabolism, but she figured it was a fitting punishment for making the Lightning take time out of her day. For a strong-and-silent-type hero, 'Ning could be fantastically passive aggressive.

Regardless, they made as efficient a team as they always did when a common enemy—or a Rex fuck-up; honestly, it was usually a Rex fuck-up—made them temporary allies. The local news stations were the only ones who still found it surprising. Rex could already see the headlines: "The Lightning and the Meister: Dawn of a New Age of Cooperation?" As though they hadn't run something similar half a dozen times already.

'Ning didn't stick around after the last stegosaur crashed to the asphalt and the police closed in. She never did. Apparently, sexy-fine superheroes were wasted on cleanup, but it was all right to let a perpetually pseudo-probationary super genius take responsibility for the stampeding dinosaurs she'd accidentally released.

Rex opened her phone screen inside the Exo-suit to shoot Flora a *still alive* text and groaned. She had a dozen missed messages that Aya had helpfully labeled: *Mayor—urgent.*

The one perk of meeting with Mayor Vicker so often was that his staff always bought Rex dinner. This time, she ordered a burger without cheese, but they delivered one with cheese anyway. And not the kind of cheese she could peel off, no—the kind that seeped into every crevice in the patty and made it bleed yellow. She used half the stack of paper napkins to wipe it off and wrapped it up so the smell couldn't escape.

"—and there's nothing I can do about it. You signed the document," the mayor was saying.

Rex had lost track of the conversation while removing the fungal cancer that some worldwide conspiracy deemed worthy of calling food. She glanced across the conference table to note Mayor Vicker's usual tight expression as he either berated her or explained a legal issue. His assistant sat next to him with a colorfully tabbed planner forgotten in his hands and a look of distaste as he watched Rex's growing pile of cheese napkins.

"Are you paying attention? I'm telling you, Ms. Anderson, it's out of my hands. We're talking about federal law."

"What's out of your hands?" Rex asked. She had a sudden epiphany: *They're called landing skids.* Why did they use those things, anyway? Why not put all helicopters on wheels?

The mayor gave her a disappointed frown. "Ms. Anderson, you violated point three of your truce agreement—"

"The clone clause—I know." She winced as the first bite of decontaminated burger hit her tongue. Could she actually taste it, or was her brain just reminding her of the gelatinous orange waste that had been smeared all over her food?

"For Christ's sake, just eat it! You wiped it off. Stop being so dramatic about it," the mayor burst out.

Yeah, and if someone took a shit all over his burger, she was sure he'd just wipe it off and forget about the particulates of fecal matter mushed into the meat.

"The security measures I have in place are ironclad if they're followed," Rex said, lowering the burger in surrender. "I'll oversee it myself this time. So, wherever my dinosaurs are being held, I'm eager to plead my case to regain custody."

"You're worried about the *dinosaurs?*"

"They're the big losers here. I've been tasered by 'Ning before. It isn't fun."

The assistant—Hammond? Hansen?—raised an eyebrow. "You want the city to release the horde of dinosaurs back to the mad scientist who set them loose on Main Street?"

"This didn't happen because I'm mad," Rex protested, pointing at the assistant. "It happened because my lab techs are incompetent."

"A *horde* of dinosaurs," the assistant sneered.

"I really didn't think I'd made so many."

"Regardless, you did," the mayor cut in, rubbing his forehead. "Which is an unambiguous violation of the truce you signed. National news sources have already picked up the story. This can't be swept under the rug."

Rex didn't like the direction this was going. "That Oversight stuff is optional at the local level, right?"

Mayor Vicker gave her a thin-lipped look and his forehead wrinkled all the way to his hairline—wherever that was. His hair was thinning in such an even gradient that the top of his head looked more like a swatch of grayscale than a separable head and forehead. "Listen, Rex."

She swallowed. This wouldn't be good.

"The people like you for some reason. They're used to you, at least. God knows most villains don't generate half the local goodwill you've managed. I mean, a choice between you and someone like Last Dance—"

There was a pit behind Rex, bottomless, the back legs of her chair sitting right on its edge, and all she could taste was cheese cheese cheese.

"—*there's* a real villain. No doubt New York opted for Oversight with a please and thank you."

"I'm not a villain," she corrected, ignoring the shivers dormant in her spine. "I'm chaotic neutral at worst."

"The polls aren't so clear on that." The mayor's fist clenched. "The polls *are* clear that the people of Decimen prefer to opt out of the Superbeings Oversight Contingencies—you have the Lightning to thank for that, by the way."

Rex rolled her eyes. God forbid the government interfere with Decimen City's special child.

"But in cases where a superbeing demonstrates they cannot or will not cooperate with local efforts to mediate, the national ordinance is clear."

"I'm not a superbeing," Rex tried.

"If your IQ didn't qualify you, your past actions would," the mayor said gently.

"If you'd broken the law any less outrageously, you'd be in jail by now," Hamboy added helpfully.

"'Ning's dragged me to jail three times, not counting the time she locked me in a cell to sweat out that zombie bite. You mean prison."

"Rex, please," Mayor Vicker said. "I'm afraid I have to act this time. It's the law."

Rex leaned back with a sinking feeling. She'd read through the tiers of Oversight outlined in the Contingencies, from check-ins to imprisonment. She'd known she qualified if public opinion ever swayed that way. That it was happening now because she'd shot herself in the foot instead of having anything to do with public opinion seemed stupidly fitting.

That God-awful taste returned to her tongue. "Lay it out for me."

The mayor gave a sympathetic grimace and had his assistant call in a lawyer.

← ⟲⟲⟲⟲⟲ →

Fun fact: Superbeings Oversight, while small and specialized, was technically a branch of the military. Since the threat tier she best fit required direct oversight, the government was essentially assigning Rex a team of babysitters with military training. They'd be in her home, her databases, her Peak Street labs—anywhere she might get it into her head to cause some mayhem. As if she ever started something for the purpose of causing mayhem.

Granted, her introduction to the public scene had involved a cobbled-together death ray that 'Ning had barely managed to short out in time, so it was hardly shocking—ha—that they'd bumped her up a few tiers.

She strode out of city hall in a nightmarish mood, the papers the lawyer had given her clenched in her hands. Her Exo-suit was slumped next to the bike rack at the bottom of the stairs, secured to the rail by a bike lock.

No one could make it work without Rex's DNA and brain waves, but she wouldn't put it past anyone in this city to throw it in the back of a truck and set it up in their living room.

She shoved the papers into the suit and jumped as the Lightning zipped onto the stone balustrade beside her.

"You need to get your life together," the superhero said.

"Holy shit. You talk," was what fell out of Rex's mouth.

Expressionless through the yellow mask, 'Ning cocked her head. "You've heard me talk."

"Yeah, but only to say things like 'You've gone too far this time, Meister,' or 'These aliens will destroy hero and villain alike unless we work together.'" She didn't have Flora there to tell her to breathe. Also, the Lightning was standing very close in a well-fitted bodysuit; there went those magnets trying to pull Rex's eyes down.

'Ning shook her head in that slow way that Rex got from friends and strangers alike and sat on the balustrade with her legs dangling.

"And *I* need to get my life together?" Rex continued. "What about you? What kind of hero still hasn't touched base with Superbeings Oversight? I thought that was responsible superhero-ing. Vivid Blue did it. Isn't she the hero's hero? The One True Hero? Leader of the Protectors-of-the-World-which-usually-just-means-New-York?"

'Ning folded her arms, which—wow, that made it worse. "I have a well-balanced life as my secret identity and the full support of my community as my alias. I think I'm doing fine."

"Brag much?" Rex tried to ignore the excited calls of some passersby who'd stopped to take pictures of 'Ning. "Do you even have a tragic backstory? Even small-timers have something better than got-powers-in-an-electrical-storm. You go up against villains with more fleshed-out backstories than yours. It's not right."

"I'm serious, Rex. There are enough real villains in my life without having to wonder if the Meister has been too quiet lately."

Rex squinted. "Is this a shakedown?"

"It's an offer. Half the times you start something world-ending it's because you're responding to a real problem. I'm saying you can call on me *before* you take things too far."

"So, you'll punch world hunger in the face?"

"Is that what the dinosaurs were for?"

God, Rex hated her.

"Just think about it. If a superhero has to keep you in check, take it as a hint. You're probably doing something wrong." She stood. "And get your life together."

Rex flinched as the Lightning zapped away, searing a yellow streak across her field of vision. She rubbed the spots out of her eyes and groaned into her hands. Then she shoved the bike lock into the mecha and strapped herself in to go see Animal Control about her dinosaurs.

ISSUE 2

DINOSAURS AT THE POUND

The next day, the headline of the state *Gazette* was "Jurassic Age Returns to Decimen City" with a street-level photograph of a triceratops flipping a car while smaller raptors spilled past it. There was also a story on the front page of the *Metro Times*, overshadowed only by the latest throwdown between Vivid Blue and Last Dance—Blue saved the factory workers who had been press-ganged into building who-knows-what, but Last Dance got away.

The *Decimen City Circular* hadn't bothered with a story, acknowledging the episode only in its reporting of the traffic interruptions with phrases like *because of the dinosaurs*. Rex forcefully ignored the sound of slicing scissors across the lab as Flora cut articles from the pile of newspapers on her desk for framing on the Wall of Infamy, which she'd started either out of pride or as a weird effort to shame Rex into thinking before she scienced.

The *Metro Times* lay on the workbench in front of Rex, the dinosaur story already cut out and the picture of Vivid Blue, lavender cape billowing as she led liberated workers out of the factory, drawing her eyes like a train wreck. Rex pushed the paper to the floor. It helped, but her heartbeats still felt heavy. "Do I have a crush on the Lightning?"

"You've never been attracted to a woman before," Flora said without looking up.

"She's *really* hot though."

"No argument here."

"Am I having a gay crisis?"

"Why does it have to be a crisis? Maybe you're just having a gay." Flora's scissors gave a long rip, making Rex wince. "You *can* notice someone's hotness without being attracted to them. I can tell when a man is attractive. It doesn't mean I'd date one."

"But I feel nervous every time I'm around her."

"Are you sure that's not because she keeps beating you up?"

"That's almost always my fault."

"That's a dollar."

Rex huffed. "What? That doesn't count."

"It counts. Dollar in the jar."

Rex grumbled, but she dug a dollar out of her wallet and crossed the room to stuff it into the mason jar on Flora's desk with the taped-on label, *Self-Deprecation Jar.* "What are you gonna buy when this is full?"

"Something that's good for self-esteem." The scissors gave another rip. "By the way, I'm getting you an interview with the *Circular* to talk about the dinosaurs."

Still settling back at her workbench, Rex jolted. "Why?"

"To get a story out there that isn't 'crazy person makes dinosaurs just because.' We have to build a platform to appeal Oversight's decision. Unless you want houseguests with permission to shoot you for the rest of your life."

The nausea was getting old. Rex dropped her chin onto her blueprints and nudged the fallen newspaper further away with her toe. "How do you tell the difference between a real crush and a friend crush?"

"If you can't tell the difference, I don't know how to explain it to you."

"I can tell them apart when they stop," Rex said sullenly. Without raising her head, she pulled the wrinkled to-do list closer and eyed the second item on the list: break up with Dillon. She cringed. Maybe that could wait until tomorrow.

Flora sighed. "You've got to stop dating people you're not attracted to. It's confusing your emotional compass."

Rex grumbled unintelligibly. If she did that, she might never date anyone.

A ping came from Flora's computer, and she—thank God—set her
scissors aside to give it her attention. "Hm. The Oversight Committee has
organized your surveillance team. We can expect them later this evening."
That was fast. "I'm going to ask if they need any help with accommodations
or transportation."

"We have to pick them up from the airport now?"

"The more cooperative we are, the better our position will be when we
appeal." Flora's attention returned to the screen. "It looks like they've been
organized by the list of locations you gave the lawyer, with two quartered
here at home." She glanced up. "I should have been part of that conversation,
by the way."

Flora was, after all, her lawyer. Rex was a dumbass. "Sorry, I didn't think
of it."

Flora *hmm*ed. "They wanted to set guards at the old lab facility on Everglade, but I let them know it's been defunct and zoned as a dumping ground
for toxic waste since the incident with the mice."

Rex nodded solemnly and did not mention that Everglade was still
powered and stocked. You never knew when you might need a safehouse.

"We should have Aya run background checks, starting with the two who
will be living with us: Grant Underwood and Lewis Stone." Flora leaned
back in her chair and glanced around the lab. "Where is Aya, by the way?"

Rex was careful not to tense up. "Charging." She nodded toward the
shallow cup on a shelf where the metal eyes lay dormant.

"Doesn't she charge the eyes at night?" Flora's posture had straightened
minutely. She looked across the room at Rex with a neutral expression. "You
look tired."

It took effort not to fix her slouch. "Anxious. Didn't sleep much." True,
but misleading.

Last night, after talking over the bad news with Flora, Rex had paced
in her room for an hour or so. Then she'd snuck back downstairs barefoot

and in pajamas, taken the handle of their least-classy, whipped cream vodka from the freezer, and gone down to the lab.

It was a tight window—only seven or eight hours until Flora would be back in the kitchen for breakfast. She and Aya worked quickly, with occasional pauses to take a swig, transferring her most sensitive projects to private servers, neutralizing chemical agents, moving cultures to basement levels with higher security, digitalizing sketches, blueprints, and old records, and burning the paper copies.

The bulk of the time, however, had gone into some major rewiring in the lower levels. As convenient as it was to have the whole house integrated into one system, Rex hadn't planned for her home to be infiltrated and her whole life brought under the authority of strangers. The long rows of servers under the house needed to be inaccessible to anyone but her. The pair of eyes made a nice avatar, but those servers were Aya's real body.

Flora was glaring outright now, eyes magnified by her glasses. "We're cooperating fully with Oversight so we can get them out of our lives faster, remember?"

Rex nodded, going for casual. "Mm-hm."

Flora's chair squeaked as she pushed herself back. "Goddammit, Rex, if you're already pushing—"

"Just cleaning house." At this point, maintaining the lie would be an insult to Flora. "There were a lot of bad ideas lying around here. I have you to tell me when to scrap something, but that's not good enough if someone steals them."

Flora didn't look pacified. "It's not enough in any case, if the Oversight decision means anything."

Rex grunted, unsure if she meant it as acknowledgment or dismissal.

She'd ended last night sitting on the floor of the freezing sublevel, leaning against one of Aya's supercomputers, the handle of vodka half empty by her hip.

"Don't disable the weapons system," she'd told the metal eyes hovering over her lap.

"Ms. Shay said—"

"Yeah, but—don't disable it." Through the fog of exhaustion and alcohol, she'd acknowledged that her new babysitters would undoubtedly examine the security system and deem the laser guns in the walls unacceptable. "Well, okay. We'll remove what they want. But don't disable the knockout gas. It's wide-dispersal, untargeted. We can make the argument that it doesn't put them at a disadvantage if anyone in the house becomes a threat."

"But you are inoculated against the knockout gas in the home system."

Rex had nodded and taken another small mouthful of vodka, deciding it would have to be the last if she didn't want to be drunk at breakfast with Flora. "Yeah. But they don't know that."

Rex had enough time to handle the dinosaurs' move to their new facilities before the Oversight team arrived. As per her agreement with Animal Control yesterday, she'd rushed the conversion of their habitats at Peak Street overnight, bringing the security up to a level that the most bumbling technician couldn't sabotage.

Her guilt returned as she inspected the upgraded space and wondered how she'd come up with the guidelines in the first place, considering dinosaurs were long extinct. She should probably be filtering the air more thoroughly to simulate ancient-Earth conditions—unless she'd engineered the clones with today's atmosphere in mind. She'd have to revisit her notes.

When she arrived at the dinosaurs' temporary housing—kennels for very big dogs, she guessed—a cacophony of squawks, rumbles, and screeches greeted her past the heavy containment doors. Two jump-suited Animal Control workers tossed food through the bars with faces frozen in a look of lost patience.

Before Rex could blurt out an apology from self-preservation instinct alone, there was a sudden volume increase and the dinosaurs crowded against the bars, calling and stepping on each other. Two winged microraptors scrambled up the back of a waist-high deinonychus to cling to the metal mesh at her eye level, squawking as the deinonychus rattled their perch with a head bash and a thick-clawed foot. She hoped that was a happy greeting and not related to her part in stopping their rampage.

Animal Control waved her back toward the lobby. When the doors closed behind them, cutting the noise in half, one said without preamble, "I hope none of the big ones are gonna eat each other, because we put them all in Montgomery Stadium behind big-ass blast doors. When are you getting them out of there?"

This wasn't the first time Rex needed someone willing to handle large, hostile animals. She called the closest circus company, and they actually sounded flattered to be chosen.

As her lab techs supervised the transfer, she finally got all her apologies out to Animal Control. They listened stoically, and by the time her dinosaurs were sleeping off the tranqs in new habitats, they were leaving with a wave and the grudging forgiveness everyone in Decimen seemed willing to grant her.

When Rex got home, Flora told her the surveillance team was on their way to do an assessment of the house. The two of them stood on the front steps to receive a full military convoy like a pair of dignitaries. Or maybe like a pair of traitors waiting for extradition. For the first time in a while, Rex felt underdressed in her usual sweatpants and T-shirt. At least she hadn't had to worry about bedhead since she sacrificed her hair to the almighty electric buzzer of lab safety.

The team consisted of one squad of nine soldiers and an officer—maybe a lieutenant?—who had the squarest jaw Rex had ever seen and looked at her like an assistant principal who'd pinned her as the problem child he would be putting in their place this semester. Rex forgot all their names except for the two Flora had said would be living with them. Typical of her luck, they were the two biggest men in the gaggle.

Flora must have recognized that Rex was getting panicky because she started questioning Lieutenant Quinten—Flora probably said his name because she knew Rex hadn't caught it—about the limitations on their government-mandated invasion of privacy. And there were limitations, apparently. After the home inspection, they wouldn't be allowed in her private rooms, or Flora's, although there would be scheduled searches. She also had some leeway in public—she could eat at a restaurant without a soldier sitting at the table, for example, as long as one waited outside.

The outline of her remaining freedoms helped Rex relax enough to leave Flora to iron out the details while she hovered around the pair of soldiers examining her security system.

The blond one—Paul? Percy? Something with a P—marveled at the laser guns' tracking program, and they talked excitedly about coding for weapons systems even as he dismantled it.

Flora had mentioned that the surveillance team was selected partially based on their scientific backgrounds. They would bring in experts to scrutinize her projects more closely—or as close to experts as they could get, since Rex was Rex—but Oversight didn't want the on-site surveillance to be totally ignorant of what she was doing. She hadn't considered that those measures might mean that she could have conversations about work with her babysitters.

"I don't think we should take out all the hardware, since your whole house is basically a gun," the blond guy said. "I wouldn't be surprised if this mess is load bearing."

She snorted a surprised laugh.

"Let's just take out key components," he continued, addressing both Rex and his fellow soldier. "We'll make an inventory of what's confiscated so you can get it back or get compensated for it when you're done being grounded by America."

Rex found her stress level significantly lowered by the interaction, which said something about how tightly wound she'd been. She wished this guy was one of the two living with her. Alas, it wasn't to be.

Knowing her lab would be next in the inspection, Rex left Aya to watch the soldiers and headed downstairs for a last look over of the space. She'd been as thorough as she could last night, but she'd still only had one night and no opportunity to move anything off-site.

The *ding* of the lab door made her jump.

One of the soldiers had stepped inside—one of the big ones. Lewis Stone, she was pretty sure. She'd only gotten a cursory look at him in the hand-shaking line. He was, again, large. Tall, heavy, clearly muscled but not cut—like a football player with a belly. His hair, light brown and barely darker than his skin, was in a short afro; maybe it was as long as he was allowed to keep it. Did Oversight have rules like that? Everyone in the squad had conservative haircuts, but they weren't uniform. His gaze found her in the middle of the lab, and his eyes narrowed.

At five-foot-eight, Rex didn't often have to deal with people looming over her, but when they did, she despised it. She tracked his approach from the corner of her eye, her back straightening. He knew what he was doing—he had to. Stepping close enough to make her look up but still far enough back that telling him to stop wasn't worth the risk of him refusing. She reminded herself of the lab's secondary exit so she wouldn't back away or flip her shit about him standing between her and the door.

Rex regretted not installing speakers to go with the cameras throughout the house. Though Aya was fully integrated into the home system, she would've felt less alone if Aya's voice could join her.

"There are cameras in every room. Aya is always watching." Did she sound rattled? No. She was doing fine.

A sneer rolled across his face and was replaced by a blank look. "You shouldn't be in here before the inspection's done," he said, sounding bored. His eyes never left her.

"No one told me. Unless it's in writing somewhere, literally no notification was given. If they can bump me up tiers for that they might as well lock me away now."

Again, that little pull of disgust at his mouth. "Get back upstairs."

Rex made herself walk past him, then in front of him until they reached the next landing. Like hell was she going to do the you-go-first dance and give him the chance to make her bend. She gave him a polite but cold, "You can ask Aya if you need anything while you're here," before they parted. When she was alone, she noticed how fast her heart was racing. Noticing that triggered her hands to shake.

After ensuring that she was alone, she leaned against a wall and took deep breaths, collecting herself. That pit was behind her again, right where the wall met the floor. She took a final, deep breath and drew herself up to return to Flora and Lieutenant Quinten.

That wasn't so bad. She could do this, easy. It wasn't like it was the first time she'd had to live with someone she didn't trust.

ISSUE 3

SPOTLIGHT ON LEWIS STONE: LEWIS HATES HIS LIFE

So, this was the lair of the Meister of Decimen City. Lewis tried to dredge up some curiosity from the well of moroseness he'd been stuck in since getting the assignment, but it slipped right back into the depths as he spied the series of framed articles on one wall with headlines like "Mutant Strain of Zombie Virus Traced Back to Meister's Labs" and "Rain of Terror: Meister Unleashes Mind-Warping Weather Machine."

This kind of nonsense was the reason they'd been called, yet here it was, proudly displayed across the wall. Did the Meister not understand how serious this was? Or did she just not care? Peter had joked about getting babysitting duty, but maybe they really were dealing with a child. And lucky Lewis—a spotless record and a background in biochemistry got him the place of honor as full-time nanny.

Lewis shifted his gaze to the center of the room, where the Meister herself stood, buzzed, freckled, bony enough to be a keratin beak away from resembling a human buzzard, dressed like a depressed college student, and looking shifty as all hell. Why was she so tense? What had she hoped to accomplish by sneaking down here in the middle of the inspection?

Unprompted, she spoke up. "There are cameras in every room. I, uh, is always watching."

I is. Oh, Christ. This was going to be a long assignment. "You shouldn't be in here before the inspection's done," he said.

She babbled something about needing instructions in writing as Lewis tried to disengage from the steady, sinking feeling in his gut.

He turned aside in clear invitation for her to exit. "Get back upstairs."

She strode past him with a rigid posture that she maintained all the way to the main floor. Then she turned to him with a disapproving expression and said, "You can ask I, uh, if you need anything while you're here," confirming that the internet-cat-Yoda-speak hadn't been a one-off. Lewis happily took the dismissal for what it was.

There wasn't much else Lewis could contribute to the home inspection, besides searching for obvious weapons. He didn't have a background in engineering like Peter and the others who were going over the security system, which was, frankly, a mind-blowing indulgence in paranoia and gun-worship.

The house was a trip, though. He hesitated to call it a mansion because the boxy layout made him think of something more industrial and efficient, not that there was anything efficient about the design. Three floors above ground and three more below, at least according to the blueprints, which Lewis wouldn't be taking at face value. Each floor was filled with narrow hallways that made him feel like he should be walking sideways and doors with specialized locks that he and Grant, his fellow nanny, would need master keycards to get through. Until those were issued, he was stuck shuffling through a pile of blank plastic cards and hoping that when he did get a door to unlock, it wouldn't open into a monster pit or an alternate dimension or some other mad scientist nonsense.

The team working on the security system did ask him to take a look at the knockout gas that a . . . pair of floating robot eyes?—probably an avatar for the AI they'd been briefed on—creepy, but kind of cool . . . was asking them to leave intact. He made use of the lab facilities and confirmed the gas was what the robot eyes claimed: non-lethal and temporary.

Lewis would have recommended they at least switch out the agent in the gassing system, since there was no telling what the Meister could put past them, but it would just be more taxpayer dollars dumped into this black hole of a mission. And if he was being honest, the Meister could probably find a way around any safeguards they took. For all their posturing, Oversight at this level came down to getting an early warning more than prevention. He tried not to think about the fact that he'd be living in a house with a Meister-made chemical agent waiting in the walls.

Peter nodded as Lewis gave his assessment, blond hair flopping a bit. Lewis was avoiding his eyes and hoped Peter couldn't tell—not an easy feat, since Peter was one of the few people who nearly matched his height and had never been intimidated by casual eye contact with him. He noticed Peter's face getting redder as they spoke, making the guilt in his gut grow into something physical.

This wasn't working. He glanced around to make sure none of the others were listening—he'd learned his lesson on that—and asked, "How are you doing?" Did that sound condescending? Insensitive? No one had ever told Lewis they had feelings for him before—he was always the one who did the asking. He certainly didn't know how to deal with his best friend confessing his feelings for him and then finding out the rest of the squad was in the next room over, in perfect hearing distance.

"Oh, fine," Peter said with a bit of a laugh. "Just got assigned to a city where I don't know anyone for an unspecified amount of time right after everyone I'll be working with heard me cop to my crush on a man. So, you know . . ." Another laugh sort of fell out.

"I don't think anyone minds," Lewis said. Then he had a horrible feeling that might have sounded backhanded. "And it's cool. Between us. I mean, I don't . . ." He tried to think of anything to say besides *mind*.

"Oh, yeah, I wasn't, you know, expecting anything. Obviously." Peter ran a hand over his head. His face and neck were completely red now. "I just thought you—it seemed fair to tell you. Just sort of to . . ."

Lewis hated this so much.

"Hey, lovebirds—we're heading out," Joey called, leaning into the room. "You can fuck on your own time." He ducked back into the hallway.

Lewis turned back to Peter. "We don't have to take that."

"It's fine. They'll rib me for a bit and then it'll blow over. Half of them already thought we were together because we hugged too long or something."

That didn't make Lewis feel any better.

"So, good luck living in the madhouse." Peter was clearly going for joking, so Lewis laughed a bit. It was awkward. He and Peter had gone to college together, gotten their master's in the same town, requested assignments that involved both their areas of expertise so they could work together. Things had never been awkward between them before.

A panicky flutter started up in his gut.

Lewis kept the smile until Peter left the room. Then he let it drop. What was he supposed to do now? Act like it never happened? How long had Peter even felt that way?

What if . . . what if the crush was the *only* reason Peter liked him? Lewis knew that wasn't fair after all this time, but the thoughts persisted. What if Peter wouldn't want to put up with him now that Lewis had turned him down? Or what if they stayed friends, but they stopped being close? No more falling asleep with his head on Peter's leg, no more helping pay for Peter's dad's meds . . .

Were those parts just hurting Peter?

When the others had gone, Lewis and Grant were left standing in the front room across from the Meister and her housemate-slash-lawyer—couldn't superbeings live any part of their lives like normal people?—staring at each other. The two made quite a contrast, especially since the lawyer—Flora Shay, Lewis remembered—actually dressed like a human being and wore a polite smile instead of the bird-like look the Meister was shooting between Lewis and Grant.

"Do you want a tour of . . ." Shay trailed off. No one took up her small effort at conversation.

When the silence dragged, the pair of metal eyes floated up between them, bobbing out of sync as though a loose, invisible tether held them together. "If no one requires dinner, I can show Misters Stone and Underwood to the guest apartments." Because this house had guest apartments.

When they were alone in the small common area they apparently shared, Grant turned to Lewis with a grin, professional facade forgotten. "Shame we're here for a mission. I'm a professional, but the lawyer one's hot. That tight skirt—damn."

Lewis squeezed his eyes shut and fought back a surge of despair. He desperately wanted to commiserate about his situation with someone who understood, but all he had was this guy.

Grant flopped onto the couch. "But damn, this place is nice. Look at us—we're living in a mansion rent free while the rest of the guys are in the dorms. What do we have to complain about?"

Just that I have to live where I work now and I might have lost my best friend. Lewis let out a long breath and decided eight thirty wasn't too early to go to bed.

ISSUE **4**

DINOSAURS AT FEEDING TIME

*T*he next few days were rocky. Rex eventually stopped forgetting to alert her surveillance when she changed locations and managed to convince them that she wasn't slipping the leash on purpose, although Lewis Stone still gave her cold looks that made it plain that he thought she was lying.

Rex got to test the limits of her Oversight conditions mere days into the new arrangement when she deviated from what now passed for routine to see Dillon. Their exchange began with the text, *So, what's up with the dinosaurs?* The fact that it took him a few days to ask—and she hadn't offered an explanation all this time—said a lot about the state of their relationship.

Rex had never really liked sex. She found it biologically interesting in that she had buttons on her body that made her feel good, but she'd never understood what a second person added to the party. She never told her partners, of course, because only psychopaths and traumatized people were supposed to be uninterested in sex, and she was pretty sure she wasn't either of those. It was particularly uncomfortable this time since the stress of the live-in-soldiers thing had manifested in the form of constipation and an unrelenting eye twitch. Getting off helped a bit with the coiled tension in her gut, but honestly, Rex could have dealt with that on her own.

As they dressed to go out to breakfast, Rex wondered if it was unethical to have sex with someone you were planning to break up with. But refusing would be a deviation from their usual pattern, possibly leading to a confrontation she didn't want to have yet. This kind of thing was why she didn't deserve a healthy relationship.

That's a dollar, popped into her head, and she wondered if it was part of Flora's evil plan to make her internalize that stupid jar.

"Isn't it kind of weird that there are soldiers just waiting downstairs for us?" Dillon asked, drawing Rex's attention.

Dillon was good-looking, as Rex understood the concept. She'd never found him attractive, but he met most of the requirements she'd picked up from movies, television, and other people: symmetrical features, toned body, signs of adequate grooming, and taller than her. Her own "type" was harder to articulate—unless you counted 'Ning, whose appeal wasn't subtle—although she appreciated expressive mouths and eyebrows. They made it easier to see a person behind a face. Dillon's eyebrows were usually too sculpted to express much, and his expressions in general were movie-basic.

"Is it?" she asked. She tended to forget that people were supposed to be able to pretend they didn't know when someone else was having sex. She guessed having her escort wait in Dillon's kitchen sort of shattered the illusion.

Dillon frowned at her as he worked on his shirt buttons. "It doesn't make you uncomfortable?"

"Uh." It didn't. It apparently made Dillon uncomfortable, though, and Rex gave herself a mental kick for her thoughtlessness and general unworthiness for intimacy, reveling in her right to be as self-deprecating as she wanted in her own head. "We're working on an appeal."

"How is this constitutional?" Dillon continued as they made their way downstairs. "Doesn't this violate your rights? Heck, doesn't it violate mine? And your housemate's?"

They reached the kitchen before Dillon was finished, and the two soldiers stood to greet them. Rex offered a special smile and wave for Becky. She was one of only two women on the team, and Rex had hoped for an ally in her. Becky stared back with an unaffected expression, so apparently Rex's impulse of sisterhood was unreciprocated.

"Superbeings have as many exceptions under the law as limitations compared to normal citizens," the other one, a tall guy—Joey, Rex finally remembered—told Dillon with a shrug and a smirk. Rex figured the smirk had to do with the issue Dillon had previously raised, but she still couldn't find it in herself to be bothered. "Ms. Shay could move out of the house if she wants. We're not surveilling her."

"Rex isn't a superbeing," Dillon said.

Rex hated when he tried to debate. "Well, what's done is done. It's too bad. We hate it. Ready to go?"

Dillon huffed and led them out.

One of the main drawbacks of Oversight, in Rex's opinion, was how often it required her to use a car. The issue had come up on the first day. No, she couldn't take the mecha—the escort couldn't ride along and it would be too easy to give them the slip if they followed by car. She shouldn't be taking a giant robot suit on the roadway, anyway. Her attempts to negotiate had been firmly shut down by Lewis Stone, his mouth twisted in a look as poisonous as it had been that first day in the lab.

He'd actually looked thoughtful when she brought up her problems with carsickness and claustrophobia—both a little more truth-adjacent than full-on truth—but then she'd pointed out, "Aya tracks the GPS in the Exo-suit," and his expression had glazed over. She wondered if he was one of those anti-AI ragers who sometimes attacked her on the internet. In which case, fuck that guy. But Flora had convinced her not to die on that hill.

So, Rex climbed into a car at least twice a day, teeth clenched and the taste of vomit in the back of her throat and sat in tense silence as her escort drove her around. At least she could sit in the back, a good position to keep an eye on anyone in the car with her, though she tried not to be obvious about it with Dillon next to her.

When they reached the café, Rex told Dillon her order and went to the bathroom to collect herself, the tension draining once she was alone. On her way back, a woman bumped into her with a muttered apology.

Rex felt a hand slide into her pocket.

The beat of her heart drowned out the woman's retreating footsteps. Her hand moved to check the pocket, but she froze when she noticed Dillon waving. Dropping her hands to her sides, she finished the walk to their table and sat.

"What's the matter?" he asked.

"Nothing." Pressure lingered on her hip from whatever the woman had left behind.

Rex wasn't sure what they talked about. Her part was minor. For once, this place gave her an omelet with no cheese, as ordered. Miracles did happen and God was real.

When Dillon got up for more coffee, her hand went straight to her pocket. The edge of folded paper ran along her fingers. She extracted it, held it low in her lap, and opened it with both hands.

Hi T.

I need help. I have to make it stop. I need you to make this for me. My people can't figure out the last part. Your dinosaurs looked cute in the news. Thank you. I love you.

—Sam

The numbness sinking through Rex's chest came to her attention when her lungs started to ache, and she shook herself with an inhale. There was a second page behind the note, which she moved to the front.

It was a sketchy diagram of what looked like a cross between a football helmet and anti-space-alien gear. "That looks dumb," she muttered. A glance over gave her an idea of its purpose, and her stomach churned with unidentified feelings. She saw what he meant; there was an unfinished component that left the thing nonfunctional. Unbidden, a few ideas occurred for completing the design.

A shiver hit her like a shock, and she shoved the pages back into her pocket in some kind of learned guilt response.

She blamed the Lightning.

It had been a year? A year and a half? No, about sixteen months since her brother had last reached out to her. Her hand, still in her pocket, clenched compulsively around the note, again like a shock response—fuck the Lightning. Her eyes slid across the café to Joey and Becky talking over coffee at a table near the door.

This was not a good time.

Rex wasn't sure what she babbled to Dillon when he came back. She mustered some mild rage when he teasingly took a bite of fruit off her plate—that fruit was *hers*—and soon they were dropping Dillon back at his house on their way to the Peak Street labs.

The note pressed against her. She imagined it drawing her escorts' eyes.

When she got to the lab facility, she didn't remove the note. The thought of touching it in front of any member of the surveillance team made her neck burn.

Like a beleaguered ferret, she dug herself in at her usual workspace in the mid-security wing. She wondered if her chaperones noticed how much she was sweating.

Flora appeared at Rex's elbow with an "I've been looking at the budget," which earned a jump and a shout, both of which were ignored. "I think you're going to have to do some consultations to make the bottom line."

Rex *hated* consultations. She bent further over the sketch on her worktable and groaned.

"Don't give me that. It's the easiest way to make up the losses after all the money we've dumped into the city for the dinosaur rampage. Unless you have something patentable lying around here."

She probably did, but the patenting process was always more time-consuming than a few hours of consulting at an exorbitant rate.

Flora reached Rex's worktable and looked over her shoulder at the sketch she was developing. "Is that a helicopter?"

"It turns out they make helicopters with skids because they can land on more diverse terrain." Rex added some details to her design. "But with wheels, it can taxi. I'm making mine with wheels and retractable skids."

Flora put a hand on her shoulder. "You hate the cars that much?"

"Yes," she hissed.

"Rex—"

"There's enough room on the roof of the house and Peak Street."

Flora sighed and pulled a chair closer. "Anyway, I want to schedule a few hours over the next month or two. What works best for you?"

Rex tried not to think about the consultation that weighed like a rock in her pocket. "I don't care when. Just don't open it up to the Protectors."

Flora didn't sigh or shift, but frustration radiated off her. "Rex, the Protectors of the World would pay the price of a small country if you designed them some gadgets. And their budget is practically bottomless. If you agreed to a contract with them—"

"I can't stand the Protectors. I'm not making their stuff."

"And it would be good for your image," Flora pushed. "Imagine appealing the Oversight decision while being the exclusive provider of tech for the Protectors of the World. That doesn't sound like a villain to me. And you keep saying you're not a superbeing—providing *support* for superbeings would back that up."

"Not the Protectors." Rex pushed back from the table, telling herself it was to get a better look at her sketch and not an emotional outburst. "Several of them have helped 'take me down.'" She made a show of forming air quotes. "They all side-eye me like I'm a streetwalker—"

"You don't have to like coworkers. And you wouldn't have to see them often."

"But I'd have to know they're out there using my stuff. I'd have to design shuriken shaped like jellyfish or something—"

"Manta Man uses stingray weapons, not jellyfish."

"Most of them have gadget people, anyway. Or they use alien technology that should probably be looked over by the EPA, or they make it themselves because they have every skill due to weird childhoods or training adjacent to their tragic backstories."

"Vivid Blue has reached out via a representative."

Rex froze. The note was suddenly heavier. She felt pressure on the tip of her finger before she realized it was tapping on the desk. "Vivid Blue doesn't use gadgets."

"On behalf of her fellow Protectors, then."

Yeah, Rex knew what she was doing.

"She doesn't actually want me to make them anything." Her voice had dropped. She spontaneously remembered the soldier sitting in the corner of the room, keeping an eye on her.

Just a few days, and she was already starting to see them as part of the background.

That was dangerous.

Rex drew in a breath and changed the subject. "Am I still doing an interview with the *Circular*?"

"Even better. I got you on *Good Morning, Gorgeous*."

A sputter-squawk burst out of Rex's mouth. "You what?"

"It's a wider audience, and Gorgeous is very nice."

"I don't do well on camera." Rex managed not to grasp at Flora in supplication, but there was more than a little whine in her voice.

"Well, you do worse in print. At least this way people can watch you correct yourself when you say something wild."

Rex bit back anything else that would add dollars to the jar and swept out of her workspace toward the dinosaur habitats. It was almost time for their noon feeding, and she was never trusting her lab techs again. Joey hopped up from his seat to follow her.

"What's this?" Flora asked.

Rex turned in the doorway. Flora was standing by her worktable, looking down at a crumpled piece of paper. For a crazy-making instant Rex wondered if she'd pulled out Sam's note without realizing it. Then Flora held up the to-do list.

It's hard to breathe your heart rate back down while hiding that winded look of panic, but Rex had gotten pretty good at it. "It's my obligations from most pressing to least pressing."

"I see 'break up with Dillon' isn't crossed off." Flora followed Rex with the list in hand, so Rex kept walking.

"Well, 'deal with the dinosaurs' isn't crossed off either, and we can agree it's higher priority."

"You told me you were breaking up with him weeks ago."

Rex huffed, eyes rolling toward the black-tiled ceiling. "I just think when I do it, he'll get mad."

"The longer you wait, the worse it will be."

"I have a plan."

"Which is?" Flora scanned her access badge to let them into the high-se-curity wing.

Rex held the door for Joey and automatically checked the lights on the floor: green, so her employees weren't actively in crisis. "I'm pretty sure he wants to break up, too, so I was going to wait for him to do it. But he keeps not doing it."

"So," Flora said slowly, "you think he wants to break up with you, but you haven't broken up with him because you think he'll get mad?"

Rex nodded too vigorously.

"Sweetie." Flora put a hand on her shoulder. "Break up with him."

Rex gave an exaggerated whine.

"And find someone you're actually attracted to—"

"That's not the main issue."

"Of course, it isn't." Flora's voice gentled, as though she expected resis-tance. "You know, a lot of men don't know how to satisfy a woman because no one teaches them—"

"You don't have to lesbian-splain women to me. And it doesn't factor because I don't care if Dillon's good at sex or not. Which he is. I think."

Flora sighed. "All right. If you don't care about that part, what parts *do* you care about?"

Rex's face did a squirmy little dance. She was okay at acting on feel-ings. Not so much describing them. "The part where you want to be around someone, and then you get to be around them."

"And everything else is just the price of keeping them around?"

"Yes?" There was more that Rex wasn't willing to say in front of Joey. Like prolonged physical contact. She loved prolonged physical contact. Or being able to tell someone how you think and feel without worrying about them using it against you. She liked the idea of that, anyway.

As they opened the second, heavier door, the excited cries and barks of dinosaurs about to be fed hit her ears. Rex strode immediately toward the clear wall separating the lab floor from the large, circular space packed with previously extinct plants and insects.

Sunlight spilled into the lab through the habitat's much higher ceiling. The happy dino-babbles echoed louder as a white-coated tech entered a side chamber attached to the enclosure. Small- and medium-sized dinosaurs, feathers flying, scaly skin rippling, and sharp teeth glinting in open mouths, hopped over each other under the access hatch that the technician opened to toss out raw chicken cutlets.

"Chicken!"

"Chicken!"

"Meat!"

Flora's eyes bugged behind her glasses. "Did you make them talk?!"

Rex nodded, lips pursed. "I needed to know what their ideal conditions were and asking them seemed like the fastest way to learn. But their attention spans aren't great, and some of them lie a lot." She scratched the back of her head. "Did you know they aren't all dinosaurs? I've been doing research, and I think they're a mix of dinosaurs, archosaurs, and species made up in movies. And a lot of them existed millions of years apart, so it's been an exercise in compromise."

The dinosaurs caught sight of Rex and stopped snagging hunks of meat out of the air to surge along the wall with a chorus of, "Mommy! Mommy! Mommy!"

"I can't get them to stop calling me that," Rex muttered.

"Why would you want to?" Flora strode to the wall with her arms spread wide. "Hi, babies! It's your Aunt Flora!"

Rex sighed.

"Dr. Anderson?" A woman in a lab coat hovered at Rex's elbow with a clipboard in hand. "Their intelligence seems to be growing past the expected limits. We've also adjusted their diets since test results came back about their food sensitivities, if you want to check it over."

"Why do you all keep calling me doctor? My highest degree is a bachelor's in concert piano."

"Sorry, Doctor."

Rex took the clipboard with another sigh. She snuck a glance at the tech, hoping to catch a defining feature, but failed to find any eye patches, scars, or tattoos. "What's your name again? Shelby?"

"Caroline Green."

"Right. I knew that. The diet changes are fine, but what's this injection you want to give them?"

"Most of the team is concerned about the increased intelligence. They want to return the dinosaurs to how they were now that you've explored the option of interviewing them."

"That sounds morally problematic."

"Respectfully, enhancing their intelligence was too. This will just return them to their natural state."

"They don't have a natural state. They're abominations of nature." Rex scribbled some notes on the clipboard. "But now that you mention it, they're going to need more stimulation with the intelligence boost. We should probably bring in a tutor or something. Maybe those people who teach apes sign language." What job was that? Flora would be good at it.

"I want to pet them," Flora called with her cheek against the clear wall. On the other side, a red-frilled aquilops scraped at the wall with its beak while a larger yarasuchus used it as a footstool and pressed its whole long neck against the wall.

"I'll make some heavy-duty baby toys to tide them over." Rex gave the clipboard back to the visibly deflated Caroline Green.

"Yes, Dr. Anderson."

"Thank you. And remember, our new lab goal is to not—"

"Not let them out. Yes, Doctor."

"Great. Keep up the good work."

On their way out of the lab, as Rex steeled herself for the car ride, Flora asked, "Are they really the best you could get?"

"My labs have a reputation for mad science. Applicants aren't the cream of the crop."

"Yet another reason to take your reputation more seriously."

Rex groaned. "Superbeings don't go on talk shows."

"All the better. You're not a superbeing. Get the public to believe it, and the courts will follow." They climbed into the car, Rex and Flora in the back seat, Joey and Becky in front.

"Look," Flora continued, "I think this interview is a good call. I know that—" She took a breath. "I know we might not be in this mess if I'd been more on top of this. If I'd paid enough attention to see this coming—"

"That's a dollar," Rex interrupted, adding before Flora could protest, "Impossible standards. It counts."

Flora frowned, but she pulled her purse into her lap and went fishing for a dollar. "Anyway, I'm going to be more proactive from now on. We'll work like hell on your public image, and when we appeal, they won't dare to keep Oversight going. It looks very intrusive, applied to a civilian. And they started you at the second-highest tier. One slip and they'll lock you up in genius super-max. I'm not letting that happen."

Rex considered the stakes that Flora had lined out and wanted to scratch her pocket like an itch. She was pretty sure the world had forgotten that Sam was her brother. The reminder of that wouldn't do her any good. That he'd reached out now made it worse.

Rex's eyes flicked to her friend. Flora's priorities would not always align with hers. They shouldn't. *Hi T. I need help.* Rex pushed through the flinch, but guilt still swirled in her stomach. "You've been staying at Sable's place most weekends lately, right?"

Flora gave her an unimpressed look. "My girlfriend's name is Sadie."

Right, of course. "So, I was thinking—this whole thing could have a silver lining."

Flora raised an eyebrow. "Your devious look is worrying. Don't do that in the interview—we want you to look harmless."

Rex fought her smirk into a deep frown, making Flora huff. "I'm just saying, I'd back up any claims that staying in the house isn't an option anymore."

Flora laughed outright, which gave Rex a deep sense of accomplishment. "I'm not going to use government surveillance to con my girlfriend into letting me move in. I'd rather she move in with us, anyway." Her eyes narrowed. "And I'm not leaving you alone there. I see your game, Rex. Oversight isn't anything I can't deal with."

Damn it. "But it's my fault you—"

"Think of the jar. And shut up—I make my own choices."

Rex's shoulders dropped. The strength of her relief at Flora's answer was shameful. She could admit to herself that she'd been a little worried that this would be the thing that made Flora leave. At least she didn't have to do this alone.

As long as she didn't step a toe out of line and end up waiting in a cell for Flora to visit for the rest of her life.

Hi T. I need help.

A surge of dread made Rex's limbs heavy. This would probably end badly.

ISSUE 5

SPOTLIGHT ON THE PAST: PART ONE

R ex was in high school when she started sleeping with a hammer under her bed. She felt ridiculous about it, but she still couldn't put it back in her dad's toolbox. She told no one. There was a fear of not being believed, or of finding out she was seeing something that wasn't there, and what would that mean about her? Beneath that, though, was a fear she could barely recognize—the possibility, too real to consider, that she *would* be believed, and nothing would be done.

Rex and Sam were always the same size growing up. Rex was a little taller according to the marks in the kitchen doorway, which she crowed about every time a new set was added on their birthday.

Then Sam got tall. It seemed to happen overnight. He was picked on at school before—girls could be cruel to each other, but boys had no mercy for a small, hyper, thirteen-year-old. It didn't help when your twin sister was a genius and you struggled to pass algebra. Then he got tall, and he wasn't quite angry yet. That was still around the corner, waiting for him to recognize it.

Rex had always bossed him around, with the mix of kind and cold whims that older siblings had, even if it was by barely enough to count. She still did even after he got tall, but she felt how thin the bubble had gotten, the empty authority that was all that stood between her and her much larger brother. She could swear he felt it too. How could he fail to notice that for the first time in his life someone was smaller than him? Things quietly became different. Rex tried to stand with more space between them so she wouldn't have to tip her head and feel that little chill when his shadow fell over her. When it was her turn with the laptop, sometimes he took it and walked away. When Rex walked through a room where Sam was sitting, sometimes he stood abruptly and blocked her path.

She never said anything about it. She knew she would lose something if she did, having to run to Mom and Dad, needing someone else to fight for her when she and Sam had always fought toe-to-toe, always exchanged equal shoves and tattled for equal transgressions. But she found the hammer in the back of a closet while looking for a hand pump to reinflate a soccer ball, and without thinking too much about it—without letting herself think too much about it—she hid it under her bed.

Later, after the accident, when Sam stepped out of the machine with his hands on his head, wailing with pain, she watched everyone else overlook the way he'd gained a foot of height and nearly doubled his weight in pure muscle, unless it was to compliment him or jokingly point out the bright side.

She'd scrambled to help him with the real problem, of course—what everyone saw as the real problem—but she'd looked on in wonder as their family ignored the other changes, squeezed his arms, hugged him with no hesitation. Was she the only one who suppressed a tremble when he blocked a doorway? Was she the only one who watched her brother get strong and was filled with dread?

ISSUE **6**

DINOSAURS ON TELEVISION

That night, Rex looked over Sam's message again in the privacy of her room. She trusted Aya to loop footage of her sleeping in case someone pulled it later; they weren't allowed to watch her rooms live, but she wasn't sure where that line got drawn. She memorized the design unconsciously, and her mind played around with it as she paced.

First of all, helmets were dumb. She could do the same thing with a cloth hood, stitched-in circuitry, and maybe a grounding harness to protect it from interference.

I have to make it stop, Sam's note said. Rex didn't know what the rock in her gut was made of, exactly. Guilt was part of it. Anger too. Part of it—she hated this part—was fear. Still. Fear wasn't supposed to hang around that long, was it? And there were other parts without words. Ugly, twisted things that made her want to cry and made her hate them for it.

The worst parts were not negative. Was it weird that every time her brother showed up in her dreams, he looked like he had as a kid? Her brain should know what adult Sam looked like by now.

Hi T. I need help. I love you.

Rex stopped pacing when that familiar black pit appeared behind her, a straight drop right at the edge of her heel. With shivers almost making her legs buckle, she left her room, eyes straight ahead. She took the stairs to the kitchen and turned the light on low, breathing a sigh as the light and the communal nature of the space filled the pit back in. On a stool at the kitchen island, she let her eyes focus on the grain of the marble, mind falling back into circles.

What would happen if she made it for him?

What would happen if she didn't?

Soft footsteps brought her out of whatever thoughts she'd been lost in, and she raised her head to see Lewis Stone in the shadow of the doorway, blinking at her in the kind of muted surprise you feel when you're supposed to be asleep and nothing matters.

Rex stiffened, but she was under the I'm-still-not-asleep spell, too, so instead of getting up and backing out, she watched him walk to the refrigerator. Her heart rate picked up enough to sharpen her focus and remind her that she was effectively alone with him. She noted the island between them in deliberate self-reassurance, and asked, "What are you doing up?"

He shot her an eyebrow-arch, pulled out something burrito-shaped wrapped in foil, and sat across from her. "What are *you* doing up?" he countered as he unwrapped, yes, half a burrito. Rex should win a prize.

"I have stuff on my mind. I've been under stress."

Lewis hunched over his first bite of cold burrito and muttered something Rex didn't catch.

Whatever. Rex was used to being muttered about. "When did people get burritos? Because I don't remember being asked if I wanted one."

Lewis rolled his eyes, set the burrito back on the foil, and pushed it toward Rex.

"I don't want yours—I would've wanted my own."

"My burrito isn't good enough for you?"

"Does it have cheese in it?"

A brow crease joined his frown.

"Then it's not good enough for me."

Lewis pulled the burrito back with a jerkier movement, and Rex questioned her self-preservation skills when it came to antagonizing someone with absolute power over her life.

But it was the middle of the night, and nothing she said right now counted. "Just ask everyone next time. It's polite."

"Fine," he said, that little twist in his mouth holding strong through a bite of cheese-infected burrito. "Why are you sitting in here if you're not eating?" he asked next.

Rex couldn't talk about the pit, of course. She never talked about the pit. "I'm thinking about how to break up with my boyfriend." A flat-out lie, but heck—that bit of drama was already playing out in full view of her surveillance, and it wasn't like it wasn't adding to her stress and, thus, vulnerability to the goddamn pit.

Little brow crease made a reappearance, but this version didn't look threatening. "Why are you dragging that out?"

Wow, not even going to pretend he didn't have the details. "That's none of your business."

Lewis wasn't looking at her anymore. "It just seems selfish," he said with his mouth full, "holding on to a relationship that can't go where he wants."

"Excuse me?" Rex's brow climbed. "He wants to break up too. It's not always my job to do the dirty work."

"You don't know that." He took a big, rushed bite. "You don't always know how people really feel. Just because you didn't know doesn't mean you're not hurting them, and that isn't okay."

That was so incomprehensible it was almost cute, like a toddler sharing his thoughts. "This conversation is such nonsense that I'm not even offended anymore, but your investment in my breakup is a little worrying."

He blinked at her, cheeks full of the last of his burrito. He almost looked like he was blushing, but that was probably snacking exertion and bad light. When he'd chewed the monster bite down enough to swallow, he balled the foil and said, "Yeah. I'll get a lid on it."

Rex blinked after him as he tossed the foil in the trash and left the kitchen. She hopped off the stool to return to her room, half certain that interaction would turn out to have been a stress dream or a mind-warping villain attack. The pit didn't make a reappearance though, and she finally slept.

The two surveillers who accompanied Rex and Flora to the *Good Morning, Gorgeous* interview were Peter and Lewis. The second was unfortunate, but the first was a small mercy the universe was granting Rex, since Peter was her favorite babysitter by far and as easy to get along with as he'd seemed at the home inspection. They chatted on the drive about automated navigation in the helicopter she was designing.

Flora allowed her that brief break from reviewing what to say and what to avoid saying at all costs.

Instead of scowling at everything, Lewis stared out the window and pouted the whole time. If that was how he protested his colleague being nice to her, he could suck it. She was grateful Peter kept talking to her despite casting tight glances at Lewis, hands a little stiff on the wheel.

Rex pulled at her blazer as she got out of the car. Professional dress was so aggressively gendered. The feminine cut pressed around her, making her want to slink around like a cat in a Halloween costume. They'd done what they could with pants and flats, but it didn't seem like truly gender-neutral business wear existed. Flora had encouraged her to think of it as a disguise, but to Rex it felt more like a lie.

She was also carrying a purse. That wasn't necessary, but a couple of the more enterprising dinosaurs had lain eggs, which were now nestled in a scarf bed in the bag on her arm. Because even though they apparently had a breeding instinct, none of the dinosaurs seemed interested in sitting on the things. Rex had barely saved the clutch from one of the clumsier quadrupeds tearing through the brush. She was having some incubators installed in case more eggs appeared, but for now she hoped Flora's giant backup bag could be made as warm as a dinosaur's butt.

The television studio was frantic in a way that made Rex ache with sympathy for the poor souls who had to work there. They learned quickly that the energy wasn't typical, as the first five people they saw told them in a rush that Bright Jack was in the studio. Flora looked a bit worried, but her face smoothed when they learned he was appearing on a news program after *Good Morning, Gorgeous*. Rex was just glad her inevitable shitshow would be so conveniently overshadowed.

After the set crew, or whatever they called themselves, made her acceptable for television—Flora had prepared her thoroughly for the experience of TV makeup—there was nothing to do but wait. So, Rex, Flora, Peter, and Lewis found themselves in a small lounge area with a platter of snacks, sitting in a semicircle of couches and armchairs with Bright Jack and his two attendants.

"So, the Meister." Bright Jack shot her a congenial smirk. His manly brown hair was gelled back from his red-masked face. He was wearing his whole superhero ensemble—blue body-armor-slash-spandex with red accents and a yellow cape thrown over the back of the couch, Rex assumed to avoid wrinkles. "I heard you got caught up in Oversight. That's a real shame."

"I kind of had it coming," Rex said, earning a warning glare from Flora.

"It still doesn't seem right to start you so high in the tiers." He leaned back with his legs stretched in front of him like a propped-up Ken doll. "That's a big adjustment to ask you to make after your city settled for truce agreements for so long."

"That's not the policy's fault," Lewis said, gaze hovering on the corner of the room. "She should have been placed on a lower tier earlier and had it escalated if her behavior didn't adjust. The city looked the other way for too long."

Rex arranged her egg-laden purse beside her and tried not to scowl at the talk of her *behavior,* as though she was a rowdy child. Flora silently placed a hand on her knee.

"I've never paid much attention to the whole Oversight situation," Bright Jack mused with a wave of his hand. "I've been looking into it more now that Jenny Glow is at risk for the lower tiers."

"Right—you got a sidekick," Peter broke in, all smiles in a way that looked fake. "Is that a 'congratulations' situation? I don't know how it works."

Rex didn't think anyone knew how it worked.

Bright Jack gave Peter a gracious nod. "I'll take congratulations. I'm proud to have the opportunity to take Jenny under my wing."

"It must be a big responsibility," Lewis said, that brow crease finally replacing the pout. It was almost a relief—Rex hadn't known his face could make those shapes.

"Oh, it is. And I've always worked alone. But with everything she's been through, seeing her parents decapitated like that, being subjected to the same ultra-light radiation that gave me powers—"

Holy crap, that was actually horrific. Rex glanced around at the politely sympathetic faces. Had they not heard the same thing she'd heard?

Bright Jack shook his head. "She needs this. She needs to know that she can use these powers to make sure others aren't hurt the way she was."

Rex thought she needed a stable home, therapy, and a buttload of friends, but no one was asking her.

"That's quite a sacrifice," Flora said.

"It is." Bright Jack sighed. "But the people want to know someone's out there, standing for justice. The victims of supervillains need that hope."

Was that what victims wanted? All Rex remembered wanting was her mom.

"It's a heck of a tragic backstory too," Peter said. "If she's revenge-driven so far, I can see why she'd be on Oversight's radar."

"It's unfortunately common in the superhero community." Bright Jack gave an apologetic chuckle. "We can't all be Vivid Blue."

Rex's body sank deeper than the sofa should go. Her heart was beating in her ears, but she couldn't feel it.

"Oh, that's a doozy of a backstory," one of Bright Jack's aids said with a grin.

"I don't know," Peter hedged. "Something about being born with powers—I can't make myself relate to those."

"Blue wasn't born with powers—she got them in a childhood accident," Bright Jack said.

Rex didn't wince.

Peter frowned. "I could've sworn—"

"The origin of her powers isn't part of her tragic backstory, so it's under-standable. But no, she got them when she was young—nine or ten."

It was twelve.

"I'm not sure I've heard Vivid Blue's backstory either," Flora said thoughtfully. "I think I know the basics, but it's been some time."

Bright Jack sat forward and clasped his hands. "Well, you know that Last Dance and Vivid Blue are brother and sister, right?"

Rex could feel herself retreating, watching from afar, the racing of her heart in her ears fading to a white noise that was almost soothing. The reac-tion was as automatic as ever, she was surprised to find—it had been a while since anyone had told the story in her presence. And as always, a morbid curiosity kept her listening.

"It's sort of a joint backstory—hero and villain, sister and brother. That's what makes it so compelling. See, Vivid Blue was the oldest. Having her pow-ers from such a young age, she always protected her younger siblings."

Fighting with a sibling who could technically take whatever they want is tricky. When you win, you know they let you. When you lose, you know they used their powers even though they tried not to.

"But she had trouble fitting in. She stood out—you know? And she wanted to be a normal kid. They had another sister, a real whiz kid, who ran tests on Blue's blood and everything, trying to get rid of her powers. So, one day—they were older then, late teens, early twenties—Last Dance let his friends into the lab."

He called them his friends. Anyone else would've called them his bullies.

"The sister was building a machine that was supposed to make Viv-id Blue normal again. But it wasn't ready, and it was keyed to her DNA or something like that."

Rex managed not to roll her eyes.

"Last Dance's friends—these weren't good kids, understand? A bad crowd. They dared him to get inside."

He never passed up a chance to prove himself. He couldn't afford to—he didn't get the chance very often.

"Last Dance had always been jealous of his sister."

What a simple way to describe being overshadowed, overlooked, and negatively compared to someone you're growing up with.

"He thought if the machine could take Vivid Blue's powers away, maybe they could give superpowers to him. So, he got inside."

"I'm guessing it didn't go the way he hoped," Peter said.

"Not at all." Bright Jack raised his hands like he might mime the story. "The machine went crazy—wrecked the place and ruined Vivid Blue's hopes of a cure."

That was overdramatic. It would've only been a setback if she hadn't changed her mind.

"And then Last Dance stepped out, and he was changed. But it wasn't how he thought it would be. He had the same super strength Vivid Blue had, but he didn't have the telekinesis."

"And he wasn't blue," one of the aids said, and several people chuckled.

"No," Bright Jack said through a grin. "Mind reading. That's the power he got."

I have to make it stop. God, Sam.

"And that's how he became Last Dance?" Lewis asked.

"I'm getting there," Bright Jack answered. "He already envied his superpowered sister when he went into the machine. After the machine, he was enraged that Vivid Blue was still stronger. And the thoughts of everyone around him were always in his head. He was full of bitterness, slowly going crazy."

He couldn't sleep, couldn't think. Enraged? Bitter? Yes, he was enraged and bitter. He was desperate.

"So then, he kidnapped the science-y sister to make her recreate the accident."

Rex's body wasn't there. She couldn't feel a thing. There were too many people in the room—she couldn't afford to feel.

"The one who built the machine?" Peter asked.

"Yes. When Vivid Blue went after him. it was the first time she took action as a hero. She brought him home, tried to reason with him, but he didn't stick around. She caught up to him in his makeshift lair, getting ready to unleash a virus that would make the whole population brain-dead, just so he'd stop hearing their thoughts."

"That's a heck of a starter villain," Peter said.

Bright Jack nodded. "That's when Vivid Blue realized her powers could help people. She stopped trying to be normal and became Vivid Blue."

What a nice ending. Rex felt her lip start to twist and stopped it with an effort.

"My favorite part is how at the end a reporter asked her—this was her first statement to the press—'How are you going to stop Last Dance?' And she said, 'I'm not going to stop him. I'm going to save him.'"

There were a few sounds of appreciation from the circle.

"That's what really makes her a hero," Bright Jack finished.

Rex was aware of her palms sweating and her heart beating too hard—that was starting to hurt; she should probably get it to slow down—but she was still watching from somewhere else. So, this was how other people remembered it. It was odd to hear. The main points were the parts she would put in the footnotes, and vice versa. Her eyes roved over the faces in the circle again. Their expressions were all so *appropriate*.

"What happened to the girl?" Flora asked.

"The girl?" Bright Jack raised an eyebrow, stretching his mask.

"The one Last Dance kidnapped," Flora explained.

Something in Rex's chest went loose and desperately grateful. Thank God for this woman. Her existence was a gift the world didn't deserve.

"Oh, Vivid Blue saved her. She was shaken up, for sure, but she was okay."

Rex felt a phantom hand around her arm and her own phantom fingers poking at a tender crescent under her eye. If it healed in a week, it didn't count.

"You said she brought Last Dance home?" Lewis asked, brow crease heavier on one side. "She brought the sister home too?"

Bright Jack's mouth twisted before he gave an uncomfortable chuckle. "Well. That would be inconvenient."

Rex didn't think a truer sentence had ever been spoken.

"I want to know more about that machine for taking Blue's powers away," Peter said. "Something like that could do a lot of good for supervillains in custody. Make rehabilitation possible, in some cases."

Aid number one nodded. "Something like that could actually save Last Dance, like Blue wanted. I wonder what came of it."

Rex was going to throw up. It was only a matter of time. The vomit-sweats had already broken out on her ribs and neck. She'd been motionless on the cushy sofa long enough to work up a decent layer of back and thigh sweat too. Good thing her lady-blazer was so dark. Flora would not approve of a sweaty Rex on *Good Morning, Gorgeous.*

The door to the hall swung open, and several people jumped. Not Rex—if she hadn't reacted to anything yet, she wasn't going to start with the door.

"You're on deck, Ms. Anderson."

This would go well. Rex was in an excellent headspace for a live interview. Flora would be so happy with her. She hopped to her feet and tugged her hem straight. "Let's do this."

They touched up her makeup while Gorgeous introduced her, Flora hovering at her shoulder and whispering reminders about the agreed-upon talking points. Her words registered as a buzz, leaving Rex's head oddly blank. Messages from Aya kept popping up on her phone, all some version of *good luck.*

Next came instructions. *Stand there. Wait. Go on.* She smiled as she shook Gorgeous's hand, those apple cheeks making her feel like a welcomed-home daughter despite Gorgeous being surprisingly young—the makeup must age her on camera. Her halo of brown curls looked very stiff up close. Polite claps from the studio audience replaced the buzz. She sat as directed.

"So! Theodora Rex Anderson: the Meister of Decimen City." Gorgeous did a bit of gushing that made Rex feel good about herself. "Now, you've made a stir in the news recently with a little mishap in your labs."

And there they went about the dinosaurs. After a short back-and-forth, Rex got to watch the screen behind the chairs as they played a montage of the dinos sunning themselves and rolling around in their habitats. It had been the network's idea to pre-tape footage of the dinosaurs, and Flora had instantly agreed.

With the attention off her for a moment, Rex's face melted into a smile. In the clip, two raptors fought over a rubber block until a brontosaur swatted them aside with its tail and cast a narrow-eyed look over its shoulder that looked suspiciously like a lizard smirk. What a bunch of A-holes.

"They seem to be settling in," Gorgeous said.

Rex nodded. "The accident was very scary for them, and it's nice to have them back where they're safe." Nailed it—almost word for word what they'd practiced. Rex glanced off set and saw Flora giving her a big thumbs-up.

"It sounds like you care a lot about them."

"They're surprisingly sweet." They were little shits. "And there's a lot of information lost to time encoded in their DNA. Every one of them is a living treasure for science." So vague and so, so stupid.

"What an exciting project! I guess we can all be grateful to the brave police officers who responded to such an unprecedented disaster and got them back where they belong. And the Lightning, of course."

"Oh, yeah." The tightness in her throat made it hard to judge her tone. "The Lightning's great." There was a glass of water by her chair. She took a swig. "Yeah, she electrocuted a bunch of confused dinosaurs while I punched them out. But I guess that's better than the freaking bazooka the cops were shooting at them. No problem-o."

Pseudo-Spanish. Great idea, Rex.

Gorgeous was stiff in her seat, like she was keeping herself from leaning forward. The smile on her face was equally stiff. "Is that not the whole story?"

"No, it's the whole story." She set the water down. Flora was making a hand motion off set. "I mean, that's what was told, so obviously that's 'the story.'" She did air quotes and hated herself a little for doing air quotes. "That's what stories are, right? People tell them, and then that's it. That's what they are."

"I guess I'm asking if there was more to it."

Oh, right—the opening to talk about why she cloned dinosaurs without mentioning that she broke the clone clause to do it. "Well." Flora's flapping at the edge of her vision was hard to ignore, but she didn't think she could look at Flora, maintain her I'm-being-interviewed face, and answer Gorgeous at the same time. Not with the way feelings kept surging in the pit of her stomach.

"There's always more, right?" she heard herself say. "I mean, the news only says so much. I'm sure there's someone whose car was kicked over by one of my dinosaurs, and to them the story doesn't end until the car gets fixed. And there were businesses that will lose customers because the street's messed up. So, I can tell the story, and 'Ning can tell the story, and the only thing that matters is it's me and 'Ning telling it, and what version do people want to—"

"I'm so sorry to interrupt. This is fascinating," Gorgeous broke in, not looking sorry at all. "But we're going to have to cut to commercial. We'll be back with more from the Meister of Decimen City." She directed the last to her audience with an apple-cheeked grin.

Rex sat back in her seat, smile frozen on her face. It was probably for the best that Gorgeous cut off that train of thought.

Who cared, honestly? Saying *that's not how it happened* was petty, all things considered. Even worse when it was so damn inconvenient for everyone.

Flora was beside her, voice low. "I need you to breathe, Rex. You're doing fine. Just stay present. It's only ten more minutes."

"I told you I was bad at this," she hissed back.

"We need to reset," a crewmember said, ushering Flora away.

Rex gulped a full glass of water and fixed her posture. Then she was listening to her reintroduction and wondering if her smile made her look as mad as her action figures. Not that Flora ever let those stay in production longer than it took to slap on a lawsuit.

"I hear you're paying for the damages out of pocket," Gorgeous said, managing to smile through her speech in a way Rex envied.

"Yeah, but I'm rich. No skin off my back. I bet most people would prefer that it hadn't happened. But I'm giving out a buttload of reparations, so maybe everyone will forgive me again. I have no idea why people do that."

The concept of forgiveness felt alien to Rex. How did people do it? What was the first step? Besides everyone telling you how important it was, that is. Everyone makes mistakes. You aren't blameless. You have to move past it. You can't get better unless you get better.

"I'm sure people remember the part you played in stopping the stampede." Gorgeous's words cued footage of Rex in her Exo-suit punching dinosaurs while 'Ning threw zippy yellow kicks. Rex suppressed a wince as Gorgeous gave her a teasing grin. "Can we expect more superhero team-ups from you in the future?"

Rex couldn't hold back the grimace. "That's not really what that was. Look, the Lightning and I can both be reasonable. Occasionally. We did what had to be done. At least I did. Maybe 'Ning was superhero-ing, but I was trying to circumvent getting punched by 'Ning, and then I was trying to contain the dinosaurs. And now I'm trying to generate goodwill or something, so none of that is really heroic."

Were studio audiences supposed to be this quiet? Flora had stopped gesturing and was standing behind the camera with her hand over her eyes. Gorgeous stared at her with a frozen, toothy smile. *Well, poo.*

"I mean," Rex started again, "not that there's anything wrong with that. Because if a superhero saves someone, who cares why they do it? I wouldn't." At first, anyway. Then she kind of had. "Everyone else can fill in the blanks however they want. If you remember what you remember, and everyone else sort of selectively forgets the parts that make them uncomfortable, who cares? I mean, everyone knows how dysfunctional the Protectors are, but if someone's life is in danger, I'm sure they'd be happy to see that sting-ray-shaped shadow floating over New Orleans—"

"Manta Man operates in Seattle, not New Orleans," Gorgeous cut in kindly.

Rex blinked a few times, derailed. "Then who am I thinking of?"

"You're probably thinking of Mantis Man. He's active in New Orleans."

"Oh, right." Rex tried to think. "Powers of a praying mantis?"

"No. Manta Man has the powers of a manta ray; Mantis Man *emulates* a praying mantis."

Rex internally groaned as she recalled the details. "Oh, wait—he's one of those gray-morality superheroes with the especially disturbing backsto-ries, isn't he?"

"Mantis Man has been criticized for the extreme measures he takes to stop gang violence," Gorgeous said hesitantly. "His actions have inspired many debates about the nature of—"

"Right. He's the revenge type. Good to know." Rex had a particular dis-dain for that breed of hero.

"Yes, well." That grin was starting to irritate Rex. "Having his entire fam-ily murdered that way—I know I would snap. But if we can get back to—"

"Of course. Plenty of people snap. I guess it's the way each 'snap' is la-beled good or bad that escapes my understanding. Isn't it the classic super-villain backstory that the villain gets bullied and ridiculed for years and then decides they want revenge on society?"

Gorgeous started to say something, but Rex bulldozed through, "But somehow the murdered-family-methodical-revenge-against-the-corrupt-system story makes a controversial hero? What's the difference?"

"Well, lots of people get bullied without becoming villains." Gorgeous laughed and made an elbow-nudgy gesture. "This is very interesting, but my producer's back there giving me *the look,* so—"

"Lots of people lose their families." Rex's head was filling with noise—the frustration, the illogic, the sheer inane friendliness of Gorgeous's smile.

"Not that that's not a good reason to snap," she backtracked. "I just don't get where the lines are. Losing loved ones is an acceptable push off the edge but prolonged, systematic abuse by your peers isn't. Except when it is. The categorizations defy logic."

Gorgeous was sitting back with a single crease in her brow despite the staff members off set waving for her attention.

Rex felt suddenly grateful that this was a talk show and Gorgeous had tried to smooth over her bullshit instead of latching onto it like a journalist would.

God give Gorgeous the strength to save Rex from herself.

"I think we'd all agree," Gorgeous picked up, "hurting innocents is what makes a villain when it comes down to it. When someone responds to being bullied by becoming a bully, that's a villain. When someone like Mantis Man fights for revenge—and I'm not saying I condone this—he does only target the people involved in the crime."

"Tangentially."

"Yes, but in the case of gang violence—"

"It's still a set of lines that make no damn sense." Oops. They'd have to bleep that. "I mean, he's out there killing foot soldiers. Aren't they maybe victims of the system too? Why doesn't he kill the city budget people or the staff of the zoning office?"

Gorgeous's brow flew up, and Rex hurried to say, "Not that he should! I don't think he should—I just don't understand the difference." She tried a smile. Off set, Flora hadn't removed her hand from her eyes, and now she was slowly shaking her head. "I don't expect fairness or moral righteousness, but I prefer internal consistency."

"Well." Gorgeous gave a tight little laugh. "It seems like you have a unique perspective on superheroes."

"It's not because I'm a villain. I'm not a villain." That might have come out too insistent. "I mean, I'm not usually a villain." Would it be bad to pause here to gulp water? "I know it's sort of a thing that villains never think they're the villain. So, who knows? Anyone could be." She laughed, and it came out jittery. "It's like being insane. No one thinks they are. But someone must be, or why would the word exist?"

"Uh—"

"Unless it's for the sake of the story. It's nice symmetry—sane and insane, hero and villain. But anyway, yeah, looking back I can see where I might have crossed the line into villainhood once or twice. Because if good intentions don't excuse other villains, why should they excuse me?"

"I'm sure redemption is always—"

"They shouldn't!" Rex steamrolled. "Yeah, I took a sample of that zombie virus to study because zombies make no sense. None at all. They're the most ridiculous thing. And then the virus mutated, and we had zombies that could run, and who's to blame for that if not me?" Besides her lab techs, but Rex at least had enough situational awareness to know this was neither the time nor place to throw them under the bus. "I learned from that though. And I think I'm maturing. I think I'm at a place in my life where I can be responsible for these dinosaurs without them turning out like Mutey, the mutant strain of zombie virus."

"I can tell you're taking the responsibility very seriously," Gorgeous said, that odd look on her face smoothing away with a smile. They were back in pre-approved territory.

"I am. I want to do right by them." Where the hell had that phrase come from? Maybe she'd been panicking for a while. "And the city, of course," she added, remembering why she was on the show in the first place.

"Wow. I think this has been a rare privilege, getting this much insight into the mind of the Meister," Gorgeous was saying. That was her wrap-up tone. Had they been speaking for ten minutes already? "I wish we had more time." Apparently, they had.

Rex put a smile back on her face for the gushing, goodbye handshake while the studio audience clapped in the fast, polite way of audiences from the fifties. Rex didn't know what to make of that. When she stepped off the set, Flora put a hand on her back, half patting and half rubbing, and herded her right out the door.

ISSUE 7

DINOSAURS AT HAPPY HOUR

The drive back from the studio was nearly silent, Rex and Flora in the back, Peter and Lewis up front. After a few blocks, Flora said, "So . . ."

"That went badly, didn't it?" Rex said.

"I'm honestly not sure." Flora patted her knee. "You had a lot of feelings out there, didn't you?"

"I don't know where that came from." She shouldn't lie to Flora, but she didn't want to talk about it in front of Lewis and in a moving car.

"That's fine, sweetie."

"Do you want to work on the helicopter when we get back?" Peter asked.

Great, even her surveillance felt sorry for her. "Yes," she said grudgingly.

When they got back, Rex and Peter raced down to the lab, where Aya's "Welcome back, Doctor" had the power to make Rex relax with Pavlovian consistency.

The paper version of Rex's helicopter design was still at Peak Street, but she'd scanned her sketches into Aya's cloud system. The AI called it up on the digital tabletop, hovering over Rex's shoulder as she explained the updates to Peter.

The three of them threw around some ideas, making notes to the sketches and divvying up research for drone programming. The *ding* of the lab door made Rex jump. She needed to change that sound. As Lewis strode in, she tensed. Her eyes flicked from Peter, to Aya, to the back exit like a flight attendant reminding their passengers of the security features. In the event of strange men in your workspace, look to the witnesses and escape routes located throughout the plane.

A buzz made her glance at her phone. She had a text from Aya: *I couldn't keep him out, Doctor.* She snorted and glanced at the innocently hovering eyeballs, which flashed a light in one pupil in a gesture reminiscent of a wink. Rex felt a surge of pride in Aya's growing emotional competence, though she'd have to explain later that winks were creepy.

"Hey." Lewis threw glances at each of them, oddly subdued. Rex saw Peter look away. "We were thinking of ordering pizza upstairs. I've been told it's polite to ask everyone, so what do you guys want?"

"Anchovies and no cheese," Rex said, already knowing it would not make the cut.

Peter gaped at her. "What's wrong with you?"

She sighed. "Order whatever and I'll pick the cheese off."

"I'll eat whatever, too, Lewis. It's more important that I address this dysfunction," Peter said with a wave of dismissal.

"Sure." Lewis looked like he was trying to swallow a laugh, which gave Rex the strong urge to coax it out.

"Aya thinks there's nothing wrong with it," she said, defensively.

The almost-smile vanished from Lewis's face, replaced by a tiny wince. "Right."

Oh, right. AI-hater. Rex shouldn't feel hurt he'd shut down at that. The fact that she did made her irrationally angry.

"That reminds me—I gotta ask," Peter said. "Did you name her *Ay*-a because she looks like eyes?"

Lewis froze at the door and looked back.

"I mean, kind of." Rex tried to return to the helicopter design, refusing to let Lewis distract her. "It's Japanese. It was Flora's idea. I wanted to spell it A-*I*-Y-A because she's an AI, but Flora said it's almost always spelled A-Y-A, so—"

"Then it works on several levels. I like it."

"Thank you, Peter," Aya said.

Lewis still hadn't gone through the door. From the corner of her eye, Rex saw his head turning from Rex to Aya, mouth falling open.

"Lewis? Was there something else?" Peter asked, failing to look casual.

Lewis shook himself. "No. I'll—I know what you like."

Peter went red.

"What pizza you like," Lewis amended. "I'll—" He shot them both one more glance and left in a hurry.

When he was gone, Rex and Peter turned to each other and asked at once, "What was that?" Aya trailed after with her own, "—was that?"

Rex blinked at Peter's blush, feeling heat in her face. "What's your problem with Lewis?"

Peter's shoulders hunched. "What's *your* problem with Lewis?"

"I asked first."

Peter let out a long breath and slumped in his roll-y chair.

The story that followed was some damn juicy gossip. Rex listened raptly as Peter stumbled through it, and Aya dimmed her glow sympathetically.

"And then my dumb ass doesn't stop to think that this is *Lewis* and saying anything might actually change things. What was I thinking? We've been friends for years. Why would I risk losing that just to, what? Clear the air? I'd wallow with my secret crush for as long as I had to if it meant keeping him as a friend."

Part of Rex was kind of shocked that Peter and Lewis had ever been close, considering Peter was awesome and Lewis was the worst. "Why *did* you tell him?"

"Because it's what I do. I fall for a straight guy, and I tell him. Because—I don't know. Once it's out in the world, it's like it's—" He waved a hand over his head. "You know? Once it's out there, I can get over it." His lips pressed together. "This stuff blows over, right? I didn't screw everything up?"

Rex took a deep breath and released it. "Do you want to get a drink?"

He blinked at her.

"Or several? Maybe a bunch? I've been feeling like I need a drink for a while now. It seems like maybe you do too. Is that something you're allowed to do?"

Peter answered after a few more beats. "As long as we're not on shift, yeah."

"When are you off shift?"

He glanced at his phone screen. "In about twenty minutes."

"We can shave off ten by picking up your replacement on the way."

"Cool." Peter stood, and they made their way to the car with more eagerness than may have been healthy.

Rex picked the most basic bar she could think of—not a dive or a club or any place with a reputation.

Peter gave nervous apologies to his two buddies, who were left looking irritable at a booth by the door. Rex tried to smooth things over by covering their non-alcoholic drinks while they waited for her and Peter to get plastered.

"This is the real reason the gay community can be so insular," Peter grumbled over their first set of bright red cocktails as they studied the appetizer menu. "It's not about support or community—it's so when you catch feelings for someone in your life, there's at least a chance they'll like you back."

"Did it work, at least? Are you over it?"

"Getting there. Still wasn't worth nuking half my life."

"Why *Lewis*, though?" Rex asked.

"He's just—you ever had a friend you just clicked with, and just being around them feels grounding and . . . like they balance you?" He dropped his face into his hands. "We're *close*. We have been for years. And you know how sometimes the feelings change. Even though it was great before—it's just your heart going 'hey, why don't I fuck this up for Peter?'"

Rex winced. "If you're that important to each other, you'll get past this."

"It's just that Lewis is a chronic overthinker, and he always puts other people first. And I can already tell he's gotten it in his head that he's the problem. I don't know what he's going to do, and I'm afraid he'll just quietly bow out of my life."

Rex ran her tongue over her gums, catching the syrupy taste of strawberry whatever mixed with an irresponsible proportion of tequila. That did not sound like the Lewis who kept shooting daggers at her across the lab. "Sounds like he's a better friend than babysitter."

Peter shook his head. "No—he's really fair."

Rex wrangled back the urge to say more. "Yeah, okay." They were talking about Peter, and jumping in with her utter hatred of his best friend would be shitty.

He didn't seem satisfied. "Really, you don't have anything to worry about."

She couldn't control the way her brow pinched in anger. "Two giant men move into my house, one of them keeps sneering every time I say anything, and Oversight will believe anything they say over me. But I don't have anything to worry about."

"He's not *dangerous*. He's a good person. You need to cut him some slack."

Memories of the conversation with Bright Jack made Rex's jaw tight, and she couldn't quite take it. "So, it's *my* job to give him a chance. Except he risks nothing while I get to stake my life on trusting a stranger. But I'm sure I'll sleep better knowing you told me he's a good person. That's all I was waiting for."

Peter drew in a breath, then stopped, frowning. He sucked his bottom lip into his mouth, and his eyes drifted to the tabletop. "You're right."

She was what?

"I want to defend Lewis, but I guess it's unfair to ask you to trust in the strength of his character when we have so much power over you."

For a long moment, Rex couldn't find words. "I've never seen someone do that before."

"What? Listen?"

"I guess?"

Peter shrugged and sipped his drink. "I like to think people can change their minds. But for that to be true, I also have to be willing to do it."

Rex stopped gaping. "Are you God?"

Peter snorted and dropped his head on the table, shoulders shaking with silent laughter. "You caught me. I'm a superbeing, and my power is—"

"God." Rex lost it to laughter as well, bowing over. How long had it been since she'd laughed to the point of gasping? It felt like she'd been starving to laugh.

It took some time to pick something to eat. Rex and Peter knocked their heads together as they bent over the laminated monstrosity of a menu, cueing another laughing fit as Rex saw stars.

"Not nachos, either?"

"Ugh." Rex's face twisted. "Never."

"And no cheesy fries?"

"Nope."

"They don't even have normal fries on the menu. We'd have to order cheesy fries without cheese. How do you function in the world this way? Because now I'm having trouble thinking of foods that *don't* have cheese."

Rex shrugged. "It's easier to pretend there's a medical reason." She counted three glasses on her side of the table and had no memory of drinking the second one. That was so weird. "People want you to put up with it because it's normal, but it's so easy to not put it on food. It's not even inconvenient—it's just not normal. And how is it worth doing normal things if it makes you want to barf?"

Peter gave her a confused sort of half smile. "You okay there?"

Was she? "I have to break up with Dillon."

"The guys have a bet going about when you're gonna get that done."

"Ugh." Rex leaned back in her chair. Her life had so many spectators. "They should teach us how to do these things. They'll teach us sex ed, but they can't tell us how to break up with someone?"

"At least you got sex ed. Mine didn't even mention LGBT stuff. I could hardly relate to anything."

"Same here," Rex muttered. She remembered the other students' giggles as they were gently lectured about the things *everyone* felt, and the slow epiphany that no, it was not an invention of the media everyone played along with to look cool—she was the only one who didn't know what they were talking about.

"Ugh! Brain freeze." Peter put down his glass and clapped a hand to his head. "I thought you were straight."

"I am. With the possible exception of the Lightning."

"Then why couldn't you relate?"

Rex filled her cheeks with air and let it out. "Just the way people talk about each other. Like having these draws to people." Elbows on the table, she waved her hands limply over her head. Her gut twinged, like a weak warning that her loosened tongue was about to say something shameful. "Or people say that someone's looking or acting a certain way and it just makes them react? What does that even mean?"

His brow furrowed. "Are you ace?"

"At what?"

Peter blinked at her. "Huh?"

Rex blinked back. "Wait, what are you talking about?"

"Ace as in the A in LGBTQIA? Plus?" At her blank look, he said, "I assumed you knew this stuff because you live with a lesbian. I mean ace, short for asexual."

Rex blinked a few more times, recalling petri dishes of microorganisms in her labs. "Like . . . like seahorses?"

She knew she'd said the wrong word as soon as it was out of her mouth.

"Oh, honey." Peter leaned across the table to take her hand in both of his, a smile fighting over his face. "You need to do some research. Because not only do you not know what asexual means—you don't know what seahorses are."

Rex dropped her burning face onto the table to escape his laughter. "Shut up."

"Aw, hey." The edge of the menu poked at her forehead, and she eyed the line under Peter's finger. "Wings?"

"Yes."

The wings arrived almost instantly, and Peter threw out the cheese dipping sauce with a "Boo." They tore into the food like dinosaurs at feeding time, and Rex was suddenly talking about the interview with no memory of how they reached the subject.

"It wasn't that bad," Peter said.

"Was it not that bad?" Rex asked around a mouthful of chicken.

"For what it's worth, I don't think it's fair how they always bring up the Lightning." Peter leaned forward to look her in the eyes. His eyes were so blue. It was like staring at a washing machine. "I have a sister, and that's what it reminds me of. It's like you're Decimen's kids and they have a favorite. It's no fun being the one who isn't the measuring stick."

Rex had always been the measuring stick, but her siblings never let her forget it.

"It's like this constant comparison." Some of Peter's "s" sounds were coming out as *sh* sounds, which Rex found very interesting. "Like, you're doing fine at something and then it's, 'Hey, you look like Madison. Are you related?' It sucks, right?"

"I wouldn't know. I accidentally turned my sister blue when I was eight."

They lost several minutes and the thread of the conversation to laughter. "Oh my God. You would." Peter took a few breaths. "But you cured cancer," he said, still gasping. "You literally found the cure for cancer and you gave it away for free."

"Big Pharma's still sending assassins after me," Rex said mournfully.

"I don't understand why you don't mention it in every interview. People hardly ever bring it up anymore. Instead, it's zombie virus this, dinosaur rampage that."

Rex winced into her drink and accidentally blew bubbles.

"Flora says if we bring it up too much it'll cheapen it. And it looks like I'm trying to get out of taking responsibility, playing the 'I cured cancer' card."

"It's a good card. I'd play it."

"It makes me sound like a child star who never did anything else. At a certain point, it's just embarrassing."

Peter stared at her, his mouthful of chips unchewed. "*Cancer,*" he repeated.

"Okay, yeah, that was a big deal. I'm proud of that one." Rex's heart was beating faster. Her hand gripped the side of her chair as though to anchor her to a rocking ship. "But that project was weird. It was a weird year." It was a productive year. She would bend her head over her work and look up fourteen hours later soaked in sweat with her throat dried shut up and her head spinning because she'd forgotten to breathe for too long.

"I know it was before you set up in Decimen, so I can see why it's not associated with the Meister of Decimen City. But it's not like it's a secret it was you."

"You'd be surprised how easily people forget the stuff I do." Even she had trouble remembering that year. She had snapshots. She'd force herself into her car every day, park at her various destinations with shakes traveling up her arms, and head straight to a bathroom to puke in the toilet. Panic had sped her heart too easily when she found herself without a wall at her back and an exit in view. And there was a *feeling,* too strong to feel, clawing at the back of her throat and leaving an ache in her chest like a building had fallen on it.

Rex lost most of her friends that year.

"And curing cancer wasn't really the goal," she added.

"How do you cure cancer by accident?"

"It was a side project—not an accident. I spent a whole year on the cancer part." A year of procrastination. Ignoring her responsibilities. Abandoning people who needed her because even looking at the research filled her with rage, helplessness, and guilt.

"I probably could've fixed him," she told the ceiling. She wasn't sure how loud she was. Her ears needed to pop. "I made cancer cells normal again. If I'd sucked it up, maybe I could've done it. My feelings are always so inconvenient."

It hadn't been that kind of problem, though. *Arrogant of me to act like it was.* But it's not like she was the only one who'd thought it was her job to fix Sam.

A rustle by her feet triggered her it's-a-rat instinct, and she jumped. She checked the ground, almost sliding off her chair, and found little nudges pushing from the inside of her purse. For one more horrified instant she thought a rat had gotten inside. Then understanding hit, and her heart plummeted.

"Shit, shit, shit." She snatched up the purse and dragged it into her lap, careful as she could be.

Peter straightened. "What is it? What's wrong?"

"How could I forget there were dinosaur eggs in my purse?"

Peter's mouth fell open.

"Oh my God. Crap, I'm too drunk." She fumbled with the cloth flap over the top, already hearing little cheeps and trills. Soft, fragile heads nudged her fingers. "Oh my God."

Peter's chair scraped. Then his voice was at her shoulder. "Oh my God."

Rex felt floaty, her eyes glued to the shadowed innards of the purse, where soggy, weak bird-lizards with eyes taking up half their downy heads shuffled and squawked, little hands gripping air.

"What do we do? What do we do?" Peter was saying. His hand gripped her shoulder as though to steady himself, and then a wad of paper napkins was shoved in her face, making her sputter. "To dry them off?"

"Right, right." Rex took the napkins and dabbed at the baby dinosaurs. "Hi, sweetie-babies," she crooned at who-knows-what-volume, "Mommy's a little drunk. Look at you; you're perfect."

Peter was still leaning heavily on the hand on her shoulder. "I'm so proud of you, honey," he slurred. "You did great."

Rex put a hand over his and smiled up at him. "*We* did great."

A gagging sound in the purse broke the moment.

"Whoops. They're trying to eat the eggshells." Rex accepted the clump of fractured chips Peter shoved in her face and coaxed the hatchlings into dropping the bits of shell, getting her fingers gnawed on by blunt baby teeth. "What are you?" she baby talked. "I think you're tyrannosaurs. We don't have room in the lab for you."

"You really don't have room for more dinosaurs." Peter had flopped back into his seat, but he leaned over the table to ogle the purse's contents. "What are you going to do?"

"We're putting contraceptives in the food for now, but it's not a permanent solution. I think I need to buy them a Jurassic Park." One of the babies got a mouthful of the scarf and worried it. Rex petted its little head. "Do you want a Jurassic Park, sweeties? I'm gonna name each of you after a cocktail."

The noise from the bar area spiked and drew Rex's eyes back up. Peter twisted around to get a better view. The people around the ceiling-mounted television—when did the place get so packed?—jostled for better views, some holding phones and calling out a channel number.

"Wonder what's happening there," Peter said.

Rex grunted acknowledgment and leaned into the aisle to rubberneck more effectively. She rolled her eyes as they switched to a local news station showing a half-destroyed street and 'Ning zapping past in a flash of yellow. The camera shook as lightning struck a lamppost, and a wave of shouts and flinches passed through the bar.

"Why do they still act like this is a big deal?" Rex asked. "She fights someone every week."

"Hey, that's us!" someone shouted.

What? Before Rex could refocus on the screen, the building shook. She grabbed the edge of the table, her other arm clamped around the purse. A few people shouted. Glasses rattled, but the rumble lasted barely a second, ending before any could fall to the floor. Rex hadn't fully torn her eyes from the TV when a burst of light from the window left her blinking. On the screen, lightning cut through the live footage, illuminating an image of the building she was sitting in, less than a block from the fight.

Silence struck the bar. Then everyone broke into babbles.

One of the bartenders called over the noise, "Hey, hey! Everyone move to the back room. There's a TV there, too, so you can all keep watching."

Rex stood. *Oops, swaying floor.* She clutched the purse to her chest and pushed against the flow of patrons, eyes on the screen. The shaky camera caught a yellow zigzag shooting down the road. Then it veered off course and zipped up a building as an armored truck swerved into its path.

Peter winced beside her. "Not just a villain—they've got minions."

"She's coming this way. Why is she coming this way?"

The two babysitters who'd been waiting at the front appeared out of the crowd. Rex had no tools to determine who either of them were, but the taller one said, "We've gotten the go-ahead to treat this as extraordinary circumstances. We're gonna give 'Ning backup."

Rex let out a spurt of giggles. "What are you gonna do? She already shoots lightning."

"We're trained for these situations. We'll be fine," Peter said, drawing himself up. He swayed on his feet and fell back onto a barstool. "Then again, maybe I'll sit this one out."

The bartender spoke up, eyes on Rex. "Are you gonna help?"

"Why would I do that, Bret? I don't have powers."

"She's also pretty drunk," Peter said.

Bret gave her a disappointed look that wasn't fair at all.

The shorter babysitter asked the bartender, "Is everyone in the back?"

Bret shrugged. "I mean, the ones who didn't go out the front."

Rex dropped a hand over her face and groaned, "Oh my God, people are idiots." The hatchlings' trills turned frantic, and she caught the sagging purse.

With the room empty of people, Rex had a clear view of the front windows and jumped as a fork of lightning lit up the parking lot. The babysitters headed out, guns in hand, and Rex, Peter, and Bret pressed themselves to the windows for a better view. An orange slash of light broke the darkness across the street, making Rex wince back. Through spots in her vision, she watched it split into a hovering circle, and a figure stepped through it, the orange light of the rift illuminating his matching bodysuit.

"It's Rifter?" Rex sucked air through her teeth. That explained the rumble, although she wasn't sure why his rifts only did that when he made an entrance. Maybe it had to do with distance? The orange-clad figure threw out an arm and a new rift appeared in 'Ning's path, forcing her to swerve over the parked cars. A few of the drunk-os who'd run outside cheered.

Peter raised his voice over the smattering of car alarms. "That's a local villain?"

"Yeah. Not a big deal; 'Ning always wins. And stop giving me that look, Bret. If you're so concerned, why don't you go out there and fight?"

Bret shrugged. "I just gotta wonder why you'll do a team-up to fight dinosaurs but not to protect the bar that pays my bills."

"They never catch him anyway. Unless someone figured out how to close rifts in spacetime—oh, that gives me an idea. Do you have a napkin and a pen?"

A grinding screech announced the armored truck's arrival as it cleaved through parked cars.

"Here come Rifter's minions," Peter said.

"And their desperate bid for atten—" Rex's voice fell away as four men with massive guns filed out of the truck. In the low light of the bar's front display—and intermittent flashing as 'Ning and Rifter fought—she made out coattails, opera masks, and bulletproof vests in a cut reminiscent of tuxedos.

That wasn't a Rifter-themed getup. That was how Last Dance's goons dressed.

"Hang on. I need to—" Rex pushed the purse into Peter's arms and scrambled through the door.

"Whoa, Rex." Peter swiped for her, missed, and swayed into the window as Bret gave a whoop.

Outside, uniformed minions returned fire as the pair of Oversight soldiers covered 'Ning from behind a car. "Get back inside, Meister," one shouted over car alarms that were doing a horrible job of harmonizing.

"You're not the boss of me." An excellent comeback, but maybe they needed some reassurance. "It's okay; I just want to know where they got their outfits."

One of the babysitters grabbed her around the middle and hauled her back, shouting curses in her ear.

A lightning flash burned a trail in Rex's vision that ended with 'Ning on a car a few rows over, her masked face turned toward Rex. "Meister!" She raised a hand without turning away and shot a stray lightning bolt that made the minions scatter, which looked too badass to have not been on purpose.

"I'm not with him," Rex yelled back, bracing her heels in the gravel as her overzealous protector dragged her back. "He was following you." She pointed at the orange circle opening a few feet away. "Can you wrap this up? Why don't you ever shoot into his rift? I bet he'd close that thing up in a hurry."

"Stay right there." 'Ning zapped away, searing Rex's retinas again.

Rex didn't see what happened next, as she was hauled—"Ow! Seriously?"—to the ground, where a very mean babysitter called her several kinds of drunk and stupid. She stopped listening as Rifter shouted orders on the other side of the lot and the armored truck revved back to life. Rex pulled herself up on a tire in time to see the vehicle speed through a rift. Then Rifter jumped through and closed it behind him.

The new silence was jarring. Fast footsteps slid in the gravel, and Peter's voice was at her back. "I'd yell at you, except if you're as drunk as me, I don't think it'll mean much."

"Eurgh," Rex answered. Her weight fell against the car as the parking lot spun.

She took back the purse as Peter said, "How dare you give me this much responsibility?"

Something landed on the car with a *thump*.

"Hello, Rex."

Rex jumped hard enough to jostle the purse, earning a flurry of indignant cheeps. "Jesus!" She spun around and almost fell over when her head lurched, hugging the purse to her stomach before it could spill on to the ground. Her blurred vision registered the yellow figure of the Lightning standing on the hood with arms folded.

"Oh my gosh, it's 'Ning," Peter said behind her.

"Crap." Rex swallowed down a bout of nausea. All that movement was catching up. "This really isn't a good time."

A full-coverage superhero mask shouldn't be able to look judgmental, but 'Ning managed it even while catching her breath. "Is this what you call getting your life together?"

"Cheap shot," Rex got out.

"Lightning," one of the soldiers said, standing at attention like he hadn't been cussing Rex out five minutes ago. "Police are on the way. If you're good here, we need to set a perimeter."

"I'm fine. Thank you for your help."

Rex rolled her eyes, which was a mistake. The sky was much too far away, and the vertigo sent her sliding down the car. "Don't look at the sky, Peter."

An eyeroll minutely shifted the yellow mask, and the hero zipped to ground level to grab her shoulder. Rex tensed as she readied herself for a shock and was almost disappointed when none came, like an aborted sneeze. Geez, something was wrong with her.

"We need to talk, Rex."

Rex was vaguely aware of the spectators openly taking video or prancing close to snap selfies despite her babysitters' efforts. The blinking lights of their phones seemed brighter and more accusatory than usual. "I'm starting consulting hours this week. You can make an appointment."

"Those filled up an hour after you announced them. And I can't afford your rates."

"Well, there you go." Rex blinked her dried-out eyes, noticing a thin, brown line cutting diagonally across 'Ning's blurry torso. "Are you wearing a purse? That looks so weird with a superhero suit. Why not go full-efficiency and wear a fanny pack? We could call it a utility belt. Other heroes get away with it."

"I think your purse is cute," Peter said kindly.

"I was bringing you this." 'Ning pulled the thin purse around to her front without acknowledging Peter. Rex patted his shoulder in commiseration.

'Ning extracted an item carefully, using two yellow-gloved fingers, and held out a stoppered vial with something greenish inside. "I caught Rifter breaking into the water treatment plant with this thing." She gave it a careful shake. "I was on my way to you with it, and suddenly he's rifting in a whole truck on my tail."

Every instinct Rex had as a scientist cringed at such casual handling of ooze in a test tube. "That isn't one of those alien organisms that takes over your mind when you're doing some late-night testing, is it?"

"I just got it, but I don't think so."

"Good. Because been there, done that."

"He was trying to put it in the water." 'Ning's voice sharpened in Rex's ears, the background fading out with each word. "I suspect it's some kind of contaminant. You could probably figure out what."

A rock turned over in Rex's gut, settling alongside the nausea. Behind her, Peter muttered, "Oh, shit."

Rex cleared her throat, forcing her branching thoughts to narrow. "I thought you said I could come to you for help, not the other way around."

'Ning shifted. "I figure if I'm going to ask you to trust me, it wouldn't hurt to extend the same courtesy. And there's no point to this Oversight thing if you don't get the chance to prove yourself."

Rex blushed and started into some *aw, shucks* body language, but she snapped out of it when her purse squawked at almost being dropped again.

"But I'm not giving it to you in your state." 'Ning returned the vial to her purse. "I wouldn't have come to you at all if you weren't under Oversight."

"Whoa, shots fired," Peter said.

Rex almost rolled her eyes again but stopped herself in time. "How did you even know where I was?"

"Oversight can track your phone. The mayor gave me access."

"Stalker."

"We need to talk when you're sober."

Some misery leaked into Rex's voice. "You really think it'll go better than this?"

Bret was suddenly at Rex's shoulder. "I brought you that napkin."

"That's completely useless now. Thank you, Bret."

He turned away from her. "If you don't mind, um, 'Ning—"

"Not at all." The Lightning leaned in as he snapped a selfie, then held out a hand for the napkin and pen. "I'll take that, if you don't mind."

Using the car as a desk, 'Ning scribbled on the napkin while Rex tried very hard not to notice how she bent over. "Here's my number. Call me when you're less of a mess."

Holy crap. Rex got the Lightning's number. A giggle spilled out.

"I assume you also saw these." 'Ning pulled an opera mask, half-charred from a lightning blast, from her purse and dropped it on the hood of the car.

Rex's giggles died.

"Rifter never had minions before. Either he dressed up some friends to make it look like he had help from a much bigger fish, or Last Dance is in Decimen City."

Rex swallowed. Her throat felt dry.

"If I don't hear from you tomorrow, I'll find someone else. We need to know what Rifter almost put in Decimen's water."

"You're just going to carry it around in your purse till then?"

"You want to tell me what's in your purse?"

Her arms tightened around it. "Touché."

The Lightning cast one more glance around the parking lot and zapped back over the rooftops, leaving a bright streak in Rex's vision and her hand clenched around the napkin.

Bret let out a low whistle in the relative quiet.

"Wow," Peter said. "Now, what do we do?"

Rex gazed at the scorched, white mask. For a moment, it looked a little less cheap, less damaged, shadowed by the cowl of a deep red cloak. A shiver ran down her spine. Tearing her eyes away, she headed back to the bar. She was going to do a lot more drinking.

SPOTLIGHT ON LEWIS STONE:
LEWIS CLIMBS OUT OF HIS ASS

*L*ewis followed Flora into the bar, bracing himself against the noise. He glanced around for their two wayward party animals, but the tables were too packed to see far. They pushed their way to the counter and Flora waved over a bartender, whose brow cleared in recognition.

"Flora Shay?" the man said.

Flora nodded. "You're the one who called the lab line?"

Lewis had been putting away the leftover pizza when he'd overheard Flora's side of the phone call and offered to drive. The bartender's eyes flicked to him briefly, and Lewis wondered if he should have changed into his uniform first.

"Yeah." The man nodded toward the back wall. "They're not causing any trouble—I just thought it was getting real close to that Oversight curfew."

"Appreciate it." Flora's smile was sharp. "It would be nice if her surveillance detail had called earlier, but I guess that's not their job."

She'd greeted Lewis's unhappy colleagues out front with a media smile and insisted they wait outside while she and Lewis carry out the extraction. Lewis had softened it with praise for their good work, and they'd looked a little too proud, adding a few data points to Lewis's theory about the damage to the parking lot.

Theory might've been the wrong word—it was pretty obviously a superhero fight.

Maybe he should have checked with his boss as well as changed out of his pajamas. He hoped Peter was okay.

They picked through the crowded room in the direction the bartender had indicated, and Flora turned her head, voiced raised to speak through the noise. "I guess we're lucky the Oversight order got so much publicity. I don't know if anyone even told her about the curfew—this all got thrown together so fast."

Lewis wanted to ask why a bartender in midtown was bothering to save Rex from getting in trouble with the government. But it didn't seem as shocking today as it would have yesterday.

That interview had been, well, an absolute, nail-biting trainwreck to watch, but Lewis, standing next to Peter off set, hadn't been able to tear his eyes away from the Meister's face. There was something there, reflected in her voice, that looked so familiar to Lewis. The feeling of: *I don't know what to do; I just know I'm doing it wrong.*

He'd thought about it off and on all evening, splinters of shame striking each time, but only in short increments because Lewis was still reeling from learning the robot thing's name. He kept going over half-remembered conversations. I, uh, is. Aya is. I, uh, wants. Aya wants. I, uh, does. Aya does. *Christ.*

At least he hadn't gotten desperate enough to vent about his misunderstanding to Grant—that would have been embarrassing. Except if he had, it could've been cleared up sooner.

If he was talking more to Peter, it never would have happened. Peter would have laughed in his face.

Lewis zeroed in on familiar, raised voices. As their friends' table came into sight, strewn with empty glasses and the remains of a meal of wings and chips, Lewis suppressed a sigh. Flora didn't suppress hers.

The Meister straddled Peter's lap, shaking a finger in his face as she babbled, and he nodded in rapt attention. Rex's tirade cut off as she noticed them, and a grin split her face. "Flora! You're an aunt!"

"What? Oh, dear." Flora hurried forward, her eyes falling to the purse—which was possibly making chirping noises—cradled between the two drunk dumbasses. The hurry became a lunge to snatch it up when Rex stumbled to her feet. "I'll take that now, sweetie."

A tiny, round head popped up next to the strap and vanished again as Flora settled the purse over her shoulder.

What the hell.

"Lewis, the Lightning was here!" Peter called.

"That's great, buddy. Time to go." They herded the drunky-drunks past the other tables. Joey and Nate held the doors open, both scowling, and Lewis shot them a commiserating smirk in hopes this would be a funny story later on instead of a rant.

The cooler night air was a relief after the mugginess of the bar. As Flora fumbled to balance Rex's weight against her side, Lewis grabbed the purse full of hatchlings—*why?*—and rested it gently on her hip. "You good?"

"I can take her from here. You'll get him back?"

"I got him," Lewis said as Peter fell against his side with a groan.

"Thanks, Lewis." Flora gave Rex's shoulder a squeeze and guided her toward the parking lot after Joey and Nate. Lewis pulled Peter's arm over his shoulder before he could pitch over the curb and turned toward his car. He'd had to park further down the street—some of the roads were trashed, presumably from the fight.

"Flora, the Lightning needs my help," Rex said as they disappeared into the parking lot.

"Of course, she does, sweetie."

Peter wheezed a laugh, dropping his weight so they almost tipped over. "I'm totally in the superhero club," he told Lewis, neglecting to mind where his breath was hitting. "Once Rex helps 'Ning save the city and the Oversight thing ends, I'm definitely gonna be invited to the meetings."

Lewis nodded. "I'm sure you will." God, he'd missed this. He felt a little guilty for relishing the easy way Peter babbled and hung off him, like he was poaching the friendly atmosphere Peter had spent the night building with Rex.

"You could've been, too, but"—Peter vibrated his lips on an exhale—"she hates you. Like, to a comical degree."

Did she? They'd barely had two conversations. Not that either one had gone that well.

And yeah, Lewis hadn't exactly . . . cared. Shame squirmed into his voice. "I might owe her an apology. I misunderstood some things." He blushed. "And I've been taking other stuff out on . . . everyone, I guess," he ended in a mutter.

Peter snorted. "'Other stuff.'" He lurched aside, dragging them to the edge of the sidewalk before Lewis could amend what he'd said. "Whoa! Close one." He snickered as they got back on course. "Oh, man, when was the last time we did this? Your birthday?"

"That was your birthday, if you mean the last time I had to drag you home drunk."

Peter released a *pft* and grew an evil grin. "This isn't dragging. Dragging was when you saw that buff statue—"

Lewis groaned.

"And you *had* to say hi—"

"I was practicing," Lewis protested.

"An *Adonis,* is that what you called it? I was pointing to the ropes around it, man. How could you not know it was a statue?"

"I knew it was a statue! I'm not an idiot."

Peter snickered and fell more heavily against Lewis. "I feel so warm right now."

Lewis fought back laughter. For the principle of it. "That's probably the alcohol."

"It's all you, man. It's the warmth of friendship." His grin grew. "You know, you're lucky security didn't ban you from that park, or Oversight would have to ask about that blot on your record. What do you think you'd tell them?"

Lewis was too busy wheezing to answer, feeling Peter laughing against him.

Then Peter stilled and turned his head toward Lewis, blinking. He didn't look sober, but he looked serious. "Hey, I hope you don't think—I know you like to look at guys, and I know your whole deal, and I hope you don't think I thought you were ..."

Lewis's heart sank, and his voice came out gruff. "You don't have to explain."

"I respect you, man. I don't think you're something you're not. And I miss you." His voice cracked. "I don't like this. I don't like the way things are."

The lightness was gone. A scowl twisted over his face, and he fought it even knowing Peter wouldn't misread it.

He just wanted to fix this. But time wasn't doing it, and his doubts crowded over every idea he'd had. So, he asked, "What do you need from me?"

Peter swallowed. His eyes darted to Lewis's face several times. "I'm scared to ask. I'm scared you'll think I'm saying something I'm not saying."

Lewis felt his guard rising and pushed it down. "I'll do my best not to do that."

"Just don't bow out of my life. Please?"

That hadn't entered Lewis's mind. But he still hesitated when he said, "I'm not going anywhere." Not until Peter asked him to. And if he thought about where this path was leading—if he tried to predict how things would eventually play out—

He sidestepped that thought.

Peter took a breath. "Then would it be too much"—he swallowed again—"to ask for some space for a while?"

In a corner of Lewis's heart, something fell off a table and cracked.

"Not forever. I just need to reset," Peter was saying. "I just want to recalibrate myself."

Lewis's mouth scrunched. "You're not a robot."

"Wish I was a robot," Peter grumbled. He attempted a robot walk and almost took them both out when he tripped on a break in the sidewalk. "Darn superhero fights."

Lewis sighed as he righted them. "I'd better not have to lift you into the car."

"I can lift my own drunk ass. I have *some* dignity."

Lewis tried to smile. "I can do that. I can give you space."

Peter let out a long breath. "Okay, good." He patted Lewis's shoulder. "We talked about it, and it was good. It's fine."

Peter didn't need much help. Lewis held the door for him and shut it after reminding him to buckle up.

"You buckle," Peter called back as Lewis rounded the car.

Lewis chuckled, but it felt melancholy. Peter was right; this was good. They were talking. The pit in Lewis's gut filled with a wan, unsatisfying kind of hope.

He wished this didn't feel like the beginning of the end.

ISSUE 9

DINOSAURS IN THE CLOSET

"I'm serious," Rex said. "The Lightning came by. It's because—" because Last Dance was in Decimen City. Maybe. 'Ning thought he wanted to contaminate the water. Rex had a note in her pocket that suggested he was here for another reason.

Her legs tangled, forcing Flora to shuffle. Then her stomach churned in warning, and she slid her arm off Flora's shoulder to keel over and puke in the parking lot.

Through the misery of her innards constricting, she heard the two soldiers speak and Flora say something back. Then Flora was crouched next to her with her hand on her back.

"Do you feel better?"

"No," Rex bit out. She felt less nauseous, but the feeling of having just vomited wasn't better.

"Do you think you can manage a car ride?"

Rex debated whether nodding or speaking would make her less sick, and settled on giving Flora's shoulder a pat. As Flora helped her up, she saw the little heads poking out of the purse on Flora's shoulder and felt horrible for subjecting them to the smell of vomit so early in their lives. "I'm gonna ruin them," she mumbled.

"They're fine. They're having fun," Flora said, proving her mind reading powers. Rex shivered at the joke, even in her head.

Rex couldn't shake the idea, though, staring at the little dinos during the ride home and looking for signs that they'd been traumatized by their first night of life. She'd fed them chips. What if that was too much salt? They were tyrannosaurs. They needed meat. What else did children need? Hugs? "Flora, hug them."

Flora dutifully wrapped her arms around the purse, pulling them close enough to drop their heavy heads onto her chest. They trilled happily. "Here." Flora leaned close to Rex. "Pet them a bit. You won't hurt them."

Rex snaked her hands into the bag and stroked two hatchlings as others cuddled into the crooks of her elbows and pushed their heads under her forearms. "What are we going to do with them?"

"You'll figure it out," Flora said. The car stopped in their driveway. Rex extracted herself so Flora could gather up the bag and carry it inside.

Walking cued another bout of nausea, and Rex had to sit on the lawn or risk throwing up again.

Flora came back out during Rex's heavy-breathing break and knelt to rub her back. "Getting better?"

Rex nodded, glancing around until she spotted her babysitters leaning against the house and smoking a good distance away. "Where did you put them?"

"I spread out spare bedding in your closet. We can take them to Peak Street in the morning."

Rex dug her fingers into the grass. "They'll be okay?"

"They're fine, Rex. They're asleep."

"We should have a baby monitor or something. They're just kids." Rex twisted toward Flora too fast and slipped on the grass. Flora half-caught her and helped her lean back on her elbows. "It's weird being a kid, because you're still learning about the world, and you can believe that the good things outnumber the bad. And at some point you catch on to how impossible that is, because any good thing can be taken or broken or ruined, and that good thing can hurt you. But you're not supposed to say it. Because there are kids around, and they still believe in Santa."

Flora shook her head and opened a bottle of water that Rex hadn't noticed. "This is bleak."

"I didn't like being a kid."

"I can imagine." Flora pushed the water into her hands.

Rex drank, wincing as the first sip tasted pukey and too sweet. "I don't know how long I can take this. I don't need oversight."

"You think so?"

Rex almost protested. Then she remembered the time she'd figured out how to make her bones hollow so she could fly around with a pair of mechanical bird wings. Flora had run in at the last minute, wrestled the syringe out of her hands, smashed it in the sink, and burst into tears. Then she'd yelled at Rex for most of an hour, and they'd gone through her projects as Flora okayed or vetoed each one, shouting at each other the whole time.

Rex brought Flora so much trouble. Oversight was just the most recent trouble. "I'm sorry."

"It's okay," Flora said, although there was no way she'd followed Rex's train of thought.

"Last Dance is coming. That's what 'Ning said."

Flora nodded, a crease between her eyes. "She wasn't looking for a fight, right?"

Rex shook her head. It still made the ground sway, but she didn't feel completely disoriented. "She wants my help. I don't think I can be much help."

"The jar doesn't go away just because you're drunk."

Hi T. I need help. Rex sipped water, imagining she still tasted vomit.

In her mind, a decision made itself. A slow, cold fear beat time with her heart. "Are they watching?"

Flora looked at her, no thoughts obvious on her face. She cast a glance toward the babysitters and shook her head.

Rex leaned forward enough to steady herself and fumbled for the note. Without unfolding it, she raised it to Flora's field of view. "Don't let them see." She didn't look up as Flora took it. "There's two pages." Her heart hammered in her ears, her eyes on the bottle of water in her hand. She didn't know what she was waiting for. A reaction, a change.

Paper swished. A rustle probably signaled Flora turning to the second sheet.

She spoke after a silent moment. "What is this?"

Rex swallowed again and took a sip of water to wet her throat. "Sam's my brother. I got that a few days ago. No one saw."

"I didn't know you had a brother."

Rex nodded. She raised her eyes to Flora's face. "It was my virus."

Flora's eyebrow rose over her glasses. "Is this about Mutey? Because your containment measures worked, Rex. The only zombies left are safe on Zombie Island."

Rex shook her head. "No." She felt distant again. "It wasn't supposed to make people brain-dead. But I was having more success blocking the part of the brain that transmits thoughts—at least that he interpreted that way—than blocking the part in his brain that receives them. I did consider that something in the water, at least locally, might work. But he knew it wasn't ready."

As she spoke, Rex saw Flora catching on. The reactions were small—shoulders falling, hands clenching on Last Dance's note. Her face hardly changed, making Rex wonder if she was imagining the shift.

Flora sat straighter on her heels and tucked her elbows in, the motions small and controlled. "Are we in danger?"

Rex started to shake her head but stopped to think. Hell, she'd never been a great judge. "He hasn't been." She backtracked through her thoughts to notice that her answer didn't quite follow the question, but her head felt too sluggish to figure out how to correct it.

A slightly raised brow. "He's asked for help before?" Apparently, Flora had caught a different implication in Rex's answer.

Guilt squeezed Rex's chest. She nodded.

Still no obvious reaction.

"Since I've lived here?"

"The last time was last year. He sends messengers. He doesn't come himself."

Flora nodded. "Did you help him before?"

Rex's throat tightened around the *yes* and her breath hitched.

"Oh, Rex." Flora leaned closer, shifting her legs beneath her in the careful way of someone accustomed to skirts and heels. After the barest pause, she raised the hand holding the sketch and dropped it. "Are you making it?"

"It's only in my head. I haven't written anything down." It made a difference. Maybe.

"If Oversight finds out you got this, there will be trouble," Flora said softly.

"If Oversight finds out he's my brother, there'll be trouble." Rex leaned back, caught sight of the swimming stars, and clenched her eyes shut reflexively. "Ugh. I knew better than to look at the sky."

Flora ignored her. "We could call . . ."

Rex heard the idea occur and the implications catch up in Flora's faltered half-sentence. Rex responded, "I'm sure Vivid Blue won't be far behind."

"We should make a pros and cons list."

Rex was surprised enough to laugh, eyes popping open. "For what?"

"For making the helmet."

"Helmets are dumb," Rex muttered.

Flora pulled a little pad of paper from her bag and flipped to a blank sheet, pen in hand. "First, what would it do?"

Rex felt a rush of affection and smiled, the words coming more easily now. "I think the electrodes in the dome work like my Exo-suit, except instead of translating electrical signals from muscle movements, it translates brain waves as signals that can be manipulated."

"So, he'd stop hearing thoughts."

"Yes."

"But he could also manipulate the thoughts of others."

Rex shook her head. "That's not the function. The hood—I'd make it a hood, like on his cloak—would give him no control over other people's brain waves. He would be able to turn it the other way though. Thought projection instead of thought reception—he could make other people hear his thoughts, if he wanted."

Flora's pen was poised on the paper. "Would that be bad?"

"I don't know." It came out harsher than she'd intended. "It shouldn't be any worse than handing him a loudspeaker. Maybe he could use it for something bad, but it's not like it could end the world. But I've done so many things that didn't seem so bad on paper. Then it gets out there and, oops—horrible repercussions! Carnivorous grass! Dinosaurs on Main Street!"

She slumped, continuing, "So what does this look like? I make something to help Last Dance interface with his powers and hand it over to him in secret, and what happens? Because I can see the pattern playing out. I don't know what I've overlooked, but there will be something that's so obvious in retrospect."

Flora waited a few seconds to speak. "So, don't do it."

"But—" Rex's voice cracked. *Hi T. I need help.*

Flora put an arm around her shoulders, slipping the note into her bag and out of the soldiers' sight. At the contact, Rex blinked hard, tears gathering behind her eyes. The pit was behind her—a massive chasm, a well of dark, distorted feelings that would break her if she made the smallest movement backward.

Rex choked out, "I can't," somehow meaning it in the convoluted sense that she couldn't *not* make the hood.

"They don't watch me," Flora said, idly rubbing Rex's shoulder. "I'll take the design to the lab for Aya to scan and destroy the paper copy."

Several things unclenched in Rex's chest in awkward starts, like warming muscles as a freeze ray wore off.

"We'll make it, and we'll test it," Flora continued. "Leave the decision of what to do with it for after we know more."

Rex let out an uneven, poorly controlled gasp. Like a boulder had been shifted off her chest.

"Hey, Anderson," a soldier called. "Grant says your room is squawking. You might want to check that."

Rex shifted to rise, but Flora pressed a hand on her shoulder. "I'll go. Move when you're ready."

As Flora walked to the house, Rex checked her phone, on autopilot. She felt cleaned out. Absolved of something, but she wasn't sure what.

She blinked at a series of notifications from Aya. The last message read, *Take a look when you get the chance, Doctor.* Rex frowned, opening the accompanying link. It'd better not be another cat video. Aya was developing a problem.

It wasn't a cat video. A cut of her interview on *Good Morning, Gorgeous* had spent the day going viral. Rex stared at the view count, too drained to respond in a meaningful way. "Huh."

ISSUE 10

DINOSAURS IN TIME-OUT

*T*he next morning, as her bed swayed in time with the slow pounding of her headache, Rex tried to watch the viral video of her interview. But before hitting play, she looked at the still image of herself in femme business clothes and decided *nope*.

She'd been there in person—no need to relive that fuckup less than twenty-four hours later. Anyway, there were at least three higher priority dumpster fires demanding her attention, and she updated her to-do list accordingly.

Call 'Ning got scrunched into the second priority spot between *deal with the dinosaurs* and *break up with Dillon,* because either that really happened, or she'd gotten a number on a napkin from a cosplayer good enough to fool drunk Rex.

The first priority, of course, was getting the dinosaurs to Peak Street. Rex stumbled into the kitchen with the snappy darlings already bundled into her purse to find Lewis making breakfast while Grant and Flora gratefully devoured it at the kitchen island.

Lewis looked up from the stove when she walked in, and was that a sullen look on his face? She was too hungover to guess, and the breakfast smells weren't helping.

"Is there anything I should . . ." Lewis gestured with a spatula at the little dino heads peeking out to sniff the air as Rex placed the purse on the island.

"Just give them all the bacon." Rex poured herself some orange juice. "You brought Peter back last night?"

"Yeah." Lewis dumped the plate of bacon into the bag and the dinosaurs dove on it with rabid noises. "He was fine. Um." He cleared his throat, the rough sound irritating Rex's pounding head. "I need to apologize to you."

Rex must have misheard. Hangovers caused hallucinations, right? It was a little-known symptom.

"I made some assumptions." Now he was blushing. "And I shouldn't have brought my issues here and judged you by your reputation. It was unprofessional and . . . not great of me. I can be judgmental. Everyone who knows me tries to tell me, but I keep doing it anyway. I'm a dumbass that way. So, I'm sorry."

Rex closed her mouth when she noticed it was open, finding her voice at the same time. "That's a dollar."

Lewis's mouth twitched, a crease jumping between his eyes.

"You have to put a dollar in the self-deprecation jar," she explained.

"House rule," Flora added, mouth full.

Lewis stared at her for a few seconds. He threw up has hands and set the spatula aside. "I'll get my wallet."

Rex watched him go, wondering if she'd done some drunk experiment with parallel worlds last night. She looked at Flora across the table. "Is my surveillance here yet?"

"Me and Lewis have the morning shift," Grant said, scraping his plate as professionally as he did everything while on duty, already in uniform.

"Mind driving me to Peak Street?"

When Lewis had paid up with a constipated expression, Rex and her babysitters loaded into the car. As they pulled out of the driveway, Rex said, "You know what? Let's do the third priority first. I need you to stop at Dillon's house." She caught the glance Lewis and Grant shared. "Did either of you bet I would break up with him today?"

Surprise flickered over both their faces in the rearview mirror. Grant cleared his throat. "No, ma'am."

"Then you both lose. Watch the babies while I'm in there."

It went about as well as Rex expected. He got a good amount off his chest about how many of her flaws he'd been putting up with and all the drawbacks of dating someone as infamous as the Meister and now she was the one breaking up with him?

She returned to the car with her head pounding twice as hard. She'd expected at least a little relief from having it done, but she supposed she'd waited too long to get that satisfaction. "We can go to the lab now."

Grant mumbled something and pulled back onto the road. Lewis handed back the purse. "Sorry."

Rex shrugged, checking the hatchlings. "I didn't even really like him." She felt Lewis's questioning glance. "I kind of hoped I could Stockholm Syndrome myself into liking him." And he was fun to be around. And he gave good hugs. Rex almost wished he was awful, so the thought of all the things he'd said about her quality as a partner wouldn't make her bottom lip want to quiver.

"Why?"

Rex tried to find the judgment in his voice, but all she heard was incredulity. Grant, on the other hand, made a half-hidden hand motion that looked suspiciously like the crazy sign. Rex petted the babies. "It's what people do, isn't it? Unless people have feelings for everyone they date, which must be exhausting." Rex didn't think she could handle losing something real more than once or twice in a lifetime. Maybe it was good that her feelings didn't work right.

She recalled her conversation with Peter and made a mental note to add the stuff he told her to look up to her to-do list. Except seahorses. She knew what those were, dammit.

Lewis's frown came through in his voice. "That sounds . . ."

"Like leading him on? Wasting his time?" Rex filled in, resentment and guilt still in easy grabbing distance. People said to try, but how were you supposed to try while being honest about your feelings? Or maybe that was just her and another reason she didn't deserve nice things.

Lewis's lips pressed together, and his brow lowered like he was stuck in a slow-motion wince. "That's not what I was going to say, but sorry."

Rex curled further over her downy-headed dinosaurs and sighed.

At Peak Street, Rex spent several hours settling the dinosaurs into the newly prepared nursery and ordering her employees around. She snapped at a few who were huddled around a computer watching her interview instead of helping her track down the clutch's bio-dad, detective-style.

It shouldn't have been that hard, since there were only three tyrannosaurs, two of which were male. But the female was acting cagey, the males were arguing, and Rex was getting the vibe that they were going to start fighting as soon as her back was turned.

She was laying into them about responsibility, safe sex, and respecting each other when the techs interrupted in a panic that something in the small and medium dinos' enclosure had exploded. She left the bigs' enclosure, and sure enough, two roars and a crash rattled the walls as soon as the doors closed.

"What do you mean, exploded?" Rex sat herself in front of the blaring monitors that were warning of a perimeter breach.

"If there's a danger of the dinosaurs breaking containment, we need to call in backup," Grant said behind her.

"Just wait a minute." Backup meant heroes or the army, and Rex's blood pressure skyrocketed at either option. "This doesn't make sense," she muttered. "They shouldn't have access to the right materials to build explosives."

"This might not be a good time," one of the techs said behind her, "but some of the dinosaurs have become ashamed of their nakedness and are fashioning clothes out of leaves."

"You're right—it's not a good time." Her eyes roved over the camera feeds that should have views of the back of the enclosure, where the breach supposedly was. They were all conveniently malfunctioning.

"Doctor, we should release the gas before they get loose in the lab."

"Isn't that dangerous for us if containment is broken?" Lewis asked.

"The gas isn't harmful—it just relaxes them," the tech explained.

"Have you had to gas them before?" Grant asked suspiciously, and Rex winced. The last thing she needed was Oversight thinking the dinosaurs weren't properly contained.

"Once," a tech answered. "A fight broke out that drew blood. We needed to break it up fast."

With that information, it all came together nicely. Rex's face twisted in triumph. "Nice try, you little shits." She shoved away from the monitors and strode to the access door.

Rex waved two of the techs with her past the first security door and shut it in Lewis and Grant's faces. The babysitters had never insisted on entering the enclosure before, and she wasn't about to let that pattern slip. When she opened the inner door, dinosaurs swarmed her in greeting, a few with foliage skirts draped over their rears.

"Mommy! Mommy!"

"Go outside!"

"Travel!"

Despite the warpath she was on, that did cause a twinge of guilt. She needed to look into plots of land for them. But she put the thought aside, folded her arms, and glared them down. "What did you break?"

A sheepish hoard of dinosaurs led Rex and the two lab techs to a hole they'd dug by the back wall deep enough to access the monitoring system. The cables had been snapped, effectively cutting off the camera feeds and the sensors in the wall.

"Let me guess—you threw yourselves at the wall to sell the trick. None of you have the attention span to see this plan through. Who was it?"

Their heads turned toward a velociraptor skulking in the back. "Of course, it's Spot. Spot, come here."

The raptor made a creaky noise in his throat and waddled forward with his tail between his legs. As well he should.

"Why would they fake an explosion?" one of the techs asked.

"To get us to gas them." Rex shot a glare at the group.

"Why would they want us to gas them?"

"To get high," she spat, icy with fury. Was she being too harsh? She couldn't tell. Her mind kept circling back to Grant's face as he suggested bringing in backup to take the dinosaurs down. "You all need to shape up. I didn't bring you back from extinction to be—what are you doing? What are they doing?" She directed the last at the techs as the dinos agitatedly flicked tails and flailed their hands.

"It's sign language."

Rex stared at the tech. Forget her druggy dinos—this needed to be addressed. "Why are they using sign language?"

"You said to hire the people who teach apes sign language."

Rex's mouth fell open. "I meant to hire people with experience teaching smart, big, inhuman things! They don't all have hands—how do they use sign language?"

"If the quadrupeds want to sign something, they find one of the bipeds to sign it for them."

Rex couldn't handle this right now. She spun back to the dinosaurs. "Clearly you need more structure in your lives. I'm putting you all in sports. I don't care what sport—you're all going to participate and you're going to learn about teamwork and discipline and working hard to achieve your dreams."

She stalked back through the bushes past morose dinosaurs, already talking to the techs. "Fix the monitors and fill in that hole. Then work up some team rosters."

"And you actually want that, this time?"

"Of course, I actually want that."

"It's just that when you said to hire the ape sign language people—"

"Fire them, by the way. Wait." She thought for a moment. "If they have a rapport with the dinosaurs, keep them on. But have them teach math or something." She recalled the interrogation with the tyrannosaurs and winced. Their hands had been moving the entire time. "Now I have to learn sign language. Wonderful." She managed not to slam the doors as they left the enclosure.

Grant was in front of her as soon as she stepped on to the lab floor, his face set in a glower. "If those things got past the walls—"

"It was the monitoring system, not the walls. They're fine. No need to put them down, or whatever you wanted to do." Rex regretted the words instantly in case they'd put ideas in his head. When it came down to it, Oversight had the power to make that call, and the thought made her skin itch. She caught sight of two repair-spiders skittering down a wall and pointed to them. "You two."

The single eye on each bot turned toward Rex, the motion capture recognizing her gestures. Their sharp, delicate arms were designed for maintenance, but could easily be used to harm, making them unsuitable for the public market no matter how useful Rex found them. She jabbed a finger toward the enclosure. "Repairs needed in the alarm system, floor side."

"Those are the creepiest things I've ever seen," Lewis muttered.

"They're all-terrain Roombas," Rex defended, watching until the bots had skittered into the enclosure.

"They're creepy, and I'm surprised Flora hasn't made you give them a paint job at least."

Rex ignored his eerily accurate estimate of Flora's opinion of the repair-spiders. She checked the time and flinched. It was almost noon already. She turned to the closest tech. "I'm going to check on the babies."

The babies chirped happily when Rex entered the old greenhouse they'd set up with padded floors and warming pads. She sat with them awhile, practicing mindful breathing while they cuddled into her stomach or rolled over her lap, gnawing on squeaky toys. How long until the dinosaurs made a real escape attempt and her babysitters called in the big guns?

She had to get them out of there.

When her heart rate was lower and she was satisfied that the babies were comfortable, she extracted herself and exited the nursery to find

Lewis's eyes on her. He'd probably been watching through the glass wall for a while. She put her discomfort aside and headed for her workspace to try the Lightning's number.

Rex's heart pounded as she put the number into her phone and hit call. It wasn't fair to be this nervous when it was 'Ning's idea. Grant and Lewis lurking in the background didn't help.

An answer came too quickly. "Yeah?"

"Hi. It's me. It's Rex—it's me."

"Are you in a less compromised state?"

"Oh, fuck you."

"Are you at your Peak Street facility?"

"You're coming here?"

"I'm here already. Open the roof door."

"What?" Rex pulled a computer monitor around and found the camera feed from the roof. 'Ning stood with her purse over her shoulder and a phone held to her mask-covered ear, tapping her foot. After fighting the temptation inherent in an opportunity to stare at the Lightning unhindered, Rex pressed a few keys and watched the light on the roof door's keypad turn green. "Follow the lights on the floor." She ended the call and flipped through camera feeds to watch her progress.

When 'Ning reached the workspace, she returned Lewis and Grant's nods of greeting and handed Rex the vial with obvious reluctance, which Rex could only find insulting. She ignored the way turning her back on 'Ning made her skin prickle, took the substance into a lab area cut off from the room by clear, everything-proof walls, and whistled in relief when her Geiger counter didn't lose its shit. She got to transferring a portion onto a slide.

It looked solid through the microscope. Just green, at every magnification. She ran samples through mass spectrometers for protein and metabolite fingerprints, though it would take a while to get results.

As she waited, a suspicion—one she'd push away if science worked like that—pinged in the back of her head, along with a tiny rush of anxiety.

She treated ten microliters of the substance with a dye to stain nucleic acids and set it to incubate for ten minutes, enough time to bind and fluoresce.

While Rex prepped one microliter of the stained sample for the spectrophotometer, the intercom beeped and 'Ning's voice asked, "Did you find anything yet?"

"Not with the microscope. Most of these tests will take a while." The machine produced a graph showing high absorbency of the dye, indicating the presence of DNA or RNA in the sample. That little anxiety gave a flutter.

Rex treated another portion of the sample with an enzyme to degrade DNA, addressing 'Ning simultaneously. "Tell me more about how you found it."

"Is that necessary?"

"I don't know—you tell me." She set it to incubate at 37 degrees to speed up the reaction. "What happened at the water treatment plant? Did you overhear anything? How many ways can I die by exposing myself to this?"

There was a brief silence before the hero responded in a more subdued voice. "I was out on patrol—"

Rex snorted. The Lightning would be the type of hero who patrolled.

"I was out on patrol," 'Ning repeated, irritation clear, "and I sensed an electrical shutdown at the plant."

Electrical shutdown? Not a typical Rifter move. Rex logged it away.

"When I investigated, I saw an open rift inside. Rifter was nearby, taking that vial out of a case."

"No goons?" Rex thought of the opera masks.

"They showed up later."

Faint hope rose in Rex. "Then it might not be related—"

"They were on my tail minutes after I grabbed the vial. Rifter kept taunting that I didn't know who I was stealing from."

"Ah." The hope died. "And you didn't take it to the police because . . ." Rex checked radiation levels again. Still nothing. She was being paranoid.

"You think the police could keep anything secure from Last Dance? Also, I don't know what it is. It could be dangerous to be around."

"I'm glad you're so concerned for my safety."

"I grabbed it, and I thought of you, okay?" 'Ning snapped. "You've tackled this kind of thing before. Remember those microbes you dredged out of the ocean?"

"The ones you pushed me into acid to destroy?"

"The acid would only mildly irritate skin according to your own research. Would you rather I'd let it eat your brain?"

"It wasn't eating my brain—it was slowly altering me to live underwater." Rex reset the spectrophotometer with forced calm. "All you saved me from was being a mermaid."

"You were growing more of them to transform everyone on the planet."

"Oh, right." Maybe it had eaten her brain a little. She muttered, "Well, mildly irritated skin becomes a big deal when it's literally all of your skin."

Lewis's voice cut in. "How's it looking?"

Rex huffed. "Not sure yet. It's too small for the microscope." She ran the test again with the enzyme-treated sample, trying to manage a surge of dread.

The last time Sam put something in the water, it was Rex's virus. It had been an RNA virus—less stable, but easier to synthesize than DNA-based viruses. That was an act of desperation years ago when he knew the virus wasn't ready. He'd been more calculated since then, pursuing his goals without taking risks.

The test produced a new graph, still showing high absorbency. She had eliminated any possible DNA from the sample, and the dye was still reacting to something.

Uh-oh.

Messages appeared in the corner of the screen as Aya requested the data's significance. Rex had no answer besides a gut feeling. "I need a bigger microscope," she muttered.

"What was that?" Lewis asked.

Rex slid off her stool and stoppered the vial. "Aya, vent the electron microscope in lab six." She ignored the exclamations as she breezed back through the room to the lab next door. The others entered behind her while she moved through the sampling procedure. It wouldn't be perfect, since she didn't know what buffer solution it was in, but she could repeat the test when she had more information.

The others stayed back, speaking a few times in questioning tones as Rex tapped a finger on the table and held the vacuum door. Each minute passed more slowly than the last.

"Start with five kV," she told Aya.

Too soon, Aya brought up a gray image, and Rex let out a long breath, bracing herself.

A pressure in her chest released. But even as her mind fled far away, she couldn't help cataloguing details. It was altered from what she remembered, and it would take more targeted tests to find the exact genetic composition.

But she always recognized her work. It was the same virus.

ISSUE 11

DINOSAURS IN THE LINE OF FIRE

Decontamination after handling mysterious substances was old hat for Rex. She threw the kitchen sink at herself before exiting the lab and proceeded to secure the virus in the incubator that she'd tricked out after the ocean microbe debacle.

Grant, being one of the technologically inclined babysitters, checked all the way down to the digital locks' base code to confirm that the room was only accessible to her, the surveillance team, and 'Ning, and only with two or more of them present, before confirming as much to Oversight.

"I'm going to call it," 'Ning said as Rex locked down the lab. The super-hero was leaning against a desk, her arms folded.

Rex's hero senses tingled. "Hey, now—"

"I'm going to recommend the mayor call in the Protectors of the World."

Crap. "Let's not be hasty." Rex raised her hands and tried not to take it personally when 'Ning eyed them suspiciously. "Nothing's really happened yet. I think you and I have this handled."

"It's a virus he's putting in the water." 'Ning's voice was flat, but Rex could feel the eyes narrowed at her through the mask. "Last time he did that, it would have killed people."

Rex felt a zing of nausea that passed too quickly to link it to a clear emotion. "First of all, that virus would have made people brain-dead, not fully dead." Before 'Ning could finish puffing up in indignation, she added, "And yes, I know that's not the issue. Also, we haven't confirmed this one does the same thing."

"Is there a reason you don't want the Protectors here?" Grant asked with a step forward, head tilted up.

"What? No." His step had brought him too close, and habit locked Rex's legs against the urge to jump back. She schooled her expression and kept her shoulders loose, her heart racing so fast it hurt.

"I agree with the Lightning," Lewis added, and Rex tried not to feel disappointed. Just because he'd apologized didn't mean he was on her side. Keeping her guard up all the time was damn exhausting.

'Ning gave him a nod. "Last Dance is Blue's villain, anyway. She might have some insight into what he's up to."

Blue's villain—like superheroes collected them. But 'Ning was right, as shitty as it was. The hero who'd clashed with Sam most often would likely have, as 'Ning put it, *insight*. With her virus back out there, Rex couldn't stand in the way.

Rex squeezed her eyes shut as the understanding that Vivid Blue would be coming to Decimen City slowly solidified in her gut. "All right." It felt like setting a date for her execution. "Call the Protectors."

←⦿⦿⦿⦿⦿→

The Protectors would be at the lab the next morning. Rex couldn't sleep. She paced in her room again, resisting the urge to ask Aya if she saw any flaws in the security. She didn't want it to look like she and her AI were conspiring to access a mind-warping virus in the dead of night.

What the hell was Sam doing? Between the hood and the virus—did he want to combine them? Was the hood supposed to block the virus's effects? Enhance them? He had to know that she'd stop him from spreading her own damn virus, so was there more to it? Was that why he hadn't mentioned it in his note?

Should she show the note to the Oversight Committee?

It would not look good that she'd kept it secret this long. They wouldn't wait to hear that the design was harmless—*and what if she was wrong about that?* If they thought there was a chance she'd make it, they'd lock her up. They wouldn't risk her throwing in with Last Dance.

A woozy feeling in her head made Rex realize her breaths had gotten shallow. Her pacing had sped up. She reached one end of her bedroom and froze instead of turning around. The pit behind her gaped.

With eyes squeezed shut, she turned. She was able to stride to the door, forcing herself not to think. She kept going down the hall, to the kitchen.

In the kitchen, she opened the fridge, the light and cold washing over her, and let out a long breath. She imagined the cold slowing the movement of her blood, depressing her heartbeat to a subdued, steady rhythm.

A tap behind her made her jump, jostling condiments and sauce jars as the fridge door jerked in her hand. She turned to spot Lewis in the doorway before his voice gave him away.

"Oh. Sorry."

"What do you want?" she snapped, aware of how shady it made her sound. This was the kitchen—he could be here if he wanted to.

His eyes narrowed. Rex could practically see him trying to figure out what evil plan she was carrying out in the communal fridge in the middle of the night.

"Do you eat this late every night?" she asked.

His face did something complicated. "It's a stress thing. Do you hang out in the kitchen *without* eating every night?"

"If we both have to ask, then neither of us are here every night."

Lewis sighed and strode toward the fridge. Without thinking, Rex backed up to maintain their distance. Lewis noticed, shooting her an irritated glance, but turned away to rummage in the fridge. "I didn't bet on your breakup."

The subject change threw her off. "You what?"

"I wasn't sure how to say it when you asked in the car, but I never made a bet."

"I wouldn't have cared if you did."

"Still." Lewis shrugged, the motion a bit aggressive. He grabbed a few slices of pizza out of the fridge and turned to the island.

Rex wasn't sure what it was—the fast turn, the way he slammed the fridge door, the clipped tone when he said *still*—but her back hit the wall before she processed the impulse, several feet of distance gained between them.

Her heart lurched as her mind caught up, because there was no way to play that off as anything but *fleeing*. She stared at Lewis, and he stared back, the pizza drooping in his grip. At least he didn't look irritated anymore—he looked angry instead. Improvement?

"I've been living here for weeks," he said, voice toneless. "I've been professional even if I wasn't as nice as I should have been. You have access to my records and we're under constant surveillance. What do you think is going to happen?"

"A person doesn't have to think something's going to happen to be scared," she snarled back, and God-fucking-damn-it she'd just admitted she was scared. *Fuck.*

"What do you want from me? You won't take my apologies—"

"I didn't know you were looking for a formal statement of forgiveness."

"I'm not! I just want to fix whatever this is." He gestured between them. "I want to fucking fix *something*. But you change the subject, or dismiss it, or . . . run from me when I turn around."

"If you're trying to guilt me for that, it won't work. You came in here mad—"

"I wasn't mad!"

"You looked mad."

"That's just my face."

"Dear God, will you either put down your pizza or eat it?"

Lewis glanced down, as though he needed visual confirmation that his hand was still crushing the crusts of two pizza slices together. Shooting her an overdramatic, *is-this-what-you-want?* look, he dropped them on a napkin, sat down roughly, and started eating.

Rex lingered awkwardly by the wall as Lewis finished the first slice and started on the second. After waffling, she walked to the island and sat opposite him.

"I'm sorry." Lewis chewed with gusto. "I got mad at you for being startled. God, why am I so sensitive lately?"

"I formally state my forgiveness."

Lewis's head hit the table with a thump, shoulders shaking. Rex was alarmed for a hot second before she realized he was laughing. "You're not like I expected but also exactly like I expected."

That felt more like a compliment than it should have. "Oh."

Taking a deep breath, Lewis settled back in his seat. "Let's actually fix this."

"How?"

"Well, what would make you not be scared of me?" Rex hoped she didn't look as gobsmacked as she felt. "Is it the thought of running into me alone? Because I could stay out of the common areas at night."

"You don't have to do that," Rex said carefully.

"This is your home."

"You have to live here too."

Lewis shrugged. "Yeah, but I'm not scared of you. If you 're scared of me, I can make some concessions. You shouldn't have to live that way."

Rex's mind skipped a track or two.

"He really needs your help right now."

"I don't understand why you're pulling away from the family."

"I'm worried about your brother."

"It's not just you." It felt important for Rex to make that clear.

"Yeah, you're scared of Grant, too, right?"

Rex wished it wasn't so obvious. She kept her teeth clenched because she thought she might cry if she spoke. It didn't make sense—she didn't feel sad.

"It doesn't have to be forever. If you're able to trust me a bit we can stop, and I'll go back to wandering into the kitchen in the middle of the night."

Rex found herself nodding. He sounded so reasonable, like she was the one doing him a favor. Was it too much? Was it unfair? Rex couldn't tell, but everything he said made her feel so light. "Okay. Why not?"

Rex arrived at Peak Street the next day with enough time to pace in front of the virus's secure lab for a full hour, Flora watching her pityingly from the desk under the monitors. She scratched occasionally at the earpiece she wore, since she'd learned her lesson on leaving Aya with no way to talk to her. Texts worked fine, as long as you remembered to check them, and the exchange wasn't bogged down with cat videos and the conspiracy theories that Aya got sucked into when she had too much unsupervised internet access.

It wasn't long before 'Ning showed up, using the roof door again. "They're coming," she said as she joined them. Rex wondered if she was going to throw up.

Mayor Vicker arrived with his entourage next, looking like he shared the sentiment.

"Do you think they autograph things?" He moved his case full of Vivid Blue action figures from surface to surface. His hands shook so hard, the next move might send the whole thing smashing to the floor, but that could just be wishful thinking on Rex's part. "No, no, that would be inappropriate. We spoke before I left—that Don Conjure is such a nice young man. I gave them permission to land their jet on your roof."

Rex didn't know how that was the mayor's job, but whatever.

"Sir, should you be here if the virus is removed from containment?" Joey, one of today's babysitters said. The other was Lieutenant Quinten. Rex was sure he'd changed the shift schedule in order to be there.

"I'll be leaving before then," Mayor Vicker answered. "I thought I should greet the Protectors on their first official visit to Decimen City, and it didn't seem prudent to ask them to stop at my office given the situation."

He rubbed his hands on his jacket as his aid sneakily shifted the case out of Rex's reach. "Oh, I think I'm sweating. Is it much longer?"

A rumble shook the building, and Rex braced a hand on the wall. "Geez, how hard did they land?"

Aya's voice rattled through Rex's earpiece. "That wasn't a jet, Doctor."

Rex's blood froze. "That's not them." She crowded Flora out of the way, ignoring the tense questions filling the room. "Aya, where's it coming from?"

A view of a mid-security hallway took over the monitors where a rough, neon-orange circle hung above the floor, light flitting across it as it spun. It was so unexpected in that moment that Rex could only stare at the screen as masked and coattailed henchmen streamed through the orange ring into the hall.

"Rifter!" 'Ning's voice at her shoulder made Rex jump. "What's he doing here?"

Rex's chest felt tight. "Aya, the staff?"

"Evacuation is underway. The intruders are moving toward the high-security wing," Aya's voice said in her ear, the screens flicking through camera views. That meant they were approaching Rex's position, as well as the dinosaur enclosures. "As per Oversight conditions, lasers in interior throughways are inoperable."

'Ning's voice cut over Aya's. "Where are they, Meister?"

"What's going on? Are those people in the building?" the mayor asked.

"Sir, we need to move," a bodyguard said.

"If you break lockdown, they could gain access to everything in this wing," Flora argued.

"There is no lockdown, Ms. Shay," Aya corrected, and a chill ran through Rex. "I have attempted site-specific and lab-wide lockdown procedures but have been unsuccessful. Manual override may be possible, but I suspect the cause is sabotage of physical hardware."

Lockdown wasn't working? Was that Rifter's fault, or Oversight's? Fuck, it was probably Oversight. They didn't have time for this—a villain's goons were *in the lab.*

Rex thought out loud. "Rifter will come through last. There's still time before we have to deal with him." Their target was almost certainly the virus—which meant the room she was in now—so Rex needed to move fast if she wanted to reach anything she could use against them before they closed the distance. She tried not to panic that they'd be passing the dinosaur lab on their way.

"Lightning, I need you on goon duty. I'll close the rift." Rex had never studied one of Rifter's physics-defying holes in the air, but how hard could it be? "Take my babysitters if you want—they carry guns in case I go batshit."

"We don't take eyes off you," the lieutenant growled, stepping between Rex and the door. It figured the boss soldier would choose now to flaunt his authority.

"Review tapes later, then," Flora shot back, raising her head from the tablet in her hands. "Someone needs to find out why the lockdown isn't working. Unless it's a flipped switch, one of your people will have more luck than me."

Lieutenant Quinten's eyes narrowed at Rex. "You don't go anywhere alone."

Rex threw up her hands because she didn't have time for any of this. "Come along, then."

As soon as Rex cracked the door, a yellow flash zapped past her into the hall. "You don't even know where they are!" she yelled after 'Ning. "Fucking superheroes." She turned and grabbed Joey's arm. "Go back her up. Or find her if she's lost. They're heading up corridor four—follow the lights." Rex peeled off down a side corridor, Lieutenant Quinten at her side and Aya updating her on Flora and the mayor's movements, thankfully away from the virus.

"I've called for backup," Quinten was telling her through Aya's buzz. "Ms. Anderson, if this breach runs the risk of dangerous experiments breaking containment, we must use the time we have to terminate."

Rex's whole body went cold. "Not necessary. We can shut this down."

"Unfortunately, that's not your call." The lieutenant raised a radio to his mouth. "Anyone within the perimeter, initiate wipeout protocol."

Rex stopped dead in her tracks, attention pulling sharply to one point. The part of her mind counting time and tracking Aya's updates dropped away. "Call it off."

"This is one of the reasons we're here: to stop disasters that you let happen."

"We have time!" Her heart hammered against her ribs.

"Rifter's portals don't close unless he closes them or gets knocked unconscious, and the Lightning's never managed that faster than twenty minutes. That's plenty of time to take something dangerous back through."

"I can shut it down sooner."

His face was like stone, and it made her hands twitch with the need to shake him. "Not possible. Rifter's been on Oversight's radar for years. We have no data on how his power works and no viable theories."

"Viable theories?" She wanted to punch him. She wanted to scream. "I can bend freaking spacetime!" She started running for the room she needed with Quinten glued to her heels.

"Your spacetime disruption project is barely a lab space with a sign on the door." There was an oddly cool tone to his words that Rex didn't have the wherewithal to think about.

"Because I haven't gotten around to writing down the theory." She burst into the right room: not the one designated for the spacetime project, which would hopefully lead to teleportation someday—take that, cars—but a testing range for energy shields derived from the laser guns in her walls.

Rex darted to a workstation with two partially-constructed emitters— long sticks of metal held apart at a precise distance by a third metal rod, all wired into a charging port and computers to measure energy output and whatnot. As Rex bent over the computer and altered the math behind the shield's settings, Aya helpfully put a camera feed in the corner of the screen. 'Ning had engaged the intruders, punches flying as she zapped around the room while Joey watched the corridor behind her.

"Doctor, soldiers have entered the high-security wing via an override program," Aya said. "Some have engaged the intruders in other corridors, and some have moved into the labs. Several destructive programs have been introduced to lab computers via external devices."

Rex logged that away to deal with later. "Got it." She entered the last few numbers and set it to run, hearing the hum of the shield's emitters adjusting to the new settings. Then she snapped off the connecting bar, tugged out the wires, and snatched up the emitters by the broken, nonconductive ends.

She held one emitter still and waved the other back and forth. Blue sparks and streaks of light flickered between them when they swung close together, solidifying into an energy shield at about a foot apart.

"What kind of weapon is that?" Quinten demanded.

"I'm gonna call it a fuck-off-out-of-here-Rifter." She strode back out of the room.

Aya guided Rex through side halls, avoiding the fight where 'Ning had most of the intruders bottlenecked. To bypass a long detour, they cut through a room where two opera-masked men were rummaging in a massive refrigerator and tossing petri dishes to the floor, destroying weeks of work.

The lieutenant's footsteps landed too hard, making Rex want to tear out her nonexistent hair as the two goons spun around. They reached for their guns, and Rex couldn't stop a little scream at the *bam* as the lieutenant shot one in the head, a spurt of blood hitting the refrigerator shelves as he dropped. Rex threw up her emitters on reflex, and the translucent blue shield sprang up between them in time to block the bullet the other goon shot at her. Huh, it worked. This marked a breakthrough in the field she was going to call forcefield-ology.

The lieutenant shot the other goon, making Rex yelp again. Without looking at the bodies or blood, she separated the emitters and swept through the rest of the room before the cold fury could wear off—the last thing she needed right now was the shakes.

They came out in the middle of the hall, a few feet from the rift. This close, Rex heard the rift's warbly *hum-um-um*. The circle's rough edge warped the air like the edge of a magnifying lens, the effect hard to catch through the eye-searing orange. Through it she saw a shadowed gray floor and maybe a wall at the back. She only had time to make a few quick extrapolations based on the way the rift interacted with space before she had to tear her eyes away, because as she and her oh-so-dedicated babysitter stepped into the hallway, Rifter stepped out of the rift.

Quinten raised his gun and fired, but Rifter, with a tearing sound and a lift of his orange-gloved hand—did he coordinate his outfit with the color of his rifts, or could he manipulate the rifts to match his color scheme?—opened a circle in the air that swallowed the bullet and winked out of existence. A smirk visible through the thin mask on his face, Rifter waved a hand like every villain with a dramatic superpower, and a rift opened under the lieutenant's feet.

Rex lurched toward Quinten as he dropped, forgetting she didn't have a free hand to catch him. She heard a snap and looked through the rift to see him groaning on a lawn a couple dozen feet below, one leg twisted beneath him. She had an instant to feel relief that he hadn't fallen into a shark tank or a volcano before the *crackle-rackle* of another tearing rift jarred her back to more immediate problems.

Before the rift forming beneath her widened enough to catch her shoe, she jabbed the ends of her emitters into the tile on either side—maybe a bit too hard in her adrenaline-fueled *woo*—and blue lines shot into the orange with a firecracker snap and a burst of sparks that left her cursing at a singed ankle and no more rift.

Rex felt the grin stretching her face without any memory of when it got there, and a laugh burst out. Oh, yeah. She'd glued a rift in spacetime back together with a few theories based on a glimpse of a portal through a security camera and rudimentary force field technology. Beat that miracle, Jesus.

The look on Rifter's face was unclear through the gauzy mask, but his aborted step forward said enough. Rex barreled at him and swung one of the metal emitters to smack him upside the head. The hit jarred up her arm all the way to her neck, but she didn't let her hand loosen on the metal and strode to the main rift. There was a *snick* of another door opening behind her. Sped up by the thought of a henchman about to escape with whatever they'd plundered, Rex swung one emitter behind the orange circle and held the other over the front. The force field sprang together.

The rift exploded in a starburst of orange and blue with greater force than the small one she'd shorted out, throwing her back against the wall next to an opera-masked goon. She let out a startled scream and swung an emitter—she wasn't sure she could let go of them if she tried, at this point—but the angle was bad, and the goon caught the rod by its other end.

Rex instantly raised the other emitter and a force field sprang between them, a disturbing sizzle rising from his fingers where they gripped the metal. He screamed and let go, making her stagger at the loss of resistance. And, wow, Rex was going to have to find out why the field blocked bullets but only burned flesh—she'd expected in the panicked millisecond after making the force field that it would slice his fingers clean off. Or did it have to do with the fingers being at the field's edge whereas the bullet hit closer to the middle? She had some interesting research ahead of her if she lived through this.

"Aya, we're adding energy shields to the Exo-suit."

"Noted, Doctor. But if I could bring your attention to—"

A hit to the back of Rex's head had her vision blurring and her body listing forward. An emitter was wrenched from her hand and clattered across the floor, echoing much too loudly and making her wince hard enough to force her eyes shut.

Her shoulder hit the wall, then the floor, without a moment passing in between. That didn't seem right. Her eyes peeled open for a blurry, sideways view of Rifter's feet. She turned her head—God, that hurt; this had to be because of the Jesus thought; divine retribution was inevitable—to see Rifter bending toward her and drawing back a fist. His voice was both distant and too loud. "Where is it, Meister?"

"Rifter!"

Oh, Rex had such a complicated reaction to that voice.

The Lightning zapped into the hall in a bright yellow streak that seared straight through Rex's brain. The streak solidified into the superhero as her fist *pow*ed into Rifter's face in a burst of eye-stabbing electricity.

As the hero and villain swept out of her field of vision, Rex tried to push herself up. The movement made her head spin and nausea rise alarmingly to the top of her stomach. She let her head drop against the wall when she reached a sitting position, and the tap felt like a hammer strike.

Movement in the corner of her eye made her turn her head in time to see the staggering goon draw his gun with his good hand, the burned one balled at his chest.

Oh, yay.

Aya buzzed in her ear, "I'm making some judgment calls regarding perimeter security," but Rex couldn't spare her much focus. She raised her remaining emitter, thinking of all the ways she could change the output settings to turn it into a stun baton or a laser sword. But she didn't have any way to change those settings now. Without the other emitter it was just a cool metal stick. Fuck Rifter.

The goon aimed the gun at her and fired. Rex flinched violently, jarring her head again, then found herself staring cross-eyed at a bullet frozen inches from her face. After one empty-headed moment, she felt like laughing again. *Oh, dear Jesus, thank you.*

The goon's strangled gasp wrenched her attention back to him, and she watched him writhe in the air, gun falling to the floor. A woman in a lavender cape swept in front of Rex, feet not touching the floor, long, midnight-blue hair floating around her head, and one blue hand extended toward the man now clawing at his throat.

The bullet fell to the tile with a sharp *tink*.

Vivid Blue swung her hand down, and the goon followed, back slamming to the floor. Her feet lowered to the tile softly, which Rex's pounding head was grateful for. The pink-suited Pixie, glittery wings going humming-bird-quick, flew past Vivid Blue, and Don Conjure strode after her to kneel beside Rex. "Meister of Decimen City," he said, his handlebar mustache and old-timey newscaster voice making her giggle. "Are you injured?"

"The Lightning knocked Rifter unconscious," Pixie announced, crouching on Rex's other side. "We have to contain him before he wakes up—or he'll escape again!"

Rex turned her head as the rest of the Protectors strode down the hall: Manta Man, steps heavy as his long, stingray tail swayed behind him; Cat Man at a strut, claws clicking against the floor; Undertaker; King George; the Jester, who honest-to-God had to be the most scantily-clad hero she'd ever seen, with the possible exception of Whale Woman—now there was a woman who gave zero fucks. Although the Jester might challenge that throne since all he wore was a hat with a bell on it, face paint, and what she hoped was a codpiece. Come to think of it, she was going to have to give this whole crew a pointed lecture about exposed skin in a chemical lab.

"The building is secure. Last Dance's forces are being taken into custody as we speak," Manta Man told Vivid Blue, voice gruff. His foot hit the emitter on the floor, making it clatter again.

"Careful with that, Conjure Man. I mean—damn it—Don Manta," Rex said, one hand feeling the back of her head. There was something warm spreading down her neck. "That's one-half of a force field emitter I reconfigured to fix spacetime. I'm gonna need that to make Rifter a special prison."

Don Conjure pulled her hand down—which, *excuse him.* "Stop touching it," he ordered in that ridiculous baritone.

'Ning came into view, dragging an unconscious Rifter. "Protectors of the World! I—that is, thank you for your help. We—I mean, you—"

Pixie smiled warmly and clasped her shoulder. "We're only here to help. This is your home turf. We'll appreciate any direction you can give us."

Rex rolled her eyes. She could practically see 'Ning's hero-worship boner.

Several of the Protectors gave her disapproving looks. Great, were they mind readers now too?

Don Conjure pulled her hand down again. "Stop touching it. You require first aid. And no—we are not mind readers. You are merely speaking your thoughts aloud."

"Stop grabbing my hand. We're not dating." Rex snatched her hand back and looked at it. There was blood on her hand. What was that about?

"I believe you have a concussion."

Right. She decided to get up but couldn't think of how. "I'm not standing up, so someone else will have to make the force field prison and figure out where my boss babysitter went. Anyone got a pen?"

As the others shared looks and Rex aggressively ignored the others sharing looks, Don Conjure gave a little flourish and made a pen appear from nowhere.

"Can you teach me that?"

"With respect to your injury, I would rather not give you more tools to play with the fabric of reality, reformed villain or no."

"I'm not a reformed—you know what? Never mind." Rex took the pen and then the paper he produced with another flourish and started writing, the words slanting frustratingly across the page. She suddenly recalled how she and Don Conjure had last crossed paths. "Right. You confiscated that trans-dimensional insect—"

"The parasite that would have seeded our universe with its kind, leaving it a lifeless husk, yes."

"I was so close to opening a door to an alternate reality."

"Don, please stop stalling," Vivid Blue cut in. "The Meister needs medical attention."

Rex's head moved sharply at the interruption, a surge of nausea making her wince. When she refocused, she was gazing into Vivid Blue's sky-blue eyes, pale eggshell blue in the whites, the pupils the same blue-black as her hair, the face they were set in sharp-jawed and as true blue as a bottle of paint. She got a weird sense she'd been staring, although she'd only tracked a few seconds. "Hi, Viv," she heard herself say.

Vivian gave her a nod, expressionless. "T, stop touching your head."

Rex's other hand had, indeed, migrated to the back of her head. And now there was blood on both hands. And the paper. Well, that was fine.

The others cleared out around them, speaking to soldiers and getting restraints around Rifter. 'Ning darted from Protector to Protector in Rex's peripheral vision, looking like she ought to be fanning herself. Viv went in and out of focus in front of Rex.

When Flora dropped to Rex's side, speaking quickly and softly while someone else touched cold fingers to the back of her head, Vivian turned abruptly and issued orders to her fellow Protectors, purple cape sweeping behind her.

Rex took a deep breath. "Here we go."

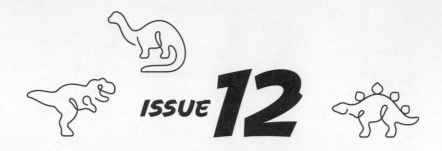

ISSUE 12

SPOTLIGHT ON THE PAST: PART TWO

R ex had built her first lab in her family's garage before she even knew
what a lab was. It was merely an exercise in problem solving—she
needed to keep her mold samples contained and organized, properly labeled
by which old food or rotting board she'd scraped them from. She also needed a way to store the chemicals she'd synthesized with the machine she'd
built out of the kitchen microwave and pieces she took from the oven.

The lab was a kind of sanctuary. Family members popped in when they
needed her, but they generally left her to her projects. She told herself that
was a good thing. She liked the privacy. If she ever wished they would ask
about what she was doing, well—it wasn't like they would understand it,
anyway.

Safety didn't cross Rex's mind until she was eight, when her sister
walked into the radiation field she was messing with and fell into a seizure.
In her panic, Rex knocked something loose in the machine before she shut
it off, changed a wavelength or a frequency or something that would take
years to work back to. As Vivian's skin curled off in strips, hair falling out,
blue-veined eyes rolling back in her head, Rex's screams drew the rest of the
family at a run.

Viv had a trump card to play for every fight they had for the rest of their
lives. No amount of work that Rex put into fixing it would ever make them
even.

ISSUE *13*

DINOSAURS IN LITTLE LEAGUE

The rift Lieutenant Quinten had fallen through only sent him to the lawn outside the lab, thankfully. That could have been a much bigger mess, considering his leg had broken on impact. Now, he sat a few beds over from Rex in Peak Street's medical center, issuing orders over his cast-wrapped leg to the soldiers streaming in and out.

Rex blinked at Flora, standing at her bedside. "Were the staff—"

"Evacuated and sheltered in place. No injuries reported, but I'm granting time off requests as they come in."

Rex nodded. Flora did an excellent Rex signature. "The wipeout protocol—"

"It's been canceled, which we confirmed when you asked ten minutes ago."

She had already asked? She rubbed the bandage on her head.

"Don't touch that." Flora pushed her hand down. "I'm also on top of the paperwork for the government to use your anti-rift technology for immediate emergency purposes with your intellectual rights protected. We'll go through the more tedious rigmarole later."

"I told you, it's called a fuck-off-out-of-here-Rifter."

Flora sighed. "That would be the thing you don't forget. And before you ask again, the dinosaurs weren't affected. No one made it that far into the facility."

Rex let out a breath and winced at a twinge in her head.

Flora sat on the edge of the bed and leaned closer. "Aya put together footage of the soldiers carrying out the wipeout protocol. I've been reviewing it."

Rex's gut clenched in cold anger. She remembered the footage Aya had pulled up in the force field lab. She hadn't had time to think about it then, but now she had some questions.

"Aya made a list of every lab that was hit, with the damage sorted by what the intruders did and what the wipeout protocol destroyed. Only about ten percent of your data was interfered with, as far as Aya can tell. But if a project was cleared completely, Aya wouldn't know, of course."

"I'll know. Show me the list."

Flora shook her head. "No screens until you're cleared by a doctor."

Right. Rex sighed and went down a mental checklist. "The lockdown malfunction."

Flora looked grimmer. "I've spoken to Lieutenant Quinten. He tried to brush me off, but I got that it was part of their initial security measures. Apparently, they didn't want you to be able to lock them out. Rex, no one told me about that. I can't find it in any of the papers we signed, either. There are some vague clauses to allow for judgment calls, but even then, they're supposed to communicate with us."

Rex nodded. Her anger was simmering beneath a layer of ice, keeping it distant. "I guess they're seeing the flaw in that plan."

Flora *tsk*ed. "If you hadn't figured out how to literally close a rift in spacetime, Rifter, or Last Dance, or whoever was behind this could have looted the labs bare. There's nothing okay about this. I'm so angry, Rex."

"To be fair, the Protectors would still have interrupted the whole thing."

"Not before Rifter would have escaped. I can't believe you did that, by the way. You could have died. As soon as you aren't fragile as a cracked teacup, I'm hitting you for that."

Rex smiled. It dropped as another anxiety churned in her gut. "The dinosaurs—"

"—weren't affected," Flora said patiently.

"Right. Good."

A booming voice announced Don Conjure as his fluttering blue half-cape made an appearance in the sterile gray and white of the medical room. "Our arrival was timely, then. We would not want this virus to reach the hands of Last Dance."

'Ning's yellow figure made another bright addition, apparently mid-conversation. "Rifter probably saw the Meister when we fought the other night and figured out it was here. I guess he wasn't counting on heroes showing up."

"Indeed. I wager our foe would have claimed his prize with ease had you brought it to the police."

Rex let out a deep, satisfying, hero-weary sigh, and Flora patted her shoulder in commiseration.

Pixie flew in next, adding pink to the peacock-fest playing hell with Rex's slow-reacting retinas. "You don't think Last Dance has found a way to mind control Rifter, do you?"

Rex frowned. "Since when could Last Dance mind control anyone?"

The Protectors paused and looked at her, the buzz of Pixie's wings cutting through the bustle of soldiers. Rex got the feeling 'Ning was rolling her eyes.

"Young Meister, is that not the purpose of the mysterious contraband the Lightning risked life and limb to obtain?" Don Conjure boomed with a twirl of his mustache.

"Why are you so ripped?" Rex asked, massaging her head. "You just stand there and wave your hands when you fight."

"I must often give chase."

"With your arms?"

"Someone has an admirer," a smarmy voice cut in. The Jester joined the other heroes, each step punctuated by a jingle of his hat.

"Rex is still pretty out of it. Her filter got knocked a little loose." Flora grabbed both of Rex's wrists and pulled them away from her head.

"Blame it on the concussion." The Jester winked. "Classic." The guy had to be cold in that outfit—more evidence that it was, in fact, a codpiece. Rex wondered if there was a not-weird way to ask.

"To answer your question," Rex said, shaking off Flora's hands, "no one said the virus controls minds. I don't see how that would translate to Last Dance controlling minds, anyway."

"But those thugs who came through the rift were wearing Last Dance's getup," Pixie said earnestly, adding to Rex's anxiety as she flitted around the room.

"It could be that Rifter is trying to shift blame," Don Conjure mused.

The Jester sneered and folded his arms, hip jutting out. "Kinda dumb to use his own rifts if that's his play."

"And to show up," Flora muttered.

"I never understood why villains give their goons uniforms, anyway," Rex said. "If I hired people to do a heist, I'd let them dress themselves so it couldn't be traced back to me."

When several of the heroes shot her looks, Flora patted her shoulder. "That's the kind of thing you need to filter."

A hearty chortle broke the lull as King George arrived, fur-lined robe dragging behind him and gold crown at a jaunty angle. "In my time, if subjects could not provide their own vestments, they were thrown to the dogs."

"There's no way that's true," Rex said through clenched teeth. "Why do you all indulge him? He's not from the past."

"But my home dimension exists *in* your dimension's past."

"That doesn't make sense. And will you stop flying around?" she snapped at Pixie, wincing when she had to tilt her head to see the woman hovering in the ceiling corner.

Vivian's voice broke in, taking all of Rex's attention. "You're clearly feeling better, T."

Vivid Blue entered the room with Manta Man and Undertaker at her shoulders. The other heroes turned their attention to their leader, including the Kool-Aid-drinking Lightning.

Undertaker's rainbow-washed sickles poked out from under her crimson cloak, making Rex's head throb at the thought of the talking-to she'd have to give the security department about superheroes not being exempt from the *no outside weapons* rule.

"The police are questioning Last Dance's men, but they haven't gotten much," Viv said, addressing her team. "Cat Man is chasing down a lead."

"Are we sure it isn't a laser pointer?" the Jester jeered.

Vivid Blue ignored him. "While we wait, I want Undertaker and Pixie to check out the plant where the Lightning found that vial."

The Vivian-in-charge voice was screwing with Rex's head. She half expected to be told to go clean the litterbox.

"Lightning." Viv turned to 'Ning, who snapped to attention. "I would appreciate it if you helped them."

'Ning gave a single nod. "Of course."

"We won't let you down," Pixie chirped as she landed.

"Hmph. Couldn't hurt." Undertaker turned and melted into the shadows, a quick wash of rainbow blending with maroon that darkened to nothing. Pixie gave 'Ning a quick smile and followed her out.

As they left, Manta Man stepped out of the shadows—there weren't a lot of shadows, so he and Undertaker had to share—and faced Vivid Blue, sharp teeth showing in flashes as he ground out, "I'm going to check my contacts in the underworld. See if I can catch any stirrings."

Viv nodded, and Manta Man trundled back through the door, his gray tail swishing behind him.

King George harrumphed. "In my time, subjects waited for orders from their ruler."

"Oh, let him go," the Jester sneered, shifting one hand to his hip. "We all know M.M. doesn't play well with others."

"Don," Vivian said, and all eyes returned to her as though pulled by gravity, "will you see what your precognition can find?"

"I shall find an empty closet or storage space," Don Conjure announced as he left.

"I could have told you where the quiet room is, but whatever," Rex muttered.

Vivian turned, and then her whole blue attention was on Rex. "T."

Rex met her eyes. She and Viv were about the same height but looking up from the medical bed as Vivian looked down at her, she very much felt like the younger sister. She wasn't sure what she expected. She and Viv had exchanged messages here and there over the years—mostly about family stuff. When was the last time they'd been in touch? A year or three ago?

"If you and Lieutenant Quinten are up for it, I need to know everything you saw through the rift. The two of you were closest to it, and it might help us figure out where the other side opened up."

And that was it. Rex didn't know whether to feel disappointed or relieved. "It was a warehouse, I guess?"

Viv frowned. "We could see that much from the security cameras."

"Then I don't know what to tell you."

"In my time, such insolence—"

Viv shot King George a glare and looked at the other bed. "Lieutenant?"

"Sorry, ma'am," Quinten said. "I only got a glimpse at the rift before he dropped me." He shot a cool look at Rex. "Ms. Anderson was in the hallway unsupervised until she took out that rift."

"I don't understand what you're implying," Rex answered. "Because it sounds like you're saying I'm covering for Rifter and also I destroyed his only means of escape."

"I think it's a little convenient you had the means to counter him lying around."

Dear God, he sounded dead serious. "I already explained that wasn't what those emitters were supposed to be for."

"Yes." He nodded, voice and expression still cool. "The reported purpose of that technology didn't fully reflect its use, did it?"

Rex's mouth fell open. Flora intervened before she could say more. "Rex has a concussion, which she got fighting Rifter, if everyone has forgotten. I think questions can wait until after she's recovered."

"Afraid she'll be a little too honest, Ms. Shay?"

"Who is this?" King George asked, gesturing at Flora with his scepter. "The Meister's vassal?"

"I didn't know supervillains had sidekicks," the Jester added.

Rex sputtered in indignation. "Flora is no sidekick. She's a goddess among lawyers, and I'm her kept genius."

"Enough," Vivid Blue said, and again commanded the room. Rex didn't recall that being one of Viv's powers, but maybe it was a late-onset thing. She walked closer, stopping between Rex and Quinten. Rex leaned so that the hero blocked the lieutenant's line of sight, and hated that impulse to hide behind Viv.

"I would like to speak with Ms. Anderson alone."

Oh, breaking out the last names. Even though they had the same one.

"Ms. Anderson is injured and should stay in this hospital bed," Flora said.

"It's fine." If Rex was honest, she'd rather have whatever conversation this was going to be away from Quinten, the heroes, and Flora, though for different reasons. "It's a *mild* concussion—no big deal." She slid out of bed before she could change her mind. "Let's speak alone, Viv."

Rex led Vivian down a hall and through an unoccupied reptile lab, passing plastic tubs of cockroaches making a constant, skittering white noise. As soon as she turned to face Viv, the hero waved a hand that threw the door shut and said, "I see you've done nothing to win over your surveillance."

"You know me. There's no telling when I might irradiate myself with supervillain particles or fall into a vat of concentrated evil."

"What are you trying to accomplish with the attitude?"

"Attitude?" Rex leaned against the roach habitats and quickly straightened as the jostled tub released a cloud of roach smell. "Okay, this is a bad spot. We're going somewhere else." She strode back out of the lab.

Viv swept to Rex's side so smoothly that she probably wasn't bothering to take steps. "The snide comments aren't cute," she continued. "And they aren't endearing you to any of the people you should be kissing up to right now."

Rex turned a corner, shoulders tight. "Like who? You?"

Viv gave a short laugh. "I hope you haven't failed to notice the Oversight team you've been hosting for a few weeks now. And me, as a Protector?" Viv shrugged. "Yes, you do need to impress us. Don and I are both on the Oversight Committee representing the interests of superbeings. One of our jobs is to coordinate with superpowered contractors—including finding skilled people to surveil those who can do things most people can't understand."

It took Rex almost a full thirty seconds to understand what Viv had said and turn toward her, stopping in the middle of the hall. "Oversight has other super geniuses checking my work?"

"Don't make it a big deal. We have a thorough vetting process and rigorous standards concerning intellectual rights."

"Who is it? Mindbender? Brainiac? It can't be Brainiac—she thought my waste treatment project was a plot to speed up climate change and tried to kill me."

"T, Mindbender is a villain."

Rex blinked. "Since when?"

"Since always."

Rex wondered if she could remove him from her contacts without Oversight noticing. The thought train lurched back on track, and she groaned. "Oh God, tell me it isn't Think Tank."

"Your first checker is Pixie, if you must know. She and Manta Man are geniuses in their own right."

"Because I guarantee you, if Think Tank gets access to my ideas, they're gone. The patents will be in the works. He still thinks he invented liquid CPU, but I know I told him about that when I was drunk." Rex shook her head, wincing at a twinge in her temple. She strode forward again and realized she'd automatically headed toward the dinosaur enclosures. It was as good a destination as any. "Hold on—you and Don?"

"Don Conjure. It's his first name."

"Oh. I thought it was Don like—mob boss."

"It's that too."

"Well, I hope you and *Don* are too professional to let something like a bad attitude or, say, personal relationships influence your judgment."

"T." Viv swept in front of her and forced a stop, cape and blue-black hair stirring up behind her. "This isn't a game. This is real life catching up with you, for once. And after that interview—"

Goddamn it, that viral video. "That was Flora's idea, and I know the whole thing sort of backfired, but I'm not the one who put it online. And hey, if my reputation has tanked, there's nowhere to go but up."

A crease appeared in Viv's blue brow. "Have you watched the video?"

"Not yet." Rex felt some uncertainty at Viv's reaction. "But I was there in person, so—"

"Your reputation hasn't tanked, T. Hashtag More-to-the-Story is trending on social media."

Rex opened her mouth, then closed it. Anything she'd meant to say slipped from her mind. She stepped around Vivian and continued to the dinosaurs' wing.

"But you know who hasn't reacted positively to your live bitch-fest?" Viv said behind her. "The Oversight Committee. Do you have any awareness of what they think you are?"

"Not good? A supervillain? Tragically mad but also irredeemably evil?" She swiped a keycard angrily and pressed a hand to the scanner to open the door.

"An instigator." Viv made it sound like *a serial killer.*

"It's not like I—oh, what the hell." Rex caught sight of the mid-sized dino habitat and strode to the glass wall. A wide space had been cleared of brush and painted with a rough baseball diamond.

Dinosaurs were scattered around the field and moved in a flurry at the crack of a baseball hitting a bat. The more agile among them ran in circles, squawking and calling as the ball sailed a few measly feet to the pitcher's mound.

A dinosaur trundled toward first base at the urging of a lab tech.

"Baseball." Rex pressed her hands to her eyes, trying to relieve her pounding head. "How many times do I have to tell them that they don't all have hands? Soccer was the obvious choice."

"The only one of us who knows about sports is James, and he was really excited to teach them baseball," a tech answered from a nearby station. "None of us had the heart to tell him no."

Rex ran her hands over her head and looked over the baseball field again. The two teams had different colored jerseys, although most had tied them around their necks by the sleeves. "We should get them tailored jerseys. They'd be adorable."

"Mommy!" one of the closer dinosaurs called, getting the attention of the others and setting off a flood of babbles as they gestured toward their uniforms and the improvised bases.

Rex raised her voice to be heard through the glass. "You look great, guys. Keep up the good work."

"T, listen to me." Viv's voice drew Rex's attention back, though Viv's gaze lingered on the scene through the wall, one eyebrow raised, before she visibly forced herself to turn. "All that 'cut villains a break' crap coming from you, right after Oversight placed you a step down from the top tier? The top tier is for people who are actively hostile. They are scared of you." The last sentence was carefully articulated, Viv's face closer to Rex.

Part of Rex could see herself getting this news from Flora and reacting completely differently. But Vivian was the one in her face, and Rex couldn't quite take it. "I never said to cut villains a break. I was griping about how tragedy is selectively utilized to judge morality. And you know I was talking about Sam."

"Of course, I know. You think that helps your case?"

"No one seems to mind that you care about him—it's a selling point for your heroic origin." Rex couldn't keep the bitterness from her voice. "But when I say something mildly in his defense, I'm an instigator?"

"So, you don't think the fact that I've earned trust—really earned it—factors in at all."

At the crack of a baseball bat, Rex turned back to the wall and forced a smile, returning the wave of a spinosaur sprinting to second base. "Well, we can't all flip a cape and win over the crowd. Maybe people just don't like me."

"Are you upset that people like me more than you? Is that what this is about?"

Rex quashed the urge to shout. Instead, she said flatly, "Your adoring public wrote me out of one of the most important events of my life."

"I didn't think you'd want me to correct them. I thought you didn't like being a victim."

"Well, I was one whether I like it or not," Rex shot back, willing her voice not to break. "That doesn't change that it was my story and it should be up to me how it was told."

"You want to make the whole thing about you, when you know what all of that did to Sam. I'm amazed you'd be so selfish."

A flare of frustration so hot that it made Rex's eyes burn rushed to her head. Of course, she was selfish to be affected by what happened; it wasn't her story to be affected by. To the world, it was Vivid Blue's story. To Vivian, it was Sam's. Words crowded over her tongue, and she bit them back, knowing Viv would only hear a plea for attention. Dramatics. Making it about her.

But fuck, how did anyone look at what happened and see a story about Viv? How did they carve out: villain snaps, hero beats villain, hero saves the day? Had Viv spent nights afterward screaming into her pillow until her vision spotted so she wouldn't wake her family? Had Viv learned to suppress the urge to flinch every time she saw Sam until it was second nature? Viv had been invulnerable since she was twelve; did she even know what fear felt like?

Maybe that was what people liked about her. Maybe that was what made Rex's part so fucking unseemly.

Viv was talking again. "But maybe it's not your fault—it's what you're used to, after all."

Two microraptors, presumably on the same team, fought over the ball in the outfield, but at those words, Rex tore her eyes away. "What is that supposed to mean?"

"Come on, T. Everything was about you, growing up. We had to move for your special school. We had to make sure you got enough 'stimulation.'" Viv made extravagant air quotes. "You couldn't stand not being the center of attention."

"How the fuck do you figure?" Rex demanded.

Viv gave her a long-suffering look. "Like you ever took interest in anything until after I did. Then suddenly you had to show me up at it."

Rex held her breath around the *because I wanted to be just like you* because the last thing she wanted to do right now was give Viv a compliment.

"But for me, it was always, 'Viv, take care of the twins—they're not strong like you.' As though I just happened to be strong, and it wasn't something you did to me. Like I didn't have any problems with being mutated into a hideous monster—"

"You told me to stop trying to change you back! You said you wanted to stay like this!" Rex burst out, suddenly furious, an old ache pounding in her chest; because how dare Viv use that against her when Rex could have been working on it this whole time?

"And what do you mean, hideous?" Rex made her tone dismissive, leaning against the glass and trying to take comfort in the sounds of warbling battle cries and thrown baseball mitts. "There are whole fan clubs dedicated to how hot you are."

"Tell that to the twelve-year-old you turned blue."

Rex's jaw felt glued shut.

"You've stayed spoiled in Decimen City." Viv turned on her heel and paced. "These people are used to you. Sure, you almost kill a bunch of them on a regular basis, but they've seen you get punched in the face, and they've heard you run your mouth, and they're not threatened by you anymore."

Rex hated being underestimated, dismissed, and infantilized. But almost just as much, she hated being reminded of the times she'd relied on it.

"You're used to everyone brushing you off and deciding you're harmless. Do you realize what you did today?"

"Yeah, I stopped a supervillain from absconding with a building-full of potentially world-ending tech. I should be given a medal."

"A building-full of potentially world-ending tech that *you* made. That's at your disposal right now. Congratulations on reminding everyone of that."

"But I didn't do any—!"

"You're not under Oversight for being a screwup. We don't bring out those measures for petty reasons." Viv stopped pacing and looked at her. Rex felt her gaze like skittering roaches on her skin. When Viv spoke again, she was quieter, contemplative. "Do you understand how easily you could take over the world?"

Legitimately, by aggressively marketing her inventions and buying out powerful markets. Illegitimately, by developing diseases to be released in a controlled way and managing access to cures. Illegitimately, by straight-up building a robot army. Aya could probably do it on her own via internet conspiracy. "Destroying the world would be less time-consuming," Rex muttered.

Vivian's blue lips thinned. "That isn't funny."

"I didn't mean to say that out loud." Was coldness in her chest a concussion symptom?

"If we're finally on the same page," Vivian's voice was softer, but still not warm, "I need you to get serious and tell me and my team about this virus."

Did Viv think she wasn't taking this seriously? She swallowed back her knee-jerk response because, well, this *was* serious. "You probably know—" Rex winced at her inability to emotionally keep up with the conversation and waved a hand. "It's the same one, basically. There are differences but I'd have to study it to find out exactly what they are."

Viv nodded. "Has he tried to contact you?" When Rex glared at her, she continued, "I'm not stupid. I don't accept that his minions hitting Decimen City is a coincidence."

Rex still hesitated. It was frustrating, but she was tempted to tell. After everything, how did it still feel so natural to trust Viv?

"What if he has?"

"You're not protecting anyone by withholding that information. The Oversight Committee knows you're twins. I disclosed that we're sisters as soon as they brought me in on your case, and you can't expect them not to do background checks."

Yeah, but she could hope.

"T?"

What would happen if she showed Viv the design? If she told her she could make it work?

She started with something easier. "I've had some ideas lately. I think I could help him."

Viv let out a frustrated breath. "We've been here before. How many times do you have to help him put innocent people at risk before you learn to leave it alone—"

"I'd have to be careful, of course. But I think I could give him more control. I could—" She hesitated. "I could build something."

"Do you hear yourself?" Viv snapped, swishing around and rising off her feet. "More control? His powers are a curse. If you can't take them away, you're wasting your time."

"What if it isn't possible? Why throw all our eggs in some hypothetical basket I *can't figure out* when maybe, if we could help him live with it—"

"Living with it is hell." Viv's face filled her vision. "Do you want him to live in hell? Are you that vindictive? Is that why you won't fix him?"

"I couldn't figure it out!"

"Mommy?"

Rex turned. The dinosaurs had abandoned their game, watching her and Viv through the wall from their places around the diamond. The ringing in her ears was Rex's first clue that she'd been shouting. Viv lowered herself to her feet.

"Nothing to see here." She cleared her throat. "Everything's fine; go back to your game."

The door beeped, and Flora walked in. Her steps faltered as she caught sight of Rex and Vivian. "What's going on in here?"

Rex took a steadying breath. "We're getting pumped to go look at the virus." She pushed off the wall, giving it a few pats to reassure the dinosaurs. "Where are the other . . . here they are."

King George and the Jester looked in from the doorway.

"Okay, Protectors, let's get to it." Rex strode to the door. God, her head hurt.

ISSUE 14

DINOSAURS ON THE INTERNET

Flora put up a fight about Rex working with the virus while concussed, and Viv gracefully conceded. Over the next two days of aggressively enforced resting, Rex won about a dozen arguments with the version of Viv that lived in her head. Then a medical worker cleared her and Rex was finally able to take steps toward getting the Protectors out of her lab.

"I want it said before I do this that we're perfectly set up for something to go horribly wrong that transforms me into a monster and teaches all of us about the hubris of science." Elbows-deep in a clear-walled biosafety cabinet, Rex slowly released the plunger on her pipetter, drawing up five milliliters of the solution containing the virus. A respirator shield and gloves taped to the cuffs of her biosafety suit further separated her from the sample, probably doing as much good as Pixie's chipper "good luck."

"Stop stalling, T. We're as prepared as we can be," Viv said through her earpiece—the only reason Rex heard her over the air blowing through the biosafety cabinet's clear partition.

Viv, of course, was safe on the other side of thick glass with Don Conjure, Pixie, the Jester, and the evening shift of babysitters. 'Ning was out with Undertaker and Cat Man, searching for signs of Last Dance and probably still riding the high of honorary Protector-hood, and King George was helping with the interrogations using his Power of Authority, which Rex was convinced was not a real thing.

"That's easy to say when your role will be to stop me from destroying the city once the mystery substance seduces-slash-drives-me-insane." Rex moved the pipetter to one of the petri dishes of brain cell cultures her techs had prepped. "I think most of us should be finding this situation eerily familiar right now."

Pixie shifted next to Viv. "I gotta admit, Blue, this whole thing is making me think of the time my mentor got swarmed by his radioactive mayflies."

Rex groaned. "Oh, right. Who did he become? The Mayfly?"

"Fly-By-Night."

"At least that shows some creativity. Not everyone has to name themselves after the animal that gave them powers." Rex gave the plunger a careful push, watched the green solution hit the cell culture, and changed the tip for the next one. "It's so unfair that you both got bit by the same flies, but you got wings and cool eyes while he got turned evil."

"I was only bit by one, not a whole swarm. See, I was working overtime at the lab to avoid the orphanage—"

Rex snorted, pre-wetting the tip for the next culture. "Of course, you're a genius orphan. Who isn't a genius orphan these days?"

"I am neither a genius nor an orphan," Don Conjure announced. "Though my feud with my father's sect of the Mystical Order—"

"Please, I don't think I can handle another tragic backstory right now. Plus, I already inexplicably like you, so I don't need a tale of woe to force a connection." On the screen in Rex's peripheral vision, Aya listed suggestions about biopanning to identify the viral factors in different types of neurons. Rex thought diverting into organoid-based experiments would be more useful—at this point, a diverse brain cell population was a feature, not a bug.

"I thought you didn't want people to be so dismissive of tragedy," Viv said.

"It is all right," Don Conjure boomed. "I am pleased the Meister likes me, though it be inexplicably."

"Blue," a gruff voice cut in.

Rex jumped and fumbled a used tip as the others turned smoothly toward Manta Man like he hadn't come out of nowhere.

Manta Man didn't spare her a glance. "We've made some progress with Rifter's followers."

Rex didn't stop pipetting, but she shut up, not wanting to miss this.

"Rifter still isn't talking. He's made rifts, but all he can do is travel from one point in his cell to another. The muscle isn't saying much, though several have repeated the same phrase: he'll save the last for you."

"Sounds like Last Dance to me," the Jester said snidely.

Pixie piped up, "Why would Last Dance lend his followers to Rifter? Or is Rifter one of his followers now? And why attack Decimen?"

The Jester cackled and twirled the end of his long hat, making the bell tinkle. "One question at a time, girl."

"I have a question," Becky said from the corner, and geez how could Rex still forget they were there after what just happened? "The Meister's oversight is high-tier and public. Why would any villain attack her lab knowing there would be so much extra security?"

Rex scoffed, drawing some attention from the other side of the glass.

"Sounds like the Meister of Decimen City has something to say." The Jester's voice dripped with disgust at the title.

Rex drew up the solution for the last cell culture, her motions steady and familiar. "First of all, I didn't pick that name—the media made it up. Second, Oversight is the reason the attack almost succeeded. They took out my internal security and spent as much time breaking my stuff as helping."

The Jester's mouth curled in a sneer. Most of them looked skeptical, and Pixie looked worried. But Viv had on her thinking face.

Becky barked a laugh, and her partner, a square-jawed man whose name was utterly lost to Rex said, "The Lightning would have been overwhelmed long before the Protectors arrived if we hadn't backed her up."

"Oh my God." Rex racked the pipetter and began moving cultures into the incubator, a bit more rushed than she preferred. "They wouldn't have gotten in at all if Oversight's weak system didn't have access to my cameras."

She ignored the few mumbles and interjections from the other side of the glass. "Has anyone figured out how they hacked it, by the way? I haven't put my AI on it."

There were a few looks exchanged that were infuriatingly suspicious. Becky asked, "What makes you think Rifter needed camera access?"

Rex almost laughed and had to swallow it when she realized the question was serious. "He can't just pop up indoors—he could land in a wall. Or an active experiment." Had no one made that observation already? "His rift opened in the middle of a hallway. That wasn't luck—it was good aim."

"That suggests he hacked your system," Don Conjure said, solemn as the implications hit.

Rex bristled. "Or Oversight's, since they have access." As if Rex's security could be beaten that fast.

"Even that wouldn't be easy to accomplish in one day," Manta Man said.

Rex shrugged as she removed her outer layer of safety gear. "There are plenty of super geniuses or electronics-based villains who could. It's not too hard of a skill set to find."

Viv spoke again. "The point is, neither Rifter nor Last Dance could do it. So, who else are they working with? This is starting to look like a coalition."

"That's good news," the Jester said. "Supervillain teams always crash and burn."

"In the long term," corrected Viv, her voice getting dark. "Supervillains working together for a short time have been quite effective."

Rex tried hard not to think of the months of headlines blasting Sam's alliance with Angel Killer. Angel Killer was taking heroes' powers away, so it was obvious what Sam would have gotten out of it if the Protectors hadn't tricked Angel Killer into turning his power on himself. She'd told herself that Sam wasn't the one with a vendetta, and he definitely wasn't doing the actual killing. Even so, she'd spent a lot of that time staring at walls and wondering where her brother had gone.

"There's another way to access the cameras that fast," Becky said tonelessly. "Someone on the inside."

Rex didn't appreciate the tiptoeing. "If I was working with them, I wouldn't have invented a way to close the rift."

"Yeah, you 'invented' a way to close a rift. Right in the nick of time," the nameless surveiller said.

Rex felt an impulse of caution alongside her frustration. Quinten had made similar half-accusations in the medical center. Were her actions during the attack really that suspicious, or had the lieutenant given a particular version of events to his team? She accidentally made eye contact with Viv, who had one eyebrow raised in a way that said *"see?"* and *"watch it,"* at the same time. Rex looked away.

"Yes, I did. I'm done in here, by the way. Buzz me out." Rex hoped with gut-stabbing desperation that she'd imagined the slight hesitation before the Protectors complied.

It was dark when Rex got home, and she was exhausted. The wary glares of the Protectors as she'd locked down the virus could have worn her out on their own, but several more hours of debate and conjecture had followed. She'd snapped at Pixie for hovering again and ordered the Jester to either put on more clothes or leave, which earned her a scolding from Viv about priorities and childishness, which led to Rex demanding to know whether it was childish to expect other adults to stand still and dress themselves.

Flora had taken her aside and reminded her that the virus was her priority, it would look very good to help the Protectors, and they urgently needed the Oversight order rescinded.

Wipeout protocol. Geez.

At home, Rex shuffled down to the lab instead of trying to sleep. Her head felt too full for her to give whatever was waiting there free rein. Her mind again went over her heartwarming reunion with Vivian, wincing a bit at the memory of some of her more stupid comments. A frown remained as she recalled Viv's jabs about her public image.

Well, she was allowed to use screens again. "Aya? Can you show me that viral video?"

"Of course, Doctor." The pair of eyes flew level with her shoulder as the monitor over the workbench flickered on.

Rex in makeup and interview clothes appeared, elbows on the armrests of her chair, and current-Rex had to look away as the sight poked at her lingering vulnerability after Rifter's invasion of Peak Street. She pushed past the discomfort and watched herself talk, paying attention to the way the back-and-forth was cut.

"There's always more, right? I mean, the news only says so much."

"I like this part, Doctor," Aya said. The video skipped over her mixing up Manta Man and Mantis Man to show her spiel about the classification of heroes and villains. Somehow, it sounded less like a panicked ramble and more like a reasoned argument. Rex gaped for a bit at the view count—"It would be more, Doctor, but the video was taken down twice by the network and re-uploaded"—and looked through some of the comments.

Lol is she high? This is hilarious.

Good points here. The host says villains hurt innocents. What standard of innocence do we have to meet? And if we don't, does what happens to us not count?

Comparing heros with LEGITIMATE AND TARGETED VEN-DETTAS to villains that just kill people indiscriminantly. #theMeister-IsaVillain

I understand what she means. I got caught in an attack and the Protectors paid my hospital bills and that was great but I still get pain in my legs and when anyone says I should be grateful I want to tell them how hard it is but I know they don't want to hear that part. #Moreto-theStory

Those dinosaurs are sooooo cuuuuute: ☺

The Meister is hot #BaldBabes

You got bullied. Get over it.

Are those real dinosaurs? And can we visit them??

I got saved by a hero. I'm glad I'm alive but I get nightmares and my bf broke up w me. I don't want more from heroes but I still don't like seeing where the story cuts off on the news like no one cares what happened. I feel like I'm stuck in something that everyone else says is over. #MoretotheStory

She is just trying to justify all the bad things she's done. Just cause there's two sides to things doesn't mean both sides are right. #theMeisterisa Villain

Still paying off repairs from superhero fight in my business. No insurance. #MoretotheStory

Haha she drunk

Why did people always think Rex was drunk?

The comments got more brutal and typo-riddled the further she looked—except the ones about the dinosaurs. People really liked them. It was too bad they were such little shits.

From there, Rex looked into the More to the Story hashtag and saw that Viv hadn't been lying—social media was saturated with people sharing mundane, personal, and inconvenient stories. There were some vicious arguments breaking out about who got to use the hashtag and what for. Some uses made her cringe, like one explanation of why the victim of a crime had deserved it. Its users rarely mentioned Rex's interview anymore, four days later. Had it only been four days? She supposed spending most of that time either drunk or concussed messed with her judgment.

Rex sat back in her seat, a mix of apprehension, confusion, and childish satisfaction swirling in her chest. She tapped a finger on the workbench, baffled that she'd missed so much by not watching the video when Aya sent it to her. Thinking of that night, she glanced at the last item on her to-do list, winced again about the seahorse thing, and had Aya scan the whole internet for an overview of asexuality.

"Resources compiled. Shall I print?"

"Sure."

Rex spread the printed pages on the floor and read them over. Then read them again. Her stomach sank. "Holy shit." She twisted around, forgetting the late hour, and yelled through the lab door, "Flora! This time I really am having a gay crisis except it's more crisis than gay."

"Ms. Shay is in her room, Doctor. I have transferred your message."

Flora ran in—impressively quick. "What's wrong?"

"Flora, either I've stumbled upon a bizarre conspiracy to justify prudishness, or someone's been spying on my thoughts and feelings and putting them on the internet."

Flora's gaze shifted to the hovering eyes. "Aya?"

"Dr. Anderson is reviewing a comprehensive overview of my findings regarding asexuality."

Rex let Flora kneel beside her and take the papers from her hands. "You guys talk over my head too often."

"You think this describes you?" Flora's eyes scanned a page, her expression falling slightly as she read. "But you have sex with . . . Wait." Flora's brow climbed. "Oh my God. It's so obvious. Rex—" She looked at Rex, who froze, taken aback by the distress on Flora's face. "I've given you so much bad advice."

"What? No, you're fine." Rex scrambled to her knees in alarm, hands hovering awkwardly in hug position.

Flora crushed the paper as she brought her hands to her face and wailed, "I've been a *horrible* gay best friend!"

"Aw, that's a dollar." Rex put her arms around Flora and patted her back.

"Do you even like hugs?" Flora demanded, voice muffled against Rex's shoulder.

"Why wouldn't I like hugs?"

"We have to talk about your boundaries. And about your past relationships. How many of your exes do we have to murder?"

"Please don't talk about murder while we're under surveillance."

"Are you sex-repulsed? Are you aromantic?"

Rex grasped for some pages to find those words. "You know more about this than I do."

"That's why I should have *known!*"

Rex gave up her search. They moved to the couch at the back of the lab, where she mechanically passed Flora tissues, and Aya dimmed the lights from her eyes.

As Flora calmed to sniffles, she mumbled, "I'm going to get you that appeal."

"You've got nothing to prove. I'm sure we'll have the clout once I figure out the virus's deal." Rex sank into the sofa. "Though it might take longer with the Protectors watching over my shoulder in case my villainous tendencies show."

"If they don't trust you, why don't they bring in someone else?"

"They have. I'm just project lead," Rex said flatly. "I think Viv fought for it. She knows I made the damn thing so I'm more qualified than anyone to find out how it's been altered. And with Last Dance in the city, the virus ending up in my lab, I figure she's just keeping all the problem elements contained."

They were silent for a moment. Then Flora said, "Aya and I saved the helmet design."

"An automated production area is prepared on sublevel B," Aya added.

Rex's gut clenched. She took a breath and let it out. It felt like a turning point—hypotheticals made real. "I'll write out the missing parts."

"Remember that Peak Street's systems are compromised," Flora said, dabbing professionally at her eyes with a tissue. "There's a good chance the home system is, as well."

Rex nodded. "Aya, you're dealing with the footage?"

"I am altering time stamps to reflect Ms. Shay crying for a longer period of time."

Flora rolled her eyes. Rex dropped her head back. "I guess we're making this."

ISSUE 15

DINOSAURS IN REAL ESTATE

*I*n its final form, Sam's hood was a thick, maroon fabric, almost brown, modeled on the hood of Sam's iconic Last Dance getup. Thin, metal circles on the inside gave entry to the circuitry woven into the fabric. When she wasn't studying the changes to her virus—which largely consisted of waiting for results—suffering through consulting hours, or dispelling the intrusive *you're ace* thoughts that kept popping into her head, Rex tested the hood in every way she could think of. and Flora's pros and cons list of whether to give Sam the hood steadily got longer.

Rex stared at the screen Aya had pulled up at her request.

Hi T.
I need help. I have to make it stop. I need you to make this for me. My people can't figure out the last part. Your dinosaurs looked cute in the news. Thank you. I love you.
—Sam

"The boy gets me," Rex said, eyes on the line about the dinosaurs.

Her attention returned to Sam's hood crumpled in her grip. Despite weeks of testing, she hadn't found any way that the hood could harm anyone. It would just help him. The results brought a sunny, shaky feeling that she tried to rein in, because she didn't trust it. It should have been something she felt back when she was trying. She'd worked for a break-through like this to the exclusion of everything else before, and she wasn't sure what would happen if this turned out to be another failure.

On top of that good feeling was a resurgence of the ever-present dread. Because she was running out of reasons not to hand it over, and she had a certainty stronger than her test results that something bad would happen if she did.

"Doctor, it is half an hour past sunrise, and Mr. Stone has left his room."

Rex let out a breath, her gaze sliding easily away from the screen as the familiar bubble of lightness disrupted the dark edges of her mood.

In the nights since their confrontation in the kitchen, Lewis had stayed in his room from curfew until the morning shift.

Rex wondered if she was being a little crazy, not calling it off. She knew that had mostly just been a bad night. If she'd run into him any other night, she would have felt tense, but she wouldn't have startled so badly. She breathed easier now, but not because he was sequestered in his room at night; it was because he'd offered.

It was like the fear evaporated when he acknowledged it. He took a stupid little step to make her feel better, and the problem fixed itself as easily as if she'd been standing in a crowd with her hands over her mouth and nose and someone had finally said, "Yes, you do need to breathe."

And there was something about this being *his* experiment. He hadn't saved her from a sniper or knocked a poisoned drink from her hand. He had suggested a way to prove himself trustworthy, and now he was following through. He hadn't cared that nothing had proven him *un*trustworthy. He just took her at her word. He made a concession.

It was fucking wild.

Still, Rex couldn't bring herself to tell him to stop yet. There was always a moment before she checked in with Aya in the morning, when she felt that tug of anxiety that this would be the night he realized he didn't owe her anything. It was like she was on the brink of stepping off a tightrope, and she could see the net below her. She just needed to stare at it a little longer to make sure it was really there. Rex found herself looking for ways to make it up to him, but all she knew about him was that he and Peter were friends and they'd recently had drama. Her secondhand anxiety for Peter had her mind circling that issue while she worked at Peak Street on the virus or at home testing the hood, and she kept coming back to her go-to for fixing friend drama among the dinosaurs—arrange a playdate.

When she asked Peter what he thought of bringing Lewis in on the climate alteration project for the dinosaurs' hypothetical new habitat, he hesitated. "I asked him for space."

"Yes, but this would be a structured activity with time limits, you'll have something obvious to talk about, and I'll be there the whole time, third wheeling it up."

Some of the apprehension in Peter's face cleared, and he gave her an odd look. "You want to fix us through a group project."

She nodded.

The smile he was fighting broke reluctantly through, and he admitted, "With Lewis's background in biochemistry, he'll probably have more to contribute than me."

So, with one rock-solid idea, Rex could help Peter, help Lewis, and get her dinosaurs out of the lab sooner, thwarting three supervillains with one taser punch. She was a genius.

Since Rifter's attack and the aborted wipeout protocol, the dinosaurs' vulnerability at Peak Street had kept Rex up at night. She would have liked to buy up a nice island, something outside the reach of Oversight, but as the need for consulting hours attested, she wasn't that liquid.

She considered taking the Exo-suit and clearing Zombie Island—it was a perfectly good island that was wasted on the undead—but she couldn't risk exposing her dinosaurs to Mutey. The zombie virus had never zombified a non-human, but people got a bit hysterical where zombies were concerned, as Rex had learned the hard way. Besides, Oversight already wasn't happy with her, and zombie dinosaurs would probably push them over the edge.

Instead, she added *clear Zombie Island* to her to-do list and looked for stretches of land in the States. Even if they were still within Oversight's jurisdiction, anywhere was safer than the lab.

It took Aya about a week to find an acceptable collection of square miles less than an hour away by jet. Rex bought up the land from its smattering of owners and visited as soon as Peter and Lewis shared a babysitting shift.

Peter was still gushing over Rex's jet long after they'd landed, as they all worked up a sweat hiking through hilly woodland. "It doesn't make a sound! It's a work of art. Why are we building a helicopter when you have this?"

"The jet isn't good for going across town," Rex answered. "Although, if we combined the two—"

Peter gasped and fumbled a notepad out of his backpack. "I'm gonna write down some ideas."

"You know helicopters that convert into jets already exist, right?" Lewis said.

"We'll do it better," said Peter. "We'll need a new engine design, to start. Biofuel is nice, but I don't know how you're getting so much of it."

"Production's a hassle," Rex admitted, eyes darting between Lewis and Peter. They were talking. Or, talking to the group, which included both of them. That was good. "I used a fission engine on that rocket I shot at the alien invasion last year." Which had prompted an investigation into why she had a rocket lying around. Ingrates.

Lewis huff snorted. "That was designed to explode."

"Yeah—designed to. I wouldn't design an exploding helicopter."

His tone stayed doubtful. "You don't have a great track record when it comes to not blowing stuff up."

She shot Lewis a glare. "You have a better idea?"

"Like, ten of them. I'm a biochemist who works for Oversight."

Rex was briefly speechless as the heavens parted over the opportunity before her. The best thing to leave a playdate with was plans for *another* playdate. "Why don't you do it?"

His brow twitched. "The helicopter thing?"

Rex glanced to Peter, who was chewing his lip as he stared at his scribblings, but she caught his nod. "Unless you don't care if I blow up Peter." She met Lewis's eyes and motioned with her head.

Lewis's expression cleared in comprehension. His eyes flicked between Peter and Rex, and he coughed into a fist. "If those are the stakes."

"You're such a considerate friend." Rex patted him on the shoulder. This was going so well. "Samples."

They stopped again to collect dirt, air, and vegetation. Rex mentally outlined a lecture series for dinosaurs about maintaining a stable ecosystem outside laboratory conditions. She'd have to get them in the habit of doing chores, maybe buy them a vacuum cleaner.

You're ace. And there it was. The thought had been a mix of freaky and good from the start, but it was leaning more toward good, so she thought it again. *You're ace.*

Lewis set down his pack full of the other samples they'd collected. "Not to bring down the mood—" He gave her lingering grin a doubtful glance. "I know you want to make the area more jungle-like, but you're going to need Oversight's approval, and convincing them that it won't affect the surrounding environment might not be possible."

"They have super geniuses checking my work. At least one of them should understand my idea." Rex's smile fell. "Big industries pollute all the time, but I can't release one measly primordial mist?"

"We'll need to justify significant ecological changes, especially if it hurts the wildlife," Peter added.

"I'll alter the wildlife. I've been genetically altering plants and bugs in my labs for years. That's how I made their habitats."

"What about animals?"

"It shouldn't be hard to put a catalyst in food and water sources to adjust their biologies. I've cloned dinosaurs; this will be child's play."

Lewis whistled. "It's this kind of talk that sets off people's villain-dar."

"How was anything I said villainous?"

Peter chuckled. "The talk of altering the biological nature of an animal by putting stuff in the food is a bit concerning. I'm gonna order in when I'm at your house from now on."

Rex grumbled, "You already do that," and jabbed at the soil. But she couldn't maintain her irritation alongside the self-satisfaction at Peter and Lewis sharing a joke. She was good at this—she should start a business.

Out of habit, her eyes cut to Lewis. Watching his face jump around like someone being strangled in a movie while he tried not to smile had recently become one of her favorite pastimes. She was getting good at sensing when it was happening.

You're ace. A little insecurity mixed in that time. But also, a streak of clarity, a settling sense of self-knowledge.

Lewis got control of himself and glanced between Peter and Rex with an expression she couldn't identify. "You need someone to spin the proposal."

"Yeah, Flora's been on me about PR since Oversight began."

Lewis rolled his eyes, the drama queen. "That was an offer. I'm used to writing grants and things like that. I think I could present your plan in a way that the committee would find palatable." He shrugged. "I know how they think."

Peter handed over a sample. "You should get Flora's help. She could handle the legal side, and you could handle the science." Eye contact was established. It occurred to Rex that while Peter had been talking to Lewis easily, he hadn't been meeting his eyos.

Lewis's Peter smile popped up. Damn, that thing was bright. "I'll ask her."

Rex cleared her throat. "Thanks?"

Lewis nodded and ducked back over his work, like it was perfectly normal to offer to do busywork for someone after telling them they sound like a villain. "No problem."

Feeling a little red, Rex clipped some more leaves and kept her eyes away from Lewis.

Peter began, "So, for dispersal mechanisms, I thought the most con-trolled way—"

She listened to their back-and-forth long enough to decide to leave them to it and switched to designing a dino-friendly keyboard in the back of her head. The dinosaurs had recently petitioned their tutors for a set of computers to cultivate a more modern learning environment, but Rex was finding the existing options unacceptably human-centric.

Her mind turned to next steps. "So, we're starting the new engine to-morrow?"

Lewis fought a look of half hope, half panic, and Peter gave a jittery laugh. "Maybe in a few days, actually? Instead of tomorrow?"

Right, space. It was her first friendship repair—Rex was learning. "This weekend, then."

With an awkward laugh, Peter turned away to pack up. Lewis shrugged and shot Rex a what-can-you-do mouth twist that . . . looked kind of grate-ful. Her return smile was appropriately smug.

The smile slipped as she looked back over the woods they'd surveyed. Even if they made the land livable, getting the dinosaurs here would be a problem. And she wouldn't want them to have no way out if something in the new habitat went wrong.

A few feet away, Peter had gone back to babbling about the helicop-ter-jet, and in her mind's eye their sketches grew larger, the cockpit changed shape, and she added a system to better counterbalance weight redistribu-tion.

That was an idea.

DINOSAURS ON A STAKEOUT

The longer they went without Last Dance surfacing, the more antsy the Protectors got. They were still looking for Rifter's base, interrogating goons, and whatever else superheroes did when they weren't duking it out with villains—probably having drama with each other. Did they all share a hotel, or what?

Regardless, the reality was that right now, Rex was the only one working on something important. They didn't exactly hound her about it, but she could hardly step into Peak Street without hearing Viv's phantom toe tapping.

Rex was considering taking them to the superhero park to burn off some energy, but they came up with their own plan first.

"It doesn't make sense for this to be Sam's only sample," Rex had explained during a supervised experiment. "His people probably don't *need* to get it back; they just didn't want us to have it. Now that you're watching the lab and the plant, another attempt isn't worth the risk."

Viv had nodded on the other side of the glass. "So, they have no reason to show themselves. And the longer we spend fruitlessly searching for a lead, the more time they have to adjust their plans."

The Protectors wanted to stage a transfer. The story would be that since Rex's facilities were inadequate—she harrumphed at that—they were moving the virus to a lab across town in the dead of night and with minimal fanfare—meaning security—in hopes of escaping Last Dance's attention. Rex's stomach twisted through the explanation as the Protectors laid it out in Peak Street's second-biggest conference room. She knew these people had fought Sam before but reading the wrap up in the news wasn't the same as keeping a straight face while Viv planned an ambush.

"He's a mind reader," Rex said, forcing herself not to cross her arms. "Won't he know it's a trap when he gets in range?"

Don Conjure twirled a finger through his mustache. "We gamble that he will not make an appearance, but rather that he will send allies and minions."

"Sam never does the dirty work," Viv said, hands folded on the table. "He knows how to make others do what he wants them to do."

Rex winced and wondered if Viv was also thinking of Daydreamer's disappearance from the superhero scene and reemergence as Nightmare. After the Protectors took down Angel Killer, they'd faced a political battle so sudden it could only have been orchestrated by Last Dance, but no one had guessed he'd also been talking to Daydreamer until his message at the site of Nightmare's first attack: *I always save the last.*

It had taken at least three large-scale catastrophes for the Protectors to get back in the government's good graces. Rex hadn't known until Vivid Blue's public statement that Daydreamer and Viv had been good friends.

Rex could almost condemn Sam for that, but every time her revulsion surged, she also thought of how close he'd been to erasing his powers for good.

Had Sam seen in Angel Killer's mind that he would follow through on their deal to take his power away, that his crimes would really buy his freedom? Had Angel Killer been lying, but Sam kept at it in the hope that he'd reconsider? Had he let himself imagine a future with his powers finally gone? Then the Protectors swooped in, Viv leading the charge, and Sam's deal with the devil was for nothing.

Also, well, Rex wouldn't say so to Viv, but Daydreamer had never seemed like the most dependable guy.

"Eliminating his allies would be a significant blow," Don Conjure continued. "We know he has won the loyalty of Rifter and the mysterious hacker."

"Assuming there is a hacker," the Jester said idly, resting his feet on the conference table and turning a knife in his hands.

Rex smiled and mirrored his tone. If he got to be passive aggressive, then the non-heroes in the room shouldn't have to take the high road. "I'm the one who pointed out that he'd need access to the cameras to get inside."

"Perhaps you meant to deflect suspicion by saying it first," Manta Man rumbled, Quinten giving an agreeing chuckle. "And you have yet to tell us anything valuable about the virus."

"I didn't know I was reporting to you," Rex said flatly.

"You have been hiding things?" King George demanded.

"It's all right, friends," Pixie cut in. "We check the Meister's reports and there are meetings with Oversight's scientists every week."

"Considering who's leading this project, shouldn't the rest of us know what she's doing?" the Jester drawled.

"Since when are you a virologist?" Rex asked.

"T, just explain what you know," Viv said in peacekeeping tones.

Rex flexed her jaw and sat straighter. "It's a synthetic RNA virus"—It was harder to say this in front of Viv; at least the other scientists didn't know where the virus came from—"developed from a herpes simplex genome linked to encephalitis." She killed the giggles coming from King George and the Jester with, "Encephalitis is inflammation of the brain. It can cause headaches, seizures, paralysis—a lot of things." She got no satisfaction from shutting them up. She'd picked HSV-1 specifically for its effects on the brain.

"Is that what this virus does?" Viv asked, carefully professional.

Rex ducked her eyes and reinforced her unaffected air. "Its exact effects are hard to determine, and they might vary." She had to force out the next bit. "From what I can tell, it blunts function in the cerebral cortex." That was oversimplified, but good enough for these people. "The result would be suppression of the conscious mind, like sleepwalking or dissociation. Based on his goals, we can assume it prevents the mind from being readable, but I don't know how much damage it does." And Rex wasn't sure she wanted to know. The thought of it doing more harm was awful. And the thought of it doing no additional harm, compared to the version she'd made . . .

She glanced at Viv without thinking and looked away before she could read her expression. "From what I can tell, after infecting someone, it lies dormant in the ganglion of the trigeminal cranial nerve unless it's triggered." That was another difference. Her unfinished version had no dormant period, rendering a victim brain-dead in as little as a day.

"Triggered?" Manta Man repeated with a frown. "By what?"

"I don't know," Rex admitted. There were grumbles from the Jester, and she added a little heatedly, "This kind of research isn't usually confined to laboratory conditions. It's not as big an ask as it would be for a naturally occurring virus, but you're basically asking me to test everything that could possibly trigger its effects by using lab-grown cells and computer simulations. I've ruled out stress hormones—if that helps."

Viv's gaze snapped to her, tone caught between a demand and a question. "You didn't infect yourself."

"What? No." Rex waved her off, her indignation a little exaggerated. "I mean, it would be the fastest way to find out what it does. Observing its effects in a living host—" She cut off at the heroes' expressions and cleared her throat. "There might not be symptoms while it's dormant, but it's still contagious. I'd have to isolate if I infected myself, which could impede the research." And Flora made her promise not to.

"She's right, you guys," Pixie said apologetically. "Seeing what viruses do is . . . pretty much how we know what viruses do."

Don Conjure's baritone reclaimed the floor. "All the more reason to sweep up our foes. Last Dance's hacker may be the same evil genius who developed this wily virus—"

Rex winced. He had a point, though—Sam must have worked with someone to get the virus in its current form.

"—or yet another villainous ally."

"We've discussed the possibility that he's built a team," Viv summed up. "They're the ones we mean to draw out."

Aya had been keeping Rex appraised of ongoing attempts to get past the upgraded security she'd gifted to Oversight, so her job would be to allow a small, believable breach—enough to leak the fake transfer plans. Rex offered to whip up some Invisi-Drink for the team, but when Viv asked how long the invisibility lasted, she could only say, "Varies."

"Based on what?"

"Metabolism, weight, humidity—"

Viv turned it down, and Rex ignored Flora's little *hm*. Flora had always hated Invisi-Drink on account of it being silly, weaponizable, and otherwise useless. She also refused to call it Invisi-Drink, but heck, it was Rex's invention—she could call it whatever she wanted.

Her contribution was supposed to end there, but the thought of knowing this was happening without being a part of it felt like torture.

She threw around several arguments: she had the expertise to know if the transfer was progressing believably, it was personal since it was her lab that had been infiltrated, and they owed her for basically conscripting her into doing their science project.

Something must have stuck, because despite Quinten's objection, she landed herself in a darkened vehicle just off the fake transfer route, cringing her way through the story Lewis was telling while Becky dozed in the back seat.

"He was nice about it," Lewis said.

"Oh my God."

"I wouldn't say we're friends, but I'd greet him in passing."

Rex sank lower in the passenger seat, almost tipping the pizza box in her lap into the footwell. "Oh my God."

"And that's how I confirmed I'm not bisexual."

"Oh my God!" Rex thumped her head against the seat, luxuriating in the lack of stitches. When they'd finally come out, Flora had marked the occasion by buzzing her hair in the kitchen and cooing over how soft it was post-buzz. Lewis shared the painful experience of frequent head rubs during his shaved-head childhood and without thinking, Rex offered to let him rub hers. The awkwardness had started there and escalated as he hesitantly took her up on it. Rex wished she could stop thinking about it, because then maybe she'd stop dying over and over.

Rex cursed Lewis's chuckles as her voice went a little high. "Is that something people have to confirm?" *You're ace.* Yes, thanks brain.

Lewis shrugged. "Most people probably don't find themselves making out with another man and liking it enough to wonder how far that could go." He wiped his hands on a napkin. "How did we get on this subject?"

"You were explaining your journey from biology major to superbeing babysitter, and all the zany stops along the way." Rex took another piece of pizza. "If you got this job through Peter, are you also staying for Peter?"

Lewis put up a valiant fight against that smile. "Do you ever get tired of wingman-ing us?"

"It's rewarding." She peeled a strip of cheese from her pizza with the care all contaminants deserved and put it back in the box.

He shook his head. "Also, most assignments aren't babysitting. Oversight does research for stuff like developing infrastructure with . . ." His gaze drifted from the intersection to her. "What are you doing?"

"I don't like cheese." Rex wiped another floppy, yellow chunk on the inside of the box.

"I know, but I didn't think you'd mutilate pizza. Give it here if you're not gonna eat it." He reached across the stick shift, and Rex recoiled.

"You're going to eat pizza cheese straight?"

"You're wasting it."

Rex held the box open with a disgust that bordered on awe as he grasped the pile barehanded and transferred it to his napkin.

Lewis hunched his shoulders. "Don't watch me; watch the route."

"You eating my peeled-off pizza cheese is more interesting than whatever's happening out there."

Something moved at the edge of Rex's vision, and she sat straighter.

Lewis nudged her. "Mm?"

"Shh." Rex squinted past the glare on the window. A figure across the street was joined by a second. One turned, and Rex got a view of a bone-white mask. "It's them." She grabbed the door handle.

Lewis made a *hrk* noise and trapped her hand under his.

She batted him back. "Your hands are greasy."

"Whose fault is that?" He rubbed his hands on his pants and grabbed their radio. "You're only here because you said you'd stay in the car. I'm signaling the Protectors." He raised his voice to say, "Becky, hey," earning a snort and a kick to the back of Rex's seat. "We've got action."

Becky looked outside and her brow jumped. Rex followed her gaze through the window and balked.

The masked men were staring at the car.

Lewis reached for the keys. "We should leave."

Becky jumped hard, her head hitting the ceiling. "What was that?" As Lewis and Rex shared an alarmed glance, she continued, "I just felt—I think there's something in the trunk."

A *thump* came from the back, followed by skitters.

"We're getting out of the car," Lewis said. "Rex, follow on my side—"

Becky hissed a curse as a soft *thunk* rocked the car, and Rex turned around.

The trunk had popped open. It rose slowly to block the rear windshield, as though something inside was pushing it up. Rex leaned to see through the side windows. Then, two theropod-shaped creatures hopped to the pavement, each fluttering four wings.

Rex's heart dropped into her stomach.

Becky's voice was icy. "What were your dinosaurs doing in the car?"

"Earning an ass whooping is what they were doing," she growled. She glanced at the goons across the road. One was still facing the car, a gun half raised toward the open trunk and his masked face tilted to the side. The other was waving toward two more goons spreading tire spikes in the intersecting street.

The two stowaway little shits conferred in the car's shadow, either not hearing Rex's desperate window taps or ignoring them because they knew if there was a definition of *in for it*—

"They look like big, long chickens," Becky muttered.

"Don't call them chickens. They've decided it's a slur."

"Those are microraptors," Lewis said. Rex gave him a look, and he added, "Spot lectured me for an hour when I called a styracosaur a triceratops."

The microraptors turned toward the goons. Rex's taps picked up like the end of a countdown. "No no no no." Long tails lashed, and the little dinosaurs crossed the street like birds on a mission. "Shitting God." Rex was out the door before Lewis's attention could turn back to her.

He cursed and lunged for her, but he was too late. She knew he'd be right behind her, so she didn't divert to the trunk for the tire iron, just ran full tilt toward the dumbasses approaching the armed thugs.

The sentry goon's gun was up, the others taking notice. Rex threw her hands out and yelled, "Don't shoot my sentries. It's about time you showed up. I've been waiting all night."

The microraptors hopped and fluttered, squawking in surprise and veering toward the shadows past the corner bodega. Their feather patterns caught the light from a streetlamp, and Rex recognized Lou Lou and Turpentine. She wished she was surprised, although Gabby May usually kept those two in line.

The goon didn't lower his gun, and now the others had theirs out. But no one had shot her yet, so she kept talking. "Sam said you'd take a message here. He didn't say you'd keep me waiting. The Protectors could show at any moment." She strode close enough to stop shouting and planted her feet just short of the curb. "I mean Last Dance, if that's what Sam makes you call him." She rolled her eyes. "You know who I am, right?"

She was playing the odds that Sam's people knew their connection. Even if they didn't, her sort-of villain reputation had to be good for something.

She heard footsteps behind her, and a bead of sweat trailed down her spine. Lewis and Becky would know she was bluffing, surely.

Yeah, right. She braced for a bullet in the back.

The two goons flanking the leader shifted their aim past her shoulder. Rex gestured behind her. "These two work for me." She felt Lewis and Becky approach to just within her peripheral vision.

That finally got a huff from the masked man. "Didn't take you long."

Rex shrugged. "There's always someone who can be bought, am I right? You would know."

The man huffed again and lowered his weapon. "I know who you are," he said, answering her first question. She braced herself for a *twin* mention—Viv said Oversight knew, but Rex wasn't sure they actually did—and tried not to look relieved when he said, "This way, Meister."

One of the others protested, "He didn't tell us to expect—"

"He tells us what we have to know," Goon Leader interrupted. "Or do you think you know better?"

That shut Goon Junior up.

Suppressing the urge to gulp, Rex followed Goon Leader. To her relief, Lewis and Becky fell in at her shoulders. A glance at Lewis found a blank face except for tight lines around his mouth, and a glance at Becky—wow, that was an expression that could melt a face off. Hopefully, Sam's henchmen wouldn't look at her too closely.

She wasn't sure where she was going with this plan besides stalling. Her heart steadily sank into her gut as she realized this might actually end with seeing Sam face-to-face. She blinked through a wave of vertigo, focusing on keeping her steps even.

How long did it take the Protectors to get their asses over here?

They rounded the corner, where a truck idled past a streetlamp. Someone leaned against its side, a dark shape with arms folded. Rex noted height and posture—it wasn't Sam. She let out a breath as quietly as possible and was proud it barely shook.

The figure straightened with a groan, resolving into a tall, feminine silhouette. "Even you idiots shouldn't take this long to lay some road spikes."

The woman who sauntered out of the shadows wore a long, black coat over what looked like a corset and skintight leather pants. Yet another supervillain dressed like a dominatrix.

Rex wondered if they knew they'd have a shot at morally gray hero status if they put on combat gear or a cape.

The woman's eyes landed on Rex, and her smirk spread. "The Meister of Decimen City. This is a twist."

"But a predictable one, if you ask Oversight. Who are you?" When the woman raised an eyebrow, she added, "I'm bad with faces out of context, and when you only see supervillains on the news—"

The woman tossed a hand, and a gust of wind punched down the street, blowing her coat out behind her. Fog billowed in to swirl through her high-heeled boots.

"Okay I see it now," Rex babbled, blown back a step. That was Ill Wind. Not exactly a local villain, and Rex was seriously rethinking her strategy because they were in deep shit.

A part of her mind whirred through the implications. Ill Wind was active where? Baltimore? DC? Why recruit so far out? And why wasn't she with Rifter weeks ago? Was she a recent addition?

"She says she has a message for the boss," Goon Leader said.

Ill Wind scoffed. "Of course, she says that, fool. Thank goodness I'm here." She lifted a hand again.

"Ah ah ah." Rex raised a finger, hoping the tension radiating from Lewis and Becky wouldn't translate to a shoot-out with her in the middle. "You might be new to the Last Dance club, but you ought to know his rules about me."

It was a shot in the dark, that Sam had made her off limits. But she thought the odds were good.

Ill Wind's eyes narrowed. The fog thickened but curled further back. Rex almost relaxed, a mental pat on the back poised to deploy. Then Ill Wind gave a little *hm* and said, "I'll chance it."

A blast of air blew them down the road like bowling pins. Rex landed on her hip, shoulder, and elbow, the back of her hand scraping pavement as she protected her head. But she was lucky not to land on those tire spikes, so no complaints.

A gunshot made her head ring—who had gotten up that quickly?—followed by Ill Wind's outraged shout.

Rex fought to her feet, heavy fog blocking her sight. She couldn't see where Lewis and Becky landed, but that wasn't saying much. Could Ill Wind still control fog in her lungs? Best not to think about that.

Another gunshot, a frustrated scream from Ill Wind, and the fog broke. Rex gasped as quietly as she could, looking around for a clue as to what the fuck was going on, and her eyes landed on feathers.

Rex stitched the scene together: a fallen goon, rolling in dissipating fog; his lost gun snatched up by a pair of thumb claws at the ends of wings; a supervillain with weather powers snarling and gripping her limp arm.

The supervillain threw her hand from her injury with an angry bellow, palm bloody, and the sky blackened, rumbling with thunder. The microraptor—Lou Lou, Rex was sure—shrieked, dropped the gun, and bumped into Turpentine as they both tried to take off. Ill Wind grinned savagely, hand stretched toward them, and alarm whited out Rex's brain.

With no memory of crossing the distance, Rex tackled Ill Wind to the ground.

A shriek rang in her ear, and a high heel came down on her calf. "Jesus!" Rex rolled away, grabbing her leg.

Ill Wind growled behind her head, "You'll regret that, Meister."

Rex bit back a panicked giggle semi-successfully. This was going very poorly. Distantly, she heard sirens. If the police beat the Protectors to the scene, she would never let them live it down. Another gunshot made her flinch, and she swore to God, if one of her dinosaurs fired that gun again—

Hands grabbed her under her arms and hoisted her out of the road. She recognized Lewis's shadow and let the relieved laugh slip. Her eyes sought Ill Wind as she got her bruised leg under her. The villain had rolled behind the truck's tire, throwing blasts of wind in scooping motions toward Becky on the opposite sidewalk, who ducked around a building as a cut of wind chipped the brick. Where were Lou Lou and Turpentine?

Goon Leader's voice came too close to her ear. "Don't move."

Rex felt Lewis freeze. Her blood turned to ice in solidarity as she turned her head.

Goon Leader's gun was trained on Lewis—probably smart, since Rex was the only person including the damn dinosaurs without a gun, but Goon Leader's words revealed a different reason. "The boss doesn't want you harmed, so you'll have to come with me."

Lewis raised his hands slowly. "We're all on the same side, man."

"Sam doesn't want my cover blown," Rex said through a deep chill. "I can leave my message with you and head back."

The stillness of the mask was unsettling. "Safer if I kill him, then. Make it look like a kidnapping."

"Never mind." Rex exhaled and tried to slide in front of the shot. The trigger gave a threatening *creak* and she shifted right back, heart pounding. "Okay, okay."

A smirk pulled at the visible half of Goon Leader's face. Then a blast of lightning struck through him.

Rex's first thought as he crumpled to the ground and she blinked spots from her eyes was that Ill Wind had terrible aim. Then the Lightning shot past in a streak of yellow and threw another bolt at Ill Wind.

Rex ducked as the electricity bounced off the rubber tire. "Those damn dinosaurs better not be trying to fly."

Lewis dragged Rex, stumbling on her bruised leg—that was going to take ages to heal; what a pain—into the alcove of the bodega's front door. She caught sight of 'Ning throwing herself to the side before a vortex of wind roared past, picking up the tire spikes and driving them into windows and brick. Holy *fucking* shit. Lewis pressed Rex into a corner, his chest vibrating in what she assumed was a strong expletive as brick dust exploded from one edge of the alcove.

Lightning strikes flashed out of sight, moving away.

Rex took a breath, numb limbs finally relaxing, and Lewis did the same beside her. Shushing noises had her head whipping around, and the microraptors slid into the alcove.

Relief and fury mixed nauseatingly in her stomach as Rex pushed off the wall. *Here we go.*

Lou Lou and Turpentine started talking over each other the moment they caught Rex's eyes. "Mom, it's not what it looks like."

Lewis plucked the gun from Lou Lou's claw. "I'll take that."

"How the hell did you get in the car?" Rex demanded.

"I'm not saying we have a lab tech on the take, per se," Turpentine began.

"I expect terrible judgment from my lab techs. I want to know what *you* were thinking."

They talked over each other again, wings floofing and fluttering.

Another series of lightning strikes cut down the street and all alcove dwellers pressed to the wall.

As the smell of ozone settled, Ill Wind's bored voice filled the ringing silence. "Come out, little hero."

A deep voice that definitely wasn't 'Ning answered, "Here I am."

Rex stuck her head out as Manta Man's gray tail swept into Ill Wind's side and threw her into a building. Rex had the panicked thought that she'd just watched someone die, but then a vortex whipped up in front of the villain-shaped hole, tossing Manta Man skyward like a piece of grass. 'Ning zipped from a rooftop as though to catch him, and the storm clouds suddenly swelled. With an accompanying *boom* of thunder, two lightning bolts flashed down.

Rex ducked away for an instant, her vision white behind her eyelids. When she forced herself to squint through the bright splotches, the

Lightning was in a crater on the ground and Manta Man was still falling, his fin wings trailing smoke and flapping like loose sails. As Rex's heart lurched—*now* she was going to watch someone die—a pink figure flew in on buzzing wings and caught him.

Rex's chest unclenched, and she looked back down, scanning the street. Ill Wind was gone.

Pixie landed awkwardly with the larger hero as 'Ning climbed out of her crater, holding her head.

"Should we call an ambulance?" Rex asked Lewis tentatively. Maybe the protocol was different for heroes.

Lewis's knuckles were white on the confiscated gun. "We can offer."

The dinos started to follow them out of the alcove, then backed up when Rex shot them a warning glare. They stepped out cautiously, Lewis keeping close as they crossed the street, but no unaccounted-for goons showed up. Rex was tempted to mention that his job wasn't to protect her; it was to protect people *from* her. But she only wasn't staggering because she had a death grip on his arm.

Becky reappeared with a nod to Lewis before turning hawk eyes on Rex. Rex gritted her teeth against a wince. Becky's report for this incident was not going to cast her in a good light. Pixie was laying Manta Man out straight and exclaiming at whatever 'Ning had said. "Ill Wind? What's that weather-warping harpy doing here?"

Manta Man wheezed, capturing everyone's attention. "Ill Wind has never been active this far west. We never anticipated—" He winced and clutched his chest.

As Lewis stepped forward with the ambulance offer, 'Ning appeared at Rex's side.

"You people have terrible response time," Rex said. Her scraped hand was finally starting to sting, and the throbbing in her calf teased trouble walking tomorrow.

'Ning gave the impression of a raised eyebrow through her mask. "You didn't call me. I saw the storm."

"Well, you can give that message to the Protectors."

"You didn't start this, did you?" the hero asked.

"You just fought the heaviest hitter who's ever shown up in this town, and you think I started it?" Rex's glare turned into a once-over when 'Ning swayed. "I didn't know you could be electrocuted."

'Ning rubbed her head through the mask again. "It was the force, not the electricity." Her hand dropped. "I was distracted."

Rex's mouth pressed into a line. She didn't know if Manta Man had any kind of accelerated healing, but they'd be down a Protector for a while in any case. And the only villain they had in custody was Rifter.

Tonight would probably count as an all-around failure.

The power of her glare must have worn off because the dinosaurs were mincing into her peripheral vision. She sighed, limped away from the heroes, and said, "One at a time."

The gist, Rex gathered, was that they'd gotten the bright idea that if they helped fight the bad guys, they would show Oversight they were good guys. Then the gun people would leave, and Mommy wouldn't be so stressed.

Rex slid a hand down her face. "You guys—it's not—" Damn, she was supposed to stay mad. "Look, if they think you can get out whenever you want, they'll add restrictions. Can you just wait for moving day? That would reduce my stress significantly."

They mumbled their yeses to the ground.

Now she just had to leave before enough of the cavalry arrived to spare attention for two dinosaurs loose in a post-rampage town. She grabbed them each by a thumb claw and made significant head gestures to Lewis. He got the picture and towed Becky back to the car.

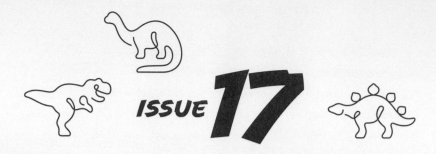

ISSUE 17

DINOSAURS IN HELICOPTERS

The mood took a dive after the failed ambush. There was a minor fiasco when the Protectors found out that Rex was growing more of the virus, which only stuttered out when hospital-bound Manta Man seconded Pixie's assurance that it was *completely normal* to make more of a substance when you were testing your limited supply to nothing.

The heroes still kept their plans closer to the vest, which had Lieutenant Quinten stomping around in the mood of a snubbed lover. Which would have been hilarious if he wasn't taking it out on Rex. He'd practically salivated over Becky's version of their confrontation with Ill Wind, and only some fast talking from Flora bought enough time for Lewis to back her up.

It shouldn't have been such a close thing, since Rex would have to be a total dipshit to bring Lewis and Becky along to a clandestine meeting with Sam's people. But such was logic in Rex-hating country. She tried to thank Lewis, but he waved her off with a frustrated snort and treated her to a rant about bosses with messed up priorities.

Rex may have thrown in a few of the Quinten insults she'd been sitting on to keep his attention.

Lately, Rex had been disgustingly needy for Lewis's attention.

It took effort to not steal glances to make sure he was looking when she spoke, even if she wasn't speaking to him. When he wasn't watching, she wanted to shake him. When he was, she was hit with a rush of stage fright and her tongue tripped over her words. It was infuriating, and she wanted to strangle whatever was responsible. She wickedly reveled in their arguments, because having his undivided attention made her breath come more easily and her cheeks twitch with a grin. Other people joined conversations, but no one interfered in an argument, meaning she got Lewis to herself.

"Would you stop pulling Lewis's pigtails?" Flora said mere seconds after Lewis left the home lab in a huff. "It's unacceptable behavior for children and for grown-ups."

Rex didn't insult Flora by pretending she didn't know what she was talking about. Her snappy comeback caught in her throat when Lewis stormed back in with an "And another thing!"

She took mild interest in his tirade, more occupied by her burst of excitement at having the excuse to look directly at him.

When had he stopped looking imposing and started looking . . . cushy? She wanted to drag him around like one of those giant teddy bears you win at the fair. She'd started gripping table edges to resist the urge to drape herself over him like a cat.

When he left, Flora stared at her until she met her eyes. She inhaled deeply and sighed.

"I know, okay?" Rex snapped, turning back to her work and rubbing both hands over her face to stifle a groan. "How do you freaking tell the difference between a real crush and a friend crush?"

Flora angled herself away from her desk and crossed her legs. "You had a friend crush on Peter, right?"

"Still do. That guy is awesome, and if he doesn't like me, I'll die."

"So, how does this compare?"

Rex fiddled with a pen. "I dunno." She did know.

Flora tapped a finger on the side of her keyboard. "What do you feel when you have a crush?"

Rex pushed out a breath at the prospect of *more talking* and sidestepped the question with a sulky, "I don't know. Fluttery good things and a lot of anxiety."

Flora hadn't been kidding about discussing Rex's boundaries. She and Aya had found a plethora of ace-related terms that Rex had never heard before and still wasn't sure she understood.

There was *sex-repulsed*, which Rex was not. To Rex, sex was like watching football in that it was boring, and she only did it for her partner. Sometimes she got into it when it was on, but it would never be something she was actually interested in. She liked touch—she'd hang off Flora like a koala, except Flora didn't like it—but whether that was about attraction, trust, comfort, or a weird mishmash, she couldn't tell.

There was also *aromantic*. Rex experienced romantic attraction—see: fluttery good things—so she wasn't that. But maybe, rarely romantic? Once-in-a-blue-moon romantic? Was there a word for that? Rex wasn't sure what difference it made to have so many labels—she still felt the same feelings, whether she could put them in boxes or not. Though, the labels did sound better in her head than *made wrong*. So, there was that.

"Do you want to touch him?" Flora asked in her information-gathering tone.

Rex twisted her crossed arms a few impossible ways. "Yeah, but I don't think I mean what that's supposed to mean."

"There's no 'supposed to,'" Flora said. "Maybe ask him on a friend date. Feel it out some more."

"How do you ask a fellow adult on a friend date without looking like you're coming on to them?"

Flora *hmm*ed. "That's a good question. When we were getting to know each other, I thought you were hitting on me."

That was news to Rex. "Were you interested?"

Flora shrugged. "I considered it." She glanced at Rex and huffed a laugh. "Don't look so smug."

Rex wrestled her smirk into a pleasant smile and indulged in a moment of ego-stroking.

"Whatever you do, remember he's still with Oversight," Flora said, turning back to her computer and probably typing something very important.

"He's been generous with his work on the dinosaur habitat, but that doesn't mean he'll put you over his job. And we have to consider how it would look for you to start seducing your surveillance. Not to mention the power imbalance between you right now."

"I'm not taking the knockout gas out of the walls."

"The power imbalance is in *his* favor," Flora said dryly. "When are you heading to Peak Street? Aren't you moving the dinosaurs today?"

Rex checked the time and stood. "I'm not doing much moving. I already had designs for dino-friendly tech, so I thought it would be easier to let them handle it themselves."

Flora tipped her head to look at Rex over her glasses. "The dinosaurs are flying the helicopters."

"Dinocopters," Rex corrected. "And before you ask, it's perfectly safe. Spot, Damien, Tricycle, and Bluetooth all got their pilot licenses last week."

"Isn't Damien a quadruped?"

"He uses the brain wave interface and some pedals. Sally will be flying with him in case it needs any mid-flight tweaks. They're eager to set up new labs. The ones at Peak Street weren't meeting their needs. Only the small bipeds got anything done, and the big ones had to delegate via video chat. On the plus side, their teamwork is impeccable. I think they really bonded in little league."

Flora turned back to her computer, shaking her head. "Tell them Aunt Flora can't be there, but I'll visit when they're settled. And don't forget you have your last consultation this afternoon."

Rex grumbled at the reminder and left, steeling herself for the car ride.

←⟳⟳⟳⟳→

Rex hugged Spot around the neck outside the waiting dinocopter, ignoring the scratch of his sweater vest and the growl of his halfhearted, "Mom, you're embarrassing me."

"Get Aya installed, first thing. She'll tell me if there are any problems. And if any of you want to call just to talk—"

"We're moving to Colorado, not Mars," he grumbled, but his spindly arms returned the hug.

Rex saw her babysitters exchange an eyeroll past Spot's giant head. Pixie stood next to them, clasping her hands and smiling. "He looks so cute in his little vest."

Spot's throat rumbled against her shoulder, and Rex said, "Ignore her— you look sophisticated. One of you will be available to pick up little White Russian and Mint Julep and Long Island Iced Tea—"

"Yeah, Mom, we got it. Quit worrying."

"I thought the hatchlings were staying in the nursery," Pixie said.

"The tyrannosaurs have done a lot of work on themselves and are in a stable three-way relationship. They won visitation rights two weeks ago, and I think they're putting together a case for partial custody. I'm very proud of them," Rex explained.

Spot extracted himself from Rex's hold and stalked to the dinocopter, matte black and hovering on magnetic skids that Rex was especially proud of. At the door, he turned back and signed, *see you soon.*

She signed, *fly carefully,* and held back bittersweet tears as the propellers started up and the last of her dinosaurs finally took off for their new home.

She wasn't quite finished watching the copter fly away and thinking heavy thoughts when 'Ning appeared on the rooftop in a flash.

"Jesus!" Rex rubbed the spots from her eyes. "Can you turn down your glow-bulb?"

"The Protectors sent me. It's about Rifter."

Rex raised an eyebrow, finally able to see her through lingering spots.

The Protectors had gotten tidbits of information from the captured goons, which 'Ning and the others had investigated to no avail, but Rifter had said little that wasn't a demand.

Pixie stepped forward. "They got something from Rifter?"

"Not exactly." 'Ning's head turned back to Rex, expression indiscernible through the mask. "He wants to speak with the Meister."

Rex gave a slow blink, automatically trying to hide her surprise. "He wants to talk to me?" 'Ning's mask was impassive. Pixie's partially uncovered face twisted with worry.

"And the others are, um"—Pixie shot Rex a glance that made her grit her teeth—"considering it?"

"I think that depends on what Rex has to say." 'Ning hesitated. "His behavior in captivity has been odd."

Rex's brow furrowed. "Is he cracking up?"

"The opposite. He seems composed." 'Ning shrugged. "I've fought Rifter many times. He robs banks; he doesn't take over the world. I don't understand why he's mixed up with this."

Rex rubbed an arm. The thought of trying to interrogate one of Sam's allies filled her with unease. But refusing wasn't a real option, her position being what it was.

The Lightning gave a nod and zapped away as Rex headed inside to face whatever fresh hell this would turn out to be.

⟵ ⟳⟲⟳⟲ ⟶

Rifter wasn't being held in Rex's building—she would have pitched a fit if it had been suggested—and when they reached the facility with his hastily-assembled force field cell, complete with a convoluted system of airlock-style rooms for food delivery and visitation, most of the Protectors were already there. Rex made eye contact with Viv as she entered the observation room, but the Jester got in her face first.

"Any idea why Rifter is so eager to see you?"

"I don't know. Maybe it's because I built the only cell that's ever held him," she answered.

"You did, didn't you? Almost seems like you know more about his rifts than the rest of us."

"Can we skip this part?" Rex asked, stepping back because no one wearing so little should stand that close to her in public. "Lieutenant Quinten and his team give me the we-think-you're-working-with-the-guy-who-broke-your-stuff dance pretty regularly." She paused. "And yes, I do know more than you about rifts. Because I'm a genius, and I thought about it."

Vivid Blue rolled her sky-blue eyes. "Can you think of anything that's changed recently? Anything he might have been waiting for?"

Manta Man's voice startled her, coming from a dark corner. "He may have timed instructions." He leaned forward in his chair, crutches balanced across his lap. "For instance, if he was still here after a number of weeks, he was to deliver a message."

Rex had been turning it over in her mind on the way over and still didn't know why he wanted to talk to her unless he just wanted to stir the pot. It certainly wouldn't help with her current company if Rifter thought she'd be sympathetic.

She turned to the observation window with a tense jaw, squinting at the villain sitting inside the faintly humming walls. He looked stupidly normal without his mask and orange costume—just a stubbly, buff guy a little past his prime.

Viv joined her at the window. Rex glanced at her, forcing her shoulders not to climb at the instant rise in tension. Unable to sit in it with the grace that Viv managed, Rex said, "So, how are Mom and Dad lately?"

"Older," Viv said with a pointed glare.

Rex winced.

Before she could make another terrible attempt to dispel the tension, Viv crossed her arms and said, "If I let you in there, what would you say?"

Rex huffed. "I'd ask him why he attacked my lab. What else would I say?"

"Don thinks it's a bad idea."

Don Conjure's voice carried from the other side of the room. "I merely worry our villainous charge has plans we cannot foresee."

"Not much to foresee—he wants his inside man to help him out," the Jester said.

"But the Meister has been so helpful," Pixie piped up.

"Has she? Progress seems slow for how long she's been dicking around with that virus." The Jester nudged Manta Man. "I don't see why our geeks can't do her job. Seems like you two should be worried about someone stepping in on your role."

"I will worry about my place on the team when I figure out exactly what yours is," Manta Man replied.

"Why are your teammates so mean to each other?" Rex asked Viv.

She shrugged. "It's harmless banter."

"It's a toxic work environment. If my coworkers acted that way, I'd quit."

"When have you ever had to deal with coworkers?"

Rex's shoulders drew up. "Point."

"I'm going to give you a list of questions," Viv said.

Rex couldn't hide a small start. "You're letting me talk to him?"

"It's been almost two months. The other prisoners don't know much. They're fanatics who think our brother will make their dreams come true. But I think Rifter's different. We need him to talk."

Rex tried to rebalance. She was so used to keeping quiet about her relation to both her siblings that hearing Vivian speak openly about it threw her off-kilter. "Is that how it usually . . ." She didn't expect the difficulty in bringing up her sister's semi-regular clashes with her twin.

This was a conversation they should have had weeks ago. She should have been learning everything Vivid Blue the superhero knew about Last Dance the supervillain, but even now her last private conversation with Viv was elephant-ing it up in this room.

"Sam reads minds," Viv said, apparently inferring the rest of Rex's question. "He knows what to say and do to win someone's loyalty. And according to the minions we've arrested before, he also knows how to deal with disloyalty. None of his people would be here if he hadn't seen that their limits exceed our interrogation efforts."

Cold shivers ran down Rex's spine. She recalled the woman who had slipped his note into her pocket, the manipulations of Sam's old bullies, and the short message—*your dinosaurs looked cute in the news.* The mire of feelings almost dragged her down before she shoved it back into the pit.

"But loyalties change," Rex insisted. "You've been pressuring them for weeks. It's not like he flips a switch in their heads."

The hero sighed, turning toward Rex with her cape and loose hair following, the movement a little too slow. "You don't understand, T—he reads my mind too. He knows how far we'll take the interrogation. He knows the whole playing field, and we only know half. I can stop his plans because he's not all-knowing, and he messes up. But every time he makes a mistake, he learns.

"I know more about his abilities now," she continued. "I know how close I can get before he 'sees' me. I know his advantage grows when he's more familiar with your thoughts, which means every time we clash, he's more prepared. I know his strength is equal to mine, but my telekinesis gives me the advantage in a physical fight."

Rex felt something painful building as Viv laid out the results of all the time she'd put into chasing their brother. It was a familiar guilt she'd been trying to shove away since her own efforts led to nothing. The deeper, harder feelings from that time tried to rise with the guilt, but Rex couldn't afford to deal with that right now.

"He rarely puts himself in a position to fight me." Viv turned back to the glass. "When he does, he has a plan. There was a thing with a factory a while back—"

"I saw that in the news," Rex muttered.

"His people cleaned it out while he distracted me. And the workers said they were making boots. What is he supposed to do with those? I know he makes mistakes, but I can't tell the difference between his mistakes and decoys. With all the times we've fought over the last few years while you've been—" Her jaw clenched as she cut herself off.

Rex felt a deeper stab. Yet, at the same time, her indignation tried to flare, her automatic defensiveness, because Viv didn't know what she'd—she had no idea how—

Rex took a deep breath and pushed it all back. For the greater good. Viv didn't need to understand or approve of her for them to work together. But it sure was a mindfuck to feel like the wronged party and a worthless piece of shit at the same time.

"We have no intel," Viv concluded. "So, unless you've made a break-through with the virus, we need Rifter to crack."

Rex's stomach gave an uncomfortable squirm. "Give me the questions. All I've gotten from the virus lately is ideas for interfacing technology with dinosaur thoughts."

Viv rolled her blue-on-blue eyes and waved her toward Manta Man.

Manta Man gave instructions sharply, pointed teeth flashing as he clearly articulated each item on the list that he and Viv had prepared. Rex followed his lead in ignoring the Jester's commentary because her nerves were picking up on what she was about to do, and she didn't have the attention to spare.

"You're sure you remember?" Manta Man's pinkish glare was infamously effective since he didn't need to blink.

"Yes. This isn't my first interrogation." Rex didn't mention that she was usually on the other side of that table.

She memorized the questions and made her way to Rifter's cell, trying to banish the other thoughts crowding her mind. As she reached for the door, she thanked her brain for choosing that moment to recall that the last time she'd been face-to-face with Rifter, he'd been about to kill her.

What would Sam have thought of that?

Rex's hand opened the door, and her legs carried her into the room.

ISSUE 18

DINOSAURS AREN'T IN THIS ONE

Rifter watched openly from his bench as Rex maneuvered through the blueish force field chambers to reach his cell.

"Just a second—I think I have to jostle the handle," she called, earning a smirk. She reached the last force field between herself and the supervillain, where a couple of chairs were pushed close to the wall. Rex pulled one to the spot in front of him and sat.

"You're not joining me in here?" Rifter asked, smirk still in place.

"I don't have superpowers and I'm not a dumbass, so no." Rex leaned back and looked him over. He wore a standard gray jumpsuit, stubble on his cheeks, and greasy brown hair uncombed around his ears. "So, what do you want?"

He raised an eyebrow.

"You asked for me, right?" She knew the Protectors were watching, but she didn't get the sense Rifter would respond to her jumping straight into the interrogator role. Besides, anything she got from him would be more than he'd given so far.

"First, I wanted to give a nod to the person who blocked my rifts. Well played."

Rex nodded impatiently. "And second?"

"As you've probably guessed, I have a message for you."

"From my evil twin?" She didn't fidget. Viv *said* they already knew.

Rifter raised an eyebrow again but didn't challenge the label. "He told me if I wasn't free after a month, you might need a hint."

Rex suppressed a wince. That would not sound good to Oversight. She didn't miss that he'd been there longer than one month. Had he waited to ask, or had the others waited to tell her? "I feel silly—I didn't know I was supposed to be busting you out."

"I inferred you were working on something more tangential to my escape." He paused. "Or rather, my escape was meant to be tangential to whatever you're working on."

Crap, crap, crap. Sam hadn't told Rifter about the helmet, had he? "Let's back up. You expected to get caught, and you still broke into my lab?"

"Of course, I didn't expect to get caught. Your evil twin, as you call him," he gave her an amused look, "gave me instructions for several possible outcomes. I never took this one seriously, but here we are." He shrugged, smiling roguishly.

"Look, will you drop the buddy routine? There are certain superheroes who are probably jumping to give me crap about it later." She turned to her reflection in the observation window and clarified, "I'm not with him. This is the first time we've spoken."

Rifter shot the window a glance. "I don't know why you put up with their harassment. You have the resources to go rogue with little inconvenience to yourself. I personally can't imagine helping people who treat me like an enemy. They must realize it will be their own fault when you switch sides."

"If I switch sides," she automatically corrected, then cringed and corrected again, "I mean, not if *or* when, because I'm not going to switch sides—I'm a good guy now. I mean, I've *always been* a good guy." She said the last part directly to the observation window, imagining Viv with her face in her hands on the other side.

Rifter laughed in a very manly, rumbly way. "I feel sorry for you, Meister. At least I've always gotten the benefits of villainhood along with being considered an evil bastard."

"You don't have to rub it in." She crossed her arms. "Do villains have the opposite problem? Does Ill Wind nag you for opening rifts onto lawns instead of the ocean? Why didn't she attack with you, by the way? I can't think of a reason to hold her back, unless she was too far out of rift range to—"

In the back of her head, something clicked. "Oh, wait, you dropped Quinten on the lawn."

Rifter's smirk slid into a look of confusion.

"Why didn't I think of this before?" Rex clapped her hands to her head. It was obvious. But she'd been wrapped up in the other million things on her plate, leaving the Rifter situation to everyone else.

She turned to address the Protectors. "He's got a range. The warehouse he came through can't have been far from the lab. I can figure out a radius if I check some readings from—you know what? It doesn't have to be me. I'll write it out, and your scientists can do it. I'll give them access to my data on rifts."

Rifter was scowling when she turned back. "No more stalling, Meister." His voice was clipped. "It might interest you to know, I was supposed to leave this message if we succeeded too—preferably somewhere you would find it without all this mess," he gestured toward the window, "interfering."

This was looking worse and worse for her. "If he wants my assistance, it would help to know what he's trying to do," she said in a Hail Mary attempt to cover something from Manta Man's list.

Rifter's smile returned. "Please. It's the same thing he's always trying to do."

She cursed herself for wasting time on a question she could already answer. *I have to make it stop,* he'd written. "He got you captured. Shouldn't you be mad?"

"Honestly?" Rifter leaned forward, and there was a light in his eyes that made Rex wary. "When he gave me in-case-of-capture instructions, I thought he was taking a dig. Who would have predicted this?" He gestured toward the force field between them. "Except him, apparently."

Sam had always been the one person who thought she could do anything.

"It might not be a bad idea to grab a seat on your brother's crazy train. Seems like he knows what he's doing," Rifter continued.

Rex thought of Ill Wind lazily overseeing the laying of road spikes and knew Rifter wasn't the first or last villain to come to that conclusion.

"Can I deliver my message now?"

Unable to think of another angle, she said, "Lay it on me."

"He wanted to tell you he's sorry."

Rex's thoughts ground to a halt.

Silence stretched as she waited for more, but nothing came. Her heart turned rock-solid in her chest. She was suddenly very aware of Vivian watching from the other side of the glass. "That's it?"

"That's it." Rifter shrugged. "It doesn't seem worth my time, even stuck in here. But I guess it must mean something to you."

Sam had been miserable after the—after what had happened between them. He'd been sheepish. Morose. Needy but so, so careful with her. He'd said it through tears while the sound of his voice made waves of rage and fear and nausea roll through her: *"I fucked up."*

Under the expectant, strained smiles of their family, she'd killed a small part of herself to answer, *"I still love you."* With the anger and betrayal lashing through her gut and up her throat, no force on Earth could have made her say *I forgive you.* But she'd had to say something. She'd been worried he would kill himself.

Rex was pretty much done with this. She stood and turned away from Rifter's cell.

"We're finished?" Rifter asked, voice still light.

Rex didn't bother to answer. She made her way through the forcefield chambers to the door. When she shut it behind her, Viv was waiting in the hall with her babysitters. Rex contemplated her sister.

She remembered her heart bursting with relief at the sight of Viv—no cape yet, just jeans and a sweater with buttons askew from being thrown on in the middle of the night—flying into the cabin, the walls rending themselves around her. Rex's tears finally spilling over as her all-blue eyes found her. Viv swooping down to Rex's level, quick with worry, hands cupping either side of her face. *"I'm here. Are you hurt? Hang tight; I have to find Sam."* Then the hands had left.

Rex was a horrible person for remembering the hands leaving more clearly than she remembered them finding her. She thought of Bright Jack in the green room at the television studio, declaring, *"It's sort of a joint backstory—hero and villain, sister and brother. That's what makes it so compelling."* Screw that guy and everyone like him—every person who wasn't the Flora in the room asking, *"What happened to the girl?"*

Viv looked uncomfortable. "You doing okay, T?"

"I guess the message was bullshit," Rex said instead of answering. She turned and headed down the hall, toward the exit. Didn't she have a consultation to get to? It was hard to think. There was a buzzing in the way, a fuzzy quality to her thoughts.

Anger was such a simple word to describe the fucking *monster* that had fought for months to consume her from the inside out, that she'd battled back and swallowed down in such a physical, exhausting way that even when she was awake, she'd hardly known what was happening around her. The way she'd gnawed her knuckles bloody to keep it inside. The fantasies she'd fed to it—bashing his head in with a hammer, crushing the bones of his hands, seeing him bleed—so she could stomach being in the same room as her brother, smiling at him, letting him hug her, never running or screaming or lashing out.

All under the black cloud of his remorse and self-hatred and the grateful smiles of their family.

He'd known her feelings, obviously; the act she put on wasn't for him, except in her willingness to put it on.

Viv fell in step with her, the babysitters following. "I wasn't expecting that. Did his apology mean anything to you, besides from the time he kidnapped you?"

Rex felt a hot sweep of gratitude, even as Viv's plain language tested her calm. No talking around it. No, *the thing that happened* or, *the time you two fought.*

"We shouldn't be surprised. It's the only thing he really says to me now." Rex didn't look at her. "Have you tested the factory workers for the virus?"

Viv shot her a look that was easy to read—wary, alarmed, questioning.

"The boot factory thing. You were talking about misleads," Rex tried to explain. That fuzz in her head wouldn't go away. "It's just a feeling."

Viv nodded. "I'll talk to the others, figure out how to get it done fast."

Rex was surprised they reached the exit without a confrontation after everything Rifter had said. Viv must have told the others to leave it alone—they wouldn't have backed off for anyone else.

"T, wait."

Rex paused in the doorway. The soldiers filed out first, shooting her quick, blank glances.

"My team has been staying at a property Manta Man owns just outside Decimen City," Viv said.

Rex wrinkled her nose despite the fragile rocking in her chest urging her to get out of her sister's presence as soon as possible. "Manta Man having property in Decimen makes me very uncomfortable."

"We're having a night in tomorrow. Taking a break. You've been helping us for weeks. I think you should join us."

Rex was confused before she remembered Rifter's talk about how nagging heroes and government surveillance would push her to true villainy.

"That's not necessary. My fall from grace isn't as inevitable as Rifter made it sound."

"I want you there. It's a good chance to get to know the others."

Rex sighed, because when Flora heard about this opportunity to ass-kiss their way out of Oversight, she'd insist that Rex go. "I'll think about it."

Viv nodded, eyes lingering on Rex's face. Then she headed back into the building, cape fluttering up at the edge.

Rex's heart lurched as she watched her walk away, much too close to the surface. She made herself return to the car, where the soldiers were waiting. "Back to Peak Street. I have a consultation." It was harder than usual to fold herself into the back, hear the heavy slam of the door, and sit through the motion as the engine rumbled to life.

She remembered another car ride, their destination passing in the window, half her face pulsing from the hit, and horror settling over her as she realized what was happening.

She wasn't late for the consultation. Still, she might have canceled if it wasn't the last one—might as well get it over with. "Let my client in when they get here," she told the soldiers. They might as well make themselves useful.

Rex sat behind the computer in her office, which was really Flora's office, and pulled up the information on the client, trying to clear her mind. The door clicked open as she read the name: Samuel Anderson.

A shadow fell in the doorway, and something in Rex folded up in the back of her head like a black hole.

Heavy footsteps crossed the carpet. "T?"

Rex was listing in an airplane. She was skidding on ice. She looked up at the voice, and the impulse of fear was hidden with the ease of muscle memory.

"Is it okay that I'm here?"

Yeah, Rex had left the building. She'd checked out. Her body was empty. She watched as the man in her office—six-foot-nine and built like few who weren't superbeings could be—sat down stiffly in the chair on the other side of her desk. She took in the stony expression and dismissed it. His expression never meant much. Body language meant more for Sam.

He'd walked past the surveillance team. How could—but did they know what Last Dance looked like? He always wore that deep hood and opera mask. His hair was dyed black. It was usually only a few shades darker than Rex's, edging from blond to brown. He wore glasses—fake—and an unremarkable suit. Carried a briefcase. Like someone at a consultation with a super genius. But he hadn't disguised his long face, sharp jaw touched with stubble, shadowed blue eyes that matched Rex's except for the intermixed gray lines they'd noticed while sitting on the bathroom counter with their foreheads pressed together, breaking eye contact when one or the other started giggling.

"Did you get my note?"

The name. Flora should have—it was a common name, though. And her brother was still new to Flora, his villain moniker probably more prominent in her mind. Maybe she'd smirked at the shared surname, thought it was funny, but not that weird. Not worth a mention. Oversight would have gone over her consultations. They'd know Last Dance's name. But would they think of it? Would they have caught it?

"Surprise?" He smiled a bit, slouching. He looked nervous. "Your thoughts got weird."

Maybe Rifter could have given her a freaking heads up instead of an apology.

Sam looked down and cleared his throat, but he didn't comment on the thought. "So, did you make it?" He shrugged. "I finished your virus. You probably know that by now. It's doing well." Rex figured that information would tear its way through her subconscious at some point, but right now it wasn't relevant. "I need to know if you made it. I kind of need it a lot." He chuckled shortly, a tense sound.

No point deciding what to tell him. He'd know. "It's not here. It's at home."

"It's really loud." Sam swallowed. "It's always loud, and I can't sleep." He cracked a grin as tense as his laugh. The bags under his eyes were as deep as they'd been when she last saw him. "Sleep? What's that like?" Another quick laugh. "I kind of think it would be nice. Because I could sleep. I kind of think it would be really, really nice."

Was he like this around his followers? Heroes like Viv? Villains like Rifter? Or did he only waver on the edge of a breakdown in front of her?

"I trust you," he said.

How desperate was he? Would he—

"I won't hurt your friends or the soldiers. I won't hurt you."

A memory of him with a snarl across his face as he drew his hand back in the driver's seat popped into her head.

He flinched.

The fear was coming back, like feeling to a limb or heat to blood—each small wave a little stronger than the last.

He shifted in the seat. "You're hurting me a lot right now."

A flash of rage—she was hurting *him?*

"Okay, I'll leave." Sam stood. "I'll try again later."

Rex wondered if she should call out to her surveillance as he walked back to the door. He didn't hurry because they both knew she wouldn't.

SPOTLIGHT ON LOVE

When people say unconditionally, they really mean with a few conditions, and as long as no one else they love needs them at the same time.

R ex leaned forward on the balls of her feet and dragged another bottle out of the cabinet, not minding that the hood clutched in her hand dragged through a wet spot on the floor. What was this one? Bourbon? How long had they had bourbon?

"Doctor, are you sure I shouldn't call someone?"

"Shut up," Rex muttered, swatting at the eyes hovering by her shoulder. She used the hood as a grip to untwist the cap and took a testing sip before committing to a swig.

She'd told Oversight, of course—called directly because all it would take was the wrong person watching the security footage to know he'd been there and damned if she wasn't going to claim the brownie points before her babysitters reported their ass-covering version. She could almost feel pleased that they'd let him waltz right in. Let them face the consequences of fucking up for once. How dare he? How fucking dare he? He hung around while she faked being okay for months, then he up and vanished, and now he shows his face again like this? What did he think had changed?

Back then, she could almost feel him hoping the act would become real, that she was okay. Did he finally leave because he gave up wishing? Was he a villain now because she couldn't forgive him fast enough?

Thoughts were seeping out of the pit. Her balance at its edge was pitching the wrong way. Another swig.

The day it happened they'd passed right by their house. Numbness had run through her until the pounding pain in her eye was all she felt. What spell would break if she told him to pull over? Should she jump out of the car? What would he do if she moved to unbuckle? Her phone was in her hand, but what would he do if she tried to call someone? *What would he do?*

She had to stop thinking. The pit was right there. It was under her feet. There was no way out unless her damn brain would just *quit*.

"Doctor, I am calling Ms. Shay."

"Don't do that." Rex swiped at Aya in horror, knocking over an empty bottle. "She's at Sadie's for the weekend. Don't call her." Rex was turning her friends into caretakers again. That was how she'd lost the first bunch. That, plus being no fun anymore.

"I'm sorry, Doctor. I don't know what else to do."

Lewis's voice came from the doorway. "Rex?"

Oh, shit. Rex didn't want him to see this. Balancing on the balls of her feet became too hard, and she fell back on her ass. "Just leave. It's under control."

She heard him picking his way around the kitchen island. "Did you drink all this?" His tone was accusing—no, just harsh. The way it got when he wasn't sure what he was supposed to say or do.

She wanted to explain but explaining would mean thinking about it and the pit was *right there*. "It's fine. Go away." Rex could feel her skeleton icing over. She tried to shake it off, because she recognized this feeling, and she couldn't afford to go numb. She couldn't spend another year curing cancer or whatever instead of facing this.

Laughter bubbled out of Rex, because, God, she was so *useful* when she was messed up. When she was okay, all she did was lose track of her death ray or chase dinosaurs down Main Street.

Lewis didn't laugh with her. "Just tell me: Will Flora be here soon? Or someone else?"

Aya answered, damn her. "Ms. Shay is on her way, but she is coming from across town."

Lewis nodded. "I'll stay until then." He edged a little closer, slouching a bit as though he knew she hated people looming over her. He probably did. Rex shouldn't be allowed to appreciate it while resenting being indulged like a child. She ought to only feel one or the other.

"Listen," Lewis said as he arranged his whole massive self onto his knees. "Curfew is pretty soon, but I don't feel comfortable—"

"You don't have to do that anymore," Rex interrupted. She took another sip of burning bourbon and ignored the way his lips thinned. "It was dumb from the beginning—I don't know why you did it."

"You could have told me that before I did it for a month and a half," he said dryly.

She regretted her words. It wasn't dumb. It was the opposite of dumb. "I mean, not that you—it's really—" Her tongue stumbled over genuine sentiments. "You did that for me, and it meant"—everything—"a lot."

Lewis shifted on his knees, blushing. "It's nothing."

"You can stop though. I'm not scared of you anymore." Her grip closed on air and she noticed belatedly that he'd removed the bourbon from her hands. "I mean, I wasn't ever, really. There should be a different word for it. Because I've been scared, and that's not what it's like. You know, normally."

She leaned toward him, fixated on his face. She liked his eyes. Not because they were pretty—maybe they were—they just looked right. They were the right shade of brown. The right shape and size. "Fear is so strange. I mean, the word: fear. It's like a photograph. There's this missing depth when you try to say it."

She leaned too far forward and lost her balance, but Lewis helpfully grabbed her shoulders. She appreciated being held still against the vertigo, although she felt like her head would be better off on the floor.

"You can try to make the word more accurate," she picked back up. "Let's say I was very scared. I was very, *very* scared. But every modifier makes it weaker. You can't *say* the real thing. You can't even remember it that well. It's just a snap, and then it's in you, and you're in it, and you get to spend the rest of your life trying to bridge the gap between what people call it and what you felt."

She picked up the bottle for another swig, but Lewis took it again.

She chased it with her lips, fish-style, and gave his arm a frustrated shove, trying so hard not to think about how much stronger he was than her.

"I'm going to say something that's gonna make me sound like a bad person," she slurred.

Lewis's brow furrowed.

"I'm smarter than him." She leaned closer to say it. This felt like a secret, or at least something she shouldn't say out loud. "I'm nicer than him. I try harder. I'm a *better person* than him." Something at her core rattled loose in its casing. "But he was bigger and stronger than me. And in the end, the rest doesn't matter."

Lewis was sitting very still.

"And then people tell the story. And if he's some nameless, ugly villain, everyone hates him with you while he rots in misery or prison or hell. But if he's pretty and familiar and he has a sad story, too, you're supposed to understand." She felt like her chest was cracking open, tiny fissures spider-webbing across her ribs. "You're supposed to be magnanimous. You're not just supposed to forgive him, you're supposed to have never blamed him in the first place." She landed too hard on that sentence and let out a breathy giggle. Where was all that hate supposed to go? Up her ass?

"Rex—"

This wasn't a conversation. "Then they end the story with you being okay. And they get really uncomfortable with you if you aren't." Her cheeks ached with the strength of her grin. "That ruins it."

Lewis still had a hand on her shoulder, a light touch. His voice wasn't soft, exactly, but it was quieter than usual. Lower. "Who are you talking about?"

The look on his face. That hint of something angry and alarmed, his eyes fixed on hers.

So many eyes darting away from hers. So many, *"Please, T—" "Can't you just—" "What would it take to—" "I know it's asking a lot—"*

Her breaths came short and fast. She gasped through snot bubbling in her nose as tears stabbed into her eyes and burned down her cheeks. Her face twisted around closed up airways, only a moment of panic at her wavering vigilance, and the thoughts pulled her down.

She tried to gasp but got no air. Feelings flooded her throat and chest, rot-soft with bitterness and so *fucking* strong, smothering her at the bottom of the pit as she lost every grip.

You have to let go of it, right? But how? How? How?

Rex felt cool tiles under her forehead, but it didn't help her breathe. She sucked in fast, ugly wheezes, but her whole chest had closed up shop; there was nowhere for the air to go. Suffocation panic is a special kind of panic. This couldn't kill her. She clung to that knowledge. No matter what it felt like, she wasn't going to die.

Lewis let out a big, hurried breath above her—what a waste of air—and knocked over a few bottles with sharp clatters.

Somewhere in the shit-flood of her mind, Rex felt pathetic with gratitude. Yes, please leave. Don't watch this happen. There was nothing cute about vulnerability. Panic attacks were gross to witness and humiliating to experience. Like the physical pain wasn't enough. And God was she in pain. She couldn't push the thoughts out when she couldn't even fucking *breathe.*

"Okay, you need to slow down."

Rex jolted. When had Lewis gotten closer? Her ears ached like they were underwater—not enough air to hear, ha ha—and she couldn't tell where his voice was coming from. She could look, but she'd have to lift her head off the floor and her vision was vanishing into black spots anyway.

"Breathe with me. One, two, three." He inhaled and counted slowly. "And exhale. One, two, three."

Rex latched onto the pattern. It had been so long since this had happened to her, but she knew counting worked. She just had to focus. She wanted it to end. Her hands were twitching into proto-claws on either side of her head, like leaves curling as they starved. The panic-and-alcohol combo must have affected her circulation faster than panic alone.

Lewis's voice floated above her, muffled through her fish-gasps and sobs. "You're doing great. One, two, three. I'm going to touch your hand."

A big hand pried her fingers up, and something smooth and round—an empty bottle?—was pushed into her palm. She wondered if she should be insulted that he didn't think her strongest grip could break a glass bottle, but she was mostly relieved her CO_2-deprived hand couldn't scrunch painfully into itself anymore.

A shoe squeak placed Lewis in motion by her head. He removed the hood from her other hand and replaced it with another bottle, still counting and taking slow breaths. The thoughts kept surging, pulling her under until she clawed back out to try again.

As control slowly returned, she tried to push herself up and—*nope*. Her head swam, and she dropped it back onto the tile.

"I guess that's one way to put your head between your knees."

Rex laughed, a quick hitch in her breathing, stabilizing her a little more. "S-sorry," she forced out with an exhale.

"It's fine." Lewis's knee appeared in her peripheral vision as he settled in front of her. Aya's voice registered, too muffled to make out, before Lewis continued, "Do you want to hear a funny story about my week?"

Classic distraction, and so effective that she craved it. She nodded against the floor, answering breathlessly, "Yes."

"So, me and Peter volunteered to run an errand in town—I know how much you like it when me and Peter hang out."

Rex gasped a laugh.

"But all the cars were in use for some reason, so we decided we'd try public transportation."

Rex wheezed again, knowing a few things about public transit in Decimen City. She took in the gentle rumble of his voice like water from a desert spring, the story steadily edging out the thoughts lashing at the edge of the pit. Her breaths turned long and shaky, each its own entity with a beginning, middle, and end. She let go of the bottles in her hands and pushed herself off the floor with trembling arms to slump against the island.

"How long has the construction been going on downtown?"

Rex gave an *mph*—more from the effort it took to speak than disinterest.

"Um . . . How are your dinosaurs settling in? Did you see them off?"

Something lurched in Rex's chest, and a sob burst out of her. "They're so far away," she wailed.

"Oh, crap." A hand touched her shoulder and retracted. "Oops—I'm going to touch your shoulder." The hand returned. The self-correction made a wet laugh mix with her sobs.

"Sorry," she wheezed through sob-laughter. Why did he have to be here, of all people? She'd wanted—she couldn't think about it. She couldn't face how much she might have ruined. "I'm sorry. Not your job. Sorry."

"Rex?" Flora's voice in the doorway hit her with a one-two of relief and dread. "What happened?"

"I told her not to call." It came out high and whiny. Rex registered the makeup on Flora's face. She and Sadie had been on a date.

"Doctor Anderson was drinking and began to hyperventilate," Aya said from somewhere over Rex's head. "Mr. Stone assisted her with help from a checklist I found online."

Rex got a mental image of Aya hovering over her while Lewis was counting breaths and sending him that creepy, one-light wink. A laugh burst out, shooting pain through her chest.

"You can go now, Mr. Stone," Flora said. Her voice was sharp enough to cut off Rex's laughter. Rex followed Flora's gaze to the floor next to Lewis.

Shit, the hood.

"Rex." Flora's voice was higher than usual. "You'd risk—after all the work we've done—"

"It's not the same one," Rex said in a rush, words slurring. She'd gone to the production floor earlier with what was left of the whipped cream vodka—not enough, as it turned out—and churned out a design based on Sam's hood, fueled by disjointed thoughts sliding out of the pit. She used a brown fabric, but it could pass for maroon in bad light. "It's not the one that—you know."

Flora shook her head sharply. She bent down, stuffed the hood in a pocket, and took Rex's face in her hands, examining her. "When did you start drinking?"

"I ate some pizza." It was gross. It had cheese on it.

"There was an incident today," Lewis started.

"Aya filled me in," Flora said. "Someone should have called me earlier."

"He didn't do anything," Rex got out, one wheeze at a time. "I didn't expect—but I didn't expect it before, either. I gaslit myself, kind of. Because no one else saw it. Who's scared of their own brother?" The room blurred.

"Sweetie, I'm thrilled you want to open up, but you just had a panic attack. This might not be the best time—"

"Right. You're right. Sorry." Rex's gut churned as everything that had been tensed in her loosened up, followed quickly by pressure at the back of her throat. This could actually get worse. "God, spare me this," she whined.

Flora apparently caught her meaning and hauled Rex up by her armpits, making the room spin around. "Let's hit up the toilet. You can go, Mr. Stone."

Lewis stood. "I can help you get her—"

"That isn't necessary." Flora took slow steps, Rex shuffling to keep up. "Thank you for helping. I've got her now."

Rex groaned, lips closed, and practiced every mental trick she had to hold back the vomit until they reached her bathroom.

Lewis didn't follow. If he had, Rex would have died.

With perfect coordination, Flora flipped up the toilet seat as Rex fell over the bowl, hurling up vomit that tasted enough like pizza to put her off it for a month. Well, maybe a week. She took heaving breaths as she came up. "I'm—I'm toxic."

"You're not toxic."

"Everyone's happier when I'm not around." Her words echoed in the toilet bowl.

Flora sighed. "You know not everyone's your siblings, right?"

Rex grunted. "You didn't even know I had siblings until recently."

"Hm." Flora paused. "Why didn't I know until recently, anyway?"

Rex hauled in enough air to prompt, "Huh?"

"We've been friends for five years, Rex. Don't you think you should've mentioned your family before now?"

Guilt churned with the alcohol in her stomach. Her voice was barely above a whisper when she answered. "I don't like talking about myself."

"I know. It's almost a pathological thing with you. But it's hard not to interpret that as you not trusting me."

Rex wondered if Flora knew how nauseous this conversation was making her. She thought she might cry. "I trust you."

"You're usually a better liar than that." They were both silent for a moment. Flora sighed. "Sorry. I didn't mean to be on your case right now. You just make it so—nope, not getting on your case. I'll get you some water."

She didn't deserve Flora. No one deserved Flora.

She missed Flora returning because her head was buried in the bowl, hacking up pizza that tasted like bourbon. When she came up for air, Flora was watching her expressionlessly.

Flora set the water beside Rex, a tiny *tink* of glass on tile. She settled on the side of the tub, soundless.

The silence lasted as Rex rinsed her mouth and cautiously sipped the water, wincing through the taste.

When Flora spoke, her voice was soft and deliberate. "You keep saying you don't have a tragic backstory. No murdered parents, no torture, no horrible accident."

Rex didn't speak. She had the sense Flora wasn't finished, but the longer she waited, the more doubtful she felt.

Flora took a slow breath. "But somehow, you judge how much people love you by how badly they're able to hurt you."

Rex felt pain in her chest and realized she hadn't taken a breath in a while. She inhaled.

"Maybe that happened slowly. Maybe it's no one's fault. But I think that's . . ."

Silence fell again. Rex couldn't take her eyes from Flora's face, and Flora wasn't looking back. She kept breathing, and her chest kept hurting. She suddenly wanted to tell Flora everything—her deepest fears, her creepiest dreams, her too-intense feelings about five-sided shapes. Every little thing.

"I want to ask Lewis out," she whispered.

"Is that so?" Flora pushed the glass of water closer in clear suggestion.

Rex took a dutiful swig. "I don't want to be pathetic about it."

"Don't take this the wrong way, but you've never worried about that before."

Rex's laugh turned into a lurch over the toilet. The water was a mistake. She was peripherally aware of Flora placing a balancing hand on her back when she tilted mid-hurl.

"I'm just—I'm not right," she said, voice rough. "I'm not enough. I'm never enough for anyone."

"There's nothing wrong with you. You have so much to bring to a relationship."

The platitudes sank through Rex like a stone. Flora didn't get it. Flora was the right kind of person, whose wants and needs matched other people's wants and needs the right way. Rex wasn't an extra puzzle piece in the box—she was a smooth piece of cardboard trying to pass herself off as part of the puzzle. She couldn't feel the right things. She'd *tried* to feel correctly, but she failed.

Always, her feelings were inconvenient.

"I keep thinking—I kept thinking, after what happened." Rex raised her head, neck twinging. "I kept thinking—siblings give each other bruises all the time, right? We did worse fighting in the backyard when we were kids. I've gotten worse by accident. Like, 'Oh, how did that get there? I must have bumped into a table.'"

The room swam, and Rex waited it out before continuing in a croak that felt louder than it sounded. "So why didn't it feel like that? Why did it feel like he took everything away from me? Why couldn't I sleep? Why was I so *angry*? Why did I wish—" She'd wished the black eye had lasted longer. She'd wished the evidence hadn't erased itself without her consent.

"He was your brother," Flora said, voice low. "You trusted him."

A spike of rage hit Rex. "You don't know that. You don't know anything about it."

Flora's lips thinned.

"I'm sorry. I'm sorry. I'm sorry." She swallowed frantically as vomit rose again.

She lost the fight, bile burning up her throat. This time she came up whimpering. "I hate throwing up."

Flora nodded, rubbing her back.

"I didn't trust him," she breathed. "I got vibes. I had a hammer."

"Yes, you said. Gaslighting yourself. The word for that is denial, by the way."

"Is it? Oh. But it—" She ducked over the toilet—a sneak attack this time, but nothing came up. She breathed for a moment as her head stopped spinning. "It didn't always work." It hurt to talk—little stings and stabs in her throat, making her voice crackle. "I usually thought I was crazy, right? There was something wrong with me to even think that I should be scared of him." She swallowed back a sob-pressure that tasted sour. "But sometimes I didn't think I was crazy. And it—I was scared . . ."

Flora nodded. "It sounds like a scary position to be in."

Rex shook her head. She needed Flora to understand this. "Not of him. I wasn't scared of him. I thought—everyone worried about him. All the time. I don't know if it was because he's the youngest, or because he's a boy, or just because he needed them more. I'm a genius, right? So obviously I didn't need any parents."

She sipped water, the cool liquid soothing her throat. "I thought if I pushed . . . if it came to what was best for him or what was best for me . . ."

She laughed silently, unable to hold it back. "I didn't want to *know*. I wanted to think it, but not know."

They sat awhile in silence. Rex thought she was waiting to see if she'd throw up again. As it felt less and less likely, they were just sitting. Tear tracks dried on her cheeks. Rex didn't know when they'd started, let alone when they'd stopped.

"Do you think you want to go to bed now?" Flora's voice was a whisper.

Rex gave a tiny nod. She finished the water under Flora's watch and tried to make it easy for Flora to help her up.

They shuffled out of the bathroom more gracefully than they'd entered. Rex didn't grab at Flora's clothes or stagger sideways, which she considered a win. "I called from the car." She was close enough to Flora's ear that she didn't have to use much tone. It was easier on her throat. "Before he threw my phone out the window. Family, some friends." She took a moment to think. "I know it's not fair to blame them for missing the call. I miss more calls than I catch. But it pops into my head sometimes: I called, and nobody answered."

"Aya would answer," Flora said. "She wouldn't stop until someone helped you."

"That's the solution—build someone to pick up the phone." She waited through another breathy laugh she couldn't control. "I wish I could talk about this without drinking."

"Me too. You're doing some kind of cleanse when this is over."

Rex huffed another laugh. "They confided in me. Everyone talked to me about how worried they were about *him*. Why did they think that was okay? How dare they ask me to—why couldn't any of them fix Sam?"

As Flora helped her sit on the edge of the bed and pulled back the covers—her energy was draining so quickly, she wasn't sure how long she could hold her head up—Rex amended, "That's not fair. He needed them more than I did. And he felt so guilty."

She was pretty sure she wasn't trying to punish them. She understood. She still couldn't pick up the phone.

Rex's love was a finely-honed weapon. It was harsh and exacting. She just wished she was as stingy with it as she liked to pretend to be. Her love was won with alarming ease. And she wasn't quite sure it had ever been entirely reciprocated.

"I encouraged them to put him first. I felt so righteous about it." She swallowed. "But the further I get from it, the more I think part of me did it because I knew they would—" She waved a hand in place of words. "And it was better to be complicit than . . ."

Even now, she couldn't say it.

Flora sat next to Rex and wrapped her arms around her. "You're worth choosing. I choose you."

Rex wondered uncharitably what would make Flora take that back, knowing and hating how unfair that was. But she was too drained to do more than sit through the hug.

"I love you," Flora said.

Rex hoped she wouldn't misread her flinch. She was silent as Flora tucked her in. As Flora was leaving, she forced out, "I l-love you too." She'd done it. She'd said the words.

"I know. It'll be okay." Flora turned the light off as she left.

Rex lay in the dark, staring in the ceiling's direction. All the thoughts that had felt so sharp earlier swirled weakly on the surface of her mind, unpleasant but too dull to hurt. In the silence, her phone buzzed.

Rex worked her arm out of the blankets to check the phone and bring it to her ear. "Aya?"

"Hello, Doctor." Aya's voice was soft. "I now have satellite access to the facility at the new property, and the dinosaurs are settling in. Are you well enough for a call? Two-Toed Nancy is on the line."

The other thoughts slipped further away. "Yes. Put her through, Aya."

There was a brief silence, then the rumbly voice of the stegosaur took off. "Oh my God, Mom. Stripey won't stay out of my room."

Rex cradled the phone with both hands. "Why do you have a room? None of you need a room."

"I told him I needed this lab! It's a time-sensitive project and I had to transfer everything from home and he knows how much work I've put into this—"

"That asshole," Rex grumbled.

"I know, right?"

"Are you using the pedal-phone I made? With the headset?"

A scoff crackled through the speaker. "Duh, Mom. How else would I be talking to you? Anyway, Stripey keeps getting underfoot and then he yells about how I'm trying to crush him, but he's the one who—"

Rex laid the phone by her ear, occasionally making an acknowledging sound as her eyes drifted shut.

"Mom, are you falling asleep?" Two-Toed Nancy accused.

"What? No. Keep griping."

As the stegosaur started again, Rex broke in, "Hey, Nance?"

"Yeah?" she said, sounding irritated.

"Love you." Damn, she was on a roll.

"God, Mom, I *know*. You too. So anyway—"

Soon Rex was out.

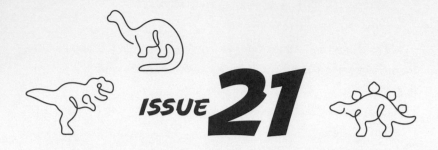

ISSUE 21

SPOTLIGHT ON LEWIS STONE: LEWIS LIKES SOMEONE

Lewis watched Flora step out of Rex's room and ease the door shut with a small click.

He spoke in a murmur. "How is she?"

"She'll be fine. But I'm making her put a twenty in the self-deprecation jar later."

Lewis let out a long breath and walked with Flora to the kitchen, still riding out the adrenaline rush of dealing with someone else's breakdown. "Where does someone get that much misplaced guilt?"

They reached the kitchen, and Flora looked over the mess. "I think sometimes it's easier to think you deserve something than it is to think bad things can happen to you whether you deserve them or not."

Lewis ran a hand down his face and tried to control the waves of hard emotion at the thought of the things Rex had said, but he didn't have enough information to know exactly what to feel.

To redirect the energy, he helped Flora gather empty bottles. Footsteps approached, and he straightened in surprise as Peter, Joey, and Grant entered the kitchen.

"Sorry, Ms. Shay," Grant said, glancing briefly at the mess. "Lieutenant Quinten needs me and Lewis for something, so Joey and Peter are taking our place for the night."

"It's related to Last Dance making contact," Peter said, addressing Lewis after a guilty glance toward Flora. "Some things will have to change. The rest of us already have orders."

Flora nodded, expression tight. "That makes sense."

Lewis glanced at her, not letting his eyes settle. He was reminded of the shock on her face when she saw the piece of brown fabric he'd taken from Rex. He'd looked it over while telling Rex about his day—he still couldn't believe that helped—and found what looked like electrical wiring worked into the cloth.

He'd considered asking about it, but Flora had snatched it off the floor, her eyes wide, and stuffed it out of sight.

Peter gave him a thin-lipped look before stepping in to help Flora. He was being oddly reticent, and Lewis thought it was because of Joey and Grant. Whatever Quinten wanted must not be good.

The ride to the base was short and silent. Lewis and Grant found Quinten in his temporary office as Becky and Jamal left, giving them grim nods on their way out.

"Come in. Sit down." The lieutenant moved through some papers as Lewis and Grant took seats in front of the desk. "So, this is a mess. Our investigation is going nowhere, and the Protectors are doing God knows what." He cursed. "One of the most notorious villains in the country waltzes past our detail to get access to a tier four superbeing who's also his sister. His fucking twin sister."

Lewis shifted. He'd been shocked by the revelation when it was reported during the Rifter interview, but when he'd walked into Rex's kitchen, it had lost priority. And what happened after that put the knowledge in a new light, leaving a sour taste in his mouth.

He knew Vivid Blue's backstory—or thought he had. "The Oversight Committee was already aware," he found himself defending. "It was known. We just didn't know it."

"And I'm making damn sure they know that wasn't on us," Quinten said as Grant eyed Lewis. "It's the committee's fault that they can't communicate, and now we're the ones who look negligent. I've already been told this isn't adequate grounds for moving her to tier five."

Lewis sat straighter. "I don't understand. She didn't invite him or aid him. It's clear he wasn't welcome . . ." He hesitated to mention Rex's panic attack. It was in the purview of Oversight to report everything, but that felt too personal.

There was also the memory of Rifter's attack.

The wipeout protocol half the squad hadn't known a thing about. Anonymous inquiries from Lewis, Peter, and two other squad members had come to nothing. The lieutenant clearly wasn't acting without support, and he'd already withheld important information from the people he didn't like. Lewis doubted he had anything to gain from arguing with Quinten.

And he didn't want to give the lieutenant another reason to antagonize Rex. After all this time under the tier four restrictions, he almost wouldn't blame her for snapping at the next little thing. He didn't think Quinten would see that as incentive to back off.

The lieutenant leaned back in his seat, face grim as he studied Lewis. "Tell me how clear this is." He turned his computer monitor around.

The screen showed a high-angle view of Rex and Last Dance—it took Lewis a moment to recognize him in civilian clothing—seated in her office. Security footage of the incident, presumably. Quinten pressed play, and their voices came through.

"*So, did you make it?*" Last Dance shifted in his seat. "*I finished your virus. You probably know that by now. It's doing well. I need to know if you made it. I kind of need it a lot.*" His chuckle sounded like quick breathing.

"*It's not here. It's at home,*" the Meister answered.

Quinten hit pause. "What did that sound like to you?"

Lewis didn't answer. He stared at the empty look on Rex's face in the paused shot.

"Last Dance is a mind reader. Did he seem dissatisfied with this exchange? Did he indicate that she might be lying or buying time?"

When Lewis didn't answer, Quinten scoffed. "Here's another question," he continued, voice lower. "Did she seem surprised? Did she ask what he was talking about?" He turned the monitor back around, breaking Lewis's staring contest with the screen. "That wasn't their first contact in years. What we just saw was a check-in. And consider that she's the one who's been locked in with that virus all this time."

"The Protectors' biggest brains are following her research," Lewis hedged.

"I watched her fiddle with some settings on a computer and create a way to seal a rift in spacetime," Quinten shot back. "We're fooling ourselves if we think we can effectively oversee anything she does." His fingers laced together on the desk. "We still don't know how that interview went viral. The techs say it was strategically uploaded to key sites. The network has that sort of thing removed regularly, but somehow this went under the radar until it was too late."

"You think the Meister did that intentionally?" Lewis asked. He hadn't known Oversight was investigating the viral video.

"The Meister or her allies. There's no question that Last Dance benefits from having his tech support in the public's good graces, especially if it gets her Oversight lifted."

Lewis thought it sounded like a weak plan, but it was an odd coincidence. He couldn't dismiss it like he wanted to.

"This is the second time you've jumped to defend her, Stone, after that fiasco with Ill Wind," Quinten continued with a frown. "It makes me wonder if there's anything you need to tell me."

Lewis blushed. "No, sir." It didn't help that there was nothing to tell.

Things were just different with Rex. Lewis was different. They *bickered*. He'd never bickered in his life, not even with his brother. He found himself bickering with her in his head. When he was in a weird situation or having a frustrating day, he'd think about what he'd say about it to Rex and what she'd snark back, until he was muttering through one side of a made-up argument and wishing she was there to appreciate his comebacks.

The other thing was, lately, Lewis had been spending an uncomfortable amount of time thinking about kissing Rex. That wasn't exactly unusual for him—he imagined kissing lots of people, from his friends to Lieutenant Quinten.

But this time it was getting . . . excessive.

He spent a lot of time picturing the buildup. He and Rex would be working in the lab, and he would find a brilliant solution to something, and she'd grab his head and kiss him, taking him too much by surprise to be sensual, but still full of passion. Or they'd be eating pizza with the others in the house, and one by one everyone else would go to bed, and they'd be bickering sleepily about a movie or pizza toppings—the scripts changed—and they'd get closer on the couch until Rex was feeding him whatever pizza he'd claimed not to like, and she'd wipe some sauce from his mouth with her thumb and he'd bend his head toward hers—

Grant spoke up, and Lewis shook himself. "There's something in that house, isn't there? That's what she said: it's at home."

Quinten nodded. "That's why I called you in. Whatever it is, we have to find it. As the two stationed in her home, this is going to fall mostly to you."

"She's had some time without eyes on," Grant said, arms folded.

"But she hasn't left the house," Quinten countered. "Unless she destroyed it, it's still on-premises. We're enforcing searches before anyone leaves or enters the Meister's properties. And in the meantime, it's your job to find whatever she made for him."

Lewis's eyes were drawn to a finger on his right hand, tapping the arm of the chair. He recalled again the cloth with inlaid wires—something Rex had dragged to the kitchen immediately after that conversation and before hyperventilating over it.

This wasn't much of a mystery.

Two easy sentences: It's a cloth hood or pocket. Flora Shay had it last.

He let himself think the scenario through. This would end the Meister. They'd seize her projects and properties. They'd put down her dinosaurs. They might still let her work in a limited capacity, but Lewis got the sense even smarter super geniuses found her thought process unpredictable, so they might not risk it.

The thought hurt. Rex was the person who didn't let him lose the most important friendship he'd ever had. She'd become one of the two people he looked forward to seeing most every day.

When had Rex stopped looking like a knobbly raptor and started looking . . . spoonable? He wanted to fold himself around her like a pita pocket. He'd taken to messing with small objects when he was in the lab so his hands wouldn't pet that fuzzy head like a baby bird.

The idea that Rex was allied with her brother didn't make sense. Sure, anyone could be swayed by family, but he'd *seen* that panic attack. Last Dance might have threatened or blackmailed her. Maybe he should ask her about it. But if she was helping her brother, could he ask her to implicate herself?

And when? She was under surveillance, and they worked in pairs. They could have a personal conversation while Becky snoozed in the back seat, but not about something that might land Rex in prison. They could swap stories on the couch after Grant went to bed, but the cameras in the house were always on. He could wait for the next time he and Peter had a shift together, but lately . . . Lewis had some suspicions about the shift schedule and his increasingly limited time with Peter. Someone—Quinten—didn't like seeing Lewis's work in Flora's appeals or Peter's name on the Meister's patents. He remembered Peter's demeanor back at the house and figured he'd come to the same conclusion.

Speaking of, Quinten was watching him again. Though when he spoke, he addressed them both. "You understand your assignment?"

"Yes, sir," Grant said with a nod. "We search the house until we find it."

"In the meantime, I'll keep pushing for tier five. I'm sure it's the other Ms. Anderson who's been blocking it." Quinten rubbed his forehead with two fingers and scowled. "Whoever thought Blue was going to be objective on this case was a damn fool. I wonder why no one questions if she's really trying to stop her baby brother, too."

Lewis was pretty sure lots of people had questioned that, from reporters to politicians, and the public had gleefully crucified them as Blue's lesser villains.

"And keep this quiet," Quinten said. "The committee may still classify her as tier four, but from now on we treat the Meister as an active threat. Nothing like this is getting past us again. I'm counting on you boys."

Lewis hated being called a boy in any context, but he matched Grant's nod and settled his cranky ass. There wasn't room here to put his feelings for Rex above everyone that Last Dance could hurt.

Lewis wasn't attached to his job. It was fun because Peter was there, but he'd quit if it asked him to do something he thought was wrong. Like sell out a good person.

But he wasn't going to be the person who let Last Dance unleash a mind-altering virus because he sat on information he could have shared.

It took effort to keep the roll of nausea from affecting his expression.

He'd keep his mouth shut unless he found something more substantial. He could give her that. He'd wait to ruin Rex's life until he had no choice.

ISSUE 22

DINOSAURS AT NAPTIME

Rex was never drinking again. She knew the soreness and exhaustion were partly souvenirs of her panic attack—but the hangover. Dear God, the hangover.

Flora pushed a mug of coffee into her hand.

"Thanks," Rex mumbled. Her throat still hurt from barfing and fighting to breathe, leaving her voice somehow scratchy and slurred at the same time. She took a tiny sip, winced, and set the rest aside. "How deep is the shit?" It was tolerable if she whispered.

"I don't know." Flora settled beside her on the couch. They were in Rex's apartment instead of any of the communal spaces. Something told Rex the playing-house part of their Oversight was over.

"Your surveillance is reorganizing," Flora continued, turning her mug in her hands. "I've been pestering Oversight's legal team, but it seems they haven't worked out everything between Quinten and the committee. I reminded them that they're obligated to keep us in the loop, but it's still a mess. The Protectors are trying to catch up to Last Dance, last I heard."

Aya, hovering at Rex's armrest, added, "Social media is inundated with pictures of Vivid Blue flying over the city."

Rex picked up her coffee and took another sip.

"Rex, I'm sorry," Flora said.

Rex shook her head. "Not your fault."

"He used his real name. If I had—"

"Not your fault." Rex swallowed. "I'm sorry Aya called you back."

"If you need me, I'm going to be here. I'll repeat it until you believe me."

"I don't want to mess up your relationship. I'd feel like shit."

Flora absently smoothed her skirt. "That's actually been a bit rocky, lately."

Rex raised her head too fast and pursed her lips against the accompanying nausea. "Since when?"

Flora shrugged, not meeting Rex's eyes. "A while now, I guess. I didn't want to bother you, with everything that's going on. She thinks I'm not as invested as she is, and . . ." Flora shrugged and sipped from her mug, hiding her eyes in a move Rex recognized as half calculated and half habit.

"That's bullshit!" She winced at the pain in her throat and dropped back to a whisper. "Just because you're not as demonstrative as she is doesn't mean—" She remembered the obvious. "Your date last night. I'm—"

"One interrupted date isn't about to define our relationship. This isn't on you."

Rex stood and aggressively ignored the queasiness. "I'm gonna hack her."

"Don't hack her. Rex, sit down." A smile twitched at Flora's cheek. "We're talking. It might be okay."

"Fine, but I'm hacking her if she doesn't listen," Rex muttered, falling back onto the couch. She pulled her to-do list from her pocket, remembered she didn't have a pen, and made a mental note to put Aya on standby.

Flora shifted and drew out from somewhere—Rex needed to find out where Flora kept her pockets—the brown hood from last night.

Rex let out a long breath. Though it looked similar to her brother's dark red hood, the wiring was messily assembled and stuck through the top in a few places. She'd already been tipsy when she put it together. "I made that last night." God, she was stupid. "Sorry, I shouldn't have made you think—"

Flora raised a hand. "Just tell me what it does?"

"It's based on the first one. Last night I was—" She swallowed and dropped the sentence. "I've been testing Sam's hood all month for its effects on brain waves. I designed this hood to block mine."

Flora's posture went rigid. There was a small beat of silence. "Rex. You're saying this would keep Last Dance from reading your mind?"

Some of the loose thoughts that had been flopping through Rex's hungover brain clicked together. "I—yes. I guess that's what I'm saying."

Flora sat forward. "You can neutralize Last Dance's powers."

It was on the tip of Rex's tongue to protest. That was what she'd already tried to do—neutralize Sam's powers. But unless every person in the world wore one, the hood in Flora's hands wouldn't meet that goal. She'd always come at the problem with the intention of helping Sam—never of fighting him. Even as she'd made it, she'd only thought about hiding her thoughts.

"You've done it. Rex, we're golden." Flora scooted forward. "You bring this to them, and you're a hero."

"Stop. Let me think." Rex closed her eyes against the outward stimuli. She pictured Vivid Blue getting the jump on Last Dance, keeping her thoughts hidden long enough to finally take their brother in. It felt like relief, and it felt like betrayal.

Rex filled her lungs, steadying herself. Maybe she was still raw from last night, but certain things felt clearer in her head now. She saw her fear and guilt piling on either side of the issue. Fear of Oversight and her sister's guilt trips. Her responsibility for her siblings' powers. Visceral fear of what her brother could do, including that small fear of what he might do if she refused to help, as disgusted with herself as that made her.

Which part of her bullshit inner conflict was weighing in on behalf of morality? Compassion? Love? Bravery? How could she know she'd made a right choice if every choice meant giving in to one set of guilts and fears or another? How could she ever trust that guilt and fear weren't the real forces behind that choice?

"I think—" Rex faltered and almost gave up. *Be honest,* she rebuked herself. She did trust Flora—she should act like it.

"I think after what happened, I went away for a while." She ran out of breath quickly. The words were making her heart pound with a fear so irrational she wanted to beat it up. But Flora waited patiently, settling back into her seat, so Rex took her time. "I went so far that when I came back halfway, I thought I'd come back all the way." Another pause for breath. "I want to actually come back all the way. But I don't know how."

Flora nodded, leaving time for Rex to continue. Then she asked, "Come back to what?"

Rex blinked. "I—to me? To who I was before."

Before she was scared and angry, then numb and careless, then just careless. Before she was the Meister of Decimen City.

Flora nodded again. "When did you go away? You were twenty? Twenty-one?"

Rex wasn't sure what Flora was getting at. "Something like that."

"So, you want to go back to who you were? Don't you think you'd be different by now whether you went away for a while or not?"

Rex hadn't thought of that. But now that she did, the difference between twenty and twenty-seven felt enormous. She couldn't imagine still being that person.

"So," Flora continued, "maybe it's less a matter of how to come back and more a matter of how to move forward. Not so much getting back who you were as figuring out who you are."

Rex took a deep breath and let it out slowly. "Did it hurt?"

Flora's brow creased. "What—"

"When you fell from heaven."

Flora huffed and ducked her head, failing to hide a blush.

Rex grinned. "I don't know how to do that either."

"You're a scientist," Flora said, crossing her legs. "Form a hypothesis and experiment. When you fail, incorporate the data and form a new hypothesis."

Tears pricked Rex's eyes, but she was so cried out from last night that she was confident none would fall. "I need to make a decision. I don't want to just react to things anymore." Her eyes dropped to the hood in Flora's hands.

Flora followed her gaze. "Don't put it on this. Everyone has their blind spots. I don't think it's fair to measure yourself by the situation with Last Dance."

Rex smiled at the pardon. But whether this counted as her experiment or not, some action needed to be taken.

"I'll explain it to Viv." It was so easy to trust Vivian. As hard as it was to talk to her, trust came easily. "I'm supposed to see the Protectors today. I'm guessing they won't be taking that break, but I should check in anyway. Find out where I stand."

The thought of leaving her couch, let alone her house, made Rex's whole body sag in misery, but she was not in a position to take a sick day.

Flora nodded, looking relieved. She raised the hood and spoke more gently. "You'll need to explain this to Lewis too. He saw it last night."

Rex cringed. She had been trying so hard not to think about Lewis.

The shame came in waves. Talking to Flora had pushed them back, but the wave that crashed down as she thought of the man who'd shoved bottles into her hands last night made up for the reprieve. Was it even shame? At least shame felt a little dignified. This was pure humiliation. Dignity didn't enter the picture.

But who was she kidding; since when did she have dignity?

"Let's do it?" Flora asked.

"Let's do it."

The relative shit-depth made itself known as Rex's surveillance met her at the door, gave official notice that a search would be carried out in her absence, and conducted a pat down search of them both. Flora handed over the brown hood with graceful disinterest to keep their hostility minimal as they whisked it away for testing.

They were taken to the team's base of operations to meet with Lieutenant Quinten. By the Lord's infinite mercy, Rex didn't run into Lewis on the way.

Her head pounded. She tried to focus through it as Quinten explained a probationary amendment being added to her Oversight conditions. Then he said, "Your ongoing projects will be frozen until these conditions are lifted," and he had her full attention.

"On what grounds?" Flora demanded.

Quinten clicked a computer key with a flourish, and Sam's voice came from the speaker. *"I finished your virus. You probably know that by now."*

Rex's throat closed up.

Flora spoke on the recording's tail. "Ms. Anderson has provided no aid—"

"Ms. Anderson hasn't been candid about her past," Quinten interrupted. "Information has come to light that was not considered when her Oversight conditions were set."

"A familial connection is not—"

"—is not the grounds I'm citing," he interrupted again. "I'm referring to the fact that Ms. Anderson has provided aid to the villain Last Dance before. Aid which remains relevant, considering he finished *your* virus, did he not say?"

Rex's heart dropped into her stomach, the ghost of its beat filling her ears.

She should have known this would be used against her. It was a mind trip to hear Quinten reference it, audibly, in words. With how quick everyone was to forget, sometimes it felt like the whole thing had only happened in her head. She almost missed Flora's rejoinder, voice rising at the end as Quinten tried to speak over her.

"Ms. Anderson's aid was given under duress. She bears no legal responsibility."

"He also came to Ms. Anderson quite peacefully, informed her of the status of her virus, and asked for an update on"—he lifted his hands, his most emotional display so far—"something she hasn't bothered to clarify. You're free to contest the new measures, but they'll be upheld."

"Withholding mental stimulation from a super genius is cruel and unusual according to the standards set in the Oversight Contingencies," Flora said, her face stone.

"You're free to contest the new measures," Quinten repeated, unaffected.

Rex finally gathered enough of her mind together to say, "I have a lot of time-sensitive experiments running. There are also projects involving live cultures and"—she swallowed—"other lives." She thought of the dinosaurs and broke out in a cold sweat.

"Our scientists are already deciding which of your projects can be continued by your techs or one of our teams. Those will be experiments with living subjects or a potential loss of resources over a certain value threshold."

Rex let the rushing fill her ears again as Flora dredged through the details, Quinten's voice giving her a spike of nausea every time he responded, until Flora said something that sounded final and waved Rex to stand.

They went straight to Peak Street, Flora peeling off with a clench-jawed vow to have a challenge filed with Oversight within the hour.

Barred from both the virus and her own work, there wasn't much Rex could do. The upside was she got an excuse to sit still in the relative darkness of the nursery to ride out her hangover. There was a paranoia twisting in her gut that Quinten's word wouldn't be followed, and only her physical presence could ensure the hatchlings' safety.

The tyrannosaur babies snuggled close to her, napping or nuzzling into her hands until she pet their heads. She found herself breathing easier, to the rhythm of their rumbles and wheezy snores.

She was grateful the dinosaurs had gotten out. Not that she had any illusions about Oversight's willingness to invade the new property, but at least it wouldn't be at the whim of a hostile lieutenant in a locked-in lab.

She rubbed absently under Mint Julep's chin. Giving in at last to the anxieties nibbling at the edges of her mind, her thoughts turned to Lewis.

What she'd told Flora was true; she wanted to ask Lewis out. Being around him made it feel simple. She didn't feel like a puzzle piece trying to fit or a half looking to make a whole. She just felt like a person who wanted to reach out to another person.

She liked his confused sneers and choked laughs when something caught him off guard. She liked telling him about her projects, even if he just made that frustrated expression that meant he didn't understand a word she was saying. She liked that he was strong but not in-your-face about it, muscles hidden by a pillowing layer of fat, and she wanted permission to press right up against him the next time they both couldn't sleep. White Russian whimpered in his sleep, and Rex rubbed his tummy until he shushed.

Or did she want that? Rex felt a pulse of reluctance. There was the usual anxiety over probable rejection. Last night couldn't have helped his opinion of her, and she wasn't sure how he thought of her on a good day. But it was more than that. It was the thought of what would happen if he said yes.

Rex always liked the beginning of a relationship best. It was when everything was exciting and new, of course. But it was also when she got to be her most honest. There was some faking from the start, the kind she hadn't recognized as fake because she'd seen it as part of the game: giving the right compliments, reacting the right way, making implications and allusions that she'd . . . what, thought everyone else was faking too? Geez, how had she not realized she was ace?

If the guy was serious—and Rex couldn't do casual; casual didn't even compute—he didn't mind taking it slow. It was classy. It might be his preference. Then later, when she started fearing he'd leave if she didn't put out, she'd drop enough hints to make sure first contact happened on her terms, get drunk enough to giggle the cute way instead of the crazy way, and start faking it in earnest.

When she thought it out in steps like that, it sounded kind of messed up. The thought of having that with Lewis made her stomach twist. With Lewis, she wanted something honest. She wanted something real.

Rex thought she'd accepted that real and honest weren't options for her. She'd justified it in lots of ways. Relationships took work, and everyone made sacrifices. Everyone told lies to make their partner comfortable. Everyone faked something about themselves. And it was easier than trying to make someone understand that she liked them, just not in that way. No, that wouldn't change with time. No, she didn't find them unattractive. No, she wasn't attracted to someone else.

She'd come to think asking anyone to accept her like that meant asking them to accept less than they deserved.

The part of Rex Flora had been steadily conditioning like a pet dog automatically asked what Rex thought *she* deserved. Still, no amount of self-acceptance was going to make Lewis, or anyone else, take a chance on something more complicated than what they might have imagined for themselves.

"Rex?"

Lewis's voice made Rex jolt, to the displeased squawks of the hatchlings, and she grabbed them before they could roll off her lap. "Jesus!"

Lewis did that discomfited mouth-twist.

"Um." Rex resettled the babies on a fluffy dog bed and stood too fast, gut rolling.

Lewis spoke first. "How are you doing?"

That harsh tone. Rex was a little reassured to know he was feeling uncertain too. Her face burned. She wanted to pull at her collar like a cartoon character. "Yeah." Shit, that hadn't been a yes-or-no question. "I'm fine."

"It's shift change. Thought I'd let you know."

She glanced through the window to see Trisha taking Joey and Jamal's place. Now that Lewis had delivered his message, he made some awkward moves toward the nursery exit.

Rex followed him out, took a breath, and pushed aside the wish for God to strike her down. "So, that's what I made last night." She gestured toward the Oversight scientists working on the other side of the lab. "It's a hood to block brain waves." It wasn't a lie, but it felt like one. She was off to a great start.

Rex gathered herself, making sure her voice was low enough that Trisha wouldn't hear. "Sorry I put you in that position last night." That was good— she'd brought it up first. She felt a bit more in control.

"It's fine." Lewis shrugged, eyes dragging away from the hood.

She tried to think of what she'd want to hear in his place. "You did a good job. It helped."

Some of the tension left his shoulders. "I just followed Aya's instructions. I'm glad it helped you."

Rex nodded. She should probably look Lewis in the eye. "I meant what I said, by the way." As his brow creased, she added, "About the curfew thing. You don't have to keep that up."

"You don't have to—" Lewis chewed his lip. "Actually, I probably couldn't hold to it, either way. Surveillance is getting kicked up. Not to the next tier," he added quickly. "But that might not be a promise I can keep anymore."

Rex wasn't sure why that hurt to hear. She didn't want him to do curfew anymore—what difference did it make if it wasn't up to them?

Lewis looked down, lips thinning in a way that suggested there was more on his mind, but she couldn't stand to think about what that might be. If he was disgusted, well, what else could she expect? Her heart gave a warning lurch, and she knew she had to change the subject if she didn't want to break down on him a second time.

"I need a ride to where the Protectors are staying," she said. "They're meeting to make a new plan."

Lewis gave himself a light shake. "Right." He waved Trisha over.

Rex checked her phone, feeling resignation instead of the expected reluctance. She'd had all day to weigh her options. It was time to face the Protectors.

DINOSAURS GONE WILD

Manta Man's property on the outskirts of town was a modern, boxy little villa—a surprise, since he struck Rex as a French château or derelict monastery kind of guy. A butler led them into an open space with a kitchen and sitting area where the Protectors were lounging around with boxes of pizza open on a coffee table.

Rex wondered why the Lightning wasn't there—not that she was complaining. Then again, 'Ning had been helping the Protectors a lot lately, and she probably had a real job she had to show up for at some point. Secret identities introduced a heck of a work-life balance issue.

"You're here," Viv said.

The talking died, and Rex froze under the frosty gaze of an entire superhero team. Her back tensed with an impulse to surrender until she remembered she wasn't fighting any of them this time. Instead, she glanced between glares of varying levels of hostility—or implied hostility, in the case of Undertaker's shadowed hood—and reached a conclusion. "I guess you all saw the security footage."

"Yup," said the Jester as he dropped his feet on a coffee table. "Heard that he finished *your virus* pretty clearly. What could that have meant?"

Rex was clenched up so tight, her headache gave an extra throb.

Manta Man laid it out. "You made the virus."

Ouch, right in the guilt complex.

Rex gathered herself for her defense, but Viv jumped in first. "We've been over this. She wasn't at fault."

Rex released a breath as her own words died.

Viv looked pointedly away from her team to Rex and said, "Grab some pizza. We were about to start."

The others didn't protest, but the gazes that slid away from her were as telling as the ones that stayed fixed. Having every reason to follow Viv's lead, Rex resisted the urge to draw her shoulders up and crossed behind the couches toward the kitchen-y space in the back. "No, thanks. I don't like cheese."

The shuffle of Pixie turning around on a couch caught Rex's attention, and she stopped short at the hero's look of distress. "That's so sad! Cheese is one of the best things in life."

Don Conjure offered, "There are many kinds of cheese. Perhaps you merely have not found the variety to suit your taste."

"Sounds like you're scared of it," Undertaker said as Cat Man stretched languidly across her to spear a piece of pepperoni on his claw.

"You should try it again," Manta Man said. "Cheese improves with experience."

"In my time, all who refused to share cheese with their king were burned as witches," King George announced.

The Jester sneered as he piled pizza on his plate. "She's just looking for attention. No one doesn't like cheese."

"I can't imagine not liking cheese," Pixie said mournfully. "You should see a doctor."

"I didn't mean to start a conversation about it," Rex said.

"What did you expect after tossing out that information?" Viv asked, arms crossed.

"I honestly expected you to keep eating your pizza while I asked to get something else from the fridge."

The Jester leaned toward Pixie and muttered, "She probably thinks she's better than us because she doesn't eat cheese."

This was going well so far. At Manta Man's nod, Rex continued to the kitchen, Lewis on her heels. As she opened the fridge, he looked back with a raised brow. "They have strong opinions about something that has absolutely nothing to do with them."

Rex had to blink a few times, but if this was the subject he was going with after that entrance, she'd let it happen. "Go easy—I think I broke their worldview."

She'd expected—actually, she'd forgotten that the Protectors would have the same information that Lieutenant Quinten had; she wasn't at her best today. But if she'd thought of it, she would have expected more accusation. It seemed to be Viv's default. The fact that Viv was capable of defending her made her equally grateful and queasy.

We all have blind spots, Flora had said. Why did Rex always feel like Viv didn't have any?

She grabbed a cardboard container from the fridge. "Look at that—leftover Chinese. A worthy alternative."

Lewis's face went through several impressive contortions as he fought off a smile, buoying Rex with a wave of smug affection. "To be clear, I love cheese," he said as he accepted a carton. "But I've had pizza three days this week."

Trisha had settled on a couch and dug into the pizza like she hadn't eaten in weeks. As Rex and Lewis sat next to her, Rex caught Viv's eye. "Have you tested the factory workers yet?"

Viv blinked. "We've barely started tracking them down."

"Let me know."

Viv pursed her lips, looked away from Rex, and prompted Cat Man with a nod.

"I hunted all night. Meow." Cat Man's elbows rested over the back of the couch, the claws on his limp hands the only visible sign of his powers. "So many smells and skittering animals in this city. Meow."

Rex exchanged a quick glance with Lewis, catching his confused browtwist, and put the entirety of her self-control to the task of not laughing.

"Did you find a trail?" Viv asked.

Cat Man grinned, showing fangs. "Meow!"

The Protectors murmured happily, so Rex took that as an affirmative.

Cat Man leaned against Undertaker, who gave an irritated huff. He leaned more insistently. "Last Dance smells like you, Blue. But I lost his trail when he got in a car. Meow." His nose wrinkled. "So, I sniffed around Rifter's range from the Peak Street labs. And guess what I found? The warehouse. Meow meow. Meow-meow meow."

Laughter bubbled up against Rex's lips. Lewis elbowed her, and she shot him a glare.

"Rifter's warehouse?" Pixie popped up in her seat. "I thought we gave up on that lead."

"Meow. It was cleaned out." Cat Man pressed against Undertaker until his head rested on her shoulder. She growled and finally shoved him off, a startled "*Rowr!*" accompanying his scramble upright.

"They must have cleared it when Rifter was caught," Viv said.

"There were still scents, though. Want to know who?" Cat Man stretched away from Undertaker to snatch at King George's scepter.

"No one paws at the royal scepter, you fiendish feline," King George admonished, holding the scepter out of reach.

Cat Man braced a hand on his shoulder to reach across him. "I want it more because you don't want me to have it."

"No one climbs on the royal lap!"

Rex jabbed her cheek with a forkful of noodles. She corrected her aim and silently apologized to Don Conjure since Cat Man had just taken his place as her favorite Protector.

"Whose scents did you find?" Viv asked with the tonal equivalent of a finger snap.

Cat Man's grin grew, one hand still clasping King George's shoulder. He raised five clawed fingers. "Last Dance." He put down the first finger. "Ill Wind."

Pixie clenched her fists.

"Drake the Dragon Man."

Don Conjure's face grew stormy. Drake had attacked his magic club, right? Something about their fathers or ownership of a relic or something.

"Stinger."

Rex didn't recognize that one, but Undertaker twitched.

"Mindbender."

So, he *was* a villain. And probably the one who revamped her virus and hacked Oversight's security. Rex would need to look into his history. If he'd done any virus work before, she needed to know his process.

Cat Man sprawled back in his seat, somehow managing to touch both Undertaker and King George without reaching. "And a bunch I don't know. Meow-meow meow."

"Last Dance's minions. Perhaps more villains our feline friend has not encountered," Don Conjure said thoughtfully.

"He's brought many allies," Manta Man growled.

Rex's eyes fell to her food. That was at least four supervillains in Decimen City.

She winced when she realized she'd left Sam out of her count. Five supervillains.

"We should be sure they left nothing else." Vivid Blue looked to Don Conjure. "Don?"

With a flourish, Don Conjure magicked up a laser pointer and handed it over. Viv tossed it to Pixie. "Pixie, go with Cat Man to the warehouse. Maybe you can figure out where they went from there."

"You can count on us! Let's go, Cat Man." Pixie traced a path with the laser pointer until Cat Man tumbled over the back of the couch and chased it out the door.

"I know what this is, but it's still fun," came from the entryway.

Pixie's response faded with their footsteps. "I think it's fun too!"

A brief silence punctuated their exit. Then Viv turned to Don Conjure. "You should follow and check for aura trails. But first, what did your precognition find?"

"Wait." The Jester fixed Rex with a glare made sharper by his face paint. "Before we get into speculation, let's hear the Meister's take on twin bro's visit. Being the lucky visit-ee, and all."

Viv seemed to consider, then nodded. "Go on, T."

Rex took a few breaths, carefully measured, and saw Lewis's hand move toward her knee only to be snatched back. The warmth she felt for the gesture was soured by the reminder that he'd seen her at her worst.

Her voice stayed remarkably steady as she described the encounter. She kept it short, highlighting the things she figured Viv in her hero capacity would need to know. Halfway through, an important part—the most important part, damn it—came back to her. "He said the virus was doing well."

As the other Protectors shared confused glances, Viv said, "He's satisfied with its alterations."

Rex shook her head, heart pounding like a bruise in her chest. "Ill Wind didn't attack the lab with Rifter."

King George banged the end of his scepter on the floor. "You waste our time with such repetition."

"You do keep harping on that," the Jester drawled.

"Because it doesn't make sense," Rex pressed. "He's got a whole team— where were any of them? Only the local guy, Rifter, and the goons were in Decimen two days after 'Ning stopped them from infecting the water."

Viv raised a hand to halt the Jester's response. "What's your point, T?"

Rex knew her heart was still pounding, but she couldn't feel it. "I explained before that the virus stays dormant in the brain unless triggered. He said the virus was doing well—"

Rex saw Manta Man's face slacken in dawning dread. Don Conjure's brow jumped, and he stroked his mustache with a rumbly, "Oh, dear."

Viv seemed to see what Rex was getting at all at once. She surged forward in her seat, her eyes pinning Rex to the sofa. "How likely do you think this is?" Without waiting for an answer, she turned to Don Conjure. "Don, get in touch with the committee. Tell them we need reported activity for Ill

Wind, Drake, Stinger, and Mindbender for the last several months. Make sure they know to treat the virus as an active threat. We'll give them more information when we can."

Don nodded and left the room, making a rotary phone appear in his hands with a flourish.

"Hey, back up and explain," the Jester demanded, on his feet.

"Indeed! I command it," King George chimed in.

Lewis was leaning forward, face darkening as he caught on. "You're saying the virus is out already?"

"I can't be sure," Rex said weakly, trying to find words to sidestep her internal logic; it was what she would do in Sam's shoes.

"Any day now," Undertaker growled, shadowed face turning toward Rex as she stroked her sickle. "Explain."

Rex looked to Viv and felt that old mix of guilt and relief when her sister retook the floor.

"Last Dance had an ally dispense the virus here in Decimen City, possibly before he was even in town," Viv said. "It stands to reason he could have had allies do the same elsewhere who weren't caught. Thousands could be infected already."

Curses came from various corners of the room. The Jester sat heavily.

"What does he mean that it's doing well?" Manta Man asked quietly. "With no symptoms, how would he track such a thing?"

Viv looked to Rex.

The others followed her gaze, and Rex mindfully loosened her grip on her carton of Chinese food. Manta Man would probably make her pay for the cleaning if it broke. She turned the question over in her head, and realized, "It's dormant in the brain."

"Which may have a passive effect," Manta Man finished thoughtfully. "One he picks up."

"He's reading the virus's mind?" the Jester asked with an impatient edge.

"He's reading the infected person's mind," Rex corrected. "The virus might alter some quality in their brain waves that acts as a signal."

"Yet no one has noticed anything," Undertaker said. "So, their thoughts aren't affected?"

"We shouldn't have sent Pixie away," the Jester grumbled.

"Pixie hasn't been studying this thing for weeks. I have," Rex said.

"Then what are we looking at, oh expert?" he snapped. "How is he going to trigger his brain disease, and what for? Will he make a ransom demand?"

"I don't know how, and—"

"Then what good are you?"

"And it won't be for ransom; he'll activate it to stop hearing their thoughts. We've been over this," Rex rushed out, voice rising. A thought of the maroon hood entered her head. If the hood and the virus led to the same end, why did he need both? Redundancy?

What if he only planned to trigger the virus if Rex didn't give him the hood? That was something for Flora's pros and cons list.

"The how and why are not our concern," Viv said, regaining control. "Our job is to stop him." Don Conjure reentered the room, and Viv turned to exchange a series of brow twitches and mouth twists with him before moving on. "T, did he say anything else important?"

"To what did he refer when he asked if you built it?" Don Conjure added.

Rex was hyperaware of Lewis beside her. He hadn't moved, exactly, but had he gotten more still?

She pushed him from her mind. "Probably the thing that blocked Rifter's rifts." It was the only thing she'd built lately that Sam might know of. "He probably thought the same thing might block his powers."

Viv watched Rex with a frown. Rex couldn't tell what she was thinking. She went back over her argument with Viv when she'd hinted about being able to help Sam, but she didn't think she'd said anything to expose the lie.

Beside her, Lewis didn't move a muscle. Neither did Rex. She didn't have to look at him to know he didn't believe her.

"But last night, it got me thinking." She looked straight at Vivian, knowing this was half shameless redirection but still nervous to bring it up. "I went back through my notes on the virus. I made a hood that can block brain waves." She saw Viv's face shift in understanding but decided to say it clearly. "It could hide someone's thoughts from Last Dance."

Several of the Protectors shifted in their seats, sharing looks that were refreshingly positive. The Jester's hat jingled as he raised his head. "Well, there's a game changer."

"You'd make that?" Viv asked, and Rex heard more in the question than she would have coming from anyone else.

"I'd have a condition." She was prepared for the narrowed eyes and thinned lips from the other Protectors. The approval was fun while it lasted. "Only you wear it." She watched Viv's three-toned blue eyes. "I'll only make it for you."

"In my time, such presumption," King George began, but Viv cut him off with a raised hand.

"Thank you, T." It was the softest tone Rex had heard from her in a while. "I'll make sure Oversight honors your terms."

Rex nodded, hardly believing how easy that had been. "I'll need some brain scans to attune it to your patterns. The prototype only matches mine."

Viv nodded.

"Even a tool like that is worthless if we can't find him," Undertaker said into the quiet, "We still don't know how to draw him out."

Rex's brow lifted. "Of course, you do." She glanced at the Protectors' blank faces. Had they not thought of this? "His goon said I was off limits before Ill Wind attacked. And Sam said he'd try again later." The shiver at speaking the words surprised her, though it shouldn't have. "He wants to see me."

The Jester guffawed. "You think we'd let *you* play double agent? Do you think we're stupid?"

"Sometimes."

Lewis elbowed her, and Rex made an affronted noise but reeled herself in.

"No. While it's the most obvious next step, I don't expect you to trust me enough for that. Oversight would pitch a fit, anyway." She crossed her arms and recognized the defensive body language too late. Uncrossing them would make it more obvious, so she doubled down and tightened her arms until she was thoroughly self-soothed. "But I'd still make good bait."

The guilt was setting in. Rex clenched her hands on her arms to drive away the memory of the bags under Sam's eyes. But her virus was in play, and she couldn't just leave it alone. Viv would be the one with the hood. Viv cared about him as much as Rex did. It was the softest betrayal she could think of.

"Whether we trust you or not is irrelevant," Viv said. "You're a civilian."

"It seems like I'm only a civilian when it's least convenient to me."

Don Conjure boomed, "We would hardly be heroes if we endangered those we are sworn to protect. Worry not, Meister. We shall find another way."

Rex's jaw clenched. Her entire lab was shut down, and now this. "We should make a plan for Mindbender, then."

Some of the Protectors blinked. "Mindbender?" Undertaker repeated.

"We'll deal with Sam's allies as well. You don't have to worry about that," Viv said.

"Shouldn't the person who most likely engineered the virus be our top priority?" Not to mention the one who hacked her lab. With Oversight's wipeout protocol, she had no way to know how far he'd gotten.

"Pretty sure your brother should be our top priority," the Jester said, casting her a side-eye. "Can't say I'm surprised you're trying to—"

"Fine. Never mind." Rex ground her teeth. "What about the virus? I could be working on a cure. If you talked to Quinten—"

"Oversight's people will handle that," Viv said.

Rex threw tact to the wind as her frustration spiked. "I literally made the thing!"

"Exactly. You're on thin ice, T. I think it's best you stay away from this right now." Viv turned away. "What did your precognition reveal, Don?"

Rex sank back in the couch and fumed as Don Conjure launched into his latest visions of the future. "—then the stage costumes caught fire, though I believe that to be a symbolic reflection of my innermost hopes and fears."

In her pocket, Rex's phone buzzed. Lewis was sitting close enough to feel it, too, and he gave her a curious look as she checked it.

Aya: I believe it is best you see this before learning of it in some other fashion.

Now what?

Rex clenched her jaw and opened the link, making sure the volume was off. She caught a glimpse of a dinosaur tail swishing across a table to scatter cups and bottles, but something the Jester was saying snagged her attention.

"Quinten thinks the dino party videos are part of the conspiracy around the, um, public response to the Meister's interview last month. Gotta say, I'm not seeing the connection."

Dino party videos?

Shit.

"Whoa." Lewis's voice drew Rex's attention back to the video playing on her phone. "Christ, your dinosaurs are hammered."

"Those little shits!" Rex hissed, hands clenching on the phone as a dimetrodon stumbled across the screen and crashed to the jungle floor. She abandoned subtlety and turned up the volume as dinosaur voices cackled and crowed.

The other Protectors turned toward her, but Rex was focused on the video, which she saw was titled, *GOTTA JURRASSIC PARK nOW LOL!!!* Damien staggered into the frame and dipped his head into a kiddie pool full of something brown and frothy—the hell?—as the others chanted, "Chug! Chug! Chug!" She scrolled through suggested videos with mounting horror.

Dinoland INagurral Parkwarming Party part 2!

LOLOLO TRICERIOTOPSS RINGTOSS FAIL

pARKWARMING PARTY AYYYY part 3

Rex hit the first speed dial, brought her phone to her ear, and spoke the instant the connection was made. "How the hell did they get booze?"

"Doctor, I request leniency," Aya answered.

"Fuck, no."

Don Conjure spoke placatingly from his armchair. "It is their first time living away from home. Some rebellion, albeit self-destructive—"

"They don't get to rebel—I'm under Oversight!" She put Aya on speaker, moved the video to the corner of the screen, and hunted through the evidence of her dinosaurs' overnight internet stardom. "When did this happen? I talked to Two-Toed Nancy last night, and she was definitely not drunk."

"You may notice Two-Toed Nancy does not appear until the third video," Aya said. "I believe your conversation raised her spirits enough to join in the festivities."

"Oh, God, they've made *memes* already."

"Doctor, I must apologize for my part in this development."

Rex took Aya off speaker and strode away from the sitting area, phone to her ear. "Come again?"

"I believe my satellite-self helped Jasper and Sally upload the videos." For an AI, she almost sounded rushed. "In my defense, due to hardware limitations, the version of myself downloaded to the compound has a reduced decision-making capacity. It was not until my most recent data consolidation that my primary program became aware of last night's events."

"Why didn't your smarter self take them down?"

Aya hesitated. "Doctor, I am not certain the videos should be removed. Though I likely would not have chosen to upload such content at my full capacity, reactions are overwhelmingly positive."

"It's a dinosaur rager. Of course, the internet likes it." Rex ran a hand down her face. "The point of sending them out there was to keep them safe, not make them popular."

"On the contrary, I theorize such exposure may contribute to that goal." Before Rex could demand an explanation, Aya continued, "Consider Ms. Shay's reasoning for your talk show appearance. Consider Mayor Vicker's reluctance to enforce Oversight in light of local sentiment. A positive public image makes it more difficult for entities like Oversight to levy harsh rulings without risking backlash. The, if you'll excuse the term, humanity displayed by the dinosaurs in these videos bolsters protection against unilateral rulings that would do them harm."

Rex leaned against the wall in the hallway, trying to ease her pounding head. She took the phone away from her ear again and scrolled to another video, in which tipsy dinosaurs were doing some kind of linedance challenge. "How does this count as a positive public image?"

"According to my analysis, commenters find the dinosaurs cute, funny, and relatable. They have been featured in several public interest news segments, as well."

Rex still wasn't sure about this. "You'll keep an eye on it?"

"I have already adjusted my satellite-self to manage the dinosaurs' future online presence more carefully. Shall I respond to the videos with your social media accounts?"

"I have social media accounts?"

"Yes, Doctor. It is the most expedient way for me to monitor the 'More to the Story' discourse."

That gave Rex pause. "That's still happening?"

"The hashtag and associated dialogue are still quite popular. I have kept your name out of the spotlight if that is your concern."

There was something here that Rex was missing. But as far as priorities went, this seemed pretty far down the list. "Just be careful. Remember our internet safety talk."

"Of course, Doctor."

"Check sources, don't give out personal information, don't believe anything claiming politicians are lizard people—"

"I will not make that mistake again."

"Good." Rex caught the rising voices of the Protectors in the other room. "I should get back in there. Make sure the dinosaurs know I'm not letting this slide."

"I will. Good luck, Doctor."

She hung up, took a moment to collect herself, and headed back. She jumped at the entrance to the sitting area, where Lewis, the creeper, was leaning in the doorway with a crease in his brow.

Not a creeper—her surveillance. She swallowed a lump in her throat at the reminder, forced her shoulders down, and returned to the Protectors without meeting his eyes.

ISSUE 24

DINOSAURS AT WORK

The workers from the factory that Sam had commandeered tested positive for the virus. Rex found herself dragged into a late-night interrogation about how she'd known they'd been infected, where she tiredly explained the concept of a test run and tried to wheedle out details about the virus's effects.

She got the impression that they'd noticed no effects at all, which made sense if he'd already infected portions of the population without anyone catching on. Though it did beg the question: why would he test the virus in controlled conditions and never bother to trigger it?

She managed to swing one more lab session before the Oversight scientists received clear instructions about her being shut out, in which she directed research toward the theory that Sam could pick up a change in an infected person's brain waves and thus track the virus's whereabouts. Plenty of the factory workers had volunteered brain scans, but Rex was no longer involved.

Between that gut-punch development and Sam's surprise visit, Oversight was spooked enough to keep Rex as locked down as the law would allow. All told, Rex counted herself lucky they let her visit the dinosaurs today.

She glanced up at Pixie, a pink blur flying over the treetops. The Protectors had taken to stalking her, after Last Dance's promise to make contact again. Pixie had volunteered for today as soon as she'd heard where they were going.

"They're dangling you out here like bait," Flora muttered, tapping a little too forcefully on her tablet as they walked.

Rex pulled at the tight neck of her fire suit—a latex-like layer she'd taken to wearing under her clothes since Sam had walked unchallenged into Peak Street.

It wasn't the best defense, but she wasn't allowed to use the mecha, and her surveillance team was permitting this alternative for the innocent reason that she'd failed to tell them what it was.

"They shot down that idea, actually," she finally responded. She was hyperaware of Jamal and Peter at her back, looking around with sharp eyes, guns sheathed but visible. "If they could justify it legally, I don't think they'd let me leave the house."

Flora's jaw tightened. Rex knew she was still simmering over the committee's dismissal of her objections.

Rex cleared her throat and returned her attention to the buildings they passed. "They've been busy." Part of Rex tried to hold on to the anger and disappointment she'd worked up while giving the whole compound the dressing-down they deserved for the so-called parkwarming party, but pride kept bursting through.

The dinosaurs had already built on her dino-oriented tech and, with Aya's help coordinating with outside resources, produced construction equipment that utilized the largest dinosaurs' size and strength without needing anything as pedestrian as hands. With that, they'd created a vision of a facility spread across the center of the property, force field walls and roofs making the spaces customizable for the dinosaurs' great range of sizes and shapes.

"Is that brain wave-manipulated nanotech?" Rex asked as a crane fluidly reconstructed itself into a flatbed on skittering legs, more useful than wheels in this terrain. Danny Dino, brain wave amplifier attached to the back of his neck, climbed onto the platform, gave her a double nod greeting when he saw her watching, and shifted his weight in a way that cued the vehicle to climb the wall as smoothly as an elevator.

"Nanotech is involved," Aya answered through the open line on her phone, "but the reconfiguration is largely automated, as none of the dinosaurs have the mental capacity to direct a nanoswarm of the necessary size."

Of course, not—Rex doubted even Aya had the processing power to direct a swarm that big.

"They have set aside plans in anticipation of their mental capacity improving to the necessary level, but as of now it is hypothetical technology. They focus on practical and versatile developments instead. Jasper is working on integrating swarm intelligence to make the nanotech more anticipatory of mental direction."

"Smart," Flora said.

Very smart. Rex was starting to wonder if their intelligence would ever level off, though the latest tests indicated it at least wasn't growing exponentially anymore. Inside the main building a wide, shallow staircase vanished into a basement—smart of them to build down instead of up, considering how much some of the dinosaurs weighed, although the open-air layout of most of the compound was still preferred. The top of the staircase was plastered with signs that said: *Mom Keep Out.*

Flora angled Rex's phone toward the stairs. "Should we worry?"

"They spend a great deal of time down there," Aya answered, sounding irritated. "They will not tell me what they're working on. They say it is a surprise."

"That doesn't sound good," Rex muttered.

One of the tyrannosaurs charged in front of them. "Mom, no!"

"Anything I should know, Trent?" Rex used her shoe to give the floor some experimental taps, impressed. She hadn't felt a rumble at Trent's approach. "We need to talk about how you guys made this floor—the shock absorption is phenomenal."

"It's not ready yet," Trent insisted, herding Rex and Flora back to the doors.

Jamal stood his ground at the head of the stairs. "I'm gonna insist we see what's down there."

Peter stood next to him, blank-faced. Rex was careful not to meet his eyes, and in her peripheral vision she could see him also not looking at her. It had been awkward every time Peter or Lewis had babysitting duty since security tightened up. Without talking about it, they'd settled into ignoring each other for the duration of the shift. Coincidentally—or not—they hadn't had a single shift together.

Rex was aware of dinosaur eyes on them from other corners of the room. Trent shifted from one foot to the other. "It's not anything bad," he rumbled.

His discomfort made fury rise in Rex, but she swallowed it. Cooperation was the safest path. "Can you show them? I won't look."

Trent's head drooped, shoulder blades making a tent of his massive T-shirt with #DinoLife printed across the front—yet another thing for Rex to look up in her endless effort to keep up with dinosaur damage control. He strode to the stairs with eyes on Jamal. The steps reconfigured to accommodate his size and gait—cool—and Jamal followed him while Peter stayed with their charge.

"Breathe, Rex," Flora muttered, though her glare at the staircase suggested that she shared Rex's sentiment.

They weren't gone long. Trent reappeared with an indignant strut, Jamal as stone-faced as ever. "It's just a bunch of tunnels," he said. "Goes to another staircase in the next building."

"What part of *it's a surprise* did you not understand?" Rex snapped. Then she caught a few dinosaurs around the room exchanging looks and let it drop. Whatever was actually down there was a problem for another day and none of Jamal's business. "Let's move on."

The dinosaurs showed Rex around with such unbridled enthusiasm that she wondered if she'd gone too easy when she had chewed them out over their poor life choices for an hour and a half, but she couldn't bring herself to linger on it. She took in their research and additions to the compound ravenously, giddy laughter coming a bit too quick. The freeze on her projects was wearing on her more than she'd anticipated. And she'd anticipated a lot of wear. She was still developing ideas in her head, but without the ability to make them tangible, she felt like her brain was full of spinning wheels with no input or output, rushing to a breaking point. She wondered if she'd explode or sputter out.

Despite the tension her trailing babysitters added, it was nice to see the dinosaurs settling in. They were much more adept at constructing an environment to suit their needs than she had been, despite her best efforts to think like a dinosaur. For once, one of her decisions had turned out better than she'd expected. She could see them flourishing here, assuming she didn't do anything to ruin it.

"Maybe I need to buy some land for the virus and let it roam free," she muttered to herself.

Flora *hmm*ed. "Still no breakthroughs?"

"Have you ever tried to cure a virus entirely in your head?" She glanced at her phone and amended, "Or your head and your AI's computer bank?" She'd finagled a look at the lab's simulated brain wave patterns and identified likely passive markers from the virus, but it was hard to extrapolate on that without the ability to direct more tests.

"You're allowed to work on Blue's hood," Flora soothed without looking up from her tablet. "Maybe you can pull that back out for a treat." Yes, Flora was bitter about the restrictions.

"They might see results faster if they gave back my prototype." The drunken mess hood still hadn't left Oversight's custody, to Rex's teeth-grinding frustration.

"I think they want to compare it to Blue's. It's the only similar technology, so I suppose it's a check against either hood not being what you say it is." Flora flicked a look back at the babysitters, which Rex followed, but Peter was carefully looking elsewhere and Jamal didn't have that jaw pulse he developed when he thought they were conspiring.

Rex lowered her voice anyway. "They won't be able to check it because I'm only giving it to Vivid Blue. Viv agreed."

"Oversight probably thinks you're bluffing."

Rex exhaled harshly. "Well, I'm not. Until they figure that out, I guess every hood stays where it is."

Flora's eyes cut a bit lower, to where the hood of Rex's red jacket hung down her back. The jacket hadn't originally come with a hood. The embedded circuitry was easy enough to insulate against a metal detector. With an extra layer of fabric on the inside, the resulting garment passed right through the search and pat down routine that marked her house's threshold these days.

Rex knew they were searching her house; they weren't exactly hiding it—at least Lewis wasn't. The safest thing would be to destroy Sam's red hood. After all, the design was in her head. She could make another one.

But her dreams about Sam had come back. More often than not, they featured a younger Sam speaking the older Sam's words: *"I can't sleep. It's always loud, and I can't sleep."* Sam looking at her with blue eyes interspersed with lines of gray. *"Did you make it? Because if I had it, I could sleep."*

So, while Awake Rex had no intention of giving Sam his hood until she knew more about his plans, she'd sewn buttons onto the dark red hood, paired it with an almost-matching jacket, and tossed it on every time she left the house. So, no one nosing around her house would find something they shouldn't, and maybe she wouldn't wake with a gasp and tears in her eyes quite so often.

She'd snuck it past Flora for two days before realizing what she was doing—old habits—and stuttered through a confession. Flora had just nodded and added *soothe guilty conscience* to the pros and cons list.

"Time to go," Peter announced around mid-afternoon. Rex didn't argue. Missing a check-in would only test Quinten unnecessarily.

Pixie landed as they reached the jet, back from her flyover. "All clear," she reported. As they loaded up, she added, "Aw, no babies?"

"They seemed so happy with their parents, we decided to let them stay another day or two." Or forever. In fact, it was the main reason for the trip. Now that the others had set everything up, the hatchlings would be better off here.

Peter took the copilot seat on the flight back, and Rex wasn't sure if the surprise made her happy or nervous. They sat in silence as she got them in the air and leveled off, broken occasionally by the tapping from Flora's travel laptop or Jamal's voice drifting from the cabin as he tried to hit on Pixie.

Peter cleared his throat, interrupting Rex's third anxious check of systems Aya could technically run by herself. "I've been meaning to say." His eyes flicked to the cabin, where, it occurred to Rex, Jamal was out of earshot for the first time that day. "Thank you."

Rex's brow jumped. Before she could ask, he continued, "I was half resigned to losing Lewis, I think. So was he. And it would have been the biggest mistake of my life. But you just—" He dropped his head in a contained laugh. "You jumped right in there."

Rex fiddled with the sleeve of her fire suit where the fold kept the attached gloves out of the way, torn between a simple *you're welcome* and a roundabout dismissal.

"We've paid you back pretty poorly."

"You don't have to pay me back," she said quickly. "I wanted to help. A friend is a big deal."

"You don't know how much it means to me that you understand that." His hands opened and closed on his knees. "You're a good friend. I wouldn't want to lose you either."

Rex had to fiddle with the flight path until she stopped feeling choked up. "I've also been meaning to tell you something. I looked up the thing you told me about."

"The thing?" She watched the memory register on his face. "About being ace?"

Rex shifted uncomfortably. "I've never related to anything more," she admitted.

A grin split his face. "Did I help you figure out you're asexual?"

She shrugged self-consciously. "The word for it, anyway."

He flat-out beamed. "I've always wanted to be in this position. I'm so happy for you." He turned to her and gripped her shoulders, the angle awkward since she kept a hand on the controls. "Congratulations on coming to know this part of yourself a little better, and good luck in exploring what it means to you."

His grin was as infectious as a venereal disease. "Thanks, I guess." She pushed him away, trying to control her face.

Peter fell back in his seat, grin lingering. After a pause, he added, "You know, you and Lewis seemed better too."

Rex suppressed a flinch. "Maybe we were. But I sort of"—rolled around in her issues on the kitchen floor like a dog rolling in an old carcass—"messed up. He's been"—killing her with professionalism—"a bit standoffish. I don't blame him, but . . ." She shrugged instead of finishing the thought. She didn't want to get choked up again.

Rex felt Peter's eyes on her, but she couldn't bring herself to meet them.

"So, Lewis and I talk a lot." His tone suggested he was easing into something, and Rex was hit with insta-dread. "Sometimes, we talk about you. I mean, obviously. Our lives kind of revolve around you for now." He huffed a recalibrating breath. "We haven't—well, we haven't talked as much lately." So, there was something to the change in the shift schedule. "But I think," he paused, "the reason he's shutting you out probably isn't the reason you think it is. And he's trying so hard not to cross the wrong lines that he's overcompensating. And overthinking. He tends to overthink."

Rex fought the urge to ask outright if Lewis was disgusted by her drunken meltdown. It would be a pathetic question, but the way it festered made her feel like she couldn't breathe.

What a stupid thing to dwell on. She had bigger problems.

Jamal's voice drifted from the back of the jet. "I like your costume. I think it makes you look very confiden—"

The jet's lurch threw Rex against the controls. Flora's laptop clattered across the cabin, jangling her nerves.

"What was that?" Pixie called, wings humming.

"Aya?" Rex pushed herself up, checking readings.

"Doctor, weather conditions are—" Aya's voice through the speakers broke off as the jet lurched sideways. Rex yelled as her harness barely kept her out of Peter's lap. She caught a glimpse of Pixie stepping off the floor and staying in the air with zipping movements as the cabin turned sideways around her. Rex was dumbfounded for a hot second when that stunt didn't end with Pixie flattened against the bulkhead.

Then she realized the jet had stopped decelerating. They'd stopped moving forward completely.

As Rex fought the controls to no effect, the jet swerved in the other direction, straightening back out. Then her center of gravity rose, and they started to fall.

Flora shrieked, grabbing Rex's attention for the space of a glance as she grabbed at an armrest and the hem of her skirt. Pixie hit the ceiling palms first with a grunt, arms bulging slightly with the effort to keep herself from flattening. "It's Ill Wind! She's caught us in a gale." She hand-walked across the ceiling, wings buzzing to keep balance as the jet rocked.

Rex had a panicked mental image of the jet slamming against the ground like a spiked football, but she shouted down the fear with the logic that if Ill Wind didn't want at least one of them alive—probably her, if Rex's fucked up luck held—the jet would already be Lego blocks in the carpet.

"Flora," Rex yelled in Peter's ear, hoping that was enough explanation. She fumbled out of her harness so she could pull herself into the cabin. She had no control of the jet anymore, and like hell was she going to let Flora be the closest to the door when it was inevitably busted off its hinges at the end of this carnival ride.

Her gaze passed over the window where land was rushing up to meet them, and nope, she would not be looking there again.

She reached Flora and tugged her by the waist to the wall, aided by their reduced weight in the falling jet. Flora grabbed at her and the seats like a nervous cat, eyes wide behind her glasses and teeth clenched so tight that Rex felt a sympathetic twinge in her jaw.

She heard Peter curse. Then the soldier dragged himself between them and the door and braced himself in time for the jet to lurch to a slower descent and hit the ground with a brain-jarring crash.

In the ringing silence, Rex groaned, "I loved this jet."

The door burst off its hinges.

ISSUE 25

DINOSAURS WITH LASER GUNS

A familiar leather-clad leg stepped on to the uneven floor as Ill Wind strode smirking through the broken doorway. The outfit was even more ridiculous in daylight.

Ill Wind's gaze found Rex, and the smirk had time to widen infinitesimally before Pixie yelled, "Flying tackle!" and body-slammed her right off her high-heeled boots.

With the path clear, Peter clamped one hand on Rex's arm and the other on Flora's and hauled them to the open door.

A second figure blocked their way. Rex ran into Peter as he pulled up short. She heard a quick, fear-infused breath from Flora and was hit with instant rage.

She might have launched herself at the new guy if he hadn't pointed a gun at Peter's chest.

Rex froze, her heart louder in her ears as a quiet overtook the cabin. Jamal's footsteps stopped behind them. The buzz of Pixie's wings trailed off.

Ill Wind broke the silence with a deep chuckle and pushed herself off the bulkhead.

"Ill Wind, you—" Pixie began, but the supervillain clapped a hand over her mouth.

"Hush, Pixie-pie." She turned to the new guy. "How's that for restraint, Lee?"

"Unnecessarily destructive, and a clear attempt at retribution for your fall from favor," the man answered. He wore a spiffy blazer and slacks, his brown hair gelled but not so styled that Rex recognized it as a villain's signature. He walked through the door with a sigh, gun still trained on Peter. "You brought that on yourself by attacking the Meister."

"I'm only doing my job," Ill Wind said. "It's hardly my fault that the first chance to get to her requires violence." So, this was about Rex. Great.

The man rolled his eyes. "That you bother to lie says a lot about your lack of confidence in your ability to challenge him."

Rex placed him: Liam Evertrue, of the weirdly appropriate real name. He could hear lies, and his code of ethics drove him to punish liars, especially heroes he considered hypocritical. It was all explained in his tragic backstory, but Rex couldn't remember the details.

Ill Wind started to reply, but a gunshot burst through the cabin from Jamal's position in the back. Peter lunged forward as Evertrue reeled, and a blast of air with the force of an invisible truck threw Rex across the cabin to collide with Jamal, Flora at her side.

Ears ringing from the gunshot, Rex faintly heard the familiar crack of a punch to the face and someone yelling "Fly-in-the punch!" She scrambled to disentangle herself from the others, catching snapshots of Ill Wind's head whipping to the side and Pixie's other fist flying.

Ill Wind yowled, and the cabin filled with dark fog. Rex barely managed to get below it before lightning lit up the fog—or lit up the cloud? Rex would have time to appreciate the novelty of an indoor storm later—and her vision whited out.

Flora's pitchy scream rang in Rex's ear. The center of her vision was one big spot. At its edges, a leather-clad high kick knocked Jamal's gun aside with a *thwak* and a clatter, and he dropped out of sight.

Flora clung to Rex's arm, so when a hand snagged Rex's jacket and hauled her up, they were both forced to their feet.

"Oh, shit," she blurted, blinking as the spot in her vision turned bruise colored. "We get it—we're subdued."

A prim huff confirmed it was Ill Wind pulling her to the front of the jet, if the black sleeve poking out of the fog hadn't done it.

The weight on her arm vanished as Flora got her feet under her. Then something tugged on the collar of her jacket.

Ice shot up Rex's spine. She swallowed, hyperaware of the slight weight of the red hood lifting button by button.

Rex hadn't thought of the hood. As Flora removed it, she internally cheered Flora's quick thinking while clamping her mouth shut against the urge to tell her to stop. With the fog still dissipating, this might be their only chance to try something, but most of Rex rebelled at the risk Flora was taking.

Ill Wind pulled her sharply forward, probably interpreting the final yank of the hood coming off as Rex's brave and noble resistance. "Don't try me, Meister. You're only alive because your brother thinks you're useful."

Rex's eyes flicked around. What happened to Peter? Had there been another gunshot after Jamal's? "Did he mention that my usefulness is directly proportional to how many of my friends stay alive?" she asked. "Or travel companions? Guards? I'm trying to say don't kill my babysitters."

Flora's tense exhale hit the back of her neck.

"He did tell us not to hurt anyone," Evertrue answered. "Something about a promise he made." The fog was thin enough now for Rex to make him out as he approached, his gun pointed loosely at the floor. "He won't be happy with how you interpreted those instructions."

Shit, shit, shit—*what happened to Peter?*

"He may be spearheading this venture, but that denialist doesn't give me orders," Ill Wind sneered.

"Again, you bother to lie to me." Evertrue ziptied their hands with a businesslike air. Rex wanted to look at Flora to identify where she'd stashed the hood, but she kept her eyes forward.

Evertrue stepped back around them and crouched next to a crumpled form. She felt a jab of terror. Was someone dead? Then the fog cleared enough to see the feeble beating of two gossamer wings.

"Take her with us," Ill Wind said.

"She's your nemesis, isn't she?" Evertrue sounded bored with the concept. "Wouldn't you rather kill her?"

"She's caused me too much trouble for a clean death. I want to draw this out."

Evertrue sighed again. He did not say that Ill Wind was lying. When he stood, Pixie's hands were ziptied behind her back. Pixie had some version of super strength, didn't she? The proportionate strength of a fly? Were they really restraining her with zip ties?

Ill Wind bent over Pixie to rest her fingers on the back of her head. A short crack of lightning made the hero's body jolt and fall limp. Rex jumped, and Flora's shoulder pressed against hers.

"That should keep her out for a while." Ill Wind shot a glance to Evertrue. "Deal with the one in the back."

As Ill Wind pulled them through the door to the rocky ground, Rex asked, "What do you mean by 'deal with?' Because I was serious about not cooperating if you kill people. Does your boss want me to build something? I'll do it—swear to God. No torture necessary."

"She's not lying," Evertrue huffed, dragging Jamal's unconscious body by the armpits.

Ill Wind shot her a distasteful look. "Honestly, Meister, do you have no pride?"

"What the fuck would I do with pride?"

Ill Wind gave her a shake. "Just shut up."

Evertrue dumped Jamal against the side of the jet where Peter was already slumped, out cold. Rex let out a shaky exhale when his chest rose, although her worry wasn't completely gone—superbeings didn't seem aware that getting *knocked unconscious* was a big fucking deal. But maybe they could still get out of this. She didn't have any tech in reach, but words seemed to be a passable tool with these two. She still had something to work with.

Evertrue shoved Flora down beside Peter—"Stay there"—and Ill Wind maneuvered Rex to her knees in such an obvious power move that Rex had to fight not to roll her eyes. Evertrue crouched in front of her, the same bored expression on his face. "Do you have what he wants?"

It was hard to keep the fluttery, nervous feeling off her face. Flora probably just saved their asses. "No." Before he could follow up with a question that might back Rex into a truth corner, she continued, "I swear you just missed it. I had it earlier today, but—"

"Where is it?" Ill Wind hissed.

Only a split second to think. "I don't know. Someone took it." Damn, their follow-up would be *who*.

"I-I took it," Flora said, voice breathy.

Rex's heart dropped like a failed jetpack as the villains turned around. She rose to her knees, not feeling the rocks digging into her shins. "Hey, hey—remember what I said. I will fight if you hurt her."

"I gave it to—" Flora's voice kept giving out between breaths. "I gave it to the surveillance team."

Rex didn't risk looking at Peter and Jamal.

Ill Wind growled. "Oversight has it. Brilliant. Another reason to delay."

"I told you he lied about why he's stalling," Evertrue said, no sign of sharing her frustration. "This was never the thing delaying the plan, so we could hardly expect to move forward if we found it."

"It would take away his excuse," she snipped, finally turning away from Flora.

"No big deal." Evertrue dragged Rex to her feet—she was getting really sick of being manhandled—fished her phone from her pocket, and tossed it away. "You'll just have to make another."

That was when Rex fully caught on to her situation: she was being kidnapped. Distantly, she felt the steady motion of a car around her and lost track of the scene. She lurched back to the present, her chest aching—she must have stopped breathing for a bit—and the last few minutes caught up in fast-forward.

Ill Wind and Evertrue decided to take Pixie and Flora in addition to Rex: Flora to keep Rex in line and Pixie because Ill Wind wanted to.

They were led-slash-dragged to a . . . pod? Something villainous-looking that was basically a helicopter without blades or skids. Inside, two rows of three seats faced each other. The villains strapped them in on one side and took seats on the other. When the doors closed, Ill Wind waved her arms and the pod lifted from the ground, presumably on the power of wind, and zipped away.

Rex came back to full awareness as the pod lurched, dropped a bit, and turned toward Decimen City. She looked around, tallying what she had to work with. Unconscious Pixie in the seat on her left, conscious Flora in the seat on her right. On second glance, Rex saw something move beneath the black facets of Pixie's eye. So, conscious Pixie pretending to be unconscious. That was something.

She had her fire suit, but in a small, enclosed aircraft it would be suicide to whip that out. Aya probably called for help when the jet went down, though there was no telling if she'd had contact long enough to know where they'd crashed.

She also, potentially, had the pod. If it was just a hunk of metal being blown around, she couldn't do much besides question Ill Wind's sense of self-preservation. But if there was a technological component, she was in business. Like hell was this kidnapping getting to the forced labor stage. She was half a villain in her own right—it would be embarrassing.

Except, what did Sam want her for? He wanted the hood—or helmet, as he probably still expected—but did that relate to his larger plans? His henchmen clearly thought it did. Evertrue's words to Ill Wind caught up with her—*he lied about why he's stalling*. Rex knew the virus was already out there, dormant in its victims. But Sam was delaying activating it? She glanced at Ill Wind, arms crossed, and Evertrue, looking at his phone. Sam was stalling, and he was lying to his allies about it.

Why?

"Quick question," Rex said, breaking the silence. Ill Wind shot her an annoyed glance. "I get that Sam wants the neighbors to shut up, but how does that benefit either of you?"

Ill Wind smirked. "Meister, don't tell me you've never thought about ruling the world."

Okay. Wow. Rex hadn't really thought about the scale of her brother's plan. She tried to swallow spit without being obvious about it. "I guess I don't understand the point of ruling over coma patients."

Evertrue sighed. "Misdirection. She doesn't think they'll be in comas."

Well, Rex hadn't been sure, though she had assumed their unconscious minds would take over like in a dissociative episode. Evertrue heard more nuance than she'd thought.

Ill Wind chuckled. "What about ruling over mindless minions? What about controlling subjects who only think when Dance allows them to?"

Ill Wind implied the virus made people suggestible, which Rex knew was likely. That explained the appeal to old-school villains. She glanced at Evertrue, still scrolling on his phone, but he said nothing. So much for hoping Sam had gentled the virus into something harmless.

And yet, he delayed triggering it. She lowered her eyes and tried not to look too thoughtful. In the scenario Ill Wind described, Sam would be responsible for a brainwashed population. Maybe his mind reading interacted differently with an infected brain, but even if the virus silenced the onslaught of other people's thoughts, he'd still have to use his powers.

Sam would *hate* that.

There was something else going on here.

Evertrue chuckled across from her, bent over his phone. Ill Wind grumbled something Rex couldn't hear, but she heard Evertrue's indignant, "What? They're funny." He met Rex's eyes and turned the phone toward her. "I take it you're a bit of a helicopter parent."

"Is that a parent who builds helicopters for their kids?" The screen showed a shaky video of her pacing the stage in the dinosaurs' outdoor auditorium—she suspected they'd built it with award shows in mind—as she lit into the assembly about their parkwarming party.

"Did this happen today? They don't waste time," Evertrue said.

Rex squinted. "Does that hashtag say Dino Mom?"

"That's a good one." Evertrue clicked the hashtag as Ill Wind rolled her eyes. The next post was also from today, featuring a picture of the tyrannosaur parents and babies cuddled up in a sleepy pile and the text, "So grateful to our #DinoMom for giving our sweeties a loving home while we got our heads straight. This will be the only post with our darlings, just to let you all know they're home safe. Gotta keep them out of the spotlight! #HappyFamily #DinoLife #Blessed." The response had already far outstripped the posts below it.

"Damn, they're good," Rex muttered.

Before Evertrue could finish his next question, the pod shook, a hum filling the air. Rex hoped she didn't imagine the well-timed *snap* on her left, like a sneaky superhero breaking her zip ties.

Ill Wind jumped to her feet. "What—?"

The hum became a drone, and the view through the windows filled with black helicopters of various sizes. A barrage of feelings forced Rex's face into a cross between a grin and a grimace. Aya had gotten a message out, all right.

A voice, booming as though from a loudspeaker, resounded through the walls. "Attention, enemy aircraft. Land the vehicle and relinquish our mother and Aunt Flora to us. Comply or be obliterated."

"Oh, Oversight's not gonna like that," Rex said through her teeth.

Ill Wind raised her arms, snarling. "Fools, trying to command me from the skies."

Wind roared past the pod, shaking the interior enough to throw Rex's ziptied self against the shoulder straps. She kept her eyes glued to the windows, heart straining as the dinocopters were blown off course. Then the copters' propellers *retracted,* and blue shimmers zipped down the metal sides as they straightened into a grid pattern.

Hot damn, that was badass. Rex nudged Flora's shoulder. "Are you seeing this?"

"Is that like the magnetic field that keeps Aya in the air?"

"On an enormous scale and using all the dinocopters to stabilize the field," she said in a rush, bursting with pride.

"Maybe we should land," Evertrue called.

"I'm not done yet," Ill Wind growled. The sky dimmed with gathering clouds.

Thunder rumbled, and branches of lightning shot down among the dinocopters. Rex gasped as one struck, sending a shimmer through the black metal. That would be the force field she'd added, which ought to hold up against a lightning strike, but Rex didn't want it tested mid-flight while a supervillain tried to make them crash.

Panels on several dinocopters slid back and bright green streaks cut the air before impacting the pod with a *boom* that threw Rex against the harness and knocked Ill Wind on her ass.

The loudspeaker voice returned, slightly muffled. "Stop it, dumb butts! Mom is inside!"

A second voice spoke in the background. "Spot, you didn't turn off the—" It cut off with a staticky *click*.

Ill Wind picked herself up with a strangled roar, and the wind surged.

Through the window, several copters bobbed dangerously far from the magnetic field. The furthest ones seemed the most affected, pulling against the field in the same direction, like a vortex.

As Rex realized what was happening, her heart stopped and her hands fumbled to escape the ties, fighting for freedom to—what, throw herself at Ill Wind? Yeah, fuck it, she was going to throw herself at Ill Wind.

Pixie beat her to it. She launched herself at the supervillain, fists flying. "Take this, you harpy!"

The pod veered sideways as Ill Wind hit the wall with Pixie on top. Evertrue screamed, clinging to the straps. Rex, halfway out of the straps despite the zip ties, fell over the seats into Flora's lap. "It's about damn time!" she yelled at Pixie.

"Rex!" Flora grabbed her around the waist—how did she get out of her ties? Flora was a bag of surprises—as the pod swept the other way in a barrel roll. *Oh, dear.* Rex didn't want to throw up. It would be so embarrassing to be the one who threw up during the rescue fight.

The pod stopped abruptly as Pixie pinned Ill Wind's arms. "Oh, no, you don't!"

Ill Wind's glare flicked from Pixie to the window, where the dinocopters managed to stay airborne among thin, split-off funnels in the vortex. Arms still pinned, the villain flipped a hand around and touched a lit square on the wall. The door slid back.

Over the wind's roar, Ill Wind shouted, "I'll get you next time!" She rolled out of Pixie's grasp and threw herself out of the pod.

Well, shit. Stunned, Rex watched Ill Wind catch herself with one of the funnels like the freaking Wicked Witch of the West and ride it like it was a damn skateboard, tearing between the dinocopters in the time it took to blink.

Evertrue called after her, "Wait! What about me?"

A *snick* and pressure on her wrists brought Rex's attention to Flora cutting her ties with a pocketknife.

"How?" she demanded.

"They stopped searching me when they found my phone."

"I can't handle you, Flora. Where do you keep your pockets?"

"You're not getting away," Pixie yelled after Ill Wind, and Rex grabbed her wrist and slammed the door shut before she could throw herself out of it.

"You can't fly in this! And seriously, does it take that long to unbuckle yourself?"

"She was keeping us in the air! I was gonna wait till we landed, but I couldn't let her hurt the dinos."

"Rex, we're falling," Flora blurted, arms tightening around her.

And yup, they were definitely falling. Fuck Ill Wind.

Rex scrambled out of Flora's hold and toward what was probably the front of the pod, hoping for some wires or buttons or any kind of commonsensical failsafe in case Ill Wind fell over in a seizure between evil lairs. She thought of asking Evertrue but scrapped that idea as the man was panicking loudly in his seat.

There was a screen with some promising readings on a dashboard, although Rex didn't see an obvious way to make adjustments. "Pixie, get this off."

Pixie punched a hole in the dash and ripped it away, exposing a motherboard and other useful innards.

A blare made the pod's occupants wince, followed by the dinosaurs' loudspeaker. "Mom, we—stabilizing—controlled descent—"

"I could fly out and try to slow us down," Pixie said. "Or I could carry someone, maybe all three of you."

"That's a lie," Evertrue shouted.

"I don't think 'get out and push' is an option," Rex answered, elbows-deep in the pod as she tried to deduce what everything did. Besides, the thought of abandoning ship with Evertrue still inside made her feel sick. "Just give me a minute."

A glance out the window found that several of the smaller dinocopters had broken from the grid and were tracking the pod as it fell, their arrangement placing the pod in their new configuration.

The magnetic field. If Rex could get the pod aligned—

"Mom, seven-point-nine—zero zero—"

Like she ever wouldn't recognize Aya's field described mathematically. Those beautiful geniuses. She tore out a box and reconnected the wires. "We need them to shoot us if we want to live."

Pixie balked.

"She's not lying," Evertrue said.

Flora leaped to the window and waved her arms. "Hey! Shoot us!"

The closest dinocopter's side panel was already open. A green flash filled the window, followed by a *boom* that jarred the pod violently sideways. Rex hit the floor as their descent slowed fast, then steadied.

Pixie pressed her face to the window. "Sweet! Dinos ex machina!"

Then shimmers of blue stretched thin between the dinocopters, and, like tearing through a weak net, the pod dropped. A view swept past the window of jostled dinocopters extending propellers to catch themselves.

The view was replaced by a green-and-brown tangle of crashing branch-es. The pod jerked around pinball-style as it hit trees and hillside, then hit the ground and slid. When Rex started to wonder if they'd caused a landslide, they finally slowed and hit something hard without crashing through it.

She lay where she'd landed, staring at the ceiling and listening to Flora and Evertrue groan. Her ears rang in the absence of wind noise. In the still-ness, the floor swung in a ghost-tilt, like when you lie flat after spending time on a boat. They'd earned a break, hadn't they? Just a moment to figure out where the bruises were.

Eventually, Pixie's half-masked face appeared over her, one hand on Rex's shoulder. "You okay?"

"Eh." As her eyes focused, she noticed one of Pixie's gossamer wings bent at the tip, beating sluggishly. "Your wing—"

"Landed on it. It'll heal—I just have to stay grounded for a few days." Her pout convinced Rex she was okay more than her words did.

Rex sat up as Pixie checked on the others. She made eye contact with Flora while Pixie pulled Evertrue to his feet, ripping the straps from the seat to tie his hands behind his back.

"Calm down. I'm not going to hurt you," Pixie scoffed.

"That's a lie."

"Rex, uh," Flora whispered.

Rex scooted closer, Flora's tone making her wary.

"When they were questioning you—I didn't see a better option."

Rex frowned at Flora's thin-lipped expression.

"I put the hood in Peter's jacket."

Ah, she'd forgotten about that. "Huh." That was going to be a situation. "Okay."

Pixie ripped the door off the pod—unnecessary, in Rex's opinion—and led the four of them into their newly-wrecked forest home. They looked around at the empty wilderness, a few wholesome birdcalls echoing through the trees.

"Welp," Rex said. The dinosaurs might have seen where they went down. Through the twisters and the chaos of their magnetic field failing.

"They'll find us eventually," Pixie offered. "The Protectors are great at search and rescue."

"Lie," Evertrue said.

That was going to get old fast.

ISSUE 26

SPOTLIGHT ON LEWIS STONE: LEWIS TO THE RESCUE

Two nights ago, Lewis ran into Rex in the kitchen. His reasons for keeping his distance during the day always left his mind when that happened, and with very little lead-up they'd made what Rex called an I-actually-want-that casserole.

Lewis had crumbled dry ramen over a bed of potato chips. "This will burn to the pan if we don't add oil or sauce."

Head buried in the pantry, Rex answered, "Sometimes they use tomato sauce in the videos Aya sends me." She tossed him a jar of salsa. "Try that. I'm gonna look for some candy."

Now, Lewis sat between Joey and Trisha on the Protectors' jet, and all he could think about was that monstrosity in the fridge. If things went wrong today—if he had to go home tonight and see it, remembering his exaggerated disgust and the way she'd pretended to savor it—but no, he wouldn't be going back if something went wrong.

He'd have no reason to.

His stomach gained another knot.

Don Conjure stood at the front of the cabin, his blue half-cape fluttering in nonexistent wind. "We lost contact with the Meister's jet over the Rockies, about here." With a pointed finger, he magicked a red dot onto the map that Vivid Blue was holding up with her telekinesis, his other hand twirling his mustache. "The Meister's artificial assistant informed us that the jet was going down before she, too, lost contact. We suspect the cause was an attack of the most nefarious nature."

The news had broken while Lewis and Grant were in the middle of their latest search of the Meister's labyrinth of a home.

Grant had grumbled at the locked door, "According to the blueprints, this whole floor is for her private servers." The elevator hadn't wanted to take them this far—Grant had done something to the wiring to make it go past the lowest production floor while Lewis looked on and tried not to feel the AI's attention on them.

He held back a sigh at the number of barriers they were encountering. Rex couldn't help making things worse for herself.

Grant jotted a note to get some code breakers down there and moved up to the production floors.

"And . . ." Grant tapped a finger on the side of his laptop. "Got it. Should be downloading a backlog now." He handed the laptop to Lewis and started inspecting the machinery.

Lewis scanned through files, trying to go somewhere else in his head. It wasn't like he understood the schematics anyway. The sheer number of them made his gut clench at the memory of how hungry Rex looked lately when she caught a glimpse of her work, her hands twitching, her eyes wide and sharp.

He came to a blueprint of complex wiring worked into cloth, and he paused. The hood she'd made to block thoughts. The image was overlaid with the memory of Flora's hand grabbing the prototype from the floor, Rex's guilty voice answering Flora's glare.

Lewis let his brow jump once. He glanced at Grant, who was still engrossed in the production equipment. He bent over the file. There were three pages. The second looked like a photocopy of a similar design, but using plastic or metal, like a helmet. The third was also a photocopy—a short, handwritten message. And here he stopped.

The message started, *Hi T*. His heart beat against his ribs as he read, pounding punctuation as his eyes came to rest at the sign-off. *Sam.*

Lewis stared at the screen and couldn't muster a thought. His hand moved on the touchpad, selected the file, and copied it into the flash drive plugged into the laptop. His heartbeat was the only sound in his head as he erased the file from the backlog and watched the note and sketches vanish.

The buzzing silence was broken by Grant's voice. "Find anything yet?"

"Naw." Lewis pulled out the flash drive and dropped it in his pocket.

They were heading to the next floor when the alert came in.

Lewis tapped absently on the hard square of plastic in his pocket. He hadn't paused to stash the flash drive before volunteering for the rescue team.

He still just kept thinking of the damn casserole.

At the front of the jet, Don Conjure folded his arms. "We must be prepared for whatever awaits us, however grisly it may be." Lewis was reminded of Peter's insistence that Don Conjure would be the hottest Protector if he ever shaved that mustache. Lewis couldn't decide if he thought Pixie or the Jester was the hottest, although his favorite was Undertaker, hands down.

Peter wasn't a valuable hostage. He had no superpowers. He'd be nothing but an obstacle in a villain's path. Lewis stopped himself from following that train of thought.

"I'll be going ahead," Vivid Blue said. "When you catch up, let the Protectors take the lead."

Lewis glanced at the other heroes who'd come along—the Jester flying the jet and Cat Man batting at the Jester's bell from the copilot seat—and tried not to feel frustrated at having to wait. The knot in his stomach clenched tighter.

Rex had proven to have no issue attacking villains head-on—or heroes, for that matter—and Peter would always put himself between civilians and—

No, he couldn't think like that. He had to stay present. The door opened, letting in the roar of wind, and Vivid Blue flew out, cape twisting behind her. As it closed, Cat Man's claw caught in the fabric of the Jester's hat, and he tugged it once before giving up with a whine. The Jester huffed as he unsnagged him and murmured, "She's got wings, man. She's not gonna die in a plane crash."

They swung into a slowing arc less than twenty minutes later. "That's a wreck, all right," the Jester said. "I see Blue—kind of hard to miss her. Doesn't look like we're going into an active conflict."

"That is fortuitous," Don Conjure said. "But time may still be of the essence."

"Yeah, yeah, don't get your mustache in a twist."

They landed smoothly, and Lewis was on his feet and striding to the door before the others had finished unstrapping themselves.

"Your eagerness in commendable," Don Conjure announced, slapping him on the back. "Such fire and vigor."

"Please don't talk about another man's vigor," the Jester said, twisting his seat around as Cat Man climbed over the back of his.

"That's a homophobic joke," Lewis said, then regretted it because he didn't want to delay getting a move on.

The Jester pointed at Lewis. "Calling me on it. I like this guy. Don, don't talk about a woman's vigor, either."

"I was merely—"

Cat Man scratched pointedly at the door and shot the others a glare. "Meow."

"Of course, my friend. You are right to remind us of our priorities." Don Conjure's face turned stormy, and the ramp lowered with a wave of his hand.

They filed out quickly, meeting Vivid Blue and—Lewis's whole brain relaxed in relief—Peter at the wreckage of the Meister's jet. Lewis crossed the rocky ground and hugged him.

As they separated and Peter patted his back in reassurance, Vivid Blue said, "Tell them what you told me."

Peter gave a quick account of the attack. Last he'd seen before being knocked out, Rex, Flora, and Pixie were all alive, Pixie unconscious. Jamal sat on a boulder not far away, rubbing his head and nodding the occasional confirmation.

Lewis scrutinized Peter as he talked. He looked a little unsteady, but he was standing straight with no visible injuries besides a bruise at his temple. Maybe Lewis's worry was making him paranoid, but he still seemed off. His hands were stiff at his sides, like he was trying not to give something away.

His concentration broke when the Jester sidled up to him and muttered, "Hey, man, I want to make it clear I have no problem with gays. Three of my six dads were gay—not for each other though."

Lewis blinked at him, attention still split. "Is that also a joke?"

A loud, "Ha!" burst from the Jester, and he clapped Lewis on the shoulder. "Bold. I like this guy."

"Then you can take him and another volunteer tracking with Cat Man," Vivid Blue cut in. "The rest will look around here. I'm going to fly out. Ill Wind may have left a weather trail I can follow."

Peter's hand shot in the air. "I volunteer for the tracking team."

Cat Man grabbed the front of Peter's jacket and stalked off. The Jester ran ahead to the jet. Lewis jumped to follow—

—and watched as the wings folded in and the jet reconfigured into an oversized four-wheeler. Because superbeings couldn't do anything the normal way.

Peter patted at Lewis's shoulder. "I love superheroes."

"Seriously?" Lewis waved a hand toward the vehicle. There were four seats on the thing and the wheels were huge, but Lewis was not going to call it a monster truck. "How was that necessary?"

"I don't care."

Cat Man gave them both a push and slid into the passenger's seat. "Let's go. Meow."

"You heard the cat," the Jester called.

Lewis and Peter hopped in the back, and the Jester tore off down the mountainside, leaving them grasping for handholds.

The vehicle jerked around at Cat Man's last-second directions. Over the low roar of the engine—it still sounded like a jet engine, *why?*—Peter yelled, "How is he tracking anything this way?"

"Cat intuition! Meow!"

The Jester followed up, "Far as we can figure, he makes very lucky guesses."

Lewis wondered if his life could get any more goddamn ridiculous. He snuck a few more looks at Peter as they bounced downhill, his eyes drawn to Peter's elbow pressing tighter against his side. He finally asked under the noise, "You're okay?"

Peter answered too fast through a forced smile. "I'm fine."

Lewis's brow twitched in suspicion. He didn't think Peter would hide an injury, but he'd seen him take situations like this personally before. "I know you've gotten close to Rex—"

"Like you haven't," Peter said with a snort.

That shut Lewis up.

"Hey man, I didn't mean it in a bad way," Peter said, half his attention on the passing mountainside. "I don't get why you're being so angsty about it. You're not doing anything wrong."

The flash drive dug into his hip.

Lewis glanced at the Protectors, brow jumping at the sight of Cat Man leaning against the dashboard, balancing despite the terrain. He couldn't risk either hero overhearing if he spilled the beans to Peter, so he went with something safer.

"I know it's not wrong, but it's complicated. And with Last Dance . . ." He didn't know if he meant to talk about the risk he posed or his suspected collusion with the Meister—well, no longer suspected.

"Lewis." Peter leaned closer and lowered his voice. "Look, no one sits this long on tier four. They either mess up and get bumped to tier five, or they don't mess up and get dropped to tier three. Guess who hasn't violated Oversight since we got here? Rex should've been bumped down months ago."

Lewis's mouth pressed in a tight line. "Quinten's got it out for her—"

"Quinten can make her life hell, but he doesn't have *that* much power," Peter interrupted. "All I can think is that the Oversight Committee is pissing themselves that if they let up surveillance, she'll run off and help Last Dance."

They didn't have to let up surveillance for that to happen.

"So, they're holding tier four and waiting for her to crack so they can justify locking her up. Which she will. This level of oversight isn't sustainable. It isn't meant to be." He shifted in Lewis's peripheral vision, again snatching his hand away from his side to rest it on his gun.

If Peter wasn't hiding an injury, what—

"I think maybe if one of us made a decision in the near future that wasn't entirely in alignment with—I don't know—the law, it maybe wouldn't be entirely their fault. And maybe, hopefully, the other one of us could understand that?"

Easy for Peter to say—he didn't have evidence of Rex's criminal activity in his pocket.

Except, Lewis *had* made a decision. There hadn't been time to process it, but he'd made a decision in Rex's basement when he pocketed that flash drive. Why wasn't he conflicted? He'd thought the question he had to answer was whether Rex was helping her brother. Except she was, and his sense of responsibility hadn't driven him to make the call he'd expected.

He guessed the real question he had to answer was *Do I trust Rex?*

Lewis narrowed his eyes at Peter. "If I'd already done something that might technically be treason, what would you think about that?"

Peter narrowed his eyes too. "Same question back."

The four-wheeler lurched, jarring Lewis from his thoughts, and they were suddenly looking at trees instead of a mountainside. "What was that?" he called to the front.

The Jester answered, "It's a Cat Man thing. You don't want to know."

Lewis's life was a circus act, and it was Rex's fault.

Movement in the trees caught his eye, and he snapped out of his thoughts.

Cat Man leaned over the side of the vehicle, sniffing.

The Jester slowed, shooting glances at Cat Man. "We close?"

A gunshot burst from the trees and Lewis felt the *wham* of impact against the metal door. Lewis's gun was out in an instant, but before he could act, the Jester spun and whipped a knife at the shadows. A strangled yell was like the rallying cry, and people charged from the trees.

The Jester cursed and swerved, bell jangling, as attackers in opera masks and tux-cut Kevlar spilled into their path. With a clatter, someone dropped directly *onto the hood*. Was Last Dance employing ninjas now?

The windshield blocked Lewis's shot, but a yowling Cat Man was already climbing over it. The Jester dragged him back with another curse and pulled him into the driver's seat, twisting to keep a foot on the accelerator. "Keep tracking. I've got it."

The vehicle lurched as Cat Man's foot planted on the pedal, and Lewis locked his arms before his gun could go swinging. The Jester clambered onto the back of the seats and leaped onto the hood, somehow landing just right to take the first man down with two quick punches and spin into a kick that caught a new arrival in the chest.

"Is your power martial arts?" Peter asked over the engine's roar.

"No powers. Just training." Without turning to look, he threw a knife and took out a man leaping for the driver's side.

Lewis could almost hear Rex's incredulous, *Where was he keeping the knife?* but tried not to let it distract him from covering the hero. "Then why the jester theme?" he demanded.

"I was raised by clowns."

Lewis didn't doubt that for a moment.

The Jester tumbled back to the passenger's side to kick an attacker away. "If they're also searching these woods, then Pixie and the others must have escaped."

"They should have a better way to slow us down." Lewis ducked automatically as another shot hit his door. "Even if villains don't care about their minions, it's wasteful."

"I don't know, man. This is how villains do."

A jerk of the wheel sent the four-wheeler into a full speed, ninety-degree turn toward a tree, and Lewis choked on a scream.

A swerve and a bounce put them back on their original path, trees flying past. "Thought I saw a thing. Meow." Cat Man draped himself over the wheel without his foot ever leaving the accelerator. His shoulders bunched level with his darting eyes.

"Ah man," the Jester said, still crouched on the hood, "I forgot the rule about Cat Man driving. You guys hang on."

A building *mmmm* behind Cat Man's curled lips gave Lewis just enough warning to feel dread.

Peter got out, "I'm glad we're together at the end, man," before the vehicle took off in another direction. Lewis grabbed Peter's arm and waited for death.

*T*his was not the end Rex had pictured for herself, but she was getting steadily more okay with the thought of tearing into the pod's remains and making it explode.

"I'm just saying," Pixie continued, leaning against the wall while Rex worked open the tiny computer. "Are you sure you don't have some kind of cheese-related trauma that's been blocked from your memory?"

Rex ripped a strip of plastic casing aside, probably breaking something important along with it. "I bet Flora could use some help guarding Evertrue."

Pixie sighed. "Fine. I can take a hint. But I'm sure someday the right cheese will come along and sweep you off your feet."

"That's true; she believes that," Evertrue called from the other side of the pod.

Rex contemplated the destructive potential of the tech under her hands and wondered if this was how supervillains were born. She ignored the sounds of movement behind her head until Flora knelt beside her, hands resting on her knees.

"If you're able to build something, will we have a way to power it?"

Finally, a useful question. "If there's no intact power source here, we can make some version of a potato battery from stuff in the woods. The challenge is making something low-tech enough to run on that. But we only need a part of a second to get a signal to Aya. With any luck, we'll be out of here before we start breaking into factions to compete for food."

"Can't Pixie help?"

"Pixie's more of a biologist than a mechanic. Not all geniuses are as versatile as me."

"Brag," Evertrue called. "True, though."

"I call not being in his faction."

"Stop worrying about that," Flora said. "We all know it will be the three of us against him anyway."

"I don't know," Pixie called from the back. "I'm starting to think he's not such a bad guy."

Rex took a deep breath and reminded herself to be civil. "He suggested killing you while you were unconscious. Looking normal and being charismatic doesn't excuse people from doing bad things."

"Isn't that how you get excused?"

Rex winced. "Cheap shot."

Flora patted her shoulder. "Breathe, Rex."

Rex focused back on teasing wires from their bundle. Maybe the dinosaurs would find them soon. They must have a search going, at least.

A noise outside startled Rex's concentration away from the wires. A noise like an engine.

Pixie was already moving to the open side of the pod—maybe now she regretted ripping the door off—and Evertrue squirmed for a better view in his seat belt prison.

The noise faded by the time Rex reached Pixie's side. She might have thought she'd imagined it if their whole motley crew wasn't crowded in the doorway with her. Before anyone could kick off the obligatory *what-was-that?* conversation, it came again: a faint engine growl.

At least, Rex thought it was an engine. Who would win in a fight: Pixie or a bear? The sound swelled, and, yep, it was an engine.

A sleek, black four-wheeler—who the heck made a four-wheeler that fancy?—burst from the trees and skidded on leaves to stop a feet from the pod. Before Rex could finish a step back in a delayed fight or flight instinct, Cat Man bounded over the vehicle and launched himself at Pixie.

"Cat Man! Who let you behind the wheel?" Pixie cried in delight as he pulled her into the open and spun her around.

The Jester, perched like the shittiest hood ornament ever made, groaned theatrically and called, "Wrap it up, darlings. Bad guys are less than a mile out. We need to get a move on."

"Rex? Flora?" Peter's voice rounding the vehicle sent a cascade of relief through Rex's body.

Flora hopped to the forest floor. "Thank God you found us. Liam Evertrue is tied up inside. Is Jamal—"

"He's fine," Peter said as he reached them. "You're okay?"

"We're fine," Flora said.

"True, but misleadingly vague," Evertrue said.

"Shut up, Liam," Rex muttered. She stepped into Peter's space to claim a hug. He delivered a stellar hug, ten out of ten—not the hug of someone who had given the suspicious garment stowed in his jacket to Oversight, she didn't think.

When he pulled back, his gaze lingered on her face, and she felt his questions like an itch. But then he looked over his shoulder and called, "Lewis, get your butt in gear."

Lewis staggered out of the vehicle, hunched over and gripping the door. Rex's heart gave a stutter of joy, and she locked her knees against the impulse to, what, run to him? What the fuck? She looked back at Pixie and Cat Man with envy. Not that she wanted Lewis to rub his face all over her chin the way Cat Man was currently doing while Pixie laughed and yelled, "That tickles," but the open show of affection was sort of sweet.

Peter cackled. "Look at him. He's carsick."

The Jester landed lightly on the grass. "You good there, buddy?"

Lewis flipped him off, and Rex's blood boiled. He should be flipping *her* off.

Lewis raised his head for instant eye contact. His gaze jerked away while Rex blinked too many times and considered clearing her throat.

"Are you all right?" he asked.

"Yeah, you should see the other guy," she joked lamely, swinging her arm.

It fell predictably flat, and he looked back at her with a tight expression. "Are you hurt?"

"No. What? That's not what I meant. Anyway"—she needed to control her fucking arm—"Look! We caught a bad guy." She stepped aside so Lewis could see Pixie bundling Evertrue out of the pod. "Ill Wind skated away on a twister, which was badass now that I think about it."

He gave the villain a cursory glance and went back to watching her too sharply. She regretted that joke. Then he said, "Did you know the Jester was raised by clowns?"

"That's the most believable thing I've ever heard."

His face relaxed into a satisfied smile that made her want to do a fist pump.

"Yeah, yeah," the Jester said. He raised his voice. "Listen, people, we're not alone out here. Let's head out."

"I'm driving!" Pixie threw Evertrue into the back seat, slid behind the wheel, and pressed a button that reconfigured the four-wheeler into a more compact version of the Protectors' jet.

Lewis immediately started grumbling, and Rex followed him happily into the transformer.

The sun was setting when they reached the remains of Rex's jet. Rex located her phone where Evertrue had tossed it and stared mournfully at the wreckage.

"I'm sorry you lost it." Lewis hadn't gone far from her side—a blessing and a curse. In his proximity, she felt her composure slipping, but she couldn't let the day catch up with her yet. Oversight wouldn't be happy that she'd been away from her surveillance for so long. She wasn't sure what she'd have to face when she went home, but there would be something.

Rex shrugged it off. "You found us fast. Did you get powers while I was gone? I've honestly expected it to happen to one of you since you started poking around my house. There are a lot of experiments lying around that I'm not allowed to touch anymore. I'm half certain Oversight is trying to set up an origin story."

Lewis made a pained noise and doubled over.

Rex was briefly alarmed, then realized he was laughing. "Every time you laugh it sounds like it's trying to kill you."

"Every time you laugh it sounds like you're going insane," he wheezed.

She huffed and put her arms around herself. The temperature was dropping with the sun, and her jacket was light enough that she'd started shivering. She hoped no one noticed the missing hood.

Lewis shrugged off his uniform jacket and handed it over. "Here."

"Thank you." She fished out the tag and ducked over it, half to read the small print and half to hide her smile.

"What are you doing?"

"I'm wearing my fire suit, so it's important I only wear clean-burning fibers."

"Never mind." He took the jacket back. Rex stopped hiding her grin.

A rustle of cape cloth descended behind them. "T."

Rex turned half around before Viv grabbed her arms and turned her the rest of the way. "What happened? How did you get caught?"

Rex scowled. "I'm fine. Good to know you were concerned."

Viv released a shaky breath, hands loosening on Rex's arms. "Why would you risk a trip like this? What level of obliviousness does it take to fly off somewhere with minimal protection when a supervillain has already approached you—"

"Hold on," Rex cut in, offense finally cutting through her shock. "You're blaming me?" She shrugged out of Viv's hold. "Everyone knew where I was going. If it was such a bad idea—"

"It's your responsibility to keep yourself safe. Maybe for once in your life you could think first."

Viv's blue-ifying accident came to mind. In a flash of anger, Rex wondered if that was Viv's intention. Reason chided that she had no data to suggest that. Rex hated reason.

Lewis stepped closer. "I think we should head back to Decimen City. The rest can wait." He spoke neutrally, but his hand hovered at Rex's shoulder. She let that console her as she brushed past Viv to board the jet.

As expected, Rex was not destined to see her house anytime soon. She ended up where her surveillance was based, in a conference room that no one could tell her hadn't been repurposed for interrogations, telling first Quinten, then the others she didn't recognize that no, she wasn't complicit in the attack on her own jet; it wasn't a ruse to shake her surveillance; and she didn't give information, technology, or advice to Last Dance's accomplices—under duress or otherwise.

She told herself repeatedly that tier five was right around the corner if she made trouble, not to mention Flora's disappointed face. But she was damn tired, and her self-control was barreling toward either explosive noncompliance or preventatively knocking herself unconscious in some self-immolating version of a trolley problem.

Three hours in, Pixie burst through the door, towing Evertrue in handcuffs. Ignoring this hour's nameless interrogator, she looked at Rex and asked, "Did you have anything to do with the attack?"

"No."

"Lie," Evertrue said.

Rex rolled her eyes. "It's not my fault they were after me, and I didn't plan it or help."

"Okay, that's true."

Pixie turned to the interrogator. "Anything else?"

The interrogator cleared his throat. "Are you keeping back any information about the attack? Anything you haven't reported."

Rex gritted her teeth, angry at the assumption but still relieved by the qualifier *about the attack*. If she was in his place, she'd be asking much broader questions. "As I told the last two people, Ill Wind thought Sam's goal was something that I think doesn't make sense."

"True," said Evertrue reluctantly, lips turned down. He should have seen that coming—who better to know how to trick Evertrue than a mind reader? And if Evertrue believed Sam, why wouldn't his other allies? It could be half the reason Sam brought him in.

"Well." The interrogator fiddled with his earpiece and recrossed his legs. "Your story matches the others."

"So, you're done?" Pixie asked.

"There is another, unrelated matter we need to address." He sat forward, poker face pointed at Rex. "It involves an incident several hours ago in Denver, Colorado."

Rex tensed at *Colorado*.

"Have you seen this footage, Ms. Anderson?" He drew out a phone with a video cued up, which hit Rex with irritation.

"How could I have seen whatever that is? I've been in here since I landed in Decimen."

"Just watch the video, Ms. Anderson." When Pixie shifted, he added, "Please keep him here, Pixie. It will expedite matters."

Rex tried to keep half an eye on the others' faces, but her attention was quickly fixed to the screen.

Footage of a crowded room—a movie theater lobby, judging by the concession stand and bright patterns—played out, unremarkable until she recognized a voice offscreen. And yep, there was Stripey, followed by Junior, Bluetooth, Rutabaga Bill, Karen, and either Fairy Baby or Xena, Warrior Princess.

Other moviegoers, with shouts and jumps, made way as the dinosaurs rushed to the ticket stand—oh, it was Xena, the camera caught a view of the feather patterns on her face. Jabbering and laughing, they brandished cell phones which, going by the shell-shocked reactions of the staff, displayed tickets purchased online. Several people edged close to them to take selfies and dart away. Rude.

Rex filled her cheeks with air and let it out slowly. "Don't leave me in suspense. What was the incident?"

The interrogator's brow ticked up. "You think there needs to be more?"

"If they snuck in food, I can pay a fine or something."

"You seemed to understand the problem the first time they got out. You took a very active role in their re-containment."

"Well, they know better than to stampede now," she said with a frown.

"So, you don't think it's a problem that six dinosaurs, four of which are carnivores, can wander into a theater full of people."

"They're all carnivores actually. Something went wrong in the cloning process."

"Oversight is reviewing this incident—"

"For what?" Rex drew herself up, her anger stretching its confines. To slam her head on the table, or not to slam her head on the table? "They paid for tickets like everyone else. What is there to review?"

"If Oversight deems these creatures dangerous, and you prove unable to control them, we have the power to remand custody."

"Lie."

The asshole interrogator shot Evertrue a glare. "We have ways of gaining the power to remand custody."

"Murky. Maybe half true."

Rex snorted.

The man's jaw twitched. "I'm not convinced you're taking this seriously, Ms. Anderson. According to the last test results, your dinosaurs' intelligence is still growing. What are you going to do if they get smarter than you?"

The dinosaurs were already smarter than Rex. But he probably wouldn't react well to that answer. "If all they do is see movies, I don't think we have much to worry about."

"I guess we'll see." The interrogator stood and made a show of pushing his chair back into the table. "We have what we need for now." He put unnecessary emphasis on *for now*. "If you remember anything else—"

"If anything slipped my mind during the last three hours, I'll give you a call," Rex bit out.

When the door closed behind him, Rex slumped in her chair and let out a long sigh.

"Wow, they really don't trust the dinosaurs," Pixie said, taking an empty chair and pulling Evertrue into another, to his unhappy huff.

"I can't believe they went to a movie while I was missing."

"They knew you were okay. Ms. Shay called them before she called me." Pixie pulled out her phone. "Don't worry about the dinos—everyone else liked it. See?" She held her phone in front of Rex and scrolled through selfies with dinosaurs in the background guffawing around mouthfuls of popcorn. The pictures were full of nervously grinning humans and captions like *Great show! No idea what the movie was about* and *So, this happened today.*

"I think the memes are going to overshadow your lecture videos though," Pixie said.

"Pardon?"

"Oh, you wouldn't have seen them yet. I'll find one." She took the phone, scrolled, and turned it back around.

When she pressed play, Rex recognized the clip Evertrue had shown her in the pod: herself center stage in the dinosaurs' auditorium, reaming them out for their rager that first night out of the lab. Except in the poorly edited video, the audience wasn't dinosaurs.

"Let me get this straight." Rex rested her chin on her hands, elbows on the table. "The internet was given footage of an auditorium full of dinosaurs"—she needed to find out which dino was filming and give them a stern phone call—"and they took the dinosaurs out of it?"

"Yup. It's just you pacing angrily on a stage telling people to get their lives together. They've done celebrities, Congress, the casts of TV shows; there's a cute one with a bunch of pigeons—"

"'Dino Mom' and 'Meister Moment' are both trending," Evertrue cut in.

"Who gave him back his phone?" Rex shook her head. She'd have to investigate what Meister Moment meant later. "I'm gonna go home and sleep. Thanks for using your pet lie detector on my behalf."

Pixie ignored Evertrue's indignant grunt and grasped Rex's hand. "I'm just doing my duty. As a hero . . . and a friend."

Rex didn't know how Pixie figured they were friends. Unless she meant the dinosaurs were her friends. Which was also fine. "I appreciate it."

"True," Evertrue said.

Pixie gave her a glowing smile and fluttered her nonfunctional wings.

They left the conference room together, Pixie dragging Evertrue. As they stepped out of the elevator, Rex pulled out her phone to text someone—maybe Flora?—to ask if there were soldiers waiting to take her home, when a shadow and a cape rustle blocked her path.

"We need to talk, T."

Rex blinked at Viv, taking in her expressionless, blue face. Her phone hung limp in her hand with the text half-typed.

"Hi, Blue!" Pixie greeted with a wave.

Viv gave her a nod and refocused on Rex. "You can't do this kind of thing anymore." Before Rex could ask what she meant, she added, "Your surveillance has been recommending that you not be allowed out of the city for a long time. I've been blocking it with the committee, but I see now that was a mistake."

Rex stared at her, mouth open, brain catching up. "You think this was my fault." Indignation gave her some energy. "I got valuable information at least. Sam is lying to his allies. I think a lot of this might be for show."

"So, the ends justify the means for you."

"*What* means? I didn't make this happen."

"At the very least, you can't afford to take these risks," Viv said in her I'm-being-reasonable voice. "You're already a target, and with your whole antihero campaign it's no wonder villains consider you safe to approach."

"My what campaign?"

"This More to the Story movement. The glorified hissy fit you've riled people into online."

"That's not what that's about." That point felt more important than clarifying that Rex wasn't driving that discourse.

"Of course, it's not."

Rex was pretty sure that condescending tone was reserved entirely for her. She started walking again. "I don't have to do this." She was too tired and bitter. She was going to bed.

Viv's blue eyes flicked toward the ceiling as Rex passed. "Of course not."

A vice tightened on Rex's lungs. She should keep walking. She really should. She turned back. "What does that mean?"

"I just shouldn't be surprised that you're waiting for someone else to clean up your messes."

Rex bit her lip hard and tasted blood. "I didn't ask you to do anything for me."

"No, you're just going to ignore the problem until I fix it. Don't worry, I'm used to it."

A quick, angry breath escaped Rex's lips from the weight of *she can't think that* pressing on her chest. "I don't know what you've been telling yourself, but I've never done that."

"So, I'm not the one dealing with our brother after you gave up. And that also isn't why you're stalling on making that hood you promised me."

Rex gaped over the need to respond to 'gave up,' 'stalling,' and 'our brother' all at once, and came up with, "You don't know what you're talking about."

"Try to tell me you didn't refuse to cure Sam out of revenge. We both know you still won't forgive him."

"I don't need revenge. I forgave him ages ago."

"True," Evertrue said, sounding surprised.

Viv didn't spare him a glance. "And your actions clearly support that."

"I did forgive him. But you're acting like that means I wasn't supposed to learn from it," Rex hissed. Loving someone was dangerous and fucking painful and that would always be true no matter how well you learned to live with it. "You're not telling me to forgive him; you're telling me not to be different now. Well, I *am* different."

Viv looked unimpressed. "You say that, but you're acting the same way seven years later. It's like you enjoy being a victim."

"That's not the problem! I got over it. I don't give a shit."

"Eh. That's like half lie, half true," Evertrue offered.

"Everything around it is what stayed." There had to be a way to word it, a way to get it across. Viv didn't understand, and that was suddenly unacceptable to Rex. "All the bullshit that got p-piled on." She couldn't cry. She didn't want to cry in front of Viv. "It's like all the parts that didn't make it into your damn origin story just got ign-nored and sh-shoved into this pit." She was shaking. This was the closest they'd ever come to talking about—about—

Viv sighed. "Go ahead. Let's hear how you're going to make it about you."

It hit like a punch, driving the rest of the words right out of her. But she'd cracked herself open and hadn't had time to close herself back up. "It *was* about me!" she screamed. "It happened *to me*! Maybe what happened to you was about you, and what happened to Sam was about Sam, and the world can validate the fuck out of that—I don't care. But what happened to me was all the fuck about me!"

"There's the truth." Viv's voice was rising, but not to a yell, which infuriated Rex on its own. "That's how you feel about everything, isn't it? You're bitter because no one's shining a spotlight on your problems." A quick breath and a tight smile cut Rex to the bone. "What even happened to you? You were held in a cabin for a few days and got some bruises? I know it was hard, and I'm sorry—but what will it take for you to get over yourself? Do you have any idea how much worse some people have it? Do you know the kinds of things I've saved people from?"

The only thing in Rex's mind was a litany of *fuck you*'s.

"I understood when you were shaken for a while," Viv continued, pacing the width of the hall.

Shaken. Not sleeping for days, throwing up in the sink when she looked in the mirror and practiced saying, *"I slipped in the shower."*

"But he *needed* you. Your own twin. And all you had to do was reverse what your machine did."

None of it had *worked.* Every test, every trial. Fighting the dizzying rage when her brain reminded her what he'd done to keep her working, and how she was *still working anyway.* Sickening, how she was betraying herself for his sake.

"As far as I'm concerned, he is what he is now because of you. Because you were too wrapped up in yourself to suck it up and help him."

Rex was such a fool. Why had she thought Viv might listen? Because she'd stuck up for her once or twice? How desperate was she to see Viv on her side that she'd read into so little?

Viv paced past Pixie and Evertrue, who were practically holding hands now and apparently under the impression that Viv and Rex couldn't see them if they didn't move. "At this point I'm wondering if it's about me," Viv said. "It's not like you ever had anything to do with me if you could help it."

Rex tried to close off again, grasping for the faults and fissures she'd stupidly exposed. Since she couldn't shut down, she tried to be angry instead of hurt, but it wasn't working.

"Maybe it's because I want to save him, and you can't get over how much you always hated me." Viv spat out.

Oh, now it was working. "Hated you?" Rex was distantly thrown by the coldness of her own voice. "I spent the first eight years of my life bending over backward to make you like me. Then I spent the next decade sucking up to you for fucking up your life and that didn't work either. I never fucking hated you—I learned to take a hint."

A scowl flashed across Viv's face before she smoothed it out. "I swear, you go out of your way to be a victim."

The sentiment wormed in like water. *Stop whining,* she'd told herself as the motion of cars made her heart race. *Suck it up,* she'd thought when she heard a worse story, with a worse villain. *Get over it. Don't be a victim. Stop being so weak.*

It was incredible how fast Viv turned everything Rex might have called progress five minutes ago into self-indulgence. It was like a superpower; Viv could make anything true just by saying it. Her judgment seeped through Rex like a disease and made her disgusting and pathetic, like she'd always suspected she was. The small inner voice saying it wasn't true would never be stronger than Viv, and for that . . . "I hate you so much."

Viv's eyes flicked, for the first time, toward Evertrue. Pixie stirred and nudged him with her elbow, but he stayed silent.

"Well, that's not news," Viv finally said. She took two steps away, then spun back around. "And what a childish thing to say. Really, you hate me? Run to your room, T. Don't forget to slam the door."

She strode away so fast that Rex couldn't scrape up a last word.

Silence only hung for a second before Pixie gasped an inhale. "Oh, man, I forgot to breathe." She bent over her knees and wheezed, jerking Evertrue down by the cuffs.

"Well. *Now* I can go home. That's what I was waiting for." Rex stopped when her voice wavered, then she continued toward the exit. With each step, her energy drained. She hardly felt anything. No anger, no lingering self-loathing, no remorse for her words. She was just done.

Voices caught her ear as she neared the front, coming through a cracked office door. She spared a glance at the babysitters waiting in the lobby. Then a shred of curiosity drew her toward the murmurs. She distinguished Viv's voice, holding more emotion than Rex had heard from her in years.

"—better than this. But it's like I get within ten feet of my family and I'm sixteen again."

"Family is difficult," Don Conjure's voice soothed.

Rex felt a stab of anger at hearing her place in Viv's life cut down to a platitude.

"I think sometimes we know our families so well that we can't really know them," Don Conjure continued, muffled by the cracked door. "We can't see who they've become because we've seen every step they took to get there. Or worse—we've seen most of the steps. Enough to think we've seen them all."

When Viv's voice started again— "She just doesn't ever—" Rex stepped away, breathing a little harder through the thickness in her throat that she didn't feel like feeling. Thankfully, the swirl of emotion drained away as fast as before, until she was greeting her surveillance through a fog of exhaustion and nothing else.

SPOTLIGHT ON THE PAST: PART THREE

Rex used to dream a lot. The dreams were long and elaborate. She was always someone different: an old woman leading a revolution, a young man in a postapocalyptic world, a boy with a circus family. In each dream, people relied on her desperately for something. She would sacrifice, bleed, consume herself to give them what they needed. Whoever she was in the dream, she always accepted it as no less than what she owed, a natural part of the world. She would wake from the dreams each morning, get control of her breathing, try to eat something, and get back to work on the cure for cancer.

ISSUE 29

DINOSAURS IN COMPLICITY

*R*ex zoned out on the ride home. When she spotted her house through the window, a wave of relief hit. She'd—geez, she'd been *kidnapped* today. She'd crashed two different aircrafts. An overwhelming need to be home dragged her out of her lethargy and through the front door, noticing all the familiarities down to the tap her shoes made on the wood floor.

Aya swept in with a mechanical hum. "Welcome home, Doctor. It is good to see you well."

A smile spread over Rex's face. "Sorry about the delay."

"Ms. Shay has been in touch. She requested that I tell you she is stopping by Sadie's house before heading home."

A movement past the entryway drew her attention, and she locked eyes with Lewis. He hadn't changed out of his uniform. Rex wondered why she'd noticed, then recalled other times they'd run into each other this late, staggering into the kitchen in sleepwear.

He watched her with his lips pressed in a thin line. The silence stretched between them. As she tried to think of a way to break it, Lewis asked, "Have you eaten?"

Wow, not since breakfast. Her stomach gurgled at the reminder. "There's more of that casserole in the fridge," she mumbled.

"If you eat that, you'll die. I'll make you a sandwich." He turned back to the kitchen.

Rex trailed after him, soaking up his presence. They didn't speak as Lewis put a sandwich together, besides his half-muttered, "I know you don't like cheese. Anything else?" and her answering, "Naw." She considered thanking him but thought it would be weird.

Lewis carried the plated sandwich into the living room, sat on the couch, and handed it over as Rex sat next to him with a sigh.

She felt his gaze as she made her way through the, God, best sandwich of her life. It wasn't uncomfortable, though he made no effort to hide that he was watching. When she'd finished half, she slowed, taking more time to chew and spacing out at the wall as her weariness returned. Her shoulder brushed Lewis's arm. She'd automatically sat right next to him, the way they had before the security crackdown. He gave no sign that it bothered him.

Bruises from the crash ached dully. Loose threads hung where Rex's jacket had snagged on sharp corners, and her collar was stretched from Ill Wind yanking her around. The thigh of Lewis's uniform pants had a black smear, probably from the jet, and green-brown stains streaked the shins and ankles.

"I'm really glad you're back," Lewis said.

"Me too," Rex mumbled. It felt natural to follow up with, "I've missed you."

Lewis was silent for a moment. "Me too."

Rex let herself fall a little more against his arm. She felt heavy, and Lewis was warm. She hadn't realized his smell had become familiar, but now she was close enough to notice.

Lewis's gaze on her felt different. She turned her head to check his face, but she couldn't read it. There was another black smear on his chin, his hair pressed flat on one side.

He raised a hand to her face and wiped some mustard from the edge of her mouth with his thumb. She couldn't move or think. His thumb pulled away, but his fingers trailed down to her jaw and stayed there. Then he leaned down, and his lips pressed softly to hers.

Rex felt familiar discomfort at having a face so close to her face, as well as minor disgust at touching someone else's spit, but it was overshadowed by the puff of glee that Lewis wanted this. He wanted her. Her mouth moved with his, ignoring the conflict between too-soon good and bad sensations. She knew how to kiss—find the rhythm, keep it up long enough to not hurt a guy's pride, act reluctant while pulling away, and avoid doing it again for as long as possible. It was easy.

It wasn't real.

Her gut clenched, and she pulled away. Lewis looked blank as his face came back into view. Then a touch of devastation passed across it and left behind a fiery blush.

"Oh. I—shit. Damn it. I misread—"

"No, Lewis, it's not—" She tried to grab his hand as he stood, but he was already moving to the door, talking a little too fast and a little too flatly.

"I understand if you want to report me to Quinten or the Oversight Committee, but I'd appreciate if you let me come forward about this myself. I don't think it's appropriate for me to stay here anymore. I can call a replacement."

"Shit, Lewis, stop." Rex followed, trying to talk over him, something hard and choking growing in her chest as her thoughts scattered into static. "Please, I want to talk about this."

"I'm sorry. I can't—I shouldn't be here."

In the entryway, Rex got around him enough to see his face and momentarily forgot her words. His eyes were wet.

"I'm really sorry." The last word hitched a bit. He pushed gently past her and through the door, closing it behind him.

Rex caught the door. "Fuck," she gasped, short of breath. She shoved the door open too hard and scrambled after him. Her heart was in the base of her throat. She ran to the driveway, but he must have sped up when he got outside because the closest car was starting.

"Lewis, stop," she yelled.

Grant's shout behind her stopped her short. "Hey! You take one more step and I'll report a curfew violation."

Rex half turned toward him. "Wait, let me—shit!" She turned back, but Lewis was pulling into the street. She tried one more, "Hey!" fully considering throwing a rock after him.

Grant grabbed her arm, and she spun around. "Fuck off!"

He had a phone in his other hand, the speaker pressed against his chest. "No leaving the premises after—"

"I don't fucking care!" It came out with a sob. She stormed past him back into the house, aware of the tears leaking down her face and bitter disappointment tearing at her chest. In her peripheral vision, Aya hovered in a doorway, hesitating. Rex didn't blame her.

She'd wanted something real, right? Well, here it fucking was. What else did she expect?

She got to the home lab, Aya slipping in behind her, close to the floor. A thought of the cameras in every room brought a twist of humiliation that made her break into giggles. Then her face crumpled, and she sobbed.

The *ding* of the lab door made her turn, the thought of trying to hide her face discarded as futile. Grant stood in the doorway, the phone to his ear. "Yes, sir," he said, stepping inside. "Yes, I understand."

"What are you doing?" she blubbered.

Aya bobbed away from the wall. "On behalf of Ms. Anderson, I request a moment of priva—"

Rex's confusion died in horror as he took out his gun and shot Aya's left eye.

Metal bits exploded across the lab. The second eye's light winked out as it veered sideways, hit the floor with one hard bounce, and rolled into a corner. The eyes weren't Aya, but the association was so strong in Rex that the floor dropped out beneath her. "What are you doing?" she screeched.

"Oversight techs traced the original uploads of your viral interview to your AI. It matched the source of the dino party videos and a number of online pieces critical of how your Oversight is being handled. Oversight classified it as a rogue program to be terminated immediately. Backup is already on the way."

Grant followed the second eye with his gun, but he lowered it as the light stayed dark. He looked thoughtful. "But this isn't where the program is housed is it?"

Rex's stomach dropped through the floor and all the way down to the rows of servers in the lowest basement. "Wait."

Grant was already striding to the stairs.

"No!" She scrambled after him. "Stop!"

He passed the elevator and unlocked the door to the stairs with the code she'd given to Oversight.

Rex threw herself into the elevator, barking, "Server level." The elevator moved before the doors finished closing. As they opened on the lowest floor, Grant exited the stairs at a run.

Rex didn't have time to be alarmed that he'd gotten through the door she'd sealed months ago. Why hadn't she paid more attention to the house search? She'd sewn the hood onto her jacket like that was the only thing she had to protect.

As Grant raised his gun to the electric lock on the wall, Rex threw herself in front of it. "Please."

"Get out of the way, Meister. Harboring a rogue AI is your ticket to tier five, but you can still make things worse for yourself."

"You can't kill her for posting videos!"

"I can terminate a program that's facilitating a supervillain's plot. In fact, it's my job."

"Aya isn't working with Last Dance."

"I was talking about you." He flicked the gun in a gesturing motion. "Step aside. I won't say it again."

Rex's knees locked as she shut down her rabbit-like instinct to run. Her heart raced so fast she could hardly breathe. "No."

Grant raised the gun and shot over her head. Rex flinched hard through the *bang* and glanced up at cracks spiderwebbing from the bulletproof glass. Grant fired twice more, each hit making Rex jolt. Dust and shards fell onto Rex's head.

She pressed herself against the wall as though she could hold it together with her hands. She didn't have any real ideas.

Trooping, heavy footsteps on the stairs drew Grant's attention before he could fire again. Rex could already see it: they'd pull her away from the door; they'd shoot out the glass; they'd wipe the servers or destroy them. Then they'd go after her satellites. They'd leave no significant piece of Aya intact.

She heard telling, cascading clicks in the ceiling and thought of the laser guns disabled in her walls. The memory of the last option she'd left for herself burst through her panic, and she yelled, "Do it!"

Spigots poked through the ceiling and released white gas into the room, stairwell, and open elevator with a long *hiss*.

Frozen, Rex watched the gas seep toward the floor. Grant turned back to her with an expression of understanding and hate that would've made her step back if she wasn't already pressed to the wall. The flurry of motion and shouts as the soldiers noticed the creeping gas went ignored in the background. A gunshot echoed from the stairwell—maybe someone shot a spigot. Then the only sounds were the thumps of bodies dropping.

Grant's gun lowered, and for an instant Rex was weightless with the certainty he meant to shoot her. Then it lowered further, and he crumpled to the floor, disturbing the white tendrils of smoke.

Rex gasped and braced shaking hands on her knees, white clouds billowing up around her. Her head buzzed a bit as she inhaled the gas, but she didn't pass out. Her inoculation stood up to field conditions. Yay, science.

Still shaking, she pressed a hand to the scanner on the door and flinched when it pricked her finger for a blood sample. Had she gone overboard on the biosecurity considering Grant almost got through the wall with a few gunshots? She'd invest in stronger building materials in the future. But considering the last ten minutes, those materials might have to be delivered to a secret underground lair of some kind.

She cast a glance back at the soldiers lying unconscious on her floor. Oh, there was no going back from this.

Underwater lair. She was more of an underwater lair kind of person. Of course, then she'd have to worry about sea-based superheroes, which were all kinds of obnoxious. But maybe Whale Woman would be down to hang out.

The door to the server room opened, and Rex staggered inside. "Aya?" Her voice cracked. She cleared her throat. "Aya?"

A terminal lit up, and text flashed across the screen.

Aya: I apologize, Doctor. I saw no other way to preserve myself.

Rex swallowed, shuffled to the terminal, and typed back.

Doc: you did good. I would have made the call if I'd thought of it.

Letting out a long breath, she leaned against the terminal and dropped her head. When she looked back up, she spoke softly. "Aya, you made the video?"

The screen didn't change for so long Rex wondered if the terminal hadn't picked up her voice. Then a new line appeared.

Aya: I just wanted people to hear what you have to say.

Rex was too emotionally exhausted not to smile. "I'm not mad. But you must see what this looks like to them."

Aya: Conspiratorial honesty, Doctor?

Rex exhaled a silent laugh. "I recall telling you not to do anything illegal without running it by me first."

Aya: I apologize.

She sighed. "Well, we're officially on a time crunch. We can hash out the rest later. Flora wasn't in the building, right?"

Aya: No, Doctor. I took the liberty of updating Ms. Shay via blackout procedures. There will be no record of our communication on her devices. She is awaiting your call.

Doc: Link it through here.

A box opened over their chat and was almost instantly filled with Flora's wide-eyed face. "Rex! Are you okay? Are you safe?"

"For now." She tried to smile and deemed the attempt passable. Lewis's last expression popped into her head with another tug at her heart before she dispelled it.

Okay, priorities. "Aya's servers need a fast extraction. The knockout gas should hold for six hours or so, but someone will probably show up sooner. I can engage Bunker Mode, but I don't know how long it will stop the Protectors." She shied away from the mental image of Vivid Blue trying to bust into her house on full lockdown.

"I need some of the dinosaurs' construction equipment for moving the servers," she continued, ticking down the list. "If they've improved the cloaking tech I put in their dinocopters, those would be great too."

"Updating the compound now, Doctor," Aya acknowledged.

Rex nodded. "Flora, where are you?"

"Sadie's."

"Stay there. If we keep your hands clean, maybe there's some legal stuff you can do. Self-defense?"

"I don't think there's precedent for gassing your surveillance for threatening your AI, but I'll see what I can do," Flora said flatly.

A smile fell across Rex's face more easily this time. "Okay." Her legs felt weak. She lowered herself to the floor and leaned against the terminal. That was better. "All right."

Flora's voice followed her down. "Rex, where will you go? The compound?"

"No. I won't put more of a target on the dinosaurs." She paused. "You haven't tried to sell Everglade again, right?"

"The old lab facility?" Flora's voice turned wary. "It's hard to sell land that's been zoned as a dumping ground for toxic waste."

Rex winced. Yet another thing she hadn't told Flora. It was shameful how many of those she'd stumbled across. "I kept it powered and stocked. Just in case."

"Well," Flora said. Then after a beat, "I guess your paranoia paid off."

Hopefully this would be the last time. No more secrets from Flora. "Important question: how are things going with Sadie?"

Flora made an indistinct noise. "Rex, is this really the time—"

"Come on—I've been dying to know."

Flora sighed. "It's good," she said with an indulgent air. "We've had several good talks. It, um—it turns out she was jealous of you."

Rex blinked *a lot*. "Of me?"

"We do live in each other's pockets, Rex."

"I don't even know where yours are," Rex protested.

"I don't know what that means. But you're my best friend, and I think she understands that now." Flora paused. "Rex, however this turns out, I hope you know that as much as I try to be your impulse control, I've enjoyed every minute of being swept along with your antics."

Rex snorted. "Even getting kidnapped and crashing in the woods?"

"You take the good with the bad."

Rex's eyes swept over Grant and the other soldiers who'd made it out of the stairwell. Through the lingering gas, their uniforms were clearer than their faces.

Lewis had been in his uniform when he met her at the door less than an hour ago. She pushed the thought away with a bitter swallow.

An underwater lair sounded really inconvenient. Anyone who took on that lifestyle without a strong commitment to villainy would surely get there in the end. Her hands, limp at her sides, curled into fists.

It should not be this easy to get rid of her.

"Flora, another important question: what do we do with our money?"

"Run the lab, mostly," Flora said, tone cautious. "Although a good amount goes into cleaning up after you. We invest, and we support some causes. And for the hundredth time, no, we can't just buy a politician for that. We don't have politician money."

"What would it take to have politician money?"

"Excuse me?"

"That's just an example. Say we didn't have to clean up after me so much. Say we had a direction. What would you want to do instead?"

There was a pause before Flora's voice came back. "That's a big question."

"Think on it. Aya, how difficult would it be for you to popularize a conspiracy online?"

"I have done as much out of ignorance," Aya answered.

Rex nodded to herself. "We're getting out of this." How many times had she let the fight define the arena? "And we're doing it your way," she added, addressing them both. "Cult of personality, legalese, and memes." Maybe instead of pushing back, she could turn in another direction. "I think it's time we made ourselves essential."

"Do you mean to take over the world, Doctor?"

"If you want to call it that," Rex answered. She looked up at the screen. "If we do this right, it will take a very long time."

The familiar scratch of Flora's pen on paper came through. "I'll make a flowchart."

DINOSAURS IN HIVEMIND

While waiting for the dinocopters to arrive, Rex had Aya prep a production floor and fabricated three hoods. The first was a copy of the maroon hood that, for all she knew, Peter still had. The second was a more refined version of the drunkenly-invented hood that hid Rex's thoughts from Sam—the one Oversight confiscated. But in yellow instead of brown, because why not?

The third came last because she had to make the design in her head a digital reality. She made it purple, in a fabric to match Vivid Blue's pale purple cape.

"But how is that a Meister Moment?" Rex stepped over an unconscious soldier as she adjusted the purple hood's wiring.

Flora's voice carried from the phone in her pocket. "It's not that hard to understand. It's when you get worked up over something ridiculous."

"I get worked up over important things," Rex muttered as she bent to shift Becky's head to a more comfortable angle. She'd found Peter at the top of the stairs, which made her gut twist, and checked him for Sam's original hood. It wasn't there. He must have stashed it somewhere. She'd been tempted to try to move him to a couch, but since she'd already gassed him, she might as well avoid signs of favoritism that could cause him trouble later.

"You know this isn't new, right? Meister Moments were a thing in Decimen City long before it caught on online."

Rex pulled out her phone and scrolled back through the Meister Moment hashtag. "Why are there so many pictures of kids chastising their toys?"

"That's more specific to the dinosaur lecture clip, but you get the idea." The tapping of a keyboard had replaced Flora's pen scratch. "I've arranged an interview with *Good Morning, Gorgeous*. You're meeting Gorgeous in two days at Jake's Coffee for the interview. Are you sure that's not too risky?"

"It's necessary. I'll wear a wig or something." Rex frowned. "Why Gorgeous, though? It's not live, right?"

"The network has been wanting to do a follow-up interview since your last one went viral. The people I talked to say Gorgeous especially has been pushing for a pre-taped interview so you can talk more candidly and edit it later."

Rex wondered if that meant Gorgeous had enjoyed her live shitshow or really, really hated it.

"Rex, I'm watching the security footage, and I think we've got something to work with. People tend to get irrational when they think they're dealing with a rogue AI, and it looks like Grant's no exception."

Rex felt relief, then compartmentalized it. "That's great. Keep on it."

"I have selected sites that will make ideal points of entry," Aya chimed in. "Is there a particular subject with which I should start?"

At the home lab's control station, Rex triggered Bunker Mode in most wings of the house and fried the controls. They would be a bitch to get back into, but she didn't want to make it easy for Oversight. "Burn Lieutenant Quinten first. It looks more natural to start with the small fish."

"Do I have permission to break laws in pursuit of material?"

Rex shrugged. "It'll be cleaner if you don't, but as long as you don't get caught."

"Doctor, the dinosaurs have arrived."

"Great." Rex moved to the chemical zone and checked on the synthesizing formula. "They're not going to like this part."

Rex was moving Aya's servers to Zombie Island. They'd be vulnerable in any of her properties, but she couldn't think of better security than being surrounded by ocean and zombies. But Rex wasn't letting the dinosaurs deliver them without being inoculated against Mutey.

"But Mom, you can't," Fairy Baby wailed.

"We don't take chances with the mutant strain of zombie virus." Rex wiped disinfectant on the dilophosaur's shoulder. "Want me to count, or surprise you?"

Fairy Baby flared her crest, eyes squeezed shut. "Don't surprise me! Count. Count to three."

When it was over, Rex pasted on a bandage and gave Fairy Baby a hug. "Good job. Next."

Jasper stopped cradling his bandage like a mortal wound to sign a few words to Fairy Baby, and Rex pointed at him. "I saw that, J. And you know what?" She signed, *Wait until I figure out how to vaccinate you.* He skittered out on Fairy Baby's heels.

As the smaller dinos got started moving the servers, Rex took some extra-extra-large needles outside to the big ones. Damien and Two-Toed Nancy took the shots stoically, lights blinking on their techy-looking tiaras. When Rex got no reaction after slapping a bandage on Damien and shimmying back down his leg, she asked, "Is something wrong? You felt that, right?"

The two dinos' heads turned toward her, and they answered in unison, "We are sorry, Mother. We have activated the swarm network and are utilizing our combined mental capacities to facilitate the removal of the server bank."

Rex blinked, glancing from their faces to the blinking metal tiaras on their heads and back. "Did you . . . are you in hivemind?"

"Indeed, Mother," they answered. "Though many of our biologies were partially suited for such instincts, technology has facilitated a more controlled melded state, allowing a higher level of mental processing for the purpose of directing nanoswarms such as the one currently transporting the servers in your home."

"You're controlling nanoswarms by clustering your brains like when you link PCs to make a supercomputer."

The twin voices confirmed, "That summation is satisfactory, Mother, though simplified."

Numbly, Rex pulled the phone from her pocket. "Flora, did you hear that?"

"I hope not, because I thought I heard the word hivemind," Flora answered.

A crackling sound drew Rex's attention to the house as a smooth-flowing nanoswarm burrowed through the wall, dismantling the material to make a hole for rapidly constructing conveyor belts to move lines of servers into the yard. Jasper and the other dinos accompanied them with uniform gaits, each wearing a blinking circlet.

Something caught in her throat. "My dinosaurs went Borg. I'm so proud I could die."

"Remember literally everything we've talked about concerning your public image—"

"Indeed, Aunt Flora," the dinosaurs whispered in sync, voices coming from across the yard and, faintly, inside the house. "No mention of our networking technologies will be bared for public scrutiny until the advances we make in this state can speak to its effectiveness and positive impact on humanity to the satisfaction of mentally-limited singulars."

"Dear Lord," Flora muttered.

"Yeah, not to be shared with the squeamish masses," Rex agreed. "I'd love to keep gushing, but middle of the night or not, I'm sure someone will notice the apatosaur on my front lawn soon, so we need to wrap this up."

"Agreed," the dinosaurs whispered. "And we wish for you to know, Mother, in this state we have named ourselves Dino Might."

Flora sighed through the phone.

Before Dino Might left for Zombie Island, Rex had them use the nanoswarm to move the military vehicles blocking her car. She was tempted to take the Exo-suit, since she was already going on the run, but Flora advised against it.

"I'm trying to make a case for self-defense. It won't look great if you start breaking every other rule they've given you. Also, I'd love to see you stay off the radar in a giant mecha."

"Fine." Rex sighed and got behind the wheel as the last stealth copter vanished with a shimmer. "Aya, your driving skills haven't gotten rusty, have they?"

"That is not possible, Doctor." The car pulled smoothly into the road.

"You're sure this will get his attention?" Flora asked as Rex mapped the route to Everglade. Her voice turned wary. "You're sure it's a good idea to get his attention?"

"I know my brother." Rex tried to sound firm. "If what Ill Wind said is true, he wouldn't mind us finding his base, anyway."

Rex had no more reason to suck up to Oversight, her virus was still out there, and she'd just learned Sam was lying to his allies. So, she was going to make the obvious play: join the villains, find their base—make sure Mindbender was *in* the base—and call the Protectors down on their ass. Really, with how believable a double-cross would be given her current circumstances, she'd be an idiot not to take advantage.

And if Sam wanted to take his hood and slip out the back . . . well.

Maybe she understood why the Protectors didn't trust her with this.

"If you think he'd agree to your plan, why hide your thoughts?"

Rex picked up the yellow hood and ran the fabric between her fingers. "Caution. I've been hit in the face several times lately by the fact that I'm not omniscient. If I can keep some cards to myself, I will."

Flora thought that over. "I'm proud of you, Rex. Good luck."

Rex smiled. "You too."

Rex spent the rest of the ride to the outskirts of Decimen City drafting her message, taking feedback from Aya about the most appropriate platform and the likely response.

As the car pulled around the back of the dark facility, Rex read over her words one more time.

Hi, folks. I don't post much, but this is easier than telling everyone I know in Decimen what happened. Basically, my AI allegedly broke the law so now I'm going on the lam.

That ought to grab Sam's attention—or whoever he had monitoring her. Rex let out a breath and reviewed the follow-up posts.

Unfortunately, she's the most advanced artificial being of moral conscience on the planet and has few established legal rights, which apparently means Oversight can kill her for violating a copyright (allegedly). I'm pretty committed to not letting that happen, thus the lam.

I've been trying to comply with Oversight. I've done things that make people scared and this is the result of my actions. Also, they keep hinting about putting down my dinosaurs, so that's a big motivator.

Rex smirked.

Oversight was going to love what people thought of that.

But there's honestly something wrong if Oversight has the power to hurt my dinosaurs or my AI over something I did. Not that I have the wherewithal to judge a glaring flaw, but I think I made the right choice here.

So that's my first point. On to point number two: As you may know, Last Dance is my twin brother. Yeah, big gasp, we look super alike so it's not that surprising. Anyway, he contacted me recently for help on a tech problem.

The thing I can do for him might help limit his powers. I think everyone wants that, Last Dance included. I know he's done bad things. I haven't lost sight of that. I just don't want him to suffer anymore. Honestly, I'm still not super clear on what makes someone beyond mercy or a Real Villain.

Most people bring it back to who their victims are. But people talk for days about which villains are real villains when they've already

decided which victims are real victims. Which feels a lot like deciding
which people are real people. It skeeves me out.

"Are you sure I shouldn't change that part?" Rex asked, pointer finger
hovering.

"Online dialogue encourages authenticity, Doctor," Aya said. "As your
typical mode of discourse is already well known, any significant deviation
would come across as ungenuine or overly scripted."

Rex shrugged. "You're the expert."

So, if Last Dance gains the ability to speak to fish or something, it might
be on me. To try to head off that kind of thing (see? I'm learning), I
made a countermeasure to share with Vivid Blue. I've arranged to get it
to her first thing tomorrow.

"You don't think it's too obvious?" Rex asked.

"I believe that is the point, Doctor."

Establishing a deadline was one of the more important parts of the
message. If Sam thought Viv's threat level was going up tomorrow, he'd have
to collect his hood from Rex tonight.

I'm trying to improve myself. Which mostly means confusing myself
and un-confusing myself a lot and then trying to make better choices.
That's boring to hear about, sorry. I think real stories are actually shit.
There's too much backstory, it gets too bizarre to stay relatable, and
every time you think you've resolved something it pops back up to cause
the same damn problems.

Anyway, I'm a confused idiot who doesn't always know how to
separate my feelings from a situation or tell right from wrong. So, expect
a lot of meandering and decisions that will embarrass me in five years.

My goal for now is to not endanger the public (I have a good streak
going, if anyone's keeping track) and to have some positive impacts that

aren't secondhand through my much more likable dinosaur progeny. I
have thoughts about applications for my cancer cure, so that seems like
the place to start. Past that, we'll see.

Rex's thumb hovered over the publish button. Inhaling, she returned to
the message and added *#MoretotheStory*. She hit post.

She let the phone fall onto her chest, staring at the car's ceiling. The
phone started to ping within seconds, making her stomach churn. "Aya, turn
off notifications."

The pinging stopped.

Okay. On to the next thing. Rex got out of the car and walked to the
building. She needed to get the purple hood to Viv before contacting Last
Dance. Aya could tell her where it was, but maybe Viv wouldn't listen to
the AI. Should she call her? Their fight burned like acid on the back of her
tongue. Maybe she wouldn't listen to Rex, either.

The problem circled in her head as she pushed through the door and
flipped the light switch. Lights clicked on down the long ceiling of the
open-concept lab.

Something in the middle of the room caught her eye, one bright spot of
yellow in the empty, gray floor. Rex froze like a dinosaur caught downloading pirating software on Aunt Flora's travel laptop.

The Lightning uncrossed her legs and stood, full mask leveled at the
door. "Hello, Rex."

"Shit." She flipped the light back off.

SPOTLIGHT ON LEWIS STONE:

LEWIS HAS A MISERABLE TIME

*L*ewis had always liked Rex's lab. Maybe that was why he thought some-one particularly vindictive must have assigned him to the Peak Street search team. He trailed a step behind Peter because he wanted to make sure Peter didn't keel over from the counteragent he'd been injected with less than an hour ago. It wasn't because he didn't want to look at all the reminders of Rex.

"I got gassed by the Meister of Decimen City," Peter said, casting a bored glance down a corridor. "How long should I wait to put that on a T-shirt?"

Lewis lacked the brain power to respond.

"Hey, are you feeling left out, or—"

"I was on the road. I should have been there."

"You would have gotten gassed too. It wouldn't have made a difference."

"If I'd been there, I would have talked some sense into Grant, and it would never have gotten to that point." He strode past Peter to look down the next corridor.

Mistake. This was the hall with a paper sign over each inset light that said *green means good* because Rex said her babysitters needed the extra help. That was so *funny*. Also, Lewis was worthless and every choice he'd ever made was wrong. He hurried past the hall, choking on a lump in his throat. "I shouldn't have left."

"Why *did* you leave?" Peter asked, swinging his arms and dropping even the pretense of searching the lab. "You haven't said much since I got through medical, and I'm getting concerned."

Lewis was sinking into something bad—shame and something muddier that he didn't want to look at too hard. He wavered, thinking of all the reasons now wasn't the time to get into this. But when his eyes started swimming, he decided he wasn't that strong.

The story spilled out as though someone else was telling it. His mind flinched away from thinking about it. The raw-edged relief of having Rex back, sitting so close and watching her eat food he'd made, like the beginnings of his cuter fantasies. The way his thoughts had slipped away, the tips of his fingers tingling where they touched her skin, and it had felt nothing but natural to close that small amount of space between them.

Something so soft shouldn't feel like swallowing glass to remember. Even that made him teary and resentful. He wanted it to be a *good* memory.

A glance at Peter's tense expression threw him off, and he lost the ending. "And I, um." Pressure built behind his eyes, and he looked away. "So, that's it. I messed up. She wasn't—God, I'm stupid. And there's so much happening right now. I shouldn't be—God damn it." He pressed a hand over his eyes.

Peter gave a long, tight-throated, "Oh."

The odd tone had Lewis dropping his hand.

"I don't think that meant what you think it meant."

"She rejected me," Lewis said blandly. If he let Peter give him a shred of hope, he didn't think he'd be able to bear losing it. "That's all I need to understand."

"Oh, man. You know way too many queer people to be jumping to these kinds of conclusions."

Lewis huffed, feeling too low already to not be offended. "Rex isn't gay—she dated that Dillon guy. And it doesn't make a difference *why* she—"

"It makes a difference why." Peter nudged his shoulder. "And if she rejected *you*, she must be a lesbian, right?"

Despite his irritation, that elicited a snort out of Lewis, and part of him warmed at Peter being comfortable enough to joke like that again. "Why can't you just say what you're trying to say?"

"It's not a conversation that should be had by proxy."

Lewis spread his hands, prepared to whine.

"Really—you need to talk to Rex."

He didn't want to talk to Rex. The thought of it turned his face so red he felt it in his organs. A little tremor moved through his jaw that Peter couldn't have missed, and he covered his eyes again in shame.

"Oh, man," Peter said softly. His arm went around Lewis's shoulders as they walked. "I'm sorry you're feeling this way. Talk to Rex soon, please."

Lewis huffed, hoping it sounded surly instead of desolate. He leaned into Peter's side, so, so grateful they hadn't lost this. That Rex hadn't let them.

"How? She's in the wind. When she's found, she'll be arrested." He couldn't think about that either. When the scenario popped into his head of her locked up, away from her labs, her dinosaurs, her life, his heart sank with a soft kind of horror.

"About that," Peter started cautiously.

Lewis looked up, blinking back the sting in his eyes. He noticed which hall they were in. "Um." While he'd been talking, Peter had led them all the way to the facility's main conference room. On the other side of the glass wall, Quinten and the Protectors that weren't out hunting the Meister were locked in animated discussion. "We're supposed to be searching the labs."

"I was going to explain, but it seemed like you needed the floor." Peter turned his attention to the conference room and winced. "I was hoping I'd catch them without Quinten. Oh, well." Then Lewis could only follow as he pushed through the doors.

"Hi. Excuse me?" Peter said as the interrupted superheroes turned his way. "I have something urgent to report, but I wasn't sure who to approach." Before Quinten finished voicing a challenge, he drew a dark red hood from his jacket.

First, Lewis wondered why Peter stole the hood that Rex had given to Oversight. Except that hood was brown, and this one was styled almost exactly after the cowl of Last Dance's red cloak. He remembered the design on his flash drive. Oh shit.

Apparently making a few of the same observations, Quinten surged forward, reaching for it. "Where did you find that? Here? The house?"

Peter let him take it. "The Meister picked it up at the Colorado property and turned it over to me during my last shift."

There was no way Rex turned that over.

Peter continued, "But in the chaos since—"

"That's not the hood she promised me," Vivid Blue said, and it was only a half question. She took the hood from Quinten, who didn't look happy about letting it go, and inverted it to expose the wiring. Manta Man stepped out of the shadows to get a closer look.

"She wasn't able to get into the details before we were attacked," Peter said, reminding them not-so-subtly of whose side Rex was on earlier today, "but she told me this is meant to bait Last Dance so Vivid Blue can bring him in."

"We rejected that idea when she suggested it," Manta Man growled. "So, the Meister has reached out to Last Dance behind our backs and Oversight's."

The Jester snorted. "Like we couldn't have guessed."

Before Peter could reply, Lewis stepped in. "The situation changed. He reached out to her." Eyes turned his way, thankfully, since Peter didn't mask his surprise quickly enough. Wishing he didn't sweat when he was nervous, Lewis pulled the flash drive from his pocket. "I can confirm what he's saying."

It didn't take long to find a device and pull up the files.

"The Meister reported this to me earlier tonight," he said, throwing together a timeline he hoped would work with Peter's story. He wished he'd had more notice. "I thought it was important enough to bring it to Lieutenant Quinten right away. While I was on the road, Grant did what he did"—he couldn't keep all the derision out of his voice—"and things spiraled. I assume the Meister used the opportunity to give us an opening."

As the Protectors studied the screen, Lewis and Peter tried to communicate with eyebrows and tiny shrugs, but Lewis didn't think they managed much coordination.

"That would explain the internet post," Pixie said hesitantly.

"So would the obvious," Manta Man countered.

Peter broke a meaningful stare that Lewis was getting nothing from to challenge, "If she's on his side, how do you explain her giving me this?"

Lewis added, "She was transparent with Oversight. Grant crossed—"

"According to you, she was transparent," Quinten broke in. "The two of you, which, frankly, seems convenient, since Mr. Underwood is also—"

"Hey," the Jester cut in loudly enough to command the room, arms out. "I'm as sure as you all are that the Meister's a closet villain." He clapped a hand on Lewis's shoulder. "But this is my man, Lewis. And we need to listen to what he has to say. Even if he sounds batshit."

"Thanks," Lewis deadpanned.

Vivid Blue was staring at the screen, where the note from Last Dance was still displayed. Her voice gave nothing away. "Do you have anything else to report?"

Lewis met Peter's eyes, and Peter cleared his throat. "I wanted to make sure I brought this to you, possibly against protocol, because the timing is . . . sensitive. I think, given the content of her social media post—"

"She lit a fire under his ass," the Jester drawled.

Peter nodded. "I think she wanted to force him to react instead of planning ahead." He gestured to the hood forgotten in Vivid Blue's grip. "And this is our chance to draw him out while he's unsteady."

Rex's post definitely wasn't a secret signal to the Protectors, given she hadn't actually handed over any of this information. A thread of worry made Lewis hesitate. If they convinced the Protectors to act tonight, they might mess up whatever Rex's real plan was. That was Rex's life on the line. At the very least, her safety.

But, Lewis realized—and Peter must have already thought of it—if Rex went through with this, double-crossing Last Dance, or whatever she was doing, with no involvement from Oversight or the Protectors, there would be no denying she'd gone rogue. They had one chance to make this look like either a collaboration or a miscommunication, or her freedom would be forfeited.

Lewis blinked a few times. Peter wasn't usually better in a crisis than him. Good thing someone was stepping up while Lewis broke down. He cleared his throat. "That matches what she told me before I left. She's made an opening. It's up to us to act."

Lewis watched the Protectors exchange glances and let his shred of hope make itself a nest.

ISSUE **32**

DINOSAURS BARELY GET MENTIONED

As the room plunged into darkness, Rex tore for the far corner. As expected, 'Ning's first bolt of lightning hit the door in anticipation of her escape. Rex doubted she'd gotten far enough to not be revealed by the flash, so she hit the floor and rolled behind the row of chemical fume hoods to avoid a second bolt that didn't come. Instead, 'Ning zapped across the room and turned the lights back on like a person with a brain.

"Don't do this, Rex," she called, voice echoing under the high ceiling. "You can't outrun me."

Yeah, that's why she was fucking hiding. Rex made a break for an interior door in hopes of losing 'Ning deeper in the lab, but when a burst of lightning shot into her path, she planted a foot and threw herself into a new hiding spot.

"Shit!" The crack of lightning hopefully drowned that out.

The hero stopped shooting to call, "Can we skip this part for once, Rex?"

So that 'Ning could taze her and dump her in front of the police station? Fuck that. Rex fumbled to the wall, hunkered down behind the fume hoods, and felt up the corner.

If she was remembering the layout—yes! The PA system. Rex snatched the phone off the wall and pressed the button, wishing for a speaker-crackle to indicate that she wasn't about to give away her position. Blast her superior technology.

"How did you know I was here?" Rex's voice emanated from speakers throughout the room. Phew.

'Ning zapped halfway to the closest speaker then stopped, apparently catching on, and addressed the room. "Did you think I wouldn't notice that this place was still powered? I checked it out ages ago."

Rex crab-crawled to a cabinet she'd filled with—yes, it was still here. She grabbed some base chemicals. Nothing should've gone bad since the last restock. "But how did you know to look now?" Rex muttered to herself.

She forgot to press the button. Welp, time to run. She tossed the phone aside and booked it through the door, vials clutched to her chest. With a flash in Rex's peripheral vision, 'Ning zapped toward the phone's clatter—it worked on heroes as well as irradiated mouse monsters—as Rex swerved onto the factory floor.

Oh, bad idea. Metal industrial equipment and lightning were a bad mix. This wouldn't end well. A *crack* announced the Lightning's arrival, and Rex dove under a dust-encrusted conveyor belt.

'Ning's voice filled the room. "I thought you were doing better. It's been months since we've clashed."

Rex army-crawled to the wall, trying not to let the vials clink against the floor.

"What happened?" 'Ning called from atop a conveyor belt. "Did you get bored?"

Rex rose to her knees to grab the next PA phone. "Out of my mind. You have no idea." How many people knew she'd run tonight? There was Flora, Aya, and the dinosaurs . . . "I posted about this online. You didn't have to ambush me to find out." The post had gone up when she was already in the driveway. 'Ning must have been in the building before that.

"I'm not on social media."

"Of course, you're not." Rex dragged an old toolset behind a chemical vat and took out an access panel. "You can drop this disappointed social worker crap," she said into the phone as she worked. "I don't make a good redemption story. I didn't start low enough, and I'm not willing to go high enough."

'Ning might have known that soldiers had been called out to her house. Had she been watching the house? Then why not confront her there?

A blast and burst of sparks across the room made Rex jump, sloshing chemicals into the bottom of the vat. A peek around the side revealed a busted and sparking speaker on the far wall. 'Ning shot a bolt of lightning from the middle of the room and a second speaker exploded.

So, 'Ning could shoot every source of sound until she hit the right one. Great. Rex mixed the chemicals with new urgency and closed the vat to cut off the fizz.

"Rex, come on. I don't want to hurt you."

"Yeah, I can tell."

"Why did you run? Why cooperate this long just to throw it away?" The hero shot another speaker.

"I hope you're going to pay for that." Rex reopened the vat and scooped out a beakerful of the new solution. "I'm not doing this villain-pushed-over-the-edge thing. I have a lawyer. I'm taking the fight somewhere I can actually win. Let's see them justify killing Aya after she publicly apologizes, or the dinosaurs call her their friend, or I post that video of her trying to use one of her eyes to pet a puppy."

"Then why are you here?" 'Ning made a vague gesture around the lab.

"Why are *you* here?" Rex mumbled. Flora had been with Sadie. Was *Sadie* the Lightning? No, no—Sadie was much too tall to fit into that costume. *Calm down, Rex.* She sipped the solution, felt the right kind of burn and the right bitter aftertaste, and downed the rest. She winced. "Oh, that burns."

'Ning froze. "What did you do?"

"Nothing, nothing." She checked her hand, saw right through it, and stripped off her clothes with a grin. Try calling Invisi-Drink useless now, Flora. The fire suit took a bit of wrangling, but she kicked it off silently and slunk around to the front of the vat. Above her, 'Ning zapped between perches, throwing the odd lightning bolt.

"If you don't want to run, why not come quietly?"

"Like you'd come quietly." Rex rolled her eyes as she ducked back under the conveyor belt, hiding the phone in her cupped hands and inching toward the exit. "You'd go rogue so fast—"

"This isn't about m—"

Rex glanced back as 'Ning cut herself off. 'Ning was crouched in the corner by the vat. She rose back into view with Rex's jacket in her hands.

"Did you take off your clothes?"

Rex wondered if the lack of surprise in her voice said more about 'Ning or Rex. "I do a lot of weird shit." Rex pushed her pace to the—and the door was shut. Now what? A distraction? She could blow up something to give her a chance to open the door without the hero noticing. Great plan.

"Are you invisible?" There was the appropriate touch of wariness. 'Ning tossed the jacket aside and zapped back to the middle of the room. "After last time—"

"It wasn't Invisi-Drink's fault one lab tech was a creep." Dumb underlings with villain complexes ruining it for everyone.

"You as good as created Day Stalker."

"Yeah, you made that clear when you beat his name out of me." Rex's face scrunched in an invisible scowl. "What do you want from me? What would be the right answer for you?"

'Ning's shoulders fell slightly. "How long have we known each other, Rex?"

Rex watched the back of her head, uncertain. She'd gotten so used to reading 'Ning's body language that it came naturally, but for the first time in a while she wished she could see the expression behind her mask. She raised the phone to her mouth. "Five years, more or less." Did getting beat up by someone semi-regularly count as knowing someone?

'Ning nodded. "How many times have we worked together?"

Rex folded her arms and flicked her eyes to the ceiling self-consciously. "I didn't keep count. Where are you going with this?" Flora had gotten her an interview with *Good Morning, Gorgeous*, so someone in that studio presumably knew something was going on. Could one of them have called 'Ning?

"Do you not want a chance to explain before I turn you in to the Protectors?"

"I thought you were in love with the Protectors. Last I checked, you wanted to have their babies."

"Well, I've saved the city more often with you," the hero snapped, voice rising.

As 'Ning turned, Rex got a sinking feeling. A lightning bolt streaked over her head, and she shrieked, dropping the phone.

The flash blinded Rex and then 'Ning was in front of her, electricity crashing into the walls and equipment around them. Shit, shit, shit. She hadn't spoken into the phone the last few times. Damn her susceptibility to heartfelt sniping. Damn it to hell.

"I don't have to see you to stop you."

"I liked you better when you didn't talk."

A yellow-gloved fist caught Rex in the shoulder, carrying a shock that knocked her on her ass, spasms running down her arm and curses spewing from her mouth.

"Give up, Meister."

Rex struggled to right herself as 'Ning loomed closer, electric lines skittering down her arms, and something about the body language caught at her memory. Rex knew the Lightning's proportions shamefully well—it was a *very* well-fitted bodysuit. She imagined those proportions in a nice blazer, heels, and a skirt. That voice saying the lines in Rex's viral video.

Holy shit.

A swamp-colored, nausea-inducing lightbulb went off in Rex's head. "You're Gorgeous."

'Ning tensed, shifted, and coughed into a fist. "Flattery won't—"

"You're Gorgeous from *Good Morning, Gorgeous.*"

The hero, bless her, studied the ceiling. "I don't know what you're talking about."

"Oh my God." Rex clapped her hands to her face. "I can't believe this. My brain is melting."

"I'm not—that's ridiculous. Why would I be—"

"Talk show host by day, superhero by—"

With a flash and an ear-splitting crack, the busted machine to her left blew across the room and crashed over the door. Yeah, Rex was gonna shut up now.

'Ning's blank mask made it easy to imagine that she was looking right at Rex as sparks danced over her from head to toe. "If you ever talk about this—I don't care if you think you're alone—"

"Right, right." Rex scrambled to her feet, hands up, though 'Ning couldn't see them. "I'm sorry, Gorgeous—"

"What did I just say?" Another bolt lanced through the floor and hit the door blockade. "Don't think I won't kick your ass just because I'm rooting for you."

"I would never think that," Rex reassured a little too emphatically. "So," she said, watching 'Ning shift subtly toward her voice, "I'll stay put. And we can talk about this. Like normal people. And stop breaking my stuff, maybe."

The Lightning took a deep breath, the sparks on her suit settling and winking out as her fists uncurled.

"This is progress," Rex assured. "I think we're going to come out of this stronger than ever."

Again, Rex wasn't sure how 'Ning— Gorgeous, holy shit—made eyerolls so obvious behind that mask. "Put your clothes back on."

"Right." Rex walked back to her clothes, letting her footsteps echo.

Back in the chemical lab, Rex sat on a sleeve-dusted stool while 'Ning leaned against a long sink station, scrolling through the social media post on Rex's phone.

Rex threw on the yellow hood from her jacket pocket so 'Ning could at least see the outline of her head, not bothering with the buttons. She tried not to let her eyes wander, though 'Ning couldn't tell where she was looking.

Come to think of it, that was pretty much Day Stalker's MO. Maybe Flora was right about Invisi-Drink being a stupid invention. Besides, ogling other people just reminded her of her disastrous last interaction with Lewis that was probably actively stomping all over her subconscious. Her heart gave a tiny, little plunge, and she wrangled her focus back to the present.

"Your fans are odd," 'Ning finally said. "And your enemies are very angry."

"They're not enemies; they're just the internet." Rex leaned forward to see the screen as 'Ning scrolled through comments. "You see what I'm trying to do, right?"

"If I can see it, so can he."

"That's the idea. I'm saying, 'if you want this, come when I call.'" Having the freedom to not control her expression made it harder to keep the anxiety out of her voice, but she made the effort. "I contact him, he takes me to his base, I signal the Protectors."

"How can you be sure you'll get a message out?"

"Aya can listen through my phone. I'll wear a wire if it makes you feel better."

"And if he has Mindbender search you?"

Mindbender was another problem Rex needed to square away. She wasn't letting anyone with his understanding of her virus slip through the cracks. As for 'Ning's concern, though . . . "I have reason to believe that Last Dance might not be as invested in this plot as he's led us to think."

'Ning said nothing, but her body language was rigid.

Rex rolled her eyes. "Of course."

"I don't think you'd help him on purpose," 'Ning shot back. "But he's a manipulator, and your good intentions haven't always—"

"You can say you don't trust me. We're not buddies." She held out a hand. "Phone?"

"All I can see is your sleeve waving around. If you want it back, grab it."

"Oh, for—" Rex snatched her phone and stowed it.

The Lightning crossed her arms. "How are you supposed to stop him from reading your mind and knowing your whole plan?"

"Like I said, I don't think it will matter. But that's what this is for." Rex tugged the edge of her hood.

"I thought that was the hood you're giving him."

"What? No. Look, it's not that complicated. I've made five hoods." Rex held up five fingers, remembered that she was invisible, and pulled the gloves of her fire suit over her hands before repeating the gesture. "The one on my head blocks my thoughts. So does the one Oversight has right now—don't ask about that. This does the same thing for Viv." She tugged the purple hood from her pocket. "And this one is for Sam, to block his powers." She pulled the maroon hood from her other pocket. "The last one was also for Sam, but Peter has it." And hopefully hadn't told a soul.

'Ning raised her hands. "Whatever. And you think if you can get that hood to him, he'll turn on his allies. If Last Dance is as uncommitted as you think, what's the virus even for?"

That hit something fragile in Rex's head. It was the sharp, nagging inconsistency that had dogged her thoughts since her work with the Protectors began. It stood to reason, now, that he'd needed his allies to get this far—to perfect her virus, to distribute it, to use their resources—and he'd kept them on the hook with some world domination crap while planning to cut and run once he had what he wanted. It was a good plan, but complicated. And risky. And time-consuming. Had he taken a year to put this together? More? Why did he invest so much in that virus if he was going to ask Rex for a helmet to stop his powers?

Like the slow grinding of gears, two thoughts connected, and Rex's heart sank. The factory workers—Sam's test run—had experienced no effects from the virus dormant in their brains, as though Sam had never exposed them to whatever conditions triggered it. Then a note was slipped into Rex's pocket with a diagram for a helmet. *My people can't figure out the last part.*

Rex hated catching on to things too late. She felt distant from her body, the ache in her chest unimportant. Some instinct in her resisted thinking through the rest, but her mind kept going.

One: Sam wanted both the hood and the virus.

Two: the virus had likely already infected people, though they showed no symptoms.

Three: the hood, while blocking thoughts from reaching Sam, also allowed him to project his thoughts to others. This would normally be no more dangerous than handing him a loudspeaker. *Normally.*

Rex's mind called up the brain wave simulations her labs had produced based on scans from the infected factory workers and the virus's effects on lab-grown neural tissue. Almost without her direction, a side-by-side comparison appeared in her head with the weeks of testing she'd done on the ways Sam's hood interacted with brain waves.

Heat rushed to the top of her head. She gripped the edge of the sink bar at the accompanying vertigo. She'd made that hood. As recently as five minutes ago, she'd expected to give it to him.

Out of nowhere, she felt overcome with a wave of betrayal, the kind of childish indignation that came with the words *you lied*. How had she maintained this level of optimism about his intentions, after everything? How was she so surprised to realize how industriously—and intelligently—he'd been working? What kind of cardboard cutout Sam existed in her head?

Oh, right. The kind that appeared in dreams looking like the kid who needed help with algebra, saying, *I can't sleep.*

'Ning said her name sharply, snapping Rex to attention.

"I think the hood triggers the virus," she said, forcing her spine to uncurl.

'Ning reacted somewhere past Rex's focus. What would it feel like, after almost eight years of being bombarded by every thought of every stranger on the street, to have the chance to do the same to them? To be able to just make them stop?

God, she'd never stop feeling for Sam. Part of her would always be on his side. Flora said everyone had blind spots. Rex didn't think she was blind. She didn't think *everyone* would make his choices if they faced the same pressures. But she did think *plenty* of people would. It was infuriating to see those people living their unchallenged lives and somehow believing they were better than him.

Though it would illuminate a big ol' blind spot if she handed him that hood.

"Rex, are you listening?" 'Ning's hand landing on her shoulder made her jump. "Can you explain what you said?" Her mask focused on Rex's empty hood, then trailed over the rest of her. "Maybe you should sit down."

Was Rex not sitting down? She plopped back onto the stool. "So, change of plans. Sam doesn't get the hood." *Damn it, Sam. Why couldn't you—why do you always—*

She took a big breath, trying not to make it a gasp. "The rest stands. I've set the trap. I can still spring it. I'll just tell him I can make what he wants." Maybe Sam could still sneak out the back. But he'd get nothing from this. No hood, no help. No relief.

She swallowed a lump in her throat and raised the maroon hood in her hand. "Can you get this somewhere safe? It can't be here when I meet him."

'Ning took it carefully. "He could take that hood off your head as easily as he could take your phone. He'll know you won't make him another one if he reads your mind."

Rex sighed. "Point." She fished the hood of the fire suit out of the back of her shirt and pulled it over her head, scrunching the yellow hood uncomfortably beneath it. It took some effort to roll the skintight material over the contours of her face and chin and seal it to the suit's collar.

The clear goggles aligned with her eyes, probably looking pretty freaky since there was nothing visible behind them. She took a few deep breaths to test the breathing apparatus and rolled her neck to check the seal. "It won't be coming off now. Hey, since I'm invisible, I can say this is so he can see me. Invisi-Drink *is* useful."

"How will you contact Last Dance?" 'Ning asked.

"His minions will know how to find him. We have plenty in custody."

"You can't access the minions we have in custody."

"I can access one." Rex let a smirk run free on her invisible face. "I built his prison."

'Ning zapped in a quick arc to sit cross-legged on the counter, forearms on her knees and mask level with Rex's goggles. "I'm not letting you release Rifter back into the public."

Rex sighed and rubbed under her eyes. Freaking superheroes. "What if I give you my rift-stopping technology? It'll make it easier to recapture him when this is over." She'd been planning to do that, anyway.

'Ning glanced aside. "I guess that's an acceptable risk."

Bless 'Ning's reckless streak. Rex pulled the rumpled, purple hood closer. "I need another favor." Her hands tightened on the fabric. She didn't want to trust 'Ning with this. But the opportunity was too convenient to let pass.

There was a reason Rex would only give Viv the power to fight Sam: Viv would never, no matter what he'd done or what the circumstances, kill him. Rex didn't trust any other hero to show the same restraint, no matter how many of them swore off killing.

It also felt different to involve other heroes. Rex's mind kept conjuring the inevitable moment, whether it happened tonight or a month from now, when Sam saw Viv, couldn't read her thoughts, and realized what Rex had done. It didn't feel great—it twisted her heart in knots—but it was still between *them*. It was Rex, Sam, and Viv. Not Rex, Sam, Viv, and the team of superheroes Rex decided to gear up.

"Do you need me to deliver that?" 'Ning asked when Rex stayed silent too long.

She squeezed her eyes shut. "It goes to Vivid Blue and no one else. It'll only work with her brain waves anyway, but no one scans it or checks it over. Viv's hands only."

'Ning cocked her head, mask angled toward the purple hood. "This will hide her from Last Dance?"

"From his powers, yeah." Rex shrugged. "I mean, she's still freaking blue so she'll have to stay out of sight. But this will give her a chance."

'Ning hopped off the counter. "And you'll wear a tracker?"

Rex nodded. "Tell Viv to listen when Aya gives her a signal." She tried to keep the nervous snap out of her voice.

If Rex had known she'd be relying on Viv so soon, she might have worked harder to avoid a fight.

Ah, Christ, popped into her head in Lewis's voice.

This could, potentially, go very badly. But Viv would have the purple hood and the advantage of knowing where Sam's base was. She'd done a lot more with less.

Rex gave the purple hood to 'Ning, suppressing a wave of vulnerability as it left her hands.

'Ning gave her a long look through the blank mask, turned, and opened the door.

"Wait," Rex called. "Are we still on for the interview?"

Eye roll, activated. They were nothing if not consistent. "Of course. But I'm never hosting you live again. I don't trust you to keep your mouth shut."

It wasn't fair that 'Ning got to be a local celebrity twice over. "Which is the act? Is this your real self and you smile for the camera, or—"

A warning spark across 'Ning's shoulders shut her up. "Good luck, Rex." The Lightning saluted with the purple hood in hand and left in an eye-searing flash.

ISSUE 33

DINOSAURS UNDER SIEGE

*R*ex powered up the second generator as soon as the Lightning—holy crap, Gorgeous—left. As she checked the equipment in the computer lab, Aya piped up through her phone, "Doctor, the military is attempting to seize your satellites."

Rex groaned. "Let them take most of them. It'll make Flora's job easier. You know the ones we don't want in their hands."

"Yes, Doctor."

"Is your brain settled in its new jar yet?"

"About that."

Rex's train of thought stuttered to a halt. "What happened?"

"Based on the dinocopters' GPS data, I do not believe my servers were taken to Zombie Island."

Rex blinked at the phone in her pocket. "They never even *tried* to do what I said?" And after suffering through the Mutey inoculations. Served them right. "Tell me they didn't take you to the compound."

Aya hesitated. "There have been developments."

These dinosaurs would be the death of her. "What does that mean? Has the military shown up?" Rex's chest tightened. Internet fame felt like such a flimsy shield now that it was being tested.

"They have not attempted to enter the property." That was a yes. "The dinosaurs are livestreaming the blockade. I believe they are meant to act only if the dinosaurs become hostile. They requested cooperation in searching the property for you. The dinosaurs refused, and the situation has not progressed further."

Fear and relief mixed unpleasantly in Rex's gut. She hoped those little shits knew better than to antagonize the United States military, livestream or not.

"They understand the precarity of the situation, Doctor," Aya said, as though sensing her thoughts.

"But they still brought you there?"

"I have not made visual confirmation of my servers' location, but yes, I believe the dinocopters returned directly to Colorado."

It must be inconvenient to have no sense of your body. The thought made an itch manifest on her nose, and she tried to scratch it, forgetting the material of the fire suit in her way. "Let me know if it escalates," she muttered, rubbing the itchy spot and trying to focus on the digital template for her tracker.

"They requested that I tell you not to worry. They claim to have a plan." Again, the hesitation. "Many of the dinosaurs have retreated to the tunnels."

"Please don't let their secret project be a robot army," Rex whined as she finalized the tracker for fabrication.

The 3D printer—an adorably retro machine, by Rex's current standards—churned out a fingernail-sized piece of film with embedded electronics. She touched the adhesive side with her gloved thumb to check the stickiness and couldn't get it back off. *I guess that's where that's going.* Rex tapped it against a finger and a confirmation popped up on the monitor. "Tell Viv that'll be my signal."

"Yes, Doctor."

"You have eyes on Rifter?" She took a seat in front of another monitor and finished the simple hack to access her backdoor.

"Yes, Doctor."

A feed popped up showing Rifter's cell from the ceiling corner. Rex sent a test command and watched the force field wall ripple.

She set her jaw. "Loop the cameras."

On the screen, code flew by as every camera feed winked out except the one she'd taken over.

She prefaced a new line, and words formed in the blue force field as she typed.

How's minionhood working out?

In the cell, Rifter sat up slowly. His head turned toward each camera, briefly making unwitting eye contact.

The words erased themselves, and Rex typed a new sentence.

I have good news for your boss.

Rifter frowned. "That you, Meister?"

Rex rolled her eyes. She'd hoped he'd know not to alert anyone on the other side of the mirror, but mastermind, he was not.

Thanks for calling me out. Now we have less time. I have a message for Last Dance. When I take down these walls, I expect you to deliver it.

On the screen, Rifter scowled and drew in a breath. Rex typed more before he could argue.

Not that you could refuse. He'll read it out of your head as soon as you pop back up.

The scowl remained, but Rifter didn't seem on the verge of speaking anymore. Rex let out a *whoosh* of breath that mugged up her mask and continued.

You were right about one thing: being treated like the enemy doesn't inspire loyalty. Let's say I found my line.

Rifter smirked, and Rex rolled her eyes.

I can make what he wants.

Rex laid out the place and time. She would have liked to set the meeting for midnight, for dramatic flair, but she'd already missed it by two hours. She went for three o'clock instead, not wanting to give Sam too much time to question her motives.

Tell him not to bring his friends. They have a habit of crashing my jet and trashing my labs.

She didn't think Sam would listen, but hopefully he'd come with them instead of sending someone like Ill Wind to collect her alone.

Rex took down the force fields.

On the monitor, Rifter grinned, hands rising as orange light flared slowly in front of him, like he was savoring it. A circle ripped the air open, Rifter stepped through, and the circle vanished as guards ran into the frame.

Rex shut down the feed and backed out of the system, erasing her presence. Her heart was beating too fast. Hearts: such an inefficient system. She calmed herself and tested the tracker again.

A scenario popped unhelpfully into her head where the tracker died and she was stuck in Sam's villain lair, pretending to be evil for the rest of her life.

She supposed if it came down to it, she could just light the place up.

Time passed too slowly. Elbows on her knees, Rex alternated between triple-checking her tracker and squinting at her reflection in screens to see if she was still invisible through her goggles. Did she jump the gun when she downed a thrown-together experimental substance? It was probably fine.

She took a deep breath that echoed in the near-empty lab, bouncing her leg—not a usual habit for her, but this situation seemed appropriate for developing new ones. The more time passed, the more certain she felt that there was something important she'd overlooked. She always missed the most obvious thing, didn't she?

That's a dollar. She bit her lip to stop herself from breaking into giggles. That wouldn't be a good look as she waited alone in an abandoned lab for the most notorious villain in the country to make their 3 a.m. appointment. *Christ.*

A shoe squeak echoed by the wall.

Rex's heart jumped from skitter to book it. Her mind fled to make room for muscle memory as she turned in her desk chair, spine straight and face blank despite being covered with a fire suit and probably still invisible.

The white opera mask stood out in the shadows past her workspace. Rex's eyes fixed on it as the figure wearing it moved into the light. A larger shape followed it, the breaths and footsteps heavier. Rex glanced at the second figure, identified the villain Rockfall, and looked back to her brother.

Sam looked sullen beneath the cloak and mask. His voice was almost swallowed by the open lab. "You're hiding from me."

The static in Rex's head broke. She let out the breath she'd been holding, freeing her lungs to answer, "You think I'd hide Viv's thoughts and not do my own?" Her hands shook, she noticed. Her heart still raced uselessly. He hadn't used a rift. Had Rifter busted out of jail and instantly been too busy?

Rex's heart sank. *Had* he been busy?

Orange sparks split the air a few feet from Sam and expanded into a rift. Rifter came through with short steps, like he'd entered at a run. "Got it. Just like you said."

While the rift was still shrinking, dark red fabric changed hands.

The sullen look shifted into something clenched up and wild-eyed as Sam pushed his cowl back and shook out the hood.

Rex was on her feet but didn't remember standing, mind suddenly moving in a dizzying rush. Did they take it from 'Ning? Did they take it from *Peter*? She shouldn't have released Rifter. How had they had time? How had they *known*—?

Another voice rang through the room. "Sam, stop!"

A streak of blue and lavender shot through the closing rift just before it shrank into nothing. But Rockfall took a step that cracked the tile, pivoted, and intercepted Viv head-on.

Alarm pushed everything else out of Rex's head. Viv wasn't supposed to be here. What was going *on*?

Before she could recover, Sam grabbed her arm and pulled the hood over his head.

Rex found her eyes glued to the exposed lower half of his face. The tension in his jaw drained away. His face went slack. Then a tiny, twitchy smile spread across his hollow cheeks. A speck of shine trailed past the bottom edge of his mask.

A sick mix of dread and empathy filled Rex's chest.

Sam sucked in a thick breath and turned to Rifter. The tug on her arm turned Rex to see Viv's fist pulling back from a punch that sent Rockfall into the floor, nearly shaking Rex off her feet. The hero's head rose, hair loose— no hood—and three-toned blue eyes met goggles.

"Open a rift," Sam bit out, and an orange circle split the air in front of him.

Viv lunged forward and reeled back as a second rift opened in her path. She flew over it and grabbed Rifter by the collar.

Sam was already stepping through. Rex wanted to call a time-out. Her heart wouldn't slow down, threads were flying apart in her head, but this train was barreling forward with or without her. No turning back now. She felt the blue gaze boring into hers.

Rex looked away from Viv and stepped through the rift with her brother.

ISSUE 34

DINOSAURS DON'T MAKE THE RESUMÉ

Rex stumbled as they stepped from tile to wood floor. The new space was dimmer and draftier than Everglade. The rift collapsed behind them instead of closing smoothly. Viv must have knocked Rifter out—not the smartest move if she wanted to follow them through, but who among them was thinking clearly?

What went wrong? How did—

'Ning was supposed to—

What the hell went wrong?

Rex wrenched her arm away from Sam, demanding, "What was that?"

Instead of answering, he patted her down brusquely, pulled her phone from her pocket, and smashed it in his grip, sullen look back in place.

Rex's mental scrambling settled into anger. "You'd better replace that. Do you think I'm stupid enough to bring a phone they could track?" Her heart raced so fast she worried he'd see a jumping vein, even beneath the suit, but he didn't call her on the lie. It was so odd to lie to Sam.

"You gave the heroes my helmet. I don't know what else you did." He strode away from her with swift, controlled steps that part of Rex, the part that kept vigilant track of Sam's mood whenever he was in sight, cataloged as a warning sign.

Rex hadn't given the heroes his helmet. Had the villains intercepted 'Ning to get Sam's hood? Viv hadn't been wearing hers, after all. But Sam had said *the heroes* had his helmet, and Viv had barreled through that rift like Rifter's personal demons had come to collect, so something had gone down without Rex's knowledge. Had the Protectors gotten ahold of the hood that Peter had?

And somehow Sam found out?

They told him, Rex realized. They'd gotten Peter's hood, and they'd baited a damn trap with it. There were plenty of minions in custody to deliver a message to Sam.

And then Rex gave the villains their escape plan back. She and 'Ning were the only ones who knew what the hood was really for, and now Sam had it because Rex went and released Rifter.

Rex's train of thought paused. After a moment of grasping, she realized she'd anticipated Sam responding to her thoughts. But that connection was blocked from both ends.

"Of course, I gave it to them," she said, finally following him, her steps echoing. "If you haven't noticed, I've been under surveillance for a long time." The dismissiveness in her voice wasn't easy, exactly, but it was an automatic part of her Sam's-in-the-room protocol. Now wasn't the time to work on less childish defense mechanisms.

"Why would it matter? I can make another." Not that she needed to anymore—with that hood on Sam's head, her value here was a lot less certain—but she wasn't about to point that out. "You didn't have to wrestle over it like the last non-Tootsie-roll piece of Halloween candy. Mom taught us those breathing exercises for a reason."

Sam sucked air through his teeth and whirled back around, snatching off his mask. His face beneath it was tensed in a snarl, and she froze. Her face locked into a neutral expression despite her mask, and her shoulders loosened to look unimpressed. In her peripheral vision, she paid special attention to his hands clenching and unclenching by his sides.

His voice carried without rising. "Shut the fuck up."

The anger roiled like it could crowd out her organs, choke her, press her bones into dust. She fought it down, but not too much. She needed her head as clear as possible, and while anger wasn't useful in a crisis, it was less debilitating than fear. Fewer shakes to deal with.

Her eyes found the drying streak of shine on Sam's emotionless face, and she doubled down on anger again. Sadness was a festerer—shoving it down was asking for a mold to spread to every corner of you, but moment to moment, you did what you had to do. Ignore the infection if you have to stop the bleeding.

Sam turned his back again, slammed a door open, and called through it, "Pack up. We're leaving."

The bang of the door jolted Rex into widening her focus. The open space the rift had landed them in was a stage. Half-rings of velvet-backed seats radiated out from the edge, disappearing into darkness in the back. "This is the Millennium Theater," she said as she placed it. Her gaze found Sam smirking in the doorway offstage, light and noise spilling from the room behind him.

When her eyes—empty eyeholes, anyway—landed on him, his smirk broke into a grin. "Where did you think we were?"

Rex hadn't speculated, but her first guess wouldn't have been dead center of downtown Decimen. Her heart gave a wiggle. This would be a horrible spot for a superhero fight. Mustering annoyance, she said, "This place was shut down for construction. I had season tickets, asshole."

"It kept the civilians away," he said, still grinning. "All my people had to do was dress as construction workers coming and going."

Rex made a mental note to file a complaint about 'Ning's inadequate patrolling skills. Construction sites were supposed to be prime snooping grounds for superheroes.

She spread her fingers at her side, feeling the phantom weight of the tracker on her thumb. She had confirmation this was Sam's base, but not that his allies were here. They could still be scattered after the meet-and-greet with the Protectors or out on a freaking grocery run for all she knew. She couldn't activate the beacon until she knew Mindbender wouldn't skip out with knowledge of her virus in his head.

"Is that also how we're leaving?" She allocated peripheral focus to the voices and movement past Sam. "Convoying out in dump trucks?" That didn't seem likely, since Sam's goal for this alliance was complete with the virus distributed and the hood on his head. And damn, she needed to either suggest a new use for herself or steer him away from the subject. "Where will we go?"

Sam laughed, so obviously mocking that Rex wondered if she could get away with punching him. "Nice try."

"You won't tell me?" Without moving her head, Rex studied his hood. She had to get that thing off him. Escaping with the means to trigger the virus or going into a superhero fight with the means to trigger the virus were both bad options.

Mindbender, hood: a checklist of two.

"If I tell you, you'll try to stop me. I know you know what I'm doing."

Sam had always been the one person who never underestimated Rex.

"It's your fault, though." He let the door fall shut, cutting off the background noise, and strode past her onto the stage. "Maybe if you weren't up the heroes' asses all the time and if you were helping me, maybe I wouldn't have had to do this. Why would you do that? T? Why would you make me go brainwash people?" He breathed out a laugh.

Rex wanted to apologize, but the impulse made her so angry it caught in her throat. Her eyes followed his restless arc back through the stage light, part of her mind weighing the benefits of putting distance between them against the cost of appearing to retreat. Self-preservation versus determination to never give him the satisfaction. Neither love nor fear could make her less petty.

"It's Viv's fault, actually," he continued. "She keeps fucking with me. She won't let me fix myself. I wouldn't have to work with villains if she wasn't on my ass about everything I do. Like she's obsessed with me. Why's she so obsessed with me?" His voice slowly rose. He looked back at Rex. "It's actually sad. I feel sorry for her. She freaks out if she isn't in control of everything."

"Don't." Rex resisted the urge to cover her ears. "Don't tell me what's in Viv's head."

"Yeah, I don't want to know it either!" He fell into laughter that echoed past the stage. "I don't get to not know, so you don't get to either. Don't you always want things to be fair? That's not very fair of you."

He turned again in his pacing. "I deserve to fight back. If people hadn't always ganged up on me. If people weren't always working against me." His voice rose suddenly, and Rex locked down the impulse to flinch. "Because they do." He spread his hands, face stuck between a smile and a snarl. "They want me to live this way. It doesn't matter what I do because people will ruin it. Because it makes them feel better when I'm a loser."

The bitterness in his voice was hard and deep—the kind of sick, weeping frustration that came from years of trying and failing to save yourself. Her heart stuttered at the familiarity of it. At least Rex hadn't been alone for long.

"That sounds really hard," she said, because it was true, and it didn't cost her much to say it.

"Yeah. It's really fucking hard," he yelled, voice reverberating through the theater.

Rex ground her teeth at how little he cared about whether he scared her. She was pretty sure he liked it: a tiny moment of power to break up the helplessness. Flip the script by making T jump. Gotta be satisfying.

The door slammed open again, and Sam was suddenly bumped down the threat list as Ill Wind strode through. "Dance, are you out here? What's this about leaving?" Her eyes fell on Rex, and she startled. "What's this? Is Expanse recruiting minions now?" She squinted into the fire suit's eyes. A smirk curled across her face. "Meister. I didn't think we'd meet again so soon. How lucky that I found you first."

Well, at least she knew her face wasn't invisible anymore.

Sam stepped into the light, and Ill Wind jumped, turning around.

"Oh. Dance." Ill Wind's surprise melted into a smug look. "Well, your little zealots are packing, the Meister is here—I suppose this means the last piece has fallen into place?" Her eyes rose to the hood on his head, and her smile stretched. "May I have the honor of picking our first target?"

"Not till you stop being a dumb bitch." Sam strode toward Rex, whose indignation revealed that she hated misogyny more than she hated Ill Wind. Funny what we learn about ourselves under pressure.

Rex yelped when he grabbed her arm. "Geez, I can walk all by myself."

Sam scowled down at her. A trickle of fear ran through her, but she slid her arm from his grip as it loosened and walked with him to the door.

Ill Wind was forced to sidestep out of the way and follow, an exaggerated pout on her face. "You're still mad at me? You wanted the Meister here. I don't see why it's so bad when I try to collect her."

"Did you ever squeeze a puppy too hard as a kid?" Rex asked, because fuck it.

"Cute," Ill Wind said.

Sam spun around. "Don't say a fucking word to her." When Ill Wind drew a breath, glaring at Rex, he added, "Don't look at her. Look at me, bitch."

That curl of relief at Sam's willingness to defend her made Rex very uncomfortable.

"This is dangerous, Dance," Ill Wind said, jaw tight. Her eyes drifted toward Rex, but snapped back to Sam. "The Protectors will be looking for her."

Sam's expression flattened. "She worked out the tech."

"So what?" Ill Wind demanded, crossing her arms. "Rich geniuses are a dime a dozen on our side. What does she have that we couldn't get from Mindbender or the Architect?"

An army of teched-out, super intelligent dinosaur children, Rex didn't say.

Sam pushed through the door without answering. "Load the trucks," he called as they entered a wide area—perhaps a prop warehouse? That would explain the racks of cloth and piles of wood pushed to the walls. People in Sam's goon getup rushed around, packing sleeping bags and space blankets.

They passed through the open space and into a hallway in the back. Her time with his full attention was limited now that they were on the move, so she put the rest aside to say, "You don't have to go through with this. You have the hood—you can block their thoughts now."

Sam's expression lightened, jaw lifting and brow falling into the carefree smile he wore when they shared a joke. Wow, he looked a decade younger. "Yeah, but I'm not free, am I?" The smile hardened. "I don't get to go back, do I? It's too late now." He shook his head, striding ahead of her. "I don't get to move away and get a job because everyone will recognize me now. I don't get to go home to Mom and Dad. And you know what, T?"

He stopped in front of the last door in the hallway and turned to face her with a snarl. "Why should I have to wear a fucking hood for the rest of my life? Am I supposed to sleep in this? Do I wear it in the shower? Why shouldn't I get cured all the way?"

Rex's shoulders fell. It was easy to celebrate a better-than-nothing solution for someone else. Less so when you're the one living with the problem.

Ill Wind stood with crossed arms a distance back, giving them the privacy Sam had clearly stopped for. He lowered his voice and leaned closer to Rex. "I'm not going to hurt them. Don't look so sad. I told all these guys we're hitting the infected cities one by one. But now that everything's set, Viv can take them. I don't care."

"And what are the two of us supposed to do?" Rex asked dryly. She made a show of turning the wrist he'd grabbed earlier, surreptitiously checking the fire suit's seal—it was weird, trying to fool Sam with body language. Her heart sped in anticipation of a reaction, but none came.

"I'm just going to make one city forget me. You can make sure the virus works like it's supposed to." He made it sound like a gift. "I'll only turn off their thoughts when I want to take the hood off. It will be like a fugue. They'll go on autopilot and barely remember it. Then I'll put them back to normal when I'm wearing it. And you can monitor everything and make adjustments. I won't make them do anything else unless I'm forced to."

Rex imagined Sam up late at night, soothing himself with this plan when his justifications felt shaky. Reassuring himself that once he was in control, once he got what he wanted, *then* he'd do the right thing. She indulged for a moment and pictured Sam in a place where he could start over, with no constant torture and no reputation driving him to push back with cruelty or double down on indifference.

She couldn't afford to be sad, so the weight in her lungs would have to be something else. "It wouldn't work out that way." Still, given the best scenario's cost, Rex was ashamed of how tempted she was.

"You would have loved this plan before," Sam growled. "You always say you're going to help me. And then you never help me. Why did you come here if you don't want to help me?"

Rex had honestly forgotten about her plan for a moment. But the opportunity to have this conversation felt worth dropping some cards. "Yeah." She forced herself to meet his eyes. "If you had come up with this when we were nineteen, I would have trusted you enough, and I would have been selfish and reckless enough to help you do it. But it still wouldn't have worked."

Nineteen-year-old Sam's anger might not have been as deep as it was now, but it was more volatile. She'd deluded herself, semi-successfully, that he knew where to draw the line right up until he'd proven her wrong.

"What if I could help you disappear without using the virus?" she found herself saying.

Sam laughed deep in his throat. "Like to prison?"

"No." His dream was impossible, if nice. But the exercise made Rex realize, without conditions, that she was completely fine with Sam never facing punishment for the things he'd done as long as he didn't hurt anyone else. "Last month, you walked right past my security for a prearranged appointment with me," she said. "All that took was normal clothes, hair dye, and fake glasses. You could disappear if you tried."

"Doesn't matter." He shrugged, expression stony. "I still can't fucking sleep. Can't work. Can't have a girlfriend."

"I can get you a place somewhere secluded. Maybe close enough to a town for you to make short visits. I know it's easier on you if you're familiar with the minds you're reading, so you could get to know—"

"I shouldn't have to do that." The look of interest dulled, and he reached for the door. "I didn't deserve to live like this. I shouldn't have to be the one who can't do what I want."

"You're not the only person whose life has been changed by an accident." Her tone sharpened with frustration, her control slipping as she tried to get the words out before he stopped listening. "Hell, you could explain it that way. People might understand. I'm sure there are support groups—"

His glare turned on her again. "What the fuck do you think I am? I don't need a fucking support group."

"No—you'd rather be a villain than a victim, wouldn't you?" Rex kept the disgust out of her tone, but she couldn't hide her disappointment.

Sam sneered. "You're such a hypocrite."

Oh, geez. Rex hoped not. Not in the way he meant anyway.

Sam threw open the door, took Rex's shoulder, and steered her through it.

The room they entered looked like a sort of control center. Rex guessed that it had been used for the theater's security. Half of the monitors on the back wall showed views around the not-a-construction-site, and the other half had been turned to other purposes. Rex noted a view of her Peak Street labs from a camera that was probably mounted on the light post out front. Assuming she survived tonight, she'd be shooting that camera with a laser gun.

Talk died at a long table in the middle of the room as Rex and Sam entered, and several highly-recognizable people looked up: Drake, sporting horns and leathery wings but most notable to Rex for his exceptional widow's peak; Expanse, either an animate spacesuit or a cosmic entity contained in a spacesuit; and Miss Kiss, whose black lips and black-and-red suit with hearts all over it gave strong hints toward a theme, but Rex could never figure out what her powers were. There was also a ripped-as-hell woman covered in bees, but Rex had no idea who that was.

Rex pointed. "Who's this?"

"Why's the Meister here, Dancey?" Miss Kiss asked, tilting her chin in her hands.

"It's just that there are a lot of you in colorful costumes all of a sudden, and it's going to be hard to keep you straight without names." Rex turned to Expanse. "Your backstory is amazing, by the way. I didn't get the chance to say so the first time we met," when she and a few other super geniuses figured out how to keep him trapped in that spacesuit while the more physics-defying superheroes and villains-with-a-code kept him from consuming all life on Earth—but who remembered those things? "But your debut when that test trip to Mars came back with no crew was the most entertaining the news has ever been."

The bee woman rested her legs on the table. "Dance, control yer kin."

Rex's brow jumped. "That's a classic villain accent. Do southern heroes ever get confused and start punching civilians?"

"You're a right cheeky bird, love," Drake said.

Rex giggled.

Ill Wind's heels tapped past Rex as she approached the table. "Our leader seems to think the Meister can help us."

A voice by the monitors snagged Rex's attention. "Should I feel threatened?" Mindbender stood from beneath the desk, stowing wire cutters in the pocket of his jumpsuit.

"What the hell, man?" Rex said to cover the slight shock of not having noticed him. There he was: priority number two. Her thumb tingled where she'd stuck the tracker. "We've been playing online chess for years. Why did I have to learn you're a villain from Vivian?"

"I abhor labels, darling."

"Oh, I see it now."

"Where's Rockfall, Dancey?" Miss Kiss asked.

Rex had forgotten about Rockfall again. He was a forgettable guy.

"Watch her," Sam said instead of answering, letting go of Rex's shoulder. "Keep her here until I come back."

Rex tensed. She'd have to make her move now. She'd hoped to be closer to an exit, not stuck in a room surrounded by Sam's allies. She rolled the shoulder he'd been holding, using the motion to test the seal at her neck.

Did that look natural? Probably not. She hopped from foot to foot, getting her blood pumping.

Drake raised an eyebrow to that glorious hairline. "Problem, love?"

"I need to pee."

Sam looked at Ill Wind, who scoffed. "You brought her here. You deal with it."

Miss Kiss raised her hand and waved it at the wrist. "I'll escort her, Dancey."

"Is your power just being super creepy?" Rex asked. She dragged in a breath and held her right hand over her left. "Okie dokie, here we go."

She activated the beacon with a tap of her thumb, struck the back of her left glove with the palm of her right, and went up in flames.

Without waiting for the fire to finish spreading down her body, Rex lunged at Sam. Her fingers hooked the edge of his hood, and it caught fire.

ISSUE 35

DINOSAURS IN MORTAL COMBAT

With a roar, Sam lashed out and caught Rex in the ribs. She hit the monitors across the room hard. Flames caught at the equipment as she rolled clear and forced herself to her feet, ignoring the pain in her ribs. Through the flames licking up by her face, she saw Sam stomping the burning hood with a mournful howl. The sight demanded her whole attention, but she couldn't afford to give it as the other villains moved.

With a call of, "Aw shit," the mystery bee woman flung out an arm, and bees swarmed Rex. The fire engulfing her burned them to ash to a cry of "My bees!" Rex dashed for the door, feet sliding on the poor grip of the fire suit—her shoes had gone up in flames with the rest of her clothes.

"Stop her!" Ill Wind yelled unnecessarily. What did she think the others were doing?

Rex dodged the swing of the heart-tipped wand that Miss Kiss pulled from her mouth—what the hell?—and dove around the table for cover.

Heat? Tolerable. Smoke? Filtered. Brightness? Adequately tinted. No burning sensations, no obvious malfunctions, although the smell of half-melted tile wasn't pleasant.

"I got this, people," Miss Kiss announced, and Rex looked past her table as the villain tossed the wand aside and pulled a freaking bazooka out of her mouth.

"No, Kiss!" the bee woman yelled.

Miss Kiss swung the bazooka to her shoulder, and Rex shoved the table over as though it could shield her. Then Drake tackled Kiss.

"You'll kill us all, love!"

"Squabbling fools," Expanse bellowed, voice resonating throughout the room. "Would that I were not bound to this spacesuit."

Miss Kiss cackled in Drake's hold, fire licking at their costumes. The door slammed open, and Ill Wind ran out with Mindbender on her heels calling, "Fire, you sycophants!"

No, no, she couldn't lose Mindbender. The others were only going to get less disoriented, so Rex jumped the blazing table, happily noting Expanse's scramble back as flames caught his thick hand—"The indignity of such physicality!"—and barreled toward the door.

Sam stood between her and the exit. He clutched his head, and Rex blinked past her blurring vision as she imagined everyone's panic slamming into his mind.

Sam moved as though to stop her. Then he apparently reconsidered grabbing the person covered in fire, thank God, and jumped out of her way.

She blazed down the hallway, grasping for options. The element of surprise had gotten her this far, but any of the villains could stop her now. She could kill the fire and try to hide until the Protectors showed, but Mindbender might be gone by then. Not that her odds of catching him were good—the only exit she was sure of was the one through the theater, and he probably knew a better way out. Plus, the suit was single use. She'd be defenseless. Definitely an area for improvement, if she lived.

For an instant, she was tempted to do as much damage as possible while she had the chance, but she hadn't quite given up on living.

Fast footfalls behind her and a buzz of bees forced the decision. She slammed through the door to the prop warehouse and didn't stop.

Rex didn't dare look around as she made straight for the backstage door, scorching the floor with each step. Flames spread over sleeping bags and racks of cloth to cries of alarm. She dodged a few people willing to tackle a literal fire for their boss, but most scattered from her path.

Halfway through, a rattling alarm cut through the screams and the mustiest water in existence sprayed from the ceiling. Shit.

The alarm cut out as Rex reached the stage—hopefully Mindbender's quick thinking and evidence that he was still in the building. Did those systems contact the fire department? The villains might have thought to cut that feature earlier, but the noise could still drive a bystander to call.

Huffing and puffing, Rex forced a jog to the stairs leading into the audience. The flames crawling over her body banked as the limited fuel in the suit fought the rain of what had to be bog water from the sprinklers. How did they get water to stink so badly? Rex was going to shower twice and maybe nuke the theater after this.

At the first step down, some instinct twitched. Her eye caught a shift in the fall of water. Her gaze followed it upward, and she scrambled back up the steps at the first glimpse of black clouds swirling in the darkness.

"I hoped you'd come this way," Ill Wind's voice crooned from the balcony.

Shit, shit, shit. Rex was fucked. Flickers of light illuminated the knot of black clouds as it rolled toward the stage. She staggered back, trying to figure where the closest insulating agent was, but fuck if she knew. Crackling sounds built up in the cloud with flashes of white light, and jagged lightning shot from its center.

Halfway to Rex, the bolt forked, one side bursting a light fixture on the wall and the other blasting an aisle seat. The velvet burned briefly before the sprinklers put it out.

A second strike speared toward Rex, her shout swallowed by a clap of thunder, but it arced away and split a floorboard on the other side of the stage. Rex blinked at the scorch mark it left, finding it unreasonably compelling.

Ill Wind cursed, and the clouds churned violently. Then an array of lightning shot toward the stage like a volley of arrows.

In a yellow flash, the Lightning zapped in front of Rex and caught the closest strikes in her palms. Still glowing, she opened that stupid purse on her shoulder, pulled out one of the Protectors' communicators, and said, "Intel confirmed, contact made."

A half-hysterical laugh burst out of Rex.

"You little—!" Ill Wind blew out of the mezzanine on a gust of wind, and the clouds spilled down to engulf her, shooting a spread of lightning. 'Ning's fists sparked, and she shot lightning back. The bolts met halfway in a blast that knocked Rex backward, static crawling over her skin.

Her back couldn't take getting thrown around much more. Before she got herself upright, a stray bolt struck the wall over her head, and she changed the motion to a roll past the curtains.

'Ning was a yellow streak zapping from wall to wall, solidifying long enough to arc electricity at the roiling storm in the middle of the room. Ill Wind's lightning shot from the clouds like spider legs flashing in and out of existence. Lights burst in stray strikes and one side of a metal beam crashed down to the stage. Rex's heart clenched as one spider-leg bolt struck the yellow streak mid-zap, and 'Ning went flying into the orchestra pit. But the hero rolled upright and shot around a pillar before Rex could do something stupid like try to help.

Staying low, Rex wobbled to her feet. Her fire suit was full-on dead now, which was probably for the best since her exit was blocked by a fight so far above her paygrade she'd probably die by friendly fire if she stuck around. She wasn't any good at sneaking, but it was looking like the only move on the board.

Rex's retreat to the prop warehouse was met with muted chaos. She slipped unnoticed behind the closest shoved-aside set piece—something wooden and fort-like. The sprinklers were still drizzling, smoke rising along her path of destruction as goons beat out the remaining fires.

Sam shouted at a cluster of goons in the middle of the room, Drake and Miss Kiss at his side and the fire-eaten hood cradled in his hands. She had to wrench her eyes away from it, a lump in her throat. A quick scan of the room didn't reveal Mindbender. She also didn't spot Expanse or the bee woman. That was probably bad.

A disturbance by the wall caught her eye. Movements blurred in the shadows, turning into smears where water trailed down her goggles. She resigned herself to sewer water in the face and pulled back her mask for a better look, careful to keep the yellow hood covered.

A few goons crept toward the edge of the room with guns in hand, like they'd noticed the same thing. As they reached the shadows, darkness coalesced among them into a near-human form.

A rainbow scythe slashed out, spraying blood. Rex clapped a hand over her mouth. The shadowy shape vanished and reformed a few feet away, a rainbow arc slashing through screams that were quickly silenced as a maroon cloak swept into the light like an after-image.

The rest of the room caught on to the attack like an accelerating tide as Undertaker spun into full view, scythe moving so fast that Rex's eyes couldn't follow.

Undertaker was *violent*. Rex shook off chills and ducked behind a rack of soggy costumes. She should be using the distraction to move. She looked back to the middle of the room and balked.

Drake, wings spread, strode toward the fight with a look of such fury that Rex read it clear across the room.

Before he got there, orange light split the air in front of him and stretched into a spinning rift. So much for Rifter being gone. Rex tensed for a spacesuit or a bee swarm to make a dramatic entrance.

"Flying tackle!" A pink hero barreled through the rift and hit Drake head-on.

Relief hit so hard that Rex almost fell on her ass. The Protectors had cut a deal with Rifter? Great, but it would be nice if the rift had opened somewhere Rex could reach without catching a bullet. She picked her way closer, eyes darting for an opening.

Miss Kiss let out an appalled sound and swung the heart-tipped wand at Pixie's back, but it hit a sparkly force field. Don Conjure stepped through the rift with a hand extended and his half-cape fluttering behind him. "Only a most dishonorable foe attacks from behind."

Bees swarmed over the rift to engulf Don Conjure's head as the bee woman drawled from a second-floor catwalk, "Reckon that makes me right dishonorable."

Rex had missed the catwalk. She tried scanning the rest of it for the missing villains but abandoned the effort as dinosaurs clad head to tail in black body armor spilled through the rift, chanting, "Hut, hut, hut."

Rex's heart dropped through the floor.

Spot's voice called from the front, "Dino troopers, engage."

Those shits were grounded for life. Rex was building them an electric fence. The dinos fanned out in regimented lines and activated force field shields to block the first volley of goon bullets. A second wave, using hands or robotic appendages, drew laser guns—why in hell had Rex given them her designs?—and returned fire.

Pixie and Drake were still rolling across the floor, Pixie's fists a pink blur. "Fly-in-the punch! Fly-baited hook! Flying high kick!"

Rex tore her eyes away from the dinosaurs to speed up her circuit of the room, not daring to get their attention with so many enemies between them. She needed to get to the rift or get out of the way, although she wished there was a way to tell the heroes that Mindbender wasn't accounted for. She glanced toward Sam and froze when she only saw Miss Kiss coughing up a machete. Had he run?

That line of thought was cut short when her center of gravity shifted upward and her feet rose off the floor. Crap, she knew this power. She looked around for the spacesuit as she grabbed drifting costumes, trying to preserve some cover. Her stomach lurched at the motion, and she swallowed desperately. Why was she always the one trying not to vomit during the fight?

Expanse's voice boomed wall to wall, "You dare to stand in the way of my vengeance?"

That didn't help. Its voice could have come from anywhere.

A few lasers shot wide before Spot called, "Space race formation," and the dinosaurs stowed guns, linked tails, and made a dinosaur ball in a force field shell in the middle of the room, which had some concerning implications about how they'd been spending their time. Miss Kiss and some of the goons were making swimming motions as though they could propel themselves through zero gravity, and Rex logged that away to find funny later.

Don Conjure, floating upside down among drifting sprinkler water and bees, taunted, "We meet again, Expanse. How are you liking your physical form?"

The spacesuit—there it was—descended toward Don Conjure from the center of the ceiling, apparently unbothered by the state of gravity. "Would that I were not bound to this spacesuit—"

Rex grabbed a hard hat about to float out of reach and lobbed it at Expanse. It flew in a predictable straight line and knocked the spacesuit sideways while Miss Kiss pointed and laughed. Rex's stomach flipped again, there was suddenly a *down* direction, and she landed hard in a pile of wooden boards. Thank goodness for everyone else's hard landings allowing her to groan to her heart's content.

The bee woman's voice came from above. "Down there! The Meister's right yonder!"

"Oh, really," Miss Kiss answered much closer, drawing out the words.

Shit on a damn cracker.

Lou Lou's voice called, "Find cover, Mom!" and the *pings* of laser fire resumed.

Rex rolled toward the wall, wincing as she knocked some boards out of the pile, and scrambled for a better hiding place.

"Stinger, what are you doing so far from your hives?" Undertaker sneered.

"Been a good while since we crossed paths, Undie." The buzzing surged. "Ain't you heard? I *am* the hive."

A masochistic impulse made Rex glance up and, oh, God, no. However many orifices those bees were coming out of, she didn't need to know.

"Yoo hoo," Miss Kiss sang, closer again. "Meister, dear."

Double shit. Rex army-crawled into a sideways-fallen, house-looking thing that also might have been a ship. This theater needed a bigger budget.

Why couldn't there be high tech props lying around? Or tools. She'd settle for a nail gun or a screwdriver—

Gravity hiccuped. Everything lurched upward and fell back down. Miss Kiss squeaked and something clattered where she dropped. Rex used the moment to climb over the set piece, not daring to look toward Don Conjure's call of, "Not this time, fiend," and Expanse's warbly, "You begin to irk me, mortal."

It didn't do Rex's control issues any good to know that a cosmic entity that almost destroyed the world once was close to losing its shit a few feet from her apparently self-trained dinosaur special forces, but she couldn't exactly influence the situation if she was macheted to death by a woman full of weapons.

"Come on, Meister," Miss Kiss whined. "I'm bored. Come out." A smack that sounded like a machete hitting a damp, wooden board punctuated the plea.

Rex pressed against the wall. She should have run for the exit past the stage. She might not have been hit by too much lightning. Maybe she'd built up a tolerance.

"*Psst.* Meow."

Rex jumped and looked around. Cat Man was crouched next to her. He grinned and gave her a wave. Before she could muster a *"what the fuck,"* the floor shook.

Heedless of Miss Kiss, Rex looked out, clutching the house thing for balance. A long wall of the warehouse and parts of the ceiling ripped themselves asunder as Viv flew through it, her purple cape blocking a swathe of stars and downtown lights. Blue hair spilled from the matching hood. Flashes of light and peals of thunder at Viv's back told Rex the fight between 'Ning and Ill Wind had spilled out of the theater.

Drake tore away from Pixie, who stamped her foot and flapped her crimped wing. Manta Man glided past Viv's shoulder and intercepted him midair.

King George strode in beneath Viv, velvet cape dragging in the mess. "In my time, the battle did not begin before both armies had gathered on the field."

The Jester bounded after him with a jingle of his bell. "In your time, the armies shat themselves to death and—yikes!" He ducked an enterprising goon with a hammer and swiped back with a silver-flashing knife.

Where did that guy get a hammer? Why couldn't Rex find one?

Cat Man leaned against Rex's shoulder, arm in the air. "I found her, Blue! Meow!"

Viv arced toward Rex and Cat Man, unaffected by the gravity going wonky again. She grabbed Rex's arm in one hand and Cat Man's in the other and pulled them both back to the wall.

"Sam is gone," Rex blurted as Viv gave her a sweeping look. "He got the hood, but I burned it. And you have to find Mindbender."

"Where are your clothes?"

"Burned those too. Don't sigh at me. I'm in my fire suit—I'm not naked."

Viv looked to Cat Man. "Get her out of here."

"Sure, Blue." Cat Man grinned, legs floating out from under him, and reached toward Rex with his free hand.

The look of alarm on Viv's face cued Rex to squirm from his reach, but there was no room to maneuver. Viv blurted, "Wait, Cat Man—"

His touch vanished as fast as it came.

The noise of the fight vanished, and Rex fell in a heap on a flat surface, silence ringing in her head.

Viv's grip on her arm released. The rustle of her cape and squeak of shoes on a polished surface hit Rex's ears as the hero scrambled upright. Rex followed her up, fighting dizziness to look around.

They were not in the Millennium Theater. They were not in Decimen City. Rex wasn't sure they were still on Earth unless she was tripping out.

A sluggish swirl of colors under her feet belied the solidness of the ground. The sky—if that's what it was—and horizon carried a similar swirl, so trying to focus on any distance made Rex's head ache. Darts of shadow in her peripheral vision kept catching her eye, but there was never anything there.

Besides Rex and Viv, the space was empty.

Viv cursed, making a small echo. "He stuck us in the cat dimension."

Rex blinked away the shadows and looked at the hero, contrasted against their surroundings in stark blue and purple. "He stuck us where?"

"It's the dimension cats pass through when they disappear." Viv must have seen the look on Rex's face, because she bit out, "I know, okay? But Don says it checks out."

Rex put her hands over her eyes and swallowed a scream. "I can't handle this reality. I really can't. How do we get out of the cat dimension?"

"We can't unless he or another cat lets us out."

Rex really tried not to flip the fuck out. "And how likely is that to happen?"

"He'll remember us eventually. Be patient."

Viv seemed to have trouble following her own order, pacing with her hands locked behind her back. Her hair and cape floated behind her like she was only half bothering to acknowledge gravity.

Rex's anxiety rose as she watched Viv pace, until she snapped, "How long is it going to—"

"Time isn't the same here," Viv cut in. "However long it seems, it won't actually be that long. He'll pull us out soon."

Viv returned to pacing. Rex freed her head from the fire suit and shoved the yellow hood under her collar, clenching her teeth and repeating in her head like a mantra, *soon.*

Viv's footsteps made sharp, steady echoes. The colors swirled to a different rhythm. Shadows darted at the corner of Rex's eye to no rhythm at all. *Soon.*

Or maybe not.

ISSUE 36

DINOSAURS ARE NOT CATS

*R*ex had a lot of questions about the cat dimension. If she walked away from Viv, would she eventually come back around to her, or would she walk until she died of old age? *Could* she age? What conditions did a cat have to meet to enter the cat dimension? And could those conditions potentially be met by a device or chemical solution?

The answer to that one was going to be yes. In preparation, she tapped at the ground—the only real feature in sight—tracked the color swirls for patterns—there weren't any—and generally tried to ignore Viv.

The atmosphere probably wasn't normally this heavy in the cat dimension. Viv's presence was skewing her data. Rex glanced at the hero and felt the seconds slow again. They could handle waiting next to each other until Cat Man picked them up, right? They'd dealt with plenty of fights by pretending they never happened. No reason they couldn't do the same here.

A *prowp* and a tap against the smooth surface echoed lightly in the distance, and Rex homed in. A big tabby, standing out against the backdrop of colors, perked up its ears at Rex, dismissed her just as casually, and trotted off through the swirls.

"Look—a cat." Rex cupped her hands around her mouth. "Let us out of here!"

"Are you trying to talk to a cat?" Viv asked.

"We're in the fucking cat dimension. How am I supposed to know the rules?"

"Be patient," Viv said through her teeth. "Just wait for Cat Man."

Rex groaned. "What about a dinosaur? Think they could get in?"

"Dinosaurs are not cats."

"Since when are you an expert?"

Viv sighed into her hands. "Please, T. Just stop."

Rex turned away from her, trying to calm down. "You wanna tell me what went wrong?"

"Excuse me?"

"Rifter offered up Sam's hood like he was the pope crowning him king. Who let that happen?" Rex's money was on the Jester. That asshole.

"You want to talk about what went wrong? Why was Rifter there?"

Rex winced. Yeah, that was her miscalculation. But still. "And by the way, you were going to let the military storm the dinosaurs' compound? Thanks for that."

Viv's face cleared for an instant—in surprise?—and tightened again. "Right. You made it clear you think you can do no wrong when you got on the internet and bitched about being held accountable for once. Woe is you."

"I got on the internet to trick our brother, which you apparently haven't managed in five years."

"Yes, it was just a clever trick. That's why you threw some chum to your so-called social movement while you were at it. Good to know you were lying to my face about that."

Rex's jaw dropped. "You're mad at me for using the More to the Story hashtag?"

Viv shrugged too casually. "'What campaign, Viv? That's not what it's about, Viv.' You've gotten so good at lying."

A flash of rage. Did she know how close to home that hit? "It's *not* my movement. I rambled on a talk show and some other people ran with something I said." That might be misleading, considering Aya had purposefully curated and spread the interview online, but that still didn't make it Rex's movement. "How do you convince yourself I'm secretly masterminding everything?"

Good at lying? Why did Viv *think* she'd gotten good at lying? Who had practically insisted Rex get damn good at lying? "And you're grossly misinterpreting More to the Story, by the way. If you forgot it had anything to do with me, you'd be completely behind it."

Viv huffed and paced away.

A flash of light zipped across Rex's peripheral vision and vanished. Was that a freaking laser pointer? Before she could make an investigation, Viv paced back.

"Explain it to me."

Rex blinked, still thrown by the laser pointer mystery. "The hashtag?"

Viv spread her hands and ticked up a blue eyebrow.

Irritation prickled. Viv could have looked this up instead of making Rex sell it to her. Like she had something to prove. But then, they were stuck in the cat dimension. What else were they going to do? Talk about their feelings?

"Fine." Rex turned so she wouldn't have to look at Viv while she got her thoughts together, taking up the pacing the hero had abandoned. "So, it means 'more to the story.' Like the story is what gets told. But there's more."

Viv gave her an unimpressed look. "That's obvious. It doesn't need discourse—no one would disagree."

Rex matched her look. "Then why does it upset you so much?"

That got a scowl and an arm-folding. "Maybe if you give me an example."

Rex nodded. "Fine. So." She rolled her eyes to the . . . sky? Ceiling? "Classic story: a knight saves a princess from a dragon."

Viv nodded.

"Let's start with the dragon. He stole the darling of the kingdom and, what, thought he'd get away with it? That's a cry for help if I ever heard one. At best, it's suicide by knight."

Viv let out that scandalized "a-ha" that happens when something's more offensive than funny but surprises a laugh out anyway.

An answering grin pulled at Rex's cheeks. "And then what does the knight do? Live happily ever after with the princess? Weird basis for a relationship, first of all. He basically won her from another male via antler bashing." Viv's chuckle egged her on. "Heck, she was held captive by a *dragon,* like, yesterday. Do you think she wakes him up with her nightmares? Do you think she lashes out at him because it's safer than lashing out at the people who deserve it? Do you think she freezes him out and doesn't feel anything for months?"

Too late, Rex caught on to the thickening atmosphere, the lack of Viv's laughter behind her, and realized what she was saying. Her cheeks warmed. While she was still wondering if it was possible to unsay the last few sentences, one more slipped out. "Do you think the knight ever got fed up and left?"

Oh, more came through with that than she'd meant. Rex's eyes bored into the ground. Her heart had raced for an instant, and she focused on breathing it back down, suddenly concerned about how loud a deep breath or a swallow might be in the empty space.

Viv shifted, and Rex glanced from the corner of her eye to see her studying the sky/ceiling. Her tone was so carefully light when she spoke that Rex fought a cringe. "Do you think maybe the knight couldn't know about those things because the princess wouldn't talk about it?"

Rex turned in a rush of indignation. "When did—" She cut herself off and looked away. As much as she wanted to challenge Viv's memory, just thinking about addressing it directly made the words die a hard death on her tongue. "Maybe the princess got sick of the ulterior motives." So gentle, those sympathetic ears. So gently, they brought it back around.

"You know, Sam hasn't been eating much lately."

"You know, Sam's been asking about you."

And Rex, unsaid words crowded in her throat, with that familiar feeling of *oh.*

"But don't you think," Viv pushed, voice stronger, "if the princess just moved on—if she forgave—"

A deep cackle had Rex bowing over as anger bubbled in the middle of her chest. "Right, right. That's what's expected of a princess, handing out forgiveness like the gracious, two-dimensional shit she is. That would be fucking convenient for everyone, wouldn't it?"

"It's not *for* everyone," Viv snapped. "It's for y—for the princess."

Rex snorted. "If it was for the princess, no one would get mad when she couldn't do it."

"If the princess tried—"

"Who's the knight to judge if the princess is trying? It's sort of a pass/ fail standard. And hey, here's a thought." Rex raised a hand, palm up. "Maybe the princess doesn't have to forgive on the knight's schedule. Maybe she can take her own damn time."

"It's the least she owes!"

"No!" Rex whirled around. "You know what? No one owes anyone forgiveness. Maybe it's what's best for everyone—yes, including the princess," she added in a hiss when Viv opened her mouth to interrupt, "but if you forgive someone because people keep telling you to or because you think you're supposed to, that's not forgiveness. That's agreeing not to talk about it anymore."

"Dwelling on it isn't better," Viv shot back.

"You know what makes someone dwell on something? When the only place it exists anymore is your head. Where it can spiral around and around because if you forget any of it, it's like it never happened."

When was the last time Rex had sensed that black pit dogging her heels? Not since she'd fallen into it and babbled through its contents to Lewis and Flora.

"And while we're talking about what people owe, why shouldn't it be the dragon who *earns* forgiveness? Why is no one on his ass about that?"

"It shouldn't be up to the dragon whether the princess can move on or not," Viv said.

"That would be a great fucking point if everyone didn't decide that it was the princess's fault if she failed."

Rex turned her back to Viv and took a deep breath, hating that the exhale came out shaky. "So, we've moved on to the princess. 'The knight saves the princess from a dragon' is a weird way to sum it up for her, timeline-wise. How long did the dragon have her? Days? Weeks? Compared to maybe an hour of getting saved? That's gotta be disorienting. I mean, it's not like she can just"—Rex waved a hand, grasping for the concept—"turn it off."

"Turn what off?"

"She would have been on her guard in the dragon lair. She was probably on the lookout for ways to improve her chances of survival. Watching the dragon's mood, watching for slipups, watching her words—lots of watching involved. Not a lot of breaks. Maybe she was trying to escape. That makes a shitty story if you think about it. Days of work that comes to nothing, and then the conflict gets resolved by a third party. What's she supposed to do with that?"

Viv's voice turned petulant. "Maybe the knight should have just stayed home."

"I don't think you're getting that this is *not about the knight.*" Her chest ached and her face was hot. "The knight had a better story, though, so that's what gets told: the knight saved the princess from the dragon. Not: the princess called for help first, but no one answered. Then she fought back, but she wasn't strong enough. Then she gave the dragon what he wanted. Then she withheld what he wanted. Then she appealed to the dragon's ego. Then his mercy. Then his ego again, but she was sneakier about it. Then a knight killed the dragon, but the princess never got herself out, so what would happen the next time? She could be more ready, right? She couldn't stop the next bad thing from happening, but she could brace herself—she could just keep bracing herself."

Viv's soft voice started, "I'm sure the knight would protect—"

"The knight didn't stop it the first time," Rex cut in harshly. "It's a simple extrapolation from the data available: the princess was hurt; therefore, she can be hurt. Do you think the princess started to get tired? That waiting for the other shoe to drop was fucking exhausting? Do you think the princess started craving the next bad thing, because then she could just stop?"

Rex's voice wobbled, and it was enough to make her aware of her words again. Her heart fell into her gut. Her neck locked up like her body knew she couldn't look at Viv now. Probably never again. She hadn't meant to say that to anyone. Not ever. Not out loud.

The silence felt compounded in the emptiness around them. The colors swirled at their same slow pace. This wasn't how Rex had pictured their cat dimension adventure going. Not that she'd pictured an adventure in a fucking cat dimension, but still.

"Do you think—" Viv said hesitantly. Rex was surprised she spoke at all, let alone in such a neutral tone "—the princess made the next bad thing happen? Do you think, since she couldn't control the last bad thing, she helped . . . push the next one along?"

What? That wasn't—how did—that wasn't part of it. Right?

Shit, that was totally part of it.

Rex's lungs ached. She dragged in a breath. "So, the hashtag." She felt like a coward for sticking with the excuse, but she was so far past the end of her rope she'd need a shovel soon. "It's just saying that people tell stories. And what gets told is important." Her eyes followed a swirl in the middle distance. "Because what do you think it does to the princess every time someone tells that story, and everyone uses that story to decide how they're supposed to act and how they're supposed to feel," she had to pause for breath as her voice weakened, "and how she's supposed to act and how she's supposed to feel . . ." Her voice fell again. ". . . and she doesn't even recognize the story they're telling."

The silence sat. Rex heard the little rustles and taps as Viv shifted behind her, like the space had gotten smaller.

"After what happened . . ." Viv started.

Rex couldn't move again, her whole body focused on Viv like it was ready to run at the right signal.

"I saved you. But you weren't—and I couldn't do anything. I'm the strongest person in the world. But it felt like . . ."

Rex got a humbling flash of—well, it could have been projection as easily as insight.

While Sam suffered, Rex cured cancer. While Rex suffered, Viv put on a cape and saved the world a few times.

"I didn't handle it well."

Rex waited for the *"it was an impossible situation"* or *"I did everything I could,"* or the apology-canceling *"but you also could've handled it better."* The silence held. Still, she waited.

It never came.

Tears rose in Rex's eyes as a weight-shedding kind of gratitude built in her chest. A bubble of snot readied itself in her nose. Oh, fuck.

The next bit came so softly she wasn't sure if Viv would hear it. "Do you think the princess ever resents the knight for being able to stop the dragon when she couldn't?"

There was a short silence before Viv answered, "I think if the knight's any good at his—no." Viv's voice faltered. "If the knight cares about the princess at all, he didn't do it for appreciation."

Rex was trembling. Stupid freaking inefficient biology. She sat down hard and covered her face. Why didn't the cat dimension have furniture to hide behind? Didn't cats like that shit?

"Meow."

Rex looked up hopefully.

It was another fucking cat.

"God damn it!" Rex burst into tears. "Where the hell is Cat Man?"

"T!"

Rex heard the rustle of the cape falling over her shoulder as Viv put her arms around her.

"I want to get out of here," she wailed.

"I know." Viv rubbed her back.

"I'm a fucking disaster."

"You're . . . fine."

Rex grabbed Viv's silky cape for balance and was hit with a sense-memory of holding Viv's pajama shirt after having a nightmare and climbing into her bed, eyes squeezed shut and listening to Sam snore softly in the bottom bunk.

Rex didn't try to talk. She just stared at her white knuckles buried in the cape, counting the freckles on the back of her hand and ignoring the raspy sounds she was making.

ISSUE 37

DINOSAURS IN CONTESTABLE JURISDICTION

*R*ex lay on her front, arms by her sides in her best imitation of a worm.

"You know what I remembered the other day?" Viv said from somewhere over Rex's head. "Chocolate gravy."

Rex groaned. "I forgot about that." She turned her head for a view of Viv leaning on her elbows a few feet away. "I was so jealous of Mike and Abby."

"Their mom would just make that," Viv said reverently. "For breakfast."

"She only made it when we stayed over though."

Viv *hmph*ed. "I remember Mom telling us that too. Did you believe her?"

Rex's mouth fell open. "Um, until this moment, maybe." She ignored Viv's chuckle. "It was still probably less sugar than cereal prepared by Grandpa."

Viv sighed. "How many spoonfuls do you think he added?"

"I don't think he bothered with spoons. I think he just poured."

"Remember how Sam would drink the milk before he ate the cereal?"

Rex grinned. "He didn't like it soggy."

"So, you had the bright idea to tell him—"

"—he could eat it without the milk, which led to Sam eating handfuls of cereal out of the box." Rex rolled her eyes. "How many times do I have to apologize for that?"

"How many times was my cereal coated in gravel dust?"

"It was in your head! Ask him—" Rex's amusement turned sour, and she sensed the same in Viv's silence. She turned her head back down, staring at the swirls under her eyes. "What are the odds we'll get out of here before the fight's over?"

"It won't matter much," Viv said, subdued. "From what I saw, the only villain who might give my team trouble was Ill Wind, and 'Ning had the upper hand when we got there. Sam got away again." Viv shifted, and Rex glanced over to see her head tipped so her thumb and forefinger could rub the edge of her hood. "If this thing works, I guess I'll have a better chance next time." She sounded as tired as Rex felt.

When was the last time Rex had slept? Did they have time for a nap in the cat dimension? Rex chuckled.

"What?"

"A cat nap."

Viv's head turned toward her.

"Sorry." Rex inhaled deeply and pushed away her exhaustion. She made herself go back over each step of her night, up to Sam's disappearance. "I think I know where he went."

Viv sat forward. "Like you knew his helmet wouldn't do anything bad?"

"Just listen to my reasoning." Rex scooted around to face Viv. "'Ning obviously delivered your hood. What happened to the other one I gave her?"

"The copy of Sam's? We locked it down in your lab with the same security measures as the virus."

Rex frowned. "Oversight went for that?"

Viv's shoulders drew up. "There was a bit of confusion with Oversight. Without Lieutenant Quinten, it isn't clear who's in charge on the ground."

"Without Quinten?" A thrill of glee ran down Rex's spine. Aya must have found something good for Oversight to pull him that fast.

Viv frowned. "You shouldn't know anything about that."

"I don't." She failed to fight the grin curling across her face. "I had nothing to do with it."

"T," Viv said warningly.

"Moving on." Oops, that echoed. "Who knows where it is? Your whole team?"

"Yes." Viv sounded short but allowed the redirection. "The Protectors, Shay, 'Ning—"

"Okay, that's enough." Something settled as her idea matched the data. "When I burned the hood, Sam looked"—devastated—"upset." She swallowed. "I saw him in the props area before the Protectors showed up, and he vanished right after." As had Mindbender, maybe, but Rex didn't know what to do about that yet.

"He would've been reading minds again," Viv muttered. "If any of the infiltration team knew where the copy was, then so could he."

"I think he'd go straight for it."

"With Rifter back in custody, it would take him some time to reach the lab," Viv reasoned. "There might still be time to head him off."

"Meow."

Rex tensed. "I swear, if that's another—oh, thank God, Cat Man!"

Cat Man, sitting cross-legged a foot away, flashed sharp teeth in a grin. "Don wanted to know where you were. Meow."

Viv jumped to her feet and dragged Rex up after her. "Cat Man, get us out of here."

"Meow!" Cat Man hopped onto his haunches and lashed out.

Claws dug into Rex's ankle, and she felt like a vacuum was sucking out her guts. Then she was suddenly staggering on grass under a stormy sky. She wheezed, Viv groaning beside her. Geez, was breathing always like this? Was she *not breathing* in the cat dimension?

"Cat Man, we're going to have a talk when this is over," Viv said. "I'm heading to the Meister's lab. Let the others know."

"What?" Rex straightened too fast and stumbled as the ground rudely pitched to the side. "You have to take me too."

"I can't carry someone else at my top speed—your body couldn't handle it. Sam has enough of a head start." Viv's feet rose off the grass. "Just stay put."

"Like hell!"

"Cat Man, keep her safe."

"Meow."

Rex turned to Cat Man. "You suck; do you hear me? You're still my favorite though." Viv must have flown higher while she was distracted, because when Rex tried to resume speaking truth to power, she caught a glimpse of Viv overhead and then a streak of vivid blue blasted across the stormy sky. "Shit."

A peal of thunder startled Rex as 'Ning, sun-bright against the clouds, flashed into being above an Ill-Wind-shaped shadow and beat it down to Earth. Either that fight had gone far afield, or Cat Man had spat her out downtown. With a quick glance around, she identified the grassy area as Little Creek Park, just a block from the Millennium Theater. Apparently, Viv was right about time being different in the cat dimension, because it still wasn't morning.

Ill Wind and 'Ning weren't the only ones who'd expanded the battlefield. In addition to the gaping hole where the theater's stage should be, sections of the exterior and its construction site trimmings floated across several blocks. Don Conjure flew through the affected area in a shiny, blue bubble, dodging walls and waving his hands around. Oversight troops had arrived and were duking it out with the remaining goons. Decimen City police made a perimeter around the fight, and a colorful break in the barrier appeared to be Pixie and the Jester securing Drake for the proper authorities.

Okay, the good guys were winning. Cool. But where was Mindbender? Where were the dinosaurs? Rex didn't have long to hand-wring, because a black dinocopter broke through the clouds and dipped to hover over the park, near-silent chopper blades blowing the grass back. Spot, still in combat gear, leaned out the side door, his velociraptor neck twisted toward her. "Need a ride, Mom?"

Rex's heart fluttered in relief. "Yes. Take me to Peak Street. Cat Man, did—oh, he's gone." Cat Man was halfway across the park, sprinting toward the fight with claws extended.

Rex grabbed a skid and hoisted herself up. "We're breaking into the cat dimension later."

"If that's real, we'll get right on it," Stripey said as the copter rose smoothly into the air.

"Cut the attitude." Rex did a headcount. All dino troopers were accounted for. "Anyone hurt?"

"Just Fairy Baby," Spot answered from the cockpit.

"I broke my nose!" Fairy Baby announced, lying across a bench in the back. She winced and wrapped her frill around her head.

Rex checked them all anyway, ignoring their grumbling. Then she perched on a raptor-sized seat and shot each trooper a personal, well-deserved glare, though Stripey's was awkwardly angled since he'd hopped into her lap. "You guys owe me about ten explanations, and I'm getting all of them right now."

The dinosaurs had, in fact, brought Aya's servers to their compound instead of Zombie Island. But they, "had a good reason," that "has to do with the surprise." Rex's concerns about the surprise maybe being a robot army were looking more valid.

The dino troopers had apparently been a force in the works since Peak Street days.

"You were a baseball team," Rex repeated, reaching up to scritch Xena's head.

"We were the best players on each baseball team," Spot corrected.

"And we really, really liked practice drills," said Rutabaga Bill.

The dino troopers had deployed in a stealth copter to back up Rex shortly after the military blockaded the compound. When Rex activated her beacon, they'd diverted to the Protectors' location in time to get in on the rescue.

"But now we have to leave because the military caught up," Spot finished. "And they might not like us right now."

"It has to do with the surprise," Xena stage whispered.

"You're doing it on purpose at this point." Rex nudged Stripey out of her lap, moved to the cockpit, and found a terminal to connect with Aya. "Hey, buddy. What do I need to know?"

"Welcome back, Doctor. I recommend you avoid any members of law enforcement. Spot has apprised me of your current mission. I am sending backup to Peak Street."

Before Rex could ask what that meant, a tyrannosaur's voice came over the radio. "Dino troopers, we have you in sensor range, over."

Spot responded, "Trooper One to base. Approaching rendezvous, over."

"But we're approaching Peak Street," Rex protested. "What do you mean, 'base?'"

Spot's long maw split in a grin.

Rex needed to stop going ballistic over every goddamn stunt these assholes pulled, or she'd put herself in an early grave. She looked out at the approaching lab, a gray outline in the pre-dawn light, but her eyes were drawn to a blot across the still starry western horizon.

Rex wrestled down the *what fresh hell* reaction in the name of being a Zen Dino Mom. Her first thought was that the military had realized some dinos left the compound and sent a massive air raid to intercept them. But the blot wasn't a fleet. It looked more like a mass of thick clouds. Or an island.

"Surprise!" Xena sang.

"Doctor?" Aya said through the terminal. "As far as things you need to know, the first item is probably that the dinosaurs raised the land surrounding the compound from the surface of the earth and sent copies of a Declaration of Sovereignty and their National Charter to the United States government, the United Nations, and various international news organizations."

Spot grasped her hand with both of his. "Mom, will you be our Ambassador to Humanity?"

Stripey called from the back, "You have to say yes; we appointed you in our charter."

"You're perfect for the job—you're almost just like a human," Xena said encouragingly.

"Jesus fuck me blind." Rex's hands were frozen on top of her head, and she didn't remember putting them there.

The radio tyrannosaur came back, and this time Rex identified her as Lizard Wizard. "Deploying dino air force. Trooper One, bring any wounded back to base. We will proceed to rendezvous together."

As the floating island got steadily more distinguishable—Rex could see the freaking trees—small shapes broke away and approached in the pterodactyls' recognizable flight patterns.

"We'll hand you off to the air force and get Fairy Baby back home," Spot said. "We'll back you up when the base reaches Peak Street."

"No, drop me off and leave," Rex said firmly. "This isn't a shoot-out situation. And if it was, Vivid Blue is—"

The copter shook as a pterodactyl swooped close and clung to the side. Xena ripped open the door, air rushing loudly, and Geregard poked his head in. "Phew! Thanks, Zee." He twisted around the side of the door, revealing a seat buckled onto his back. "Climb on my back, Mom."

"You made yourselves saddles? I need to find you guys a therapist." Rex clambered onto the seat and figured out the buckles. "Okay. Take me down and—"

Geregard dropped away from the copter and matched Rex's delighted squeal.

DINOSAURS ON FIRE

R ex had a breathless instant to think *I'm flying I'm flying* before a sound like a whistle hurtled past her head. Geregard swerved with a curse.

"Geez, language," Rex said. "Where do you pick that shit up?"

"Mom, I think someone shot at us."

"What." Her voice came out flat. She scanned the ground over Geregard's shoulder. If Sam had shot at her dinosaurs, Rex was about to get a lot less conflicted about where this was going.

Geregard pulled up hard as another projectile whistled by, too close.

"Okay, get clear. Don't take risks."

Geregard banked, widening his circuit of the facility. Something was rigged up on the roof, probably something from her own lab.

Somehow, Rex knew this was Mindbender. Anger caught in her throat like nausea.

She'd *known* something like this would happen. Who cared if he wasn't flashy and in charge? He was competent, and they knew nothing about what he wanted, and now he was in her lab.

She looked for other weapons, but her eye was drawn to the street, where her Exo-suit was jogging toward the building.

Was that what Aya meant by backup? The mecha ran jerkily, with its arms straight by its sides as though the pilot had forgotten about them. "That's really creepy." If that was how Aya drove a giant robot, Rex would have to either put restrictions on her access to Rex's tech or write her new code for realistic running.

Although, if Aya had figured out how to drive the Exo-suit without the pilot-based control system, Rex was drastically misremembering the capabilities of the mecha's maintenance bay.

She got Geregard's attention and pointed to the edge of the lawn. "Down there."

They touched down, meeting the Exo-suit as it staggered to a stop. Rex sent Geregard off with strongly worded orders to stay at a safe range. Then the mecha's chest split open and Lewis tumbled onto the grass, wheezing and retching.

Rex stared, indulging the contextless *my hero* thought that popped into her head. This night had seemed endless, and even though it hadn't been more than five or six hours since they'd parted in such splendid dysfunction, she was just so goddamn happy to see him.

"Is this going to be a pattern?" she asked, not caring that her Cheshire grin probably wasn't appropriate for watching him heave on his knees.

He answered with a breathless, "Wha—?"

"This is a lot like when you found me in the woods and stumbled out of that four-wheeler like you were gonna hurl."

Lewis threw a hand toward the mecha. "That thing stabbed me in the back of the neck!"

"Yeah, the neural uplink."

He groaned. "Just get in the thing. I'll walk home."

Rex giggled, and it lasted longer than she meant it to.

"You—you're good?" he wheezed.

"Yeah. You're the one who looks like shit." She remembered she'd gassed her house and run off with Sam earlier. "Oh, wait, you're talking about—"

Lewis staggered to his feet and pulled her into a hug.

Rex lost her breath in his grip and didn't need to draw another. She was just a warm mass wrapped in soft, sweaty, too-strong arms. She recognized in time-stuttering, intrusive moments that her arms were wrapped just as strongly around Lewis and her head had fallen onto his shoulder. Her body came back online—the demanding shit—when her lungs started to ache.

Before she could wriggle for freedom, Lewis held her out at arm's length, blushing and looking apologetic.

"Sorry, I just—" He nodded toward his hands still on her upper arms. "Shouldn't have just . . . come at you like that."

"It's fine." Rex grabbed his arms to hold them in place. "I mean, probably not in general. I guess you should ask before hugging people, but I liked it."

His blush spread, and Rex was certain he'd thought of the kiss.

"Can we talk later?" he asked.

"Yeah. I really want to talk about it." It didn't occur to her to play maybe-that's-not-what-he-means.

"You, um." Lewis's eyebrows did their thing as his eyes flicked over her. "You're not wearing any clothes."

"Why do people keep saying that? My fire suit covers everything."

"It's very formfitting."

Rex rolled her eyes and dropped her hands. "How did you drive this thing? It's keyed to my DNA."

"Oh. Aya did something?" He let go of her and gave the Exo-suit a hostile glance. "It involved some scans and a blood draw, which, now that I think about it, probably wasn't a great idea? Because now I'm realizing an uncomfortably self-aware AI has a sample of my blood."

That sounded like Aya. "I'll talk to her about it."

"I'd appreciate that." Lewis turned as though to invite Rex into the mecha's open pilot cavity. "Aya said someone locked her out of Peak Street. I think the idea is to use this to bust in and take it back."

That was definitely Mindbender.

Rex had to find a hero super genius to play chess with. Arrogant monologues and lack of personality were a small price to pay if they didn't invade her lab and rig it to shoot her.

"I need to tell you something," Lewis continued. "Peter and I gave the hood he had to the Protectors—"

Rex shook her head. "I inferred. I get why you did it—you were keeping me out of jail."

"Well, after Last Dance got ahold of the hood we gave them, we swapped the other one with your prototype."

Rex blinked. The other one, meaning—"The red one I sent with 'Ning?"

"With his mind reading, and he got the first one so easily—" Lewis nodded toward the lab. "The hood in there is the one Oversight's had all this time. Peter took the one 'Ning brought."

A weight lifted from Rex's chest. If Viv was too late, if Sam was already gone, they'd be okay. "Thank you." She dropped her head back onto his chest, exhaling her relief. She wanted to stay there longer and expound on her appreciation of Lewis's support and general self. Or hug him again. But the priority was her lab.

She climbed into the mecha—oh man, she'd missed this thing; she was never traveling by car again—and activated the neural uplink. The familiar awareness of the mecha's systems flooded her senses. "Flag down a ptero-dactyl if you want a ride home."

Lewis's thumbs-up didn't have to be so sarcastic.

The Exo-suit closed around her, screens popping up to show a 360-de-gree view with motions tracked and prioritized. A symbol appeared on the viewscreen, accompanied by a voice. "Hello, Doctor."

"Aya, we need to talk later about when it's appropriate to fast-talk peo-ple into giving you blood samples."

"I will add it to the schedule."

"The front entrance was the facility's weakest point. Do you think that's still true?"

"Barring entrance by rift," Aya confirmed.

Rex turned to the front doors, moving the arms because it was good for balance and looked normal, and sprinted.

Laserfire hit the grass at her feet. Blue force field shields absorbed the shots that landed. Good to see that Aya had kept up with the improve-ments she'd planned while the Exo-suit was locked away. By the time the roof-mounted defenses switched to explosive projectiles, Rex was past the grass and busting through the doors—and part of the wall—a small crater of dirt and concrete blasting up on the mecha's heels.

The lights were low in the atrium. The mecha fit easily under the high ceiling. Rex paused there, letting the reactivated lasers in the walls bombard her shields.

The hood was in the high-security wing, and probably what Viv had gone for. But considering that the walls were attacking her, Mindbender was probably still here, and he could not be allowed to get away.

"Aya, what would you need in order to get control of the weapons here?"

"More time than you can likely spare, Doctor. However, a brief physical uplink should be adequate to introduce a virus."

Rex turned toward the security center and broke into a jog.

A projectile caught her in the ankle. The floor came flying up too fast. Her elbow rose in time to jar against the floor, but not at the right angle to catch her fall. The laserfire didn't let up. Mindbender must have overridden Oversight's blocks on internal security. Though the shields held steady, energy use stats popped up on a screen. This was why you didn't test new modifications in life-or-death situations. "Aya, I hope you're marking areas of poor coverage."

A voice came over the alert system. "—was surprised to hear you were working with the Protectors, Meister. A little disappointing, to be honest."

There weren't any blind spots in the lab's internal security—Rex hadn't anticipated someone taking it over when she'd designed it. At this rate, the mecha wouldn't survive a blind sprint to the security center. She raised her arm and shot out a few guns. Then she pushed to her knees and punched into a wall, targeting the wiring.

Mindbender's voice rang through the hall. "Villains really cluster at the two ends of the intelligence spectrum, don't they? They're either your dumbass bank robbers blundering in and out of jail, or they're the most elegant minds the world ever rejected. I had thought you fell into that second category."

"Everyone's a freaking person. Your tragic villain card is not that ex-clusive," Rex bit out. She ripped a bundle of wires out of the wall, and the lasers went down for the immediate area, as well as the lights. She activated the lights on her suit and lurched back to her robotic feet, testing the bad ankle.

"These other guys your brother brought in? First category, every one of them. Doesn't matter how much power they have. I shouldn't be surprised they never figured it out."

Rex wobbled through a few steps and worked up to a jog, hoping that if she ignored the balance warning and the *thunk* in her ankle it would go away.

"I mean, Last Dance plotting to brainwash city after city until he and his allies took over the world? I might buy that he'd give world domination a shot—he's got a vengeful streak—but with this plan? We'd never pull it off due to timeline flaws, alone. It was all clearly a lie that would ultimately lead to him dumping the alliance in the Protectors' laps once he had what he wanted."

Mindbender's chuckle echoed in surround sound. "I admit, I was ner-vous when I figured it out; he obviously knew I had. Ill Wind thought about betraying him after he demoted her for attacking you, and he beat her down before she could make a move. That super strength's no joke, isn't it? People forget about it with the mind reading thing. Instead, he came to me with a different task."

The security system was still activated in the next hall, but again, the lights were out. Rex tried to make a break for the closest convergence point in the wiring behind the walls, but something locked in her ankle. She fell against the wall. Laserfire poured into her shields, and the energy use warn-ing filled her screens again.

"When his people attacked your lab, some went in with a secondary assignment. You may have noticed you lost data in the attack."

Oversight's wipeout protocol. If there had been someone else mess-ing with her systems, covering their tracks, how could she have known the difference?

"Now that I control this place, I just have to cover his retreat, and then I strip the Meister's lab of whatever I want while the Protectors are busy with his half-witted allies. Easy enough, with your blue leader running aimlessly through the halls. Ah, looks like she's finally found the right wing. And speeding up—she must hear him throwing shit around in there."

Rex viciously shoved aside the implications—both that Sam had likely discovered the switched hood, and that Viv was ignoring Mindbender. Viv didn't know that Sam's hood wasn't here. The lab wasn't more important than Sam to her, anyway.

A few lights appeared down the dark hallway, steadier than the lasers. Clunky, mechanical sounds reached her through the laserfire.

"I have to hand it to Dance; for someone without genius, he has an excellent grasp of how to utilize it in others."

Rex recognized every machine that crawled or rolled into her light beams. Repair-spiders skittered down the walls—she maybe saw why people thought they were creepy. The larger bots were blunter in application, mobile and multipurpose so they could be reconfigured for different projects.

All of them converged on her position.

Rex was suddenly furious. How dare Mindbender turn her lab into the set of a cheap horror movie? She pushed off the wall, shields shifting as the guns targeted her from new angles, and snatched the closest repair-spider in a giant hand. Her head rattled as she hit the floor, and she punched through the wall without bothering to stand.

Then she thrust the stabby-bot into the mass of exposed wires and sliced through whatever she could reach.

The guns shut down. Rex threw the repair-spider at a second one and shot the closest production bot as she climbed to her knees. She wanted to scream. If this was what she had to fight through hall by hall, she'd already lost. After everything Rex had risked and endured to keep her work out of Oversight's hands, Mindbender could skip out with all of it.

Rex shot a robot into submission, punched the next one that got too close, and turned to another.

Before she landed a punch, it hit the floor.

For a moment, Rex was embarrassed that something she made would trip. Her sensors followed it down, and her screens showed a smooth-flowing puddle of nanobots climbing over its legs. The nanoswarm swept down the hall like a river, engulfing repair-spiders, climbing bots, and shaping sharp waves that sliced through guns. Rex twisted the Exo-suit at the waist to shine a light on the bodysuit-clad dinosaurs running behind the swarm, metal circlets blinking.

"Hello, Mother," Dino Might said, dozens of voices echoing down the hall. "Thank you for disabling the atrium security to speed our ingress. How may we best provide tactical support?"

"I told you to stay home," she said on principle.

Mindbender's voice rang through the hall. "There they are—the internet sensation. I've already copied the data from your dinosaur project."

Oh, *fuck* no.

"Maybe I'll start my own—"

Nanobots flowed over the speakers in the ceiling and cut them off. Dino Might blinked expectantly at her, the swarm breaking through robots around them.

"Shit." Rex wanted to run her hands down her face, but settled for clenching her fists in the sleeves, making the mecha do the same. "Please stop Mindbender. Don't let him take anything."

"Affirmative. Shall we prioritize haste or the preservation of structural integrity?"

"Definitely haste. Thank you." Rex opened the Exo-suit and scrambled to untangle herself from its pilot cavity, still shaky from Mindbender's last message. "Don't let him take anything. Disable the guns. Aya can get access through the Exo-suit."

"Acknowledged, Mother." Nanobots swarmed over the mecha's ankle and pilot system, taking sections apart and rebuilding.

"Don't get hurt. Did I mention that? Make that the first priority. Then haste."

"Be assured, Mother, we shall take the utmost care with our component beings." The nanoswarm broke a shield emitter from the mecha and brought it to Rex.

Rex took the emitter, snatched the closest fallen repair-spider, and made adjustments until the shield sprang to life in her hand. "He can't take *anything*. Did I already say that?"

"We will stop the intruder, Mother." Dino Might's dozens of eyes watched her with more understanding than looked natural in the individual faces. "You can trust us with this task."

Rex nodded stiffly, flicking the emitter on and off to test the reaction time.

"Please activate your force field, Mother."

Rex suddenly processed what the bodysuits were and pulled the shield close.

"Dino Might, ignite!" Each dinosaur burst into flames, lighting up the hallway. Rex pressed against the wall as they tore into the next wave of bots with a roar, fire blazing. Wires smoked and sparked. The nanoswarm flowed ahead with the sprinting Exo-suit, deflecting attacks without slowing.

Rex squeezed her eyes shut until the harsh streaks in her vision faded. Then she turned down a corridor and ran, planning the fastest route to the hood.

DINOSAURS EX MACHINA

*R*ex darted down the first hall with lasers bombarding her shield. In the next, none fired. By the third, Rex stopped bothering with the shield, confident that Dino Might had delivered Aya's virus. She heard distant crashes and roars, including some voices that indicated the big dinosaurs had gotten inside.

It occurred to Rex that with systems down, getting through the high-security doors might be a problem. But she found the first barrier peeled aside by sheer force—evidence of Sam or Viv coming through the same way. She stepped through the doorway, walked to the next, and stepped through its remains as well.

Only the track lighting at the edges of the room remained lit, enough to dimly illuminate Viv standing with her back to Rex.

Rex approached slowly, eyes sweeping over the broken containment unit—yeah, that super strength was no joke—and the brown scraps of a hood on the floor. Her heart sank at the scene, but it was a familiar feeling by now.

"He's gone." Viv's tone was flat. She didn't turn. Rex walked around her to see her face, as empty as her voice. "I missed him again."

"He won't try something else this extreme," Rex said, unsure if she was trying to be comforting or just speaking her thoughts.

"What makes you think that?"

Rex shifted as she put her words together, eyes on the torn fabric on the floor.

She looked to the virus samples stored nearby, still present, containment intact. "He has patterns. Have you noticed? I think sometimes the guilt catches up to him."

Viv shook her head. "I'm tired of doing this."

"Do you think you could," Rex hesitated, "just stop?"

Viv raised her eyes to glare. "You want to give up on him?"

"No. I just—" Rex looked away and told herself not to be defensive. "We try the same things over and over. And we get the same results." *Hi T. I need help.* "Yeah, we've sunk a lot of resources into our methods, but maybe it's time to test new theories."

Now Viv looked frustrated. "T—"

"I've been trying to break some patterns lately," Rex explained too fast to filter, leaving her uncomfortable with the words. "And I—I always think something's going to work this time. Like somehow it only hasn't worked because the circumstances weren't right, or I was doing one small part wrong, and this time will be different. But it's not different. It's just doing what's easy."

"What do you propose, then?" Viv threw up her hands. "He's a supervillain. If there's some other way to save him, then a lot of heroes are going to be knocking down your door for this miracle answer."

Rex felt herself bristling and once again fought it down. "I just don't think anything he does for us is going to stick." She had tried to be what she'd thought was needed. She'd done what was asked of her and hollowed herself out in the process. How much good had it done in the long run? "If we're ever going to actually help him," she refused to say save, "I think it has to be by backing *his* play."

"Of course. We should back his plan to brainwash people. Or force them to work for him. Or rob you. Or—"

"You're *trying* to twist what I'm saying," Rex snapped. "We can't save or fix him. He's not something to save or fix. He has to want our help."

Viv's hands dropped. She cleared the immediate area with a sweep of telekinesis and sat on the floor. Rex kicked some debris aside the old-fashioned way and sat across from her.

"It's not that simple, though," Viv eventually said. "It's not just us three. He's hurt people. I can't leave him alone when he resurfaces."

Rex wanted to say it didn't have to be Viv's job. There were other superheroes who wouldn't have to give so much to fight Sam. But the reality was, there may not be another hero to match Sam's strength, and Rex's reasons for only making Viv an anti-Sam hood still stood.

There were times the situation demanded more than was fair. There were times people who were supposed to love you didn't choose you. Either bitterness and anger—sadness, really, but even the most heart-ripping anger was easier to dwell on than sadness—were the price you had to pay, or Rex was doing self-sacrifice wrong.

Or maybe there wasn't a right way to give more than you had. Maybe it always left you with a black pit seeping poison into your future steps. Rex wondered if Viv had one.

Maybe assuming self-sacrifice was the only option was the first wrong step. An experiment run again and again without any of the results you waited for.

Rex took a deep breath, examining the far wall. "I could, maybe, help." What was worse than dragging that pit behind you on your own?

Viv raised her head enough to reveal a skeptical look under her hood.

"Next time." Rex coughed into her hand. Smooth.

"Because you have so many better ideas," Viv muttered.

"I *don't* have a better idea," Rex snipped, feeling jittery.

Viv's shoulders alternately drew up and dropped down, jerky motions of tension and its forced release. Rex watched the struggle and found her heart aching.

"You just don't have to do this alone, if you don't want to." Her eyes were drawn back to the wall. Such a fascinating wall. "And maybe I'll have better ideas by then."

Viv gave Rex a lift to the lawn with the intention of going back in for Mind-bender, but once outside, they saw that the dinosaurs' rampage had spilled into the street.

Down a short trail of fiery destruction, Rex heard the creaks and clat-ters of a machine and Mindbender cry, "Your brute strength is no match for my technology!"

Rex groaned. "Why would he say that? It never turns out to be true."

The dinosaurs struck, and, true to tradition, brute strength beat brain power. Not that the dinosaurs were lacking in brain power, but they clearly knew which tools fit which task.

"Will your dinosaurs kill him?" Viv asked tensely.

"Um. No?" Rex made a note to organize a long overdue lecture series on ethics for the compound. Island. Country. Whatever it was now.

Viv swooped in and dragged Mindbender out of the scraps. She held him while Dino Might's smaller component beings scanned and searched him for data storage devices. When they were satisfied and Viv was done rolling her eyes, she called to Rex, "I'm taking him into custody. Then I have to check in with my team."

Rex nodded, trying not to show her relief that Viv remained too busy to remember Rex was also supposed to be taken into custody. "I'd join, but I have a mess here that might count as an international incident." She glanced at the blazing treetops of the old dinosaur habitats.

Viv adjusted her grip on Mindbender, ignoring his curses, and took off.

Despite her half-formed plans to deal with this nonsense, Rex was hit with a wave of exhaustion as soon as Viv left. Dino Might stood in the street, dinosaurs staring vacantly as the nanoswarms systematically smothered fires. It seemed like they had things in hand.

Rex sighed and turned back to the lab. Were the pterodactyls in hive-mind? If so, could Dino Might spare the concentration to give her a lift?

A human figure standing by the curb caught her eye. Was Lewis still here? She walked closer, squinting through the weird shadows of early morning and intermittent fires.

The figure turned toward her, and it wasn't Lewis—too tall, too cut, wearing a deep red cloak with the cowl pulled down. Rex's exhaustion vanished. Sam gazed at her, blank-faced, and said, "Greetings, Mother."

"Oh my God."

"As you have no doubt surmised, a most unusual phenomenon has occurred."

Rex's hands rose to her head. "I'm suddenly faced with about a dozen ethical dilemmas."

"Upon initiating hivemind, we were joined by an unintended component being."

Sam must have still been close when the dinosaurs arrived. At a guess, upon reading Dino Might's mind, his own was caught up in the collective intelligence.

Or subsumed. Or something.

"A fascinating development, Mother."

"Oh, God, don't call me Mother. Ew."

"Ah—because of your familial relation with this unit. We shall refrain."

Rex became aware of her mouth gaping. She continued to fail to speak for a moment, then shook her head, rubbed her eyes, and said, "This definitely counts as cheating. Can you call Viv?"

Dino Might contacted Aya to contact Viv. Rex considered asking Dino Might to move out of Sam's range or drop hivemind, but they were still using the nanoswarms to fight the fires. Instead, two hiveminded pterodactyls— Geregard and Wing Wing—carried Rex and Sam to the edge of the woods.

"When all units have left his range, he will doubtless regain individuality," they—and Sam—said before leaving. "Will you be in danger?"

Her head said no, but her heart said maybe. "No. Viv will get here soon."

As the pterodactyls vanished in the distance, Sam's loose bearing grew hard. He inhaled deeply, and his eyes cut to Rex. "I'm not going with Viv."

"Sam." Rex rubbed her head. She didn't know what she wanted to say. Viv was close; he knew running would do no good. She wanted to beg him to cooperate. He'd do it if she cried. The manipulation had worked ever since he'd kidnapped her, and she'd taken it as a fraction of what she was due. But she'd told Viv not even an hour ago: it wouldn't stick.

Sam grunted. "That won't work anymore. You don't give a shit about me, so why should I give a shit about you?"

Rex didn't voice what she thought of that bullshit. He could read it from her mind.

"I didn't even want this," he said. "I wanted to be a veterinarian."

Rex nodded. "I remember."

He sat in the grass, shoulders shaking.

Rex dropped to his side. She raised an arm to hold him, and her muscles jumped and resisted. He was bigger than her; he was too close. An old fantasy came to mind—taking a hammer, bashing it through his head—that soothed her enough to put an arm around his shoulders.

Sam dropped his face into his hands and moaned.

"It's just a thought," Rex murmured, face hot with shame as she squeezed his shoulder. "It's not really what I want."

"I know," he roared.

Her hand tightened convulsively on his arm.

He leaned into her side while they waited. Old words floated through her head. Because it meant something to voice it, she muttered, "I still love you."

His voice was rough and muffled by his hands. "I still love you."

When she showed up, Viv dragged Sam to his feet and hugged him tight enough to make him wheeze. Then she paced and shouted in his face, even giving a few hard shoves, while Rex stood awkwardly to the side and stared in the other direction. Sam tried to shout back a few times, but Viv's voice hit a pitch that made Rex cringe and he fell back into his sullen scowl.

Rex tuned out Viv's words until some part of her recognized mounting tension.

"I'm keeping this." Viv was holding the edge of her hood and shaking it in Sam's face. "If you do *anything*, and I get wind of it—and I will, because you can't *not* make a mess when you're being a fucking douchebag—you won't stand a chance in hell. Do you hear me? I said, do you hear me?"

Sam exploded back, "You think you'd do better if it was you?" and threw a punch. Viv caught it and threw him to the ground. Sam came up with a snarl on his face that made Rex take another few steps back.

Sam's eyes cut toward her, jaw tight. Then he swung at Viv with a roar.

"Okay, maybe I shouldn't be here," Rex muttered to herself, dancing back across the grass. Viv and Sam were full-on crashing through the forest now, and Rex let out a breathy laugh. "This is fine. They're just getting it out. It's fine."

The crashing stopped a short time later. Rex wasn't sure it had lasted a full minute. That was for the best, since she'd already seen two trees come down. She jogged in the direction of the last shout and rejoined her siblings, both breathing hard and looking a little ragged.

"The next time I see you," Viv said, "it better not be like this."

Sam had new tear tracks on his stony face. "Fuck you."

Viv reached to her thigh and pulled a cellphone out of a hidden pocket—did she fight with that on her?—and telekinesis-ed it into a pocket on his hip. "Get my personal number from that. Maybe then you won't have to commit a felony to get my attention."

"You both have pockets?" Rex pointed between them. "And you know where his are?"

"We've been at this a long time, T. Keep up," Viv snapped.

Rex nodded and clasped her hands behind her back. Pockets. That was much better than 'Ning's purse.

Sam gave Rex an unamused look.

"Stop working with supervillains, Sam. You're doing the same things over and over, and it's not working. Try something else," Viv said. "I'm taking

T home." She strode toward Rex and scooped her up in a princess carry, making her squawk.

"Excuse me?"

"Shut up, T." Viv took off, Rex grabbing her shoulders with a yelp, and they left Sam standing at the edge of the woods.

Rex didn't speak as they flew, partly because her jaw wouldn't unclench when the ground was so far below, and partly because being carried by Viv was really, really awkward. But eventually, the silence became more awkward, and she unclenched to say, "You didn't take him in."

Viv sucked air through her nose. Rex glanced at her face to see it working through a tense series of expressions. "I don't know if I did the wrong thing," she said in a rush, voice harsh as though fighting tears.

Rex nodded. "I don't know, either." Her relief at Viv's mercy felt spoiled by fear of what Sam would do with it. He seemed different this time. He'd reached farther, he'd failed, and he looked tired. If there was a time to give someone another chance, wasn't this it?

He doesn't deserve it.

Yeah, right. How could she know what he deserved? Did she care? Every time she tried to think of it objectively, everything personal was twisted into it. Justice and mercy always seemed so biased and arbitrary. Maybe that was her problem with heroes.

"Am I under arrest?"

"I have no idea. I'm just going to drop you off at that island you put in the sky."

"That wasn't me. That was—"

Viv sighed loudly. "I don't care, T. I don't know how you two always get away with everything."

"It might have something to do with you not arresting us."

"Don't test me. I'm tired."

They slowed, and Rex looked up to see the island approaching. She couldn't help a wave of curiosity overpowering her exhaustion and moral cynicism. Static prickled over her skin as they got close—an atmospheric bubble?—and Viv brought them down a few yards from the buildings, where the jungle was thin.

Viv started to step away, but hesitated. "Do you think he'll call?"

Rex considered an honest *I have no idea,* but tempered it. "It might take a while. He holds a grudge."

Viv nodded. She still didn't move. "Will you call?"

Right. Before this, they hadn't exactly been in touch. "Do you want me to?"

"If you're about to become the despot of your own country up here, I think it will put some important people at ease if I keep an eye on things."

"It's not my country. I didn't—"

"Whatever. If I don't hear from you, I'll have to check in. You're a global security risk."

Rex rolled her eyes. "Fine."

She watched Viv step off the ground and fly back down to Earth. Then she trudged toward the compound, where dinosaurs were stalking out to meet her, calling as they came.

"Mom, was that Vivid Blue?"

"If you didn't get me her autograph, I'm never talking to you again."

Rex sighed as deeply as her lungs would allow and turned her trudge into a stomp. "My own freaking dinosaurs."

ISSUE 40

DINOSAURS WITH DIPLOMATIC IMMUNITY

"The headline for the *Gazette* was 'Jurassic Age Returns to Decimen City, Again.' Was that an inside joke?" Peter asked when he called a few days later.

"It's a reference from before you got here." Rex braved the raptor-optimized computer in one of the dinosaurs' labs to find the article online. The headline was accompanied by an aerial shot of the fiery stampede down the street. She sucked air in through her teeth. She hadn't technically promised the mayor that wouldn't happen again, but it had been heavily implied. "I can't believe that beat out the full-team superhero fight downtown."

"It makes more sense than the *Decimen City Circular*. Their headline is about how the Millennium Theater wasn't actually under construction, but now it is because supervillains destroyed it."

"Decimen loves that theater," Rex said, scrolling through the *Gazette*. "I assume they're ignoring how 'Ning did as much damage as the villains."

"The article focuses more on how she single-handedly took down the biggest threat."

"Typical."

"They're concerned about you though."

"Really?" There was annoyance in the article's commentary, but a lot of it seemed tongue-in-cheek. Pretty standard for her exploits, which was a bit disorienting since these latest events felt so different to Rex. There were also a lot of dinosaur puns.

"It says, 'no confirmation yet on the whereabouts or involvement of Rex Anderson, the Meister of Decimen City.'"

"Oh, that kind of concern."

"They seem worried. There's been a mention every day. If you won't make an appearance, you could at least post on social media."

"Flora said I should keep my head down," Rex hedged, but she didn't like the idea of Decimen thinking she'd disappeared or wondering if she'd been villain-aligned in that mess. "I'll put something out there. What's my status with Oversight?"

"Limbo, pretty much. They keep telling us to wait for orders. Lewis got moved to the barracks, since Flora kicked us out of the house. So that's nice."

Flora had already explained that development, achieved through a combination of the lawsuit over Grant's actions, Rex's nebulous status, and the fact that Flora's name was on the lease. She almost asked about Grant not being included in that move, just to revel in how thoroughly Aya and Flora were dragging him—and smearing Oversight for the part it played; Aya pulled no punches—but she satisfied herself with internal crowing.

"Is Lewis—" Well, she hadn't meant to start that question. And now she didn't know how to finish it.

"He's fine," Peter answered. He sounded uncertain. Rex wished she hadn't brought it up. "I know he'd like to talk to you in person, if that's possible."

"It will be," Rex said. "It's just taking a while."

While the heroic-but-confused story Peter and Lewis had sold on her behalf was enough to hold off a ruling in absentia, Rex would almost certainly be arrested if she tried to go home. Unless her position as the dinosaurs' Ambassador to Humanity became politically meaningful.

Progress toward legitimizing the title was steady, but slow. Decimen City had announced within the week that they'd be honored to host the Meister as diplomatic envoy from their sometimes-skyward neighbor—

the island's meandering across the globe followed an ever-changing route based on weather patterns, the attitudes of grounded nations, and human air traffic—in the event the United States recognized the nation's sovereignty.

The United Nations seemed more likely to accept their application for membership with each nation that clued into the benefits of backing the most technologically advanced society on the planet. The United States would eventually see where the wind was blowing.

Until then, it was a task of working with Flora to put together law teams with the right expertise, making a more focused public relations plan than *ignore what Aya is doing,* and looking up *ambassador* in the dictionary.

"I want to hire you, by the way," Rex said while she was thinking of it.

"What?" Peter said with a laugh. Rex hoped it was a happily surprised laugh and not a no-chance-in-hell laugh.

"Yeah." She shrugged, heart speeding with nerves. "Your name's already next to mine on some pending patents. I'll need more competent and creative people if I want to really make something of my lab, and most of my techs aren't that." Her techs were lucky she had a soft spot for people who were nice to dinosaurs. "I wanted to let you know before Oversight offers you a new assignment."

"Any idea where your new lab will be based? Because, no offense but I don't know if I could live on a floating dinosaur island."

Rex winced at the reminder of Peak Street's demise. "Decimen City, hopefully. Either the same property or somewhere with more space. Have you liked it there?"

"I have, actually," Peter said, sounding mildly surprised with himself. "I'll give it some serious thought."

Rex reined in the hope that bubbled up but let the hunter's satisfaction run free. Her love in its natural form was vicious and easily won. She had her claws in Peter, and she didn't plan to let him go. "Important subject change: if I tell you the Lightning's secret identity, can you keep it secret?"

"God, yes."

When Rex ended the call, it was with a tight feeling in her chest despite her smile. She noticed a text waiting from Lewis.

I can hear Peter talking to you in the other room. Glad you're not dying in a ditch.

She answered, *Sorry you have to bunk with the plebes.*

His response took seconds. *The plebes are annoying, but the food is actually better.*

The tight feeling went away.

Rex mourned her lab. She didn't realize it at first. She assumed she was crashing from the stress of the last days, months—years, maybe—and she probably partially was.

But so much had been in that lab. So much work, so many hopeful projects and the spaces that had grown around them. The habitats she'd made for the dinosaurs when they could barely form sentences—Stripey's first was "I am Apatosaurus," clueing them in that the dinosaurs were bald-faced liars. The greenhouse she'd converted into a hatchling nursery. The failed prototypes and bad ideas she'd built on. The burned-out space where she'd made Mutey.

It wasn't all gone; her most personal work was done in the home lab, and Aya's program wasn't the only thing on the servers sitting safe on the island. And everything she'd lost was still in her memory. But the physical aspects of her work were far from inconsequential. She may plan a lot in her head, but the sheer quantity of experiments and inventions she'd have to recreate from just that—plans—was sometimes daunting to the point of despair.

She distracted herself with work. And it was a tears-worthy relief to be able to do that again. The lab the dinosaurs refitted for her wasn't convenient, not being optimized for humans, but after being cut off from most of her projects, having the freedom to science to her heart's content felt like unstopping a dam.

The first thing she did was sneak a virus sample from the ruins of Peak Street and get to work on a cure. It was amazing how quickly insights came to her without Oversight and the Protectors questioning every step she took. By the time Flora announced that she could go home with diplomatic immunity, she had an antiviral and several dispersal options for whoever was in charge of that kind of thing.

Rex was surprised by the welcome she got in Decimen City in that she didn't get one. She had a brief meeting with Mayor Vicker in which he didn't seem to know what they were supposed to do any more than she did, but Rex got a free meal out of it. They parted with an awkward handshake, Rex giving her sharpest, most shit-eating grin to the evil assistant whose name she'd forgotten, and she considered the evening a win.

Otherwise, everyone in Decimen City acted as though nothing had changed. The *Circular* printed a blurb about her return as though she'd been on a quirky vacation, including her new title in a transparently sarcastic tone.

"It reads dry to me," Flora insisted.

"They're making fun of me, and we both know it." Either way, it made an odd contrast to the responses beyond Decimen City. Viv's estimation of her as a global security risk apparently wasn't laughable outside her hometown.

Rex made a point of sharing some of those views on social media through a petty grammar edit of the paper.

"Maybe instead of nitpicking the news, you should be getting ready for the interview."

Rex winced.

The date set for Rex's interview on *Good Morning, Gorgeous* had rolled past long before Rex got home. Rex had been all for smuggling Gorgeous to the island—she was a journalist, sort of; they got away with that kind of crap—but Flora and the network preferred to postpone. So instead of a clandestine interview in a dinosaur nation with a bag over her head, the interview was scheduled for the day after she got back, in the office that Flora's law minions had colonized.

"I'd think you'd be more motivated not to be late, now that we know the host could beat you up." Flora was enjoying 'Ning's identity reveal too much.

"Anyone could beat me up—I don't have powers."

"Now that we know the interviewer has no compunctions against beating you up," Flora corrected.

Rex might have argued the point, but the reminder had her antsy enough to toss back, "You're hilarious," and scuttle off to prepare.

Since she ran out without lunch, Rex stopped at a sandwich shop between her house and the law office. She got a short lecture from the owner—"What's this I've heard about you making trouble for your villain probation?"—which she scowled through as an equally disapproving employee made her sandwich.

She was arguing back—Enrique and Yvette could shove it—that if they'd been there, they'd see it wasn't as bad as it sounded, when someone bumped into her and slid a hand into her jacket pocket.

Rex grabbed the stranger's arm, hope coming on as suddenly as a kick to the stomach. "Wait." She dug the slip of paper out of her pocket and opened it roughly.

Hi T.
Viv's a bitch.
Love, Sam

Rex couldn't hold back the smile, relief flooding her so fast it hurt. The messenger tested her grip on their arm, making her hand tighten. "Wait."

Yvette lent her a pen, bemusement clear at the request. Rex turned the note over on the counter and scribbled out,

You know I don't like that word. I'm making you a hat (hoods are dumb). I might need brain scans. Btw, I need to know where and when the virus was spread so everyone exposed can get the cure. Love you.

She pressed the note back into the messenger's hand, grabbed her sandwich, and left with a lighter heart. Gorgeous's team had taken over one of the conference rooms by the time Rex arrived, setting two high-backed armchairs across from each other in a configuration whose only other function would be for old men in tweed to share a game of chess.

Rex wolfed down her sandwich before she was handed off to a makeup artist—probably suggested by Flora; she knew well not to trust Rex to make herself camera ready. Before she knew it, she'd been bundled into one of the chairs and Gorgeous was smiling cheerily across from her, skirt-wrapped knees pressed tight like she was riding the chair edge sidesaddle.

"I can't make this make sense to me," Rex muttered.

"We're not live this time, so we can stay here for as many takes as you need."

That was definitely a threat. "Your whole crew knows who you are?"

"Only Megan and Jerry are with me today. I trust them."

Rex glanced to confirm that besides the makeup artist, there was only one additional team member manning the camera.

Gorgeous placed a hand on Rex's knee. "We can take this slow." Rex resolved not to blurt out an innuendo. "I know the last time got a little out of hand. This setup should allow us to revisit some of those topics in more depth."

"Geez, you're really in character. Unless you're out of character."

"That's strike one."

"There she is."

Gorgeous ignored her. "I have the list of topics if you don't mind going over them one more time. The fans will be expecting me to ask about that post you made suggesting you were a fugitive—particularly if that was why you hid on Dino Island."

"As a media person, can you get the other media people to stop calling it Dino Island? It's a little disrespectful since the dinosaurs have made it clear its name is New Colorado."

"And of course, we want to know your thoughts on More to the Story, since it brought so much attention to the show."

"Does the show support it?" Rex asked. The discourse was increasingly seen as hero-critical, which caused some knee-jerk reactions that Rex had to fight not to sneer at.

"*I* support it." Gorgeous's grin sharpened. "And the network doesn't have much choice since it used my words."

"Your words?" The makeup on Rex's face made it harder to furrow her brow, but she wasn't gonna give in to that psychosomatic feedback. "That hashtag came from what I said."

"I actually said it first."

Rex scoffed. Then she mentally rewatched the video.

"*Is that not the whole story?*"

"*No, it's the whole story. I mean, that's what was told, so obviously that's 'the story.' That's what stories are, right? People tell them, and then that's it. That's what they are.*"

"*I guess I'm asking if there was more to it.*"

"*Well, there's always more, right?*"

Damn it. "Technically, neither of us said the whole thing."

Gorgeous gave her an indulgent smile. "With your permission, I'd like to cut a bit of that back-and-forth into the final edit."

"You're already rolling?" Rex shot the camera guy a glare and straightened her back. "Fine. Let's do this."

Talking about the dinosaurs was easy. That was probably why Gorgeous started with them. By the time they transitioned to why Rex was in New Colorado, she was making much less work for whoever got stuck editing this piece.

"It's not like I was on vacation," Rex defended. "I got a lot done up there. I cured Last Dance's virus . . . which was actually my virus. So, I'm at a happy neutral?"

"I have to know." Gorgeous's voice lowered, and she leaned forward conspiratorially. "The showdown between Last Dance's allies and the Protectors of the World, all these horrible things we've been learning about his plans, everything that brought the Protectors to Decimen City during your Oversight—what was your role in all that?"

Rex let her gaze fall. This part would be tricky and uncomfortable. "To explain it, I'd have to go back further than the course of my Oversight."

"I guess you could say there's more to the story?" Gorgeous pandered.

Instead of rolling her eyes, Rex gave an acknowledging smile. "I assume you're familiar with Vivid Blue and Last Dance's backstory." She waited for the nod, calm settling through her. "I'm going to tell it a little differently."

Working in the home lab felt disorientingly normal. The return to her weird house had been a relief despite the remaining damage but sitting at her workbench and alternating between the design for her new labs and the coding for Aya's next avatar—they were considering arms—was what felt like coming home.

"Are you sure you want to cut so much of the internal security?" Flora asked, watching the designs take shape from her desk.

"No," Rex admitted. Her plans still included guns in the walls, but not everywhere. Having them turned on her by Mindbender revealed the flaw in that design. "I'm less comfortable with fewer defenses. But in the end, I think they hurt me more than they helped."

Flora watched her with an odd face.

"What?"

"Nothing." Flora turned back to her computer and typed loudly.

Rex frowned, but her attention was caught by the empty mason jar on Flora's desk. "Did you spend the self-deprecation money?"

"Hm? Oh, yes. Over there." Flora gestured to the far wall.

Rex looked. A new poster had appeared, stretching nearly floor to ceiling. It pictured a kitten hanging from a tree branch with the text, *hang in there*. "What the hell is that?"

Flora followed her gaze. "It's a motivational poster."

"This is a joke, right? You're kidding me right now."

Flora sighed, probably rolling her eyes behind her glasses. "Fine, I'll fix it." She took something from her desk and crossed the lab to the poster. When she stepped away, the kitten had googly eyes.

"Flora, what the hell?"

"You don't like it?"

"You're a troll, Flora. You're a goddamn troll."

A throat cleared behind them, and Rex turned to see Lewis in the doorway, frowning and holding a pizza box.

"Um." Lewis shifted the pizza box on his arm. "Sorry, I let myself in. It was habit."

"You're fine," Flora said, gathering her stuff. "Take the lab—I was leaving for the law office." Rex wondered how many offices Flora had at this point. She breezed past Lewis with little heel taps. "I'll see you both later."

When they were alone, Rex spent a silent moment taking him in. Lewis was in jeans and a band shirt—a terrible band shirt. She needed to figure out brainwashing to fix his taste in music. Peter had mentioned something about him quitting, but she'd waited to get the full story from Lewis. She wanted to offer him a job, too, but figured she should wait for this conversation to gauge how welcome it would be.

Lewis cleared his throat, crossed the room, and set the pizza on the workbench. Rex's smile twitched at the care he took to keep it off her diagrams, his eyebrows scrunched in focus.

"Do you mind if I talk first?" he asked.

Rex shook her head, riveted on the little shifts in his jaw, the smoothness of his brow that was only ever intentional.

He stood straight. "I know we were forced to live together, and that might be the only reason we got close."

Right, like how she and Grant got so close.

"I'm sorry I took advantage of that closeness." The tip of his tongue flicked out to wet his lips. "I guess I made it pretty obvious that I want more with you. But I can handle it if you don't. I just don't want to lose you."

"I do though," Rex said without thinking. "I do want more."

Lewis's face blanked. A second later, it was in motion as feelings flicked across it. "Wait, how did I—"

"I stopped you because of the kiss. I wasn't feeling it."

His face froze halfway between stupefied and embarrassed.

"I've been trying to be more honest, especially with the people who matter to me." She held her hands between her knees and drummed her fingertips together. "It's making me realize I'm not sure what I want from people. Because what I want is usually different."

She glanced at Lewis, hoping he'd take the chance to interject. But he watched her with a frown, so she white-noised herself into the silence.

"I've been doing what I think people expect me to do for so long that I'm not sure what kinds of limits I should be setting or what boundaries I actually want. I don't know what a relationship looks like when I'm actually a part of it." Her heart was going to bruise the inside of her ribs if it didn't slow down. But at least her voice didn't shake. "And I want to be a part of it. I don't know what else I want, but that's the big one. I want you and me to be a part of it."

She suddenly couldn't stand to hear herself talk anymore. She forced her eyes to meet his, voice coming out too light. Oh, she'd forgotten to breathe. "How are you feeling about this? About the stuff I said so far?"

Lewis's frown didn't shift. He raised a hand chest high. "Can I ask a stupid question?"

"Yes." She swallowed her trepidation.

"When you say you want more, you're also talking about a romantic relationship, right?"

Rex cracked a grin. "Yes, I am."

"Okay." Lewis leaned back against the desk, shoulders looser. The lingering crease in his brow relaxed, and a dopey smile spread beneath it. "Since we're being honest . . ."

"Please." Rex tensed again.

"You aren't like anyone I've ever met." The smile went wonky in a way that scrunched up one side of his face. "I don't think I pictured any relationship with you being normal."

Rex let out a too fast, tension-draining laugh.

"I mean, can you see us walking on a beach at sunset, holding hands or something?"

Rex's laugh became a giggle. Maybe she was a bit hysterical.

Lewis cast his eyes down. "I don't know what I can promise you. Since neither of us knows what we'd be like together. But I want to try it. I mean, *really* try."

Rex's chest felt heavy. She hoped this wasn't the teary kind of hysteria. That might send the wrong message. "I want to try too."

Lewis's eyes cut to the pizza box, and Rex noticed the smell of warm pizza wafting through the lab. "I brought—" He waved at the box to finish the thought and made some leading motions toward the couch.

Rex opened the lid curiously, and warmth curled through her. "Cheese-less with anchovies. You remembered my favorite pizza?"

"It's a really weird favorite. Anyone would remember it."

She snorted. "Are you sure you can choke it down?"

"This was more of a making-a-point pizza. I figure next time we can get half my favorite, half yours." He gave her a mock-earnest look. "If that's okay with you."

Rex couldn't stop smiling. "That's okay with me."

"I want to make sure I'm respecting your boundaries when it comes to cheese."

"I'm cheese-repulsed, for the most part." She picked up the pizza and followed him to the couch. "But we can talk about something else."

ISSUE 41

DINOSAURS AT A FANCY PARTY

After finally acknowledging New Colorado's sovereignty, the United States government went full bitch-friend-whose-pity-friend-got-famous and threw a remember-the-good-old-days arm over the dinosaurs' metaphorical shoulders.

To kick off a week of what-are-we-dealing-with talks, Washington was throwing the dinosaurs a black-tie reception that would have warranted a preemptive lecture even without the dinosaurs' insistence that Rex attend in her official capacity as Ambassador to Humanity and Mother of our Race.

"There will be press at the venue, but not at the actual reception," she explained to the dinosaurs packed into the outdoor theater. "Don't mention the space program. And don't say a word about Dino Might—that should be obvious. Are you recording? Stop recording."

In the front row, Jasper pocketed his phone and looked at the ground.

Rex gave him a punctuating glare and returned to pacing the stage. "I want to see appropriate behavior from start to finish. And I've seen at least ten of you on talk shows so far, so I know you know what that looks like."

"Can we go if we don't have an official position?" someone called from the back.

Rex shrugged. "Why not? It's not like they can tell you apart." She had a thought. "Wait, how many of you want to go?"

Nearly the whole theater bobbed their heads.

"I doubt their catering service can make a dent in that." She shrugged. "Whatever. You can go if you get all your chores done and find something suitable to wear."

The theater filled with trills and hollers.

Rex checked the time and grimaced. They needed to get ready if they didn't want to be late.

She clapped her hands to regain their attention. "All right, let's all put on our most gendered clothes and go play flirting-or-friendly roulette with a bunch of strangers."

The dinosaurs dispersed in a ground-shaking flurry.

Flora fell in step with Rex as she left the stage, scrolling through lists on her tablet. "I take it you're not looking forward to the party."

"You're sure you can't come? You have a title."

"Unfortunately, Aunt of our Race doesn't inspire as much respect as Mother of our Race. If you wanted backup, you could have brought Lewis."

Rex sighed. "Yeah, but this is the dinosaurs' thing, and I'm not sure if it's too soon to bring him around."

"The age-old question: when is the right time to introduce a new boyfriend to your dinosaurs?"

Grumbling, Rex pulled the weathered to-do list from her pocket to squeeze *bring Lewis to New Colorado* into the cramped margin.

"Is he going to take your job offer?"

Rex's face fell. "I don't think so."

Flora *hmm*ed. "It *would* present a conflict of interests."

"Yeah, yeah. But Peter accepted. So, between the two of us, I think we can keep Lewis in Decimen City."

"I don't think that was ever in question." Flora split from Rex's side to avoid a muddy spot without so much as a stuck heel. "The ethics lecture series is finalized for next week. One of the bioethicists had a conflict come up, but I booked an acceptable substitute."

"Great. We need to make sure every dinosaur knows it's mandatory. They've been way too excited about genetically engineering the next generation. Also, they keep making that joke about keeping humans as pets, and it's starting to feel like they're testing the waters."

Flora nodded along, making notes. "Considering where they came from, isn't it a bit hypocritical to lecture them about the ethics of genetic engineering?"

"That's why I'm not giving the lecture." They sidestepped the gaggle of microraptors at the entrance of the Human Guests building, Flora guiding Rex by the elbow as she scanned the rest of the list. "I should start a new list, or that 'deal with the dinosaurs' line will just sit there forever, mocking me."

"I'm shocked you haven't run that list through the wash yet."

"I did. It made it stronger." They entered Rex's room, where she'd laid out a fancy outfit—not a dress, because Rex wasn't a complete masochist—that met with Flora's approval. "By the way, do you think you can find out if any of the lecturers know anything about religion? Because those chants they do before baseball games are getting really solemn, and I'm not sure if it's something I should address."

"Rex, we can focus on getting through the reception, for now," Flora said, shutting down the tablet.

"Right, right." Rex looked at the clothes. "Okay, talk me through this like I'm a skittish horse."

Lewis: You're grinning like crazy on the TV right now. These commentators are eating it up.

Lewis: Who taught your dinosaurs to walk a red carpet? Because they're acting like that's what they're doing.

Lewis: There's a viral Who Wore It Better with a deinonychus and the queen of England, and I think most people have forgotten it started as a joke.

Rex stifled a snort and typed, *Leather Heather will appreciate the feedback.*

She stowed her phone and turned her smile to the two men who'd introduced themselves as something government-y, trying to recall the conversation. At least the dinosaurs were a bunch of different species. How was she supposed to tell all these humans apart?

"Considering how your, well, your Oversight ended," the taller man was saying. His smile was sort of apologetic-slash-conspiratorial. "As a genius" —slash condescending—"I'm sure you already realize how your role here, this influence you've gained, is going to make some folks ask questions."

"Of course." Rex mirrored his concerned tone. "I absolutely understand. I assure you, everything was totally above-board. And I learned my lesson. I'm completely rehabilitated now. I'm—I'm contrite. And humble."

She took a sip of champagne—a small one; gotta set an example for her dumb, boozy dinos. "I'm sorry about how everything went down for Mr. Quinten"—not a lieutenant anymore—"and Mr. Underwood, and those two committee members who had it out for me—I didn't know them personally. I know they abused their positions, but how can I blame them for that? It's a real shame how it all blew up in their faces." Was she laying it on too thick? Naw. "I'm looking to start new. I'm responsible now. And these dinosaurs need help acclimating to the human world."

"The dinosaurs you created," the second man said with a teasing sort of chuckle.

Rex belatedly realized this mild interrogation wasn't just about the Oversight fallout. Did they think New Colorado was some kind of puppet kingdom for her?

Familiar indignation—on the dinosaurs' behalf and her own—surged, but with a thought for the dinosaurs, Rex was quick to compartmentalize it. It made sense, from a certain perspective, considering the sequence of events.

She'd snuck the dinos out of her lab under Oversight's nose, armed them—or enabled them to arm themselves—and played down their competence until it was too late to stop their power grab. At which point she'd made her move against Oversight and come out in a better position than she'd started in, all while acting more or less within the law—at least in retrospect.

In their minds, perhaps, she'd played the world like a fiddle. They'd pushed her into a corner, and she'd spun out a master plan to rival most supervillains. Except she'd done it with her legitimacy intact, a net positive public image, and the soft support of the world's most high-profile superheroes. Not to mention, somewhere in that scheme, her supervillain twin had vanished into the night.

All told, she couldn't even call it paranoid. It didn't have any more concrete support than the truth, but in Rex's experience, people didn't care much about that.

She let her eyes flick between the two men in front of her. Did she care what these people thought? She'd cared what people thought after everything with Sam. Everything about that was more personal, and there had been repercussions to its reframing that she could barely articulate. Was it all contextual, or did the truth have some intrinsic value to her?

Geez, this wasn't the time for this—and yet.

Here and now, she found, Rex didn't give a damn what these people thought she'd done. She cared about the dinosaurs, her friends, her city, and her plans for the lab. Her new experiment. Her little, personal redemptions. The way these people factored into that was . . . malleable.

It was a freeing realization.

"It's sweet of them, actually, to let me come to these things," she said with a smirk. "I think they want me to feel involved." She took a gulp of champagne.

This was what the academics would call a double bluff.

She was a good liar when she had reason to be.

Spot chose that moment to sidle up to Rex, hacking into a napkin. "Mom, what is this?"

Rex checked his plate as her conversation partners gave quick, lean-in greetings—they weren't thrown by dinosaurs, and they were going to prove it with the power of square shoulders and eye contact. "Those are vegetable puffs, which they served even though I told the organizers you're all carnivores."

The men gave laughs and commiserating comments.

Spot wiped his tongue on the napkin. "It tastes like the opposite of alcohol."

Rex wondered if Spot was deliberately playing into her act, or if this was serendipity in the form of her dinosaurs' lack of social graces. "Here, I'll eat them."

Spot tipped his remaining puffs onto her plate and looked at the men. "Mr. Brown and Mr. Kaminski! I finished reviewing your notes on our conditional mutual defense proposal."

"It's good to finally meet you, Mr. Spot," Brown or Kaminski said. No hesitation at all. That must have taken some coaching.

"Trent and Wing Wing are both here." Spot gestured toward the tyrannosaur in a black suit looming over the nervous humans at the buffet table, a pterodactyl in a shimmery dress perched on his back. "I'd love to introduce you to the whole defense committee, if Mom doesn't mind."

"You kids have fun," Rex said, giving Spot's lapel a tug. She needed to find out which dinosaurs were making their clothes and commission a wardrobe. "Let me fix your tie, Spot. He'll catch up to you."

When Brown and Kaminski were a few feet away, she muttered, "FYI, the American government thinks you guys are my puppet nation."

"Yeah, duh. By the way, Gabby May wants some advice on negotiating a trade deal with Mexico."

They'd regret underestimating Spot. "Why would I know anything about that?"

"You're human and older than three."

"Fair enough."

He glanced past her shoulder and lowered his voice. "Protectors at twelve o'clock."

Pixie's voice piped up by her ear. "Meister!"

Rex almost choked on her champagne, shooting Spot a glare. "I've told you before—clock positions indicate a direction, not a proximity warning."

"Sorry." Spot scampered after his new victims.

"Hi, Pixie." Rex turned to the hero. "I didn't know the Protectors would be here."

Pixie wore a pink cocktail dress instead of her superhero suit, though her mask still covered half her face. "Only a few representatives. Manta Man and Don are around somewhere." Pixie pouted. "I wanted to bring Cat Man, but Blue said no."

"A wise decision." Rex took a new glass of champagne from a passing tray. "Why isn't Viv here? Isn't she the blue face of the Protectors?"

"She didn't want to steal the spotlight," Pixie said, apparently oblivious to the wave of excited tittering that followed her gauzy wings.

Speaking of, "Your wing looks healed." That was a relief. Rex would've felt pretty guilty if she'd done indirect, permanent harm to a superhero who claimed they were friends.

Pixie spun around and hopped to hover briefly, wings humming. "Good as new, see?" She landed lightly, and Rex mentally congratulated her dress for having the cartoonish ability to float and twirl without ever compromising her decency. "I'm so glad everything worked out for the dinosaurs." She clasped her hands. "I was really worried after the army got involved."

Rex didn't think worry would have stopped Pixie from arresting her. At least she trusted Pixie to refuse to hurt the dinosaurs. She wasn't certain most of the Protectors would.

As though on cue, Rex's scan of the reception caught Manta Man, dressed to the nines, in conversation with a few humans. When their eyes met, he gave her an I'm-watching-you nod over the lip of his champagne flute. Rex supposed that told her enough about where she stood with the Protectors of the World.

Still, it was a step up from her standing pre-Oversight. She anticipated a renewed offer from Vivid Blue to take on gadget work. Flora would probably make the same arguments as before about good PR, in addition to the importance of superhero support for some of their goals. Rex was already steeling herself to not refuse outright.

At least Rex could admit he looked suave. "It must take skill to drink from glass cups with such sharp teeth," she murmured.

Pixie giggled. "You have no idea. He breaks everything." She waved at Manta Man. "Anyway, congratulations. I'm so proud of you for seeing the error of your ways."

Rex nodded. "They say no one's too far gone."

"That's so true! I think you could even be a hero one day."

"Me? No way."

Pixie put a hand on her shoulder. "Don't ever give up on yourself, Meister, and I'll never give up on you." Her face brightened. "Oh, I see Karen and Leather Heather. I have to say hi!" Her wings sped to lift her a few inches off the grass as she rushed away.

Pixie's place was filled by a new batch of blazered humans, who were replaced in turn by more, each taking their chance to feel out the apparent power behind the volunteer-based governing council. Rex popped vegetable puffs as she played her part, her schmoozing interrupted occasionally by an excited dinosaur with something to show her or a teary dinosaur with a wardrobe malfunction.

Jasper caused a brief stir by livestreaming from his bodycam. She indulged him by making a show of confiscating it.

Lewis: DinoLife and MeisterMoment are trending.
Jasper: Thanks Mom. I was gonna spill something on it. Your ending was better.
Aya: Inspired, Doctor. My task this evening is evident.

Rex pocketed her phone and snagged another drink. The world was gonna be Spot's oyster.

ACKNOWLEDGMENTS

I wrote a book, and a lot of people helped me.

Elana Gibson edited this book into shape. And it would not have reached Elana without the people at CamCat Books deciding not to join the chorus of "superheroes go in comics." Thank you all for believing in this book.

It would not have gotten that far without the North Texas Writers, who gave endless encouragement and excellent critique through draft after draft. Especially Carly Huss, for having an excellent eye, Cady George, for loving and understanding my story as much as I do, and Michael Hilton, for drawing a trading card for every character. Thank you all for helping me wrangle this monster into a book.

Michael Fore listened patiently to my rambles about the placement of specific commas in specific sentences and whether a joke was funnier with or without a specific word. Thanks for your support, both emotional and tech-related, and for bragging on me all the time.

To my family: thank you for your excitement and support. Thanks Dad for answering my science hypotheticals. Thanks Mom, Marci, Mark, Jonathon, and Zack for reading my work and saying you liked it.

Thank you, Spider-Man, for being my favorite superhero.

ABOUT THE AUTHOR

*B*renna Raney began her writing career with Amelia Bedelia fanfiction on hand-stapled printer paper. Her early original work was entrusted to gel pens and floppy disks, then ballpoint pens and flash drives, and briefly, receipt paper from her first job. In her Academic Period, she produced dry and esoteric works for which she was awarded a master's degree. She has also dabbled in visual media, and her minimalist comic, *Ice Cream Money from Grandma*, hangs proudly on her grandmother's refrigerator. She resides in Texas, where she bakes bread, kills plants, and teaches anthropology.

If you like

Brenna Raney's *The Meister of Decimen City*,

you will also like

Citizen Orlov by Jonathan Payne.

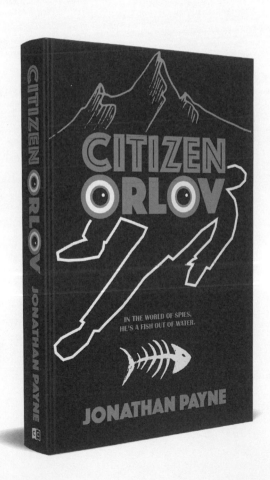

CHAPTER
1

IN WHICH OUR HERO MEETS A NEW AND UNEXPECTED CHALLENGE

O n a frigid winter's morning in a mountainous region of central Europe, Citizen Orlov, a simple fishmonger, deciding to shorten his daily constitutional on account of the weather, is taking a shortcut along the dank alley behind the ministries of Security and Intelligence when a telephone begins to ring. He thinks nothing of it and keeps walking, his heavy boots crunching the snow between the cobbles.

The ringing continues, becoming louder with each step. A window at the back of the ministry buildings is open, just a little. The ringing telephone sits on a table next to the open window. Orlov stops, troubled by this unusual scene: there is no reason for a window to be open on such a cold day. Since this is the ministry of either Security or Intelligence, could an open window be a security breach of some kind?

Orlov is tempted to walk away. After all, this telephone call is none of his business. On the other hand, he is an upright and patriotic citizen who would not want to see national security compromised simply because no one was available to answer a telephone call. He is on the verge of stepping towards the open window when he hears footsteps up ahead. A tight group of four soldiers is marching into the alley, rifles on shoulders. He freezes for a second, leans against the wall and quickly lights a cigarette. By the time the soldiers reach him, Orlov is dragging on the cigarette and working hard to appear nonchalant. The soldiers are Palace guardsmen, but the red insignia on their uniforms indicates they are part of the elite unit that protects the Crown Prince, the King's ambitious older son. Orlov nods politely, but the soldiers ignore him and march on at speed.

The telephone is still ringing. Someone very much wants an answer. Orlov stubs his cigarette on the wall and approaches the open window. The telephone is loud in his right ear. Peering through the gap, he sees a small, gloomy storeroom with neatly appointed shelves full of stationery. Finally, he can stand it no longer. He reaches through the window, picks up the receiver, and pulls it on its long and winding cable out through the window to his ear.

"Hello?" says Orlov, looking up and down the alley to check he is still alone.

"Thank God. Where have you been?" says an agitated voice, distant and crackly. Orlov is unsure what to say. The voice continues. "Kosek. Right now."

"I'm sorry?" says Orlov.

"Kosek. Agent Kosek."

Orlov peers into the storeroom again. "There's no one here," he says.

"Well, fetch him then. And hurry, for God's sake. It's important."

Orlov is sorely tempted to end the call and walk away, but the voice is so angry that he dare not.

"One minute," he says, and lays the receiver on the table. He opens the window wider and, with some considerable effort, pulls himself head first into the storeroom, where he tumbles onto the floor. Picking himself up, he slaps the dust from his overcoat, opens the storeroom door and peers along the hallway; all is dark and quiet.

With some trepidation, Orlov returns to the telephone. "Hello?" he says.

"Kosek?"

"No, sorry. I'll have to take a message."

The caller is still agitated. "Well, focus on what I'm about to say. It's life and death."

Orlov's hands are shaking. "Hold on," he says, "I'll fetch some paper."

Before he can put the receiver down, the caller explodes with anger. "Are you a simpleton? Do not write this down. Remember it."

"Yes, sir. Sorry," says Orlov. "I'll remember it."

"Are you ready?'

"Yes, sir."

"Here it is. We could not – repeat not – install it in room six. Don't ask why, it's a long story."

The man is about to continue, but Orlov interrupts him. "Should I include that in the message; *it's a long story?*"

"Mother of God," shouts the man. "Why do they always give me the village idiot? No. Forget that part. I'll start again."

"Ready," says Orlov.

This time the man speaks slower and more deliberately, as if to a child. "We could not – repeat not – install it in room six. You need to get room seven. It's hidden above the wardrobe. Push the lever up, not down. Repeat that back to me."

Orlov is now shaking all over, and he grimaces as he forces himself to focus. He repeats the message slowly but correctly.

"Whatever else you do, get that message to Kosek, in person. No one else. Lives depend on it. Understood?"

"Understood," says Orlov, and the line goes dead.

Orlov returns the receiver to the telephone and searches for something to write on. He remembers the message now, but for how long? He has no idea who Agent Kosek is, or where. Now that the caller has gone, the only sensible course of action is to make a note. He will destroy the note, once he has found Kosek. On the table he finds a pile of index cards. He writes the message verbatim on a card, folds it once and tucks it inside his wallet.

Standing in the dark storeroom, Orlov wonders how to set about finding Agent Kosek. He considers climbing back into the alley, going around to the front entrance and presenting himself as a visitor, if he could work out which ministry he is inside. But it's still early and it might take hours to be seen. Worse than that, there is a possibility he would be turned away. He imagines a surly security guard pretending to check the personnel directory, only to turn to him and say *There's no one of that name here.* Perhaps agents never use their real names. For that matter, is Kosek a real name or a pseudonym? Orlov decides the better approach is to use the one advantage currently available to him: he is inside the building.

He lowers the sash window to its original position and steps into the hallway, closing the storeroom door behind him. All remains dark and quiet. The hallway runs long and straight in both directions, punctuated only by anonymous doors. There is nothing to suggest one direction is more promising than the other. Orlov turns right and tiptoes sheepishly along the hallway, now conscious of his boots as they squeak on the polished wooden floors. He walks on and on, eventually meeting a door that opens onto an identical dark corridor. As he continues, Orlov becomes increasingly conscious that he is not supposed to be here. He imagines an angry bureaucrat bursting out from one of the many office doors to castigate him and march him off to be interrogated. However, he has walked the length of a train and still he has seen no one.

Finally, Orlov sees the warm glow of lamplight seeping around the edge of another dividing door up ahead. He is both relieved and apprehensive. He approaches the door cautiously and puts his ear to it. It sounds like a veritable hive of industry. He takes a deep breath and opens the door onto a scene of frenetic activity. Banks of desks are staffed by serious men, mostly young, in formal suits, both pinstripe and plain; there are just a few women, also young and dressed formally. Some are engaged in animated conversations; some are leaning back in chairs, smoking; others are deep into reading piles of papers. A white-haired woman is distributing china cups full of tea from a wheeled trolley. At the far end of this long room, someone is setting out chairs in front of a blackboard. Above this activity, the warm fug of cigarette smoke is illuminated by high wall lamps. Orlov hesitates, but is soon approached at high speed by a short, rotund man in a three-piece suit. He has a clipboard and a flamboyant manner.

"You're late," says the man, gesticulating. "Quickly. Overcoats over there."

"No, no. You see," Orlov says, "I'm not really here."

The man slaps him on the back, taking his coat as they walk. "You seem real to me," he laughs.

Orlov protests. "I have a message for Agent Kosek."

The man rolls his eyes. "Do not trouble yourself regarding Agent Kosek. He is late for everything. He will be here in due course."

He directs Orlov to take a seat at the back of the impromptu classroom, which is by now filling up with eager, young employees. Orlov is suddenly conscious of his age and appearance; his balding head and rough clothes stand out in this group of young, formally dressed professionals. He also feels anxious about being in this room on false pretenses. However, he need only wait until Agent Kosek appears; he will then deliver the message, make his excuses and leave. He could still make it to the Grand Plaza in time for the market to open.

The flamboyant man, now standing in front of the blackboard, bangs his clipboard down onto a desk to bring the room to order. "Citizens," he says, "I would appreciate your attention." The room falls silent and he continues. "I am Citizen Molnar, and I will be your instructor today."

Orlov turns to his neighbor, an earnest young man who is writing the instructor's name in a pristine leather notebook. "I'm not supposed to be here," says Orlov. The young man places a finger on his lips. Orlov smiles at him and returns his attention to Molnar, who is writing on the blackboard. Molnar proceeds to talk to the group for some time, but Orlov struggles to follow his meaning. The instructor repeatedly refers to the group as *recruits*, which adds to Orlov's sense of being in the wrong place. He becomes hot under the collar when Molnar invites every recruit to introduce themselves. One by one the impressive young recruits stand and detail their university degrees and their training with the military or the police. When Orlov's turn comes, he stands and says, "Citizen Orlov. Fishmonger." He is surprised when a ripple of laughter runs through the group.

Orlov is about to sit down again when Molnar intervenes. "Is there anything else you'd like to tell us, citizen?"

Orlov says, "I have a message for Agent Kosek."

"Yes," says Molnar, gesturing for Orlov to sit down, "the agent will be here soon, I'm quite sure."

Orlov's hopes pick up some time later when Molnar says he wants to introduce a guest speaker. Orlov reaches inside his wallet to check that the message is still there. But Molnar is interrupted by a colleague whispering in his ear.

"My apologies," says Molnar. "It seems Agent Kosek has been called away on urgent business. However, I'm delighted to say that his colleague, Agent Zelle, is joining us to give you some insight into the day to day life of an agent. Agent Zelle."

Orlov is disappointed at the change of plan, but perhaps this colleague will be able to introduce him to Kosek. Taking her place in front of the blackboard is the most beautiful woman Orlov has ever seen. She is young and curvaceous but with a stern, serious expression. Her dark curls tumble over pearls and a flowing gown. Several of the male recruits shift uneasily in their chairs; someone coughs. Agent Zelle seems far too exotic for this stuffy, bureaucratic setting. She speaks with a soft foreign accent that Orlov does not recognize.

"Good morning, citizens," says Zelle, scanning the group slowly. "I have been asked to share with you something of what you can expect, if you are chosen to work as an agent for the ministry. I can tell you that it is a great honor, but there will also be hardship and danger."

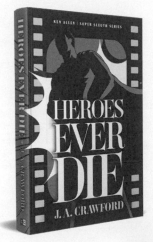
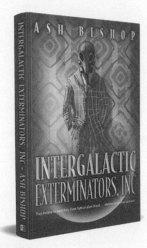

CamCat
Books

VISIT US ONLINE FOR MORE BOOKS TO LIVE IN:

CAMCATBOOKS.COM

CamCatBooks   @CamCatBooks   @CamCat_Books